Realm Of Fear
Mirror Wars Book 3

Melina

Time to face your fears

Alan

Also by Alan Bayles

Double Jeopardy
Oracle's Vision

MIRROR WARS
REALM OF FEAR

**SURVIVING IS
A NIGHTMARE**

ALAN BAYLES

Copyright © 2025 Alan Bayles
All rights reserved.
Alan Bayles has asserted his rights under the Copyright, Designs & Patents Act 1988
to be identified as the author of this work

The characters and events portrayed in this book are fictitious. Any similarity to real persons, living or dead, is coincidental and not intended by the author.

No part of this book may be reproduced, or stored in a retrieval system, or transmitted in any form or by any means, electronic, mechanical, photocopying, recording, or otherwise, without express written permission of the publisher.

ISBN: 9798263941949

Cover design by: Emily's World Of Design

For Monica
(Whose patience and understanding are without limits)

ACKNOWLEDGMENTS

I wish to express my utmost thanks to my editor, Lesley Jones, for her heroic editing skills in helping me make this book a one that readers can enjoy.

Special thanks to my amazing proofreaders; Teresa Walsh, James Adamson & Tanya Malcolm for allowing to me to use their super-powered vision.

> "Fear can be a friend or an enemy. It all depends on how you choose to face it."
>
> – Stephen King

PROLOGUE

How long were they going to be kept waiting? Detective Inspector Dave Barnes impatiently tapped his foot while he stared at the closed door, his mind fixated on that thought. Twenty-five minutes had elapsed since his friend, Karen Logue, someone he had given up for dead, had left through that very hatch. But to Dave, those minutes had felt like an eternity. He glanced over his shoulder at Claire to assess her well-being, but what he saw troubled him. Since Karen's departure, Dave had noticed a change had come over Claire. Her normally bouncy exuberance was gone. It had been replaced by a more subdued look. She was munching on a bar of chocolate someone had given to her, but it was as if a dark cloud had been cast over her.

He must have been staring at her for too long because she lifted her head and flashed him a thin smile. He returned her smile with a forced one of his own and a curt nod. But there was something in her behaviour that bothered him. Something didn't feel right, and he wasn't sure what it was. Over his extensive career as a law enforcement officer, he'd seen that same type of smile many times in career criminals or sociopaths. It didn't seem genuine; it was devoid of any feeling toward him. Not only that, but Claire also looked tense, as if she was struggling with something. But, if he was being honest with himself, he guessed she must be struggling with

everything that had happened to them since they first met. Of course, he was sympathetic to what she must have been feeling, because he felt the same way. It had been a rough couple of months for them. Their worlds had been turned upside down, and it felt as if they had been pushed beyond breaking point.

As he thought back over what had happened to him, Dave shook his head and blew out a dispirited sigh. Two months ago, his life had been relatively mundane – fifty-seven years of age, divorced, thirty-five years' service in the police force and three years from retirement. But everything changed just after he began investigating a double murder and was soon introduced to Claire Tulley, the brown-haired, fifty-something history professor standing behind him. Dave quickly learned that the case he was investigating had a surprising connection to several decades-old cases, one of which just so happened to involve the death of Claire's twin sister, Emma. It hadn't been long before their case had taken them down an even stranger rabbit hole.

While working alongside his friend and colleague Detective Sergeant Andrew Jenkins, Dave met the statuesque, flame-haired police constable, Wendy Cooper. He later found out she was secretly working for a multinational clandestine agency, which had a base hidden deep beneath Durham Cathedral – codenamed the Castle. Wendy introduced Dave and Claire to John Payne, commander of the Castle, and Sophia Collins, the British prime minister. It was through them he learned that the world was secretly being invaded and people like Sophia were being replaced by doppelgängers. Things took an even darker turn when Dave met his own doppelgänger, the devious and scheming Colonel David Barnes. It was through Barnes that Dave learned the other-worldly invaders were being controlled by a malevolent sentient AI known as Oracle.

For over two months, Dave and his allies in the resistance could only watch in horror as Oracle tightened her grip on every country across the globe. Despite several minor victories against Oracle's forces, things came to a head when Oracle mercilessly attacked the underground complex, which resulted in the base being destroyed in a nuclear explosion.

A seemingly benign omniscient being known as Custos intervened in the last nanosecond, saving Dave and Claire from being incinerated.

Dave shuddered to himself as the memory of being engulfed in a sea of fire and the pain of his skin blistering came flooding back to him. Panting heavily, he squeezed his eyes shut and ran a hand through his thinning hair. If he was sure about anything in his life, being engulfed in nuclear fire was not something he would forget anytime soon, and it was possible he would never sleep soundly ever again. And waking up and discovering he was in a parallel reality – it was a lot to process. Dave ground his teeth in frustration. Everything seemed to be happening so fast, going from one perilous situation to another. When would it all stop?

'You realise I can hear your teeth grinding from over here,' Claire grumbled irritably between chewing. 'Pack it in.'

'Pardon me for living,' Dave huffed. He raised his hands in apology and exhaled a melancholic sigh. 'Sorry. I still can't forget our last moments on our Earth. The whole nearly burning to death, an' all that.'

Claire visibly shuddered, wrapped her arms tightly around herself, and gave a sullen nod. 'Yeah,' she answered in what sounded like a despondent tone. 'I don't think either of us will ever forget that feeling of being burned alive.'

Dave thought he caught a glint of terror flash in Claire's eyes and guessed she was thinking back to the same moment as he was. There was an air of vulnerability about her, something he hadn't seen before. She normally had a vibe about her, giving him the impression that nothing could shake her. He'd seen her survive an attack from a deadly beast and never once had he witnessed her panic – even when they had been trapped under tons of rubble. However, the sight of the ghost of indecision briefly crossing her face tore at Dave's heart, and he felt an overwhelming desire to reach out, grab her in his arms, and console her. But just as he was about to do so, he paused as he recalled Claire's revelation from moments earlier, informing him of her previous encounters with Custos, that the entity had subconsciously manipulated him into sleeping with her shortly after they first met. For him, from now on, every time he made a move toward Claire,

he would be forced to second-guess himself and wonder if he was doing it of his own volition or if something was subconsciously guiding him.

The idea that he had been manipulated into doing something he normally might not have done filled Dave with a mixture of anger and humiliation. What gave Custos the right to believe it could treat people this way? How dare it do that to him? His temples throbbed as another troubling thought occurred to him. The night he and Claire slept together – did that mean he had raped her? He let out a tired groan and massaged his forehead. He hated feeling this way, having to second-guess himself. Why hadn't Claire kept her mouth shut? Would he have been better off not knowing? Dave snarled and pounded the side of his head in frustration. Stupid. Stupid. Stupid. He had no right to blame Claire. She was just as much a victim as he was, probably more so. Following an injury sustained in an attack, she had pushed him away without explanation. Initially, Dave had blamed himself because he thought it was something he had done, but after learning Custos was the reason for her standoffish attitude, it added more fuel to his fire of hate for Custos. As far as he was concerned, Custos had damaged their relationship. He still wasn't entirely sure if they would ever get back to how they were before, or if that was even something Claire desired.

Dave stiffened in surprise as he felt a hand touch his shoulder, followed by Claire's soothing voice, which also had a slight scolding tone to it.

'Hey, you,' she said, spinning him around. 'I can tell what you're thinking and I'm telling you to stop it right now. I've done enough self-flagellation over these past two months, without you doing it, too.' She made a wide sweeping motion with her hands, which was followed by a harsh glare. 'No more second-guessing ourselves. Got it?'

Feeling like he was being told off by a strict schoolmistress, Dave felt his cheeks burn in shame and he hung his head. He thought if his chin dropped any lower, it would touch his stomach.

'Yes,' he replied meekly. He drew in a long breath and let it out slowly. 'I just feel like we've lost so much. I'm not sure how we can get it back.'

Her eyes blazing with annoyance, Claire reached out and grabbed Dave's face, pulling it toward her with such aggressiveness it took him by surprise. Dave thought he was imagining it, but he was sure her eyes contained something like desire. But the strange thing was, Dave couldn't see the usual warmth or tenderness associated with desire in Claire's eyes. In fact, her eyes looked positively cold, devoid of any emotion. He was positive he'd seen that same look in people before, but for the life of him, he couldn't remember where, which only added to his concern. Was there something wrong with her?

Before Dave could say anything, Claire leaned in and placed her lips on his right cheek. The movement was so unexpected, it left Dave speechless as he felt her smooth lips brush against his stubbled face. A ridiculous thought popped into Dave's head, and he wondered how long it had been since he'd last shaved. But any thoughts about shaving evaporated as he felt Claire's lips slowly move towards his. Silently chastising himself for believing something was wrong with her, he closed his eyes and savoured the feeling, returning Claire's kiss with some urgency.

On hearing her quickening breaths, Dave felt his heart rate quicken while her tongue danced sensuously with his own, like two combatants testing each other in some erotic display of combat. His desire building, he lifted his hand and caressed her neck, smiling as he felt her squirm from his touch.

Caught up in the moment, Dave smiled to himself at the absurdity of what they were doing. It hadn't been that long ago when they had both been in a coma. He wondered if Custos's healing aura was the cause of their sudden need to act like a pair of hormonal teenagers. Despite his earlier concern for Claire's strange behaviour, he couldn't stop himself from laughing at the ridiculousness of it all.

'You were never like this before,' he murmured between bouts of heavy kissing. 'Maybe I should thank Custos.'

As soon as he heard the words leave his mouth, Dave realised he had just made a huge mistake. In his excitement, he'd accidentally spoken

out loud, voicing his internal thoughts.

Oh ... ballocks, I'm in for it now, Dave thought on seeing the murderous expression etched on Claire's face as he reared back in shock and watched her eyes sharpen, becoming flint hard. His blood froze as she took a step back, her cheeks blossoming into a deep shade of red. Dave was in no doubt that her flushed face wasn't from their passion but as a response to what he'd just said. He gulped on seeing the withering stare being aimed at him, so deadly it would have rivalled the mythical stone-inducing gaze of Medusa.

'And just what's that supposed to mean?' Claire snapped with such unrestrained vitriol, Dave imagined he could feel the heat behind her words.

Strangely intimidated by a woman shorter than him, Dave hung his head and tried to focus on anything but Claire's venomous stare. He shook his head and tried to laugh his faux pas off with a half-hearted laugh. 'It was nothing,' he insisted, holding up his hands in apology. 'It was just a joke.'

'Oh, no,' Claire answered in a tone that matched the clear indignation expressed across her face. 'I know perfectly well what you meant. Back in our reality, I saw it every time you looked at me. You thought I was a frigid ice queen.' She aggressively jabbed the same finger into Dave's chest. 'Don't lie. I could see it in your eyes.'

Not believing what he was hearing, Dave felt his eyes grow wide but could only stare at her with his mouth hanging open, lost for words. Had she lost her mind? What the hell was she talking about? She was the one who came on to him! Sick to death of Claire's petulant attitude, Dave lost his temper and threw up his hands in exasperation.

'Oh, for Pete's sake, Claire,' he snapped back. 'It wasn't like that at all. I was just caught up in the moment, that's all it was.' He exhaled a long, heavy sigh and held out his hands. 'Come on, stop acting like a drama queen.'

Claire's face turned crimson and her eyes tightened into thin slits. 'Drama queen! Drama queen! I'll show you who's a drama queen,' she

hissed, shooting Dave a murderous glare so deadly that if her eyes had been loaded with ammunition, there was a chance they would have killed him where he stood. 'Let this drama queen explain it to you in words you can understand. One, the moment has most definitely passed, and two, this shop is now closed for business.' The words came out of her mouth with such force, they left Dave with no doubt she meant what she said. Then, as if for extra gravitas, Claire folded her arms across her chest, which told Dave she wasn't in the mood to compromise. She held up her head, sniffed and spun round with her back facing him.

Feeling a migraine coming on, Dave grimaced and massaged his temples. 'Hell's teeth, Claire. Now you're just being stupid,' he moaned in exasperation.

Again, Dave regretted the words as soon as they left his mouth. He wrinkled his nose in disgust and inwardly groaned. *Well done. You're two for two so far. Do you want to go for broke and tell her she's fat too? I'm sure that will set her off even more.* Ashamed of what he'd said, he took a hesitant step forward and reached out to Claire, but paused as she jerked her head back and fixed him with a tearful stare. Seeing the expression of pain and hurt etched on her face only deepened his shame even further.

For several long seconds, an uneasy silence filled the room while they stared at one another, neither one giving in. Unsure if there was anything he could say or do that would make up for what he'd just said, Dave finally lowered his gaze and drew in a heavy sigh. The damage had been done, and it was possible their relationship would never be the same. Pursing his lips, he tried to push that defeatist thought to the back of his mind. No, he couldn't believe that. There had to be a chance he might be able to salvage something. Swallowing his pride, he straightened and took an awkward step forward with his hands held together in a penitential gesture.

'Claire, I—'

Dave's attempt to make amends was rudely interrupted by three firm knocks. They sounded like they were coming from the other side of the room's access hatch. Dave bristled in annoyance and tried to ignore it.

Whoever it was, they had lousy timing, but he was adamant he would not let them stop him from making it up with Claire. He reached out and tried to place his hand on her shoulder. But she continued to give him the silent treatment while he pleaded with her.

'Listen, Claire, I didn't mean—'

Three more loud knocks cut him off, only this time they sounded more insistent.

Dave pressed his fingers against the bridge of his nose and let out a long, measured breath, struggling to contain the growing frustration within him. Blast it! Why couldn't they leave them alone? But he realised whoever was knocking wasn't going to go away in a hurry unless they received an answer. His irritation getting the better of him, Dave spun around and shouted at the hatchway with more force than he intended.

'What is it?' he barked impatiently.

The person on the other side of the hatch must have recognised the tone of displeasure in Dave's voice because the knocking suddenly stopped. There was a pause, and then a woman's voice piped up, speaking with what Dave thought sounded like an Italian accent. 'Hello? I apologise if I'm disturbing you.' Dave raised an eyebrow curiously as he listened to the stranger's voice continue. 'But Karen told me you were ready. So I'm here to escort you to our conference room.' Despite the Italian accent, he thought her voice sounded oddly familiar.

Just as he was about to answer, something wet landed on Dave's face, startling him. *What the actual fu*— He angrily pulled the damp cloth off his face and lifted his eyebrows in surprise at the realisation it was a washcloth. Bewildered as to why it had landed on his face, he slowly turned, looked over to Claire. She was making strange scrubbing motions with her hands. He realised he'd been so focused on the hatchway he hadn't seen her race over to the sink and grab the cloth. Dave still had no idea why she'd thrown it to him. He scratched his head, looked at the cloth, and stared blankly at Claire. What was he supposed to do with this? He wondered if Claire's throwing things at him was caused by her strange mood swings.

'Wash. Your. Face,' Claire hissed through gritted teeth, angrily gesturing to the cloth in his hands.

Still not understanding what she meant, he continued to give Claire a blank stare, frowning, 'Huh?'

'Give me strength,' Claire muttered, pinching the bridge of her nose. She scowled and made angry gesturing motions to her lips and right cheek.

Dave instinctively reached up to touch his face and felt his eyes grow wide as he felt something sticking to his cheek. *Oh, that's why she threw the cloth,* he thought, the penny dropping. *She must have got chocolate on me and wants me to wash it off.* He acknowledged Claire with a sheepish grin; she answered with a snort and a roll of her eyes. The murderous glint was still there in her eyes, giving him the impression that she must have thought he was an idiot and that she was probably mentally calling him all the names under the sun.

Frantically rubbing the damp cloth over his face, Dave answered whoever was behind the door. 'Um, yeah,' he said, trying to keep the panic from registering in his voice while he looked for a place to get rid of the cloth. 'W-w-we're ready for you. Y-y-you can come in.'

'Here, give it to me,' Claire growled, snatching the cloth out of Dave's hands and hurling it across the room into the washbasin.

Relieved to have got rid of the evidence of their recent moment of passion, Dave placed his hands behind his back and tried to look as innocent as possible. Out of the corner of his eye, he saw Claire plant her face in her hands while muttering something under her breath. Fed up with her strange behaviour, Dave bit back a retort as the hatch swung open and a statuesque, athletic woman stepped into the room.

Dave guessed she must be at least six feet three inches in height and was probably in her late twenties or early thirties. She was wearing the same military fatigues as he and Claire. An eyepatch covered her right eye, which somewhat obscured the right side of her narrow face, giving her a sinister vibe. But as he drew his eyes up to her short red hair, Dave frowned. He was struck by a strange sense of recognition. Why did he feel

like he knew her?

'Oh, my god!' Claire exclaimed. 'The resemblance is uncanny.'

Dave blinked and gave Claire a puzzled glance. 'Huh? What the hell are you—'

Then it hit him.

Of course, now I can see it! Dave felt his eyebrows climb up his forehead, and he was unable to stop his mouth dropping open in stunned shock as he realised why the woman looked so familiar. He swallowed and blew out a slow whistle of astonishment, then took a step closer to get a better look. Apart from the eyepatch, the stranger bore a striking resemblance to Wendy Cooper.

'Wendy?' Dave asked, cautious not to offend the woman. He sucked in a long breath as he tried to regain his composure and gave an embarrassed cough. 'Sorry, please forgive us for staring like this – it's just that you bear a striking resemblance to someone we know.'

The corner of the stranger's mouth quirked up, and she gave a slight bob of acknowledgement. 'Perfectly understandable. But to answer your question, yes, I'm your Wendy's doppelgänger,' she said, laughing. 'Or she's my doppelgänger. It can get very confusing.'

'So, do we call you Wendy too?' Claire enquired, the expression on her face matching Dave's own curiosity.

A shadow briefly crossed over the doppelgänger's face and for a moment Dave got a sense that the statement had annoyed her. He shook his head. No, not annoyance. It was something else, but he wasn't sure what. However, no sooner was it there than it was gone, and her expression appeared to soften.

'I don't go by that name anymore,' she answered cryptically, flicking her wrist in a dismissive manner. 'But that's a long story, which we don't have time for. So for now you can call me Cooper.'

The name Cooper sparked a memory within Dave, and he thought back to the conversation he had had with his own doppelgänger, Colonel Barnes. An unsettling feeling churned inside his stomach as he recalled the colonel saying his Cooper was not only a general but was somebody who

should be feared. A mixture of panic and confusion rose within Dave as he narrowed his eyes and studied the woman in front of him. Hadn't Karen said something about this place belonging to some sort of resistance unit? If that was true, then what was Cooper doing here? The hairs on the back of Dave's neck tingled, and he had the sense that something was off.

'Forgive me,' Dave asked, careful to keep the suspicion from showing in his voice. 'But you wouldn't happen to be General Cooper, would you?'

The question appeared to take Cooper by surprise; she stiffened in shock and blinked. This lasted only a few seconds before it was replaced by a hint of amusement as she held up a finger and nodded slowly. 'Ah, I see you've met the delightful Colonel Barnes,' she said in a tone so thick with disdain, Dave could almost imagine it dripping off her tongue. Dave gave a silent nod of confirmation, to which Cooper responded with what he thought sounded like a regretful sigh. 'Yes, it's true I was previously known as General Cooper.' She shook her head and laughed mirthlessly. 'Or that cold-hearted bitch, or the whore of the URE. Take your pick. I've been called many things over the years. But that all changed following a near fatal encounter with an acquaintance of yours.'

A hint of understanding flashed across Claire's face, and she gave Cooper an enquiring side eye. 'That wouldn't be Oracle, would it?'

As Cooper held up her hands and gave a thin smile, a light bulb sparked to life within Dave's brain. He shook his head and laughed out loud. 'Oh, I see. You saw how the wind was blowing, so you switched sides.'

If Dave's assessment insulted her, Cooper didn't show it. Instead, she pulled a sour face and lifted her shoulder in a half shrug. 'Erm, not quite. I know it sounds confusing, but please believe me when I say I'm no longer that person.' She straightened proudly and made a wide sweeping gesture with her hands. 'These people took me in, gave me a home and a role as acting commander until E—' She seemed to stop herself, coughed and carried on. 'Until our leader heals from injuries she sustained during an attack by Oracle. I promise you, if you follow me, I will answer all your

questions.

Despite any reservations he may have had, Dave got a sense Cooper wasn't being deceitful with them. He rubbed his chin in thoughtful introspection and cast an eye at Claire, who answered him with a grunt and a shrug. Every instinct told him that Cooper was somebody who could be trusted, so he decided to go with his gut. It wasn't as if they had any other choices anyway.

'Fine,' he said and bobbed his head at the open hatchway. 'You lead the way.'

Cooper raised an eyebrow, then cocked her head curiously and asked, 'Do you need a moment to freshen up or anything?'

Claire's nostrils flared, and she eyed Dave with clear disdain. 'No,' she answered in a caustic tone, pushing past Cooper and stomping through the hatch. 'That moment has most definitely passed.'

Ignoring the bewildered glance coming from Cooper, Dave exhaled the tension gathering in his lungs and his shoulders sagged in defeat. It was obvious Claire still harboured a grudge, and she wasn't going to let him forget about that comment anytime soon. As he followed Cooper through the hatchway and into the corridor, Dave found himself wishing he hadn't survived the nuclear explosion.

As he followed Cooper through the maze of interconnecting corridors, Dave felt a sense a déjà vu. He wasn't sure whether it was because of the lighting or the way the corridors interconnected with one another, but they reminded him of the Castle's layout. For a second, he thought he'd woken up from a dream and was once again walking down its familiar corridors. Of course, he realised that was insane because he and Claire had had an up-close personal front seat to its destruction.

'Mind if I ask?' he said, tapping Cooper on the shoulder. 'But are we in an underground complex of some kind?'

Her gaze still fixed on the corridor ahead, Cooper gave a brusque

nod in reply. 'Yes. Emperor Hadrianus originally built this structure about two thousand years ago as part of what would later be known as the Hadrianus Deterrent.'

'Impressive,' Dave answered, nodding. That wasn't a lie; he was impressed by the idea that something this size had survived for so long because on his Earth what remained of the equivalent, Hadrian's Wall, was in ruins.

Dave glanced over at Claire to gauge her reaction because she was a history professor who specialised in Roman history, but she only answered with an indifferent shrug of her shoulders. Her reaction disappointed him; he'd thought she would have jumped at the chance to learn more about this world. He pressed his lips together and focused back on the corridor in front of him. Claire's moodiness had him worried, but he was at a loss as to how he should handle it. If he pressured her, it might just put her into a deeper spiral. The only solution he could think of was to give her some space and hope she would eventually let him in when she was ready.

But before Dave could give it any more thought, an excited cry of delight came from behind him, breaking him out of his troubled thoughts. He glanced over his shoulder; a slim, raven-haired young woman was racing down an adjacent corridor toward them, waving her hand in wild excitement at Cooper. As she got closer, Dave realised she was in her mid-teens. At first, he thought she must be related to someone on the base, but then he heard her accent. He was positive he could detect what sounded like broad Durham in her voice. Did that mean she was also from his Earth? Had she been abducted too?

'Zoe,' Cooper said, giving the teen a stern look. 'What have I told you before about running in the corridors?'

Coming to a sudden stop in front of Cooper, Zoe hung her head and stuck out her bottom lip. 'Sorry,' she replied in a surly tone. 'It's just that I heard from Karen the new arrivals are awake and that you're on your way to see them.'

Cooper laughed and playfully slapped Zoe's shoulder. 'You're too

late. We're just on our way up to the conference room to see the others.' She turned slightly to her left and indicated Dave. 'Detective Inspector Dave Barnes, this is Zoe Murray, who, as they say on your Earth, is from your neck of the woods.'

At the mention of Zoe's full name, Dave felt himself stiffen in recognition, sparking a memory of a conversation he'd had with Andy shortly after meeting Claire. He guessed Cooper and Zoe must have seen his reaction because an odd look passed between them. He gave an embarrassed cough and waved his hand, giving a weak smile.

'Sorry,' he said. 'I must apologise for my reaction, but I suddenly realised why I recognised your name, Zoe. Are you the same Zoe Murray who was attacked by a strange creature while inside a deserted building a few months ago?'

Zoe's eyes grew wide as saucers. 'How'd you know about that?' she gasped.

'My detective sergeant had the pleasure of speaking to your doppelgänger,' Dave said in a solemn voice.

A flash of understanding flickered in Zoe's eyes, and she gave a small bob of her head. It seemed as if she was on the verge of saying something but stopped; her eyes narrowed into tight slits and she scowled at something. At first, Dave thought she was looking at someone she knew, but as he followed her eyeline, he realised she was looking at Claire. He wrinkled his brow in puzzlement. Did Zoe know Claire? Had they met previously?

If she was aware of the hostility emanating from Zoe, Claire gave no sign; instead she remained silent while Dave introduced her. 'This is my friend, Professor Claire—'

'Oh, I'm perfectly aware of who that cow is,' Zoe cut in, her voice dripping with unmistakable contempt.

'Zoe!' Cooper exclaimed in shock.

A mixture of hurt and confusion swept across Claire's face, and she took a step back. 'I-I-I'm sorry?' she stammered. 'Have we met before?'

'Nobody wants you here,' Zoe spat, her face echoing the disdain

in her voice. 'Why don't you do us all a favour and drop—'

'Zoe Murray, that's enough!' Cooper shouted, her face incandescent with rage. 'You will apologise to Claire right now, missy.'

Zoe stuck out her bottom lip and folded her arms across her chest in petulant refusal. 'No. I won't. You can't make me.'

Her face thunderous, Cooper straightened to her full height and took two steps toward Zoe. Dave thought he saw a crack appear in Zoe's angry exterior as she craned her head back and met Cooper's gaze. The colour drained from Zoe's face while Cooper spoke in an obviously deliberately slow voice, which had an edge to it. Dave couldn't blame Zoe for her reaction to Cooper's steely gaze and the harsh tone of her voice. He imagined that if he'd been on the receiving end, his testicles might have shrivelled up inside him out of fear.

'Let me make it plain to you, Mistress Murray. You will go back to your quarters. Once there, you will sit and wait for me to arrive. Is that understood?'

A glimmer of uncertainty flickered in Zoe's eyes, and she gave her head a weak shake. 'Hil—'

'Is that understood?' Cooper shouted with such force, Dave was sure that most of the base must have heard it.

All the fight seemed to vanish from Zoe and her shoulders sagged, apparently in defeat. After shooting Claire a hateful stare, Zoe turned and slowly made her way back down the corridor. Dave was sure he'd seen a glint of a tear roll down her cheeks. If he hadn't witnessed her rude behaviour, he might have even felt sorry for her.

Once the sorrowful-looking teen was out of sight, Cooper shook her head sadly, pinched the bridge of her nose, drew in a deep breath, held it and then let it out. Dave cocked his head and studied the enigmatic woman before him. He got the sense that it had been hard for Cooper to shout at Zoe that way and wondered if she cared deeply for the girl. Maybe they treated each other as siblings – Zoe, the younger sister and Cooper, the eldest. Dave recalled Andy and the Wendy from his reality visiting Zoe in hospital to interview her after they received a report that a strange

creature had attacked her. Andy and Wendy both felt Zoe had acted strangely throughout the whole interview. A couple of days later, they learned people were being abducted and replaced with doppelgängers. That had happened just over two months ago, so Dave guessed that between then and now the resistance had rescued Zoe. Furthermore, while interrogating his doppelgänger, Colonel Barnes, Dave discovered that General Cooper was his commanding officer. It wasn't difficult to figure out that Cooper must have been caught by the resistance around the same time as Zoe was rescued. He scratched his head while he tried to understand how such a relationship could have developed in such a brief space of time. The only explanation he could think of was that something must have happened for them to have such a strong bond with one another.

But before he could give it any more thought, Cooper turned and held up her hands in apology to Claire. 'Claire, I must apologise for Zoe's attitude toward you,' she said in what sounded like a sincere tone. 'I keep forgetting how young Zoe is and that she can sometimes be hot-headed. Rest assured, though, her rudeness will not go unpunished. You have my word on that.'

'Oh, I wouldn't worry,' Dave said, smiling and flicking his wrist in a dismissive gesture. 'I'm sure Claire understands we all did stupid things at that age.'

Dave smirked while he tried to imagine what Claire must have been like when she was Zoe's age. He shook his head and let out a small chuckle as he leaned toward her to give her a playful nudge with his elbow. A dirty look from Claire stopped him in his tracks, and a wave of sadness overtook him as he realised she had put up an invisible barrier between them. He exhaled a despondent sigh and followed the two women back down the corridor.

A short time later, after being led through an impressive-looking command

centre, the trio came to a stop outside a closed hatch. Dave lifted a curious eyebrow as Cooper rapped on the hatch just before pushing it open, only pausing to glance back at them both.

'Please brace yourself,' Cooper said, her voice containing a twang of excitement. 'It may come as a shock, but this person has been waiting a long time to see you.'

Recalling Karen saying the same thing, Dave was curious as to who on this world would be waiting to see them, and cast a surreptitious eye at Claire. He felt a pang of sadness, which was mixed with disappointment on seeing Claire's uninterested body language. He'd expected her to show some emotion, excitement even, but there was nothing. Since their earlier spat, it seemed as if Claire had grown colder than ever, as if she'd given up and was indifferent to what was happening around her.

Deep down, Dave had a fair idea of understanding what Claire must have been going through, because he was going through it too. He was also mentally struggling with his recent near-death experience and was just barely hanging on. He usually considered himself to be a patient and caring man, but Claire's entire attitude was wearing him down, and he was sick of it. He ground his teeth and snapped his gaze away from her. As far as he was concerned, she could do what she liked. He had enough on his plate without adding Claire's worries to them as well.

Focusing his attention back on the hatch, he hadn't realised Cooper had been waiting for him to give the go-ahead. He shrugged and made a sweeping gesture to let her know she could enter.

As soon as he walked into the medium-sized conference room, Dave sucked in a sharp breath at the two people waiting inside. Then it dawned on him what Cooper had been trying to tell them. It wasn't both of them they'd been waiting to see. It was Claire. Once he'd got over the initial shock, Dave focused on the people in the room. Standing behind a conference room table was an impressive, but also very intimidating, dreadlocked bear of a man. He must have been close to seven feet in height. Dave felt a twinge of inferiority at seeing the thickness of the bruiser's arms, and he imagined he could easily snap him in two without even

breaking a sweat. To his surprise, the barrel-chested stranger turned toward him and bowed his head, which Dave acknowledged with a nervous smile.

However, it was not the intimidating man whose appearance had rattled Dave. No, it was the woman sitting behind the table. She was identical to Claire. Her brown hair was shorter, and from the toned muscles in her arms, he got the impression she was more physically athletic than Claire. But the resemblance in her face and eyes was uncanny. His first thought was that she must have been Claire's doppelgänger, but then the synapses in his brain fired and he remembered Zoe's reaction to Claire, as well as Cooper's and Karen's words about someone having waited a very long time to see Claire. Eventually, putting two and two together, Dave had a jarring epiphany.

It was Claire's twin sister.

Emma.

Alive and well.

On this world, all this time.

Struggling to find his voice, Dave took a step forward and held up a trembling finger at Emma. 'Emma Tulley?' he croaked.

Emma turned to Dave and fixed her eyes on him. For a split second, Dave thought he detected something within them. He wasn't sure, but he was positive it was a mixture of recognition and anger. But no sooner than it was there, it was gone, and her expression softened as she gave a nod of confirmation. He frowned while he thought about her reaction to him and concluded she must have met Colonel Barnes at some point in her life. From the time he'd spent with his counterpart, he had a fair idea as to the reason for her initial hostility toward him and wondered what Barnes must have done to her to warrant such a reaction. Whatever it had been, he guessed it wouldn't be long before he found out.

As Emma rose from her chair, Dave thought he saw her wince in pain and touch her chest; he assumed she had recently sustained an injury and was still recovering. A touch of concern flashed across the big man's face, and he reached out to grab her as if to offer his support. Emma shook her head and waved him away before grabbing hold of a cane. The big man

scowled and took a step back, but as he did so, Dave thought he caught something glint in his eyes. It was small and only lasted an instant, but Dave was sure it was a hint of affection, which told him that the big man cared deeply for Emma. Were they lovers or just good friends?

Emma hobbled around the table, coming to a stop in front of an impassive-looking Claire. A wide smile beamed across Emma's face, and she extended a hand to Claire. 'Hey, Cee.' Emma grinned with apparent nervousness. 'Long time no see, huh?'

Dave held his breath, crossed his fingers, and waited for Claire to respond. He silently wished that seeing Emma might be the push Claire needed to break her out of her funk. However, and much to his sadness, Claire's face was an unreadable mask, and she just stood motionless, fixing Emma with an unblinking gaze. There was no outward display of emotion of any kind. If anybody had chosen that moment to walk in, it was highly likely they would have assumed she was a mannequin.

Dave thought he detected a faint hint of hurt flash across Em's face as she took a step back from the emotionless Claire. Her pained expression changed to a heavy frown, and she turned to share a puzzled look with Dave, who held up his hands in silent exasperation, to which Emma responded with a confused but sympathetic nod.

As if to clear the cloud of awkwardness that hung over the room, Emma coughed and made a sweeping gesture with her hands. 'We've a lot to talk about,' she said in a blunt, matter-of-fact tone. 'So please take a seat.'

David pulled out a chair as instructed and sat down. Cooper and the burly stranger each took a seat on either side of Emma. Out of the corner of his eye, Dave noticed Claire had remained where she was, still standing fixed to the spot, her unblinking eyes fixed on Emma. A wave of despair overtook Dave. Even though he had told himself he no longer cared what she did, he had to admit he was lying to himself. He still cared deeply for her, and it was killing him inside seeing her act this way. It felt like he was slowly losing her and was powerless to stop it.

If Emma gave any outward sign that Claire's behaviour was troubling her, Dave could not see it. Instead, she leaned forward with her fingers steepled together and began explaining what had happened to her, with Cooper occasionally jumping in to add something. As he leaned back and listened to Cooper and Emma tell their stories, an unsettling feeling grew inside him as he realised that maybe they had jumped out of the frying pan and into the fire.

ACT ONE
Ten weeks earlier …

-1-

Reality 672
Terra (Counter-Earth)
10th November 5775

Choking on a scream, Gwendovaria 'Wendy' Cooper gasped for breath and sat up in her bed; her left hand clutching her chest. Her heart was pounding so hard, she thought it was going to burst. Her face was clammy with sweat and her clothing felt uncomfortably damp. Squeezing her eyes shut, Cooper leaned back, rested her head against the metal headboard and inhaled several breaths to help control her pulse.

'It's okay. It's just a dream,' Cooper muttered to herself. 'Oracle can't get you. You're safe.'

But despite trying to reassure herself, a part of Cooper deep down knew that wasn't true. Ever since she had woken from her week-long coma just under a week ago, she'd been having the same nightmare over and over. It always ended the same way, with her heart being ripped out of her chest, and it left her with a sense of dread. It was that same dread she was experiencing now, because she understood if Oracle ever learned she was still alive, then it would stop at nothing to find her.

With her heart rate under control, Cooper exhaled and tried to open her eyes, but discovered that she could only open her left eye. Her sleep-deprived brain still confused from its rude awakening, Cooper lifted

her left hand and gently probed the area surrounding her right eye. She furrowed her brow as her fingers came into contact with a soft fabric. Something was covering her eye. Why would—

Then her mind fog lifted, and she remembered that her right eye had sustained damage during her fight with Oracle. Even though the medics at the rebel base had tried to repair the damage with a biogenetic healing agent, they were unable to save the eye. The medics in the base's infirmary were all volunteers and only had limited knowledge of treating minor injuries, so were not skilled at tending major wounds. Cooper did not harbour any ill will toward them; she understood they had tried the best they could under difficult circumstances. It was common knowledge that all experienced medical personnel had been drafted into the URE's service, but there were still some who tried to assist the resistance whenever they could. If it hadn't been for the fear of reprisals against their families, many doctors would have joined the resistance's cause.

Cooper lifted her right arm and inspected the thick biogenetic healing pad wrapped around it. She tried to wiggle her fingers and smiled when she saw them move. *At least I still have my arm.* Even though her forearm had been shattered by Oracle, Cooper was delighted that it was nearly fully healed. She closed her eye and said a silent prayer to Parentes, her household spirit, to thank her for showing her some mercy.

But as she pulled herself up to move off the bed, Cooper exhaled sharply at the discomfort brought on by that slight movement. She delicately probed her ribs with her fingers and winced at their sensitivity, even though they were nearly fully healed. Cooper grumbled. Oracle had really done a number on her. But, she conceded, at least she was still alive. Things could have gone very differently during the fight, and she could have either ended up being an unrecognisable bloody mess on the footpath, or worse – she could have ended up as one of that thing's mindless minions.

Clenching her teeth and trying to ignore the protest of pain coming from her ribs, Cooper swung her legs over the edge of her bed. She inhaled a deep breath and stood up. *Okay,* she thought, *so far, so good. I'm upright. But why does the room suddenly feel like it's tipping to one side?* Overcome by vertigo, Cooper staggered forward and placed her hand on the wall to steady herself. Resting her head against the wall, she closed her good eye and took deep breaths while she waited for the vertigo to ease. *Well, this just won't do. I can't stand here all day against the wall acting like a piece of furniture. You're better than this. Now get a hold of yourself and suck it up!*

Cooper gave a disgruntled sigh. Now that she had joined the ranks of the monocularly sighted, she reluctantly accepted that she was going to have to wait until her body had adjusted to her partial loss of sight. She blew out her cheeks and exhaled slowly. *Well, this is just great.* All those skills she had learned, becoming proficient in every style of weapon and unarmed combat, were now going to waste. She was going to have to retrain her body and start all over again from scratch.

It suddenly hit Cooper where she was, and she let out a bitter laugh. She massaged her forehead and stared up at the ceiling. Had she just thought that she was going to retrain herself in using weapons? She scoffed and shook her head. There was no chance her new friends would let her anywhere near their weapons, never mind train with them. They were more likely to force her to stand in front of a wall and use her for target practice!

The vertigo subsiding, Cooper opened her good eye and gingerly made her way over to the handbasin across from the bed. Not long after she had regained consciousness, Cooper had discovered that she had been moved into one of the side rooms of the infirmary. These rooms were normally designated for patients who were critically injured, but Cooper was in no doubt that they had done this for her own protection from any reprisals by certain members of the resistance whose families had been harmed by the URE's overzealous troops. She couldn't blame them, really. There were a lot of things her former self had done that left Cooper feeling ashamed, wishing there was some way she could make up for her past self's deeds.

Cooper rested her hands on the edge of the handbasin and peered into the mirror that hung on the wall. She rotated her head from side to side and examined her reflection. Her once glossy short red hair was now unkempt and damp with sweat. Although the bruising on her face was almost gone, there was still an unhealthy appearance to her complexion, giving her a jaundiced look. Cooper tilted her head and ran her fingers over the patch covering what remained of her right eye.

'You would have loved this look, wouldn't you, General?' Cooper hissed, scowling at the reflection in the mirror. 'Oh, I know what you would have been thinking – that it made you even more intimidating. You were one piece of work, you heartless bi—'

Cooper froze as she noticed something in the mirror. Just over her left shoulder, it appeared someone had nudged the door open and was peeking into her room. On recognising the pair of emerald eyes peering through the crack, Cooper gave a discreet nod in acknowledgement. *Right on time*, she thought, smiling secretively. Zoe seemed to have gotten into the habit of peering into Cooper's room at the same time every morning. Never coming in, just remaining outside, staring into the room as if she was working up the courage to enter. Cooper couldn't fathom what the young woman wanted, but she hoped today might be the day she would find out, although she couldn't blame Zoe for being afraid to enter after the way she'd been treated when she first arrived on this world.

A pang of sadness filled Cooper as one of her former self's memories came unbidden to her, of her first meeting with Zoe Murray. The poor girl had been abducted from Counter-Terra, but instead of receiving a warm welcome, she had been tortured and abused at the hands of General Cooper. Cooper's stomach churned in disgust as she pictured her own hands inflicting suffering on someone so young and innocent.

Exhaling deeply, Cooper despondently shook her head to clear the memory away. She set her jaw and nodded thoughtfully at her own reflection. Maybe it was time she made the first move and offered an olive branch to Zoe; perhaps it might make things easier for them both. Although she knew it would take a lot for people to forgive the acts of violence committed by the general, Cooper reasoned that if she could make Zoe see that she wasn't the same person, then maybe that would help pave the way to her redemption.

'I can see you are there, Zoe,' Cooper called out softly. She turned and motioned for Zoe to come forward. 'It's okay, you can come in.'

Zoe's head jerked away, but Cooper could still make out her shadow on the infirmary's floor. Was she trying to decide to run, Cooper wondered, or was this the day she would take that step forward? Even though she had been stuck in the infirmary, she was very much aware of

the ill feeling toward her from those in the base. It was hard to miss the hostile glances of people who passed her room, so it didn't take a genius to guess she wasn't well liked. It was going to be no easy task to win the confidence of the rebels, but she reasoned all she had to do was to start small. If she could earn the trust of someone she – sorry, her other self – had abused, then it could help to show the rest of them she meant them no harm. As her father once told her when she was a young girl – *'To build a sturdy alliance, you first must start with a firm foundation of trust.'*

'It's okay, child, I'll not hurt you,' Cooper said encouragingly. 'I promise, you've got nothing to be afraid of.'

Cooper held her breath as the door slowly opened and Zoe edged carefully into the room. Analysing Zoe's body language, the way her chin just about touched the top of her chest and how her eyes were locked on the floor, Cooper could tell Zoe was struggling in the presence of someone who had inflicted so much pain and misery. Despite feeling ashamed for what had been done to Zoe, Cooper admired the youth. It must have taken a tremendous amount of effort for her to take those final few steps.

But Cooper wondered what was motivating her to do this. She could have easily avoided her. Why was Zoe so persistent in seeing her? Did she want to look Cooper in the eye and demand an apology from her? She glanced down at Zoe's hands – this time, there was no weapon being held in them. So, one thing was certain: Zoe wasn't here to kill her.

Cooper gave Zoe a warm smile and took a step forward. 'I'm pleased you've come. Firstly, can I just sa—' The words died in her throat. Zoe recoiled from her, and Cooper nodded in understanding. She held up her hands in a placating gesture and slowly edged back to her bed. 'I'm sorry. I didn't mean to startle you. If it makes you feel any better, I'll stay on this side of the room. You came to me, so we'll take it as slow as you want.'

Zoe shuffled her feet and gave a small shrug. 'It's alright,' she mumbled back. 'Um, I just wanted to see how you were doing. Um, if there was anything you needed … um … whatever.'

Cooper cocked her head and stared at Zoe with mild curiosity. She strongly suspected that was a lie and there was a different reason for Zoe's visit. Although the general's personality was no longer in control, Cooper

still retained her instincts and perceptiveness. Something was troubling Zoe, but rather than force the issue, she decided to make small talk and hoped Zoe would open up in her own time.

'So, how are you doing?' Cooper asked. She smiled and gestured to the open door. 'I see you've made some new friends. Are they treating you well?'

'Um, yeah,' Zoe muttered back, 'they're treating me like one of the family.' She lifted her head and let out a small laugh. 'There's this big bloke, Isaac. He's very protective of me, treats me like his sister or something. Then there's Em. You've already met her. She's this group's commander or leader, or whatever – you know what I mean. She's just amazing.' Zoe rolled her eyes and sighed heavily. 'She's always mothering me. Telling me to do this, do that. Making sure I'm eating enough. I'm not complaining though, me and my mam didn't have what you would call the best of relationships. So it's nice to have someone like Em looking out for me.'

The corners of Cooper's mouth quivered in amusement as she noticed the colour in Zoe's cheeks redden slightly every time she mentioned Em's name. From what Zoe was saying, it sounded like Em had taken Zoe under her wing and they had developed a mother-and-daughter bond. Cooper tapped her chin thoughtfully as one of the general's memories drifted to the surface. It was from the psychological profile that had been carried out on Zoe while she had been a prisoner. From the information that the general had gleaned, it was apparent that Zoe had come from a broken home and things were strained between her and her mum. Seeing Zoe had finally found someone who could be the mother she deserved filled Cooper with a warm sense of joy. Maybe some good had come from Zoe's abduction after all.

Realising she had let herself get distracted, Cooper blinked, focused her attention back on Zoe. She was grateful that Zoe appeared not to have noticed her momentary lack of concentration. In fact, she appeared to be more at ease and was beginning to open up.

'Em's awesome,' Zoe continued, appearing to come more out of her shell. 'She's showing me all this really cool technology you guys have. She even let me drive a hover car!' She let out a small squeal of delight and clapped her hands. 'Can you believe it? A real live hover car! That's fire!

Well, I ...' Zoe stiffened and her cheeks flamed up in embarrassment. She lowered her head and gave Cooper a sheepish look. 'Sorry, I forgot myself there. I shouldn't have told you all that.'

'It's okay,' Cooper said, grinning. She leaned forward, gave Zoe a sly wink, and lowered her voice to a conspiratorial whisper. 'I won't tell anyone if you don't.'

To Cooper's surprise, Zoe let out a loud bark of laughter. Then, as if suddenly realising who she was speaking to, she pulled her gaze away from Cooper and stared at something on the floor. Her lips tightening into a thin line, she lapsed into an uncomfortable silence and began pacing slowly around the small room. Wondering what was going through Zoe's mind, Cooper gave a small nod and pretended to idly inspect her fingernails. *Don't push her. Take it slow.*

After a few minutes of uneasy silence, Zoe stopped her pacing and moved closer to Cooper. Cooper kept her face neutral as Zoe positioned herself on the edge of the mattress. She was so close, Cooper had to restrain herself from reaching and placing her hand on Zoe's shoulder. Zoe exhaled and then spoke in a hesitant tone, all the while continuing to stare at the floor.

'Um, General. May I—'

Cooper held up her hand, cutting Zoe off. 'Sorry, but please don't call me that,' she snapped angrily, but immediately regretted almost biting Zoe's head off. It wasn't Zoe's fault that she didn't know Oracle had had Cooper's personality altered when she was a child, and only recently restored it to normal. If she was going to act like this every time people called her General, she was going to have to develop a thick skin and try not to lash out. She held up her hands and exhaled a heavy sigh. 'Sorry, I didn't mean to snap at you. What I mean to say is that person no longer exists.'

Zoe lifted her head and stared at Cooper in bewilderment. Cooper could see the confusion etched across her face as she shook her head. 'I don't understand. What do you mean, that person no longer exists?'

'That's ... a long story.' Cooper laughed, giving a dismissive wave. 'Let's just say I was brainwashed by Oracle and leave it there. Right now, this is about you.'

From the dubious expression on Zoe's face, Cooper could tell she wasn't sure what to make of her. Zoe tilted her head, narrowed her eyes, and regarded Cooper with clear suspicion. Cooper wondered if Zoe thought she was playing some sort of game. She couldn't blame her really after everything she'd been through. Being honest with herself, if their situations had been reversed, Cooper reluctantly conceded that she probably would have reacted the same way.

'Huh-huh, o … kay,' Zoe replied slowly, giving Cooper a guarded look, 'so, if I can't call you General Cooper, what do I call you?'

Cooper blinked and stared at Zoe in mild surprise. Even though she'd been expecting Zoe's query, it was one she didn't have an answer to. She stuck her tongue between her lips and stared at the ceiling thoughtfully. That was a good question. What should Zoe call her? As far as she was concerned, the name Wendy Cooper had been stolen from her a long time ago. Wendy Cooper was associated with fear, pain and intimidation, everything she wanted so badly to distance herself from that. Unfortunately, there wasn't a lot she could do about changing her name … Cooper arched an eyebrow. Or was there?

You silly girl, Cooper thought, slapping her brow in disgust. *Just go back to using your original name.* She widened her mouth into a knowing smile as the solution to her problem had been staring at her the whole time. It was a name from so long ago, from a time before Oracle and the URE had corrupted her – Hilaria Cooper. It was the name her parents had given to her just after she was born. She'd forgotten that when they had been forced to sell her into the URE's service, those in charge insisted that her name be changed to one that represented ideals of the so-called Universal Roman Empire. A name they felt personified strength and courage. And so, she became Gwendovaria Cooper, soldier of the URE. But it was only a few months before her fellow recruits eventually shortened it to Wendy.

'Tell you what. You can call me Hilaria. My parents used to call me their little Hilaria when I was a small child, because they said I brought them so much joy.' Hilaria smiled warmly and extended her hand to Zoe. 'Hello, Zoe Murray. My name is Hilaria. Pleased to meet you.'

Still looking confused, Zoe stared down at the offered hand. At first she appeared unsure how to react, but then her face clouded with

anger, and she slapped Hilaria's hand away. Totally unprepared for the reaction, Hilaria could only stare with her mouth open as Zoe jumped up and looked down at her with eyes filled with suspicion and anger. She hissed at Hilaria through gritted teeth. 'You think using a different name will make people forget the things you've done?' she snarled. 'You've got some nerve, General ... Cooper .... Hilaria or whatever you want to call yourself. I don't know what game you're playing at, but I'm telling you now, you won't fool me again.'

Trying to hide the hurt she was feeling, Hilaria blinked away the tears and tried to regain control of her emotions. Whether it was because of Zoe's hostile attitude toward her or the weariness she was feeling, anger was bubbling inside her. Was this how it was going to be for the rest of her life? Was she going to be forever forced to wear the stain of General Cooper's actions? Struggling to rein in her anger, Hilaria shot up and jabbed her finger into Zoe's chest. Her eyes growing wide in shock, Zoe backed away, apparently taken completely by surprise by Hilaria's fury.

'I'm getting fed up with having to defend myself to you people,' Hilaria growled, her face almost touching Zoe's. 'Don't care if you believe me or not, but if you want me to apologise for General Cooper's actions, I will.' She took a step back, held up her hands and exhaled slowly. 'Zoe, I apologise for everything that was done to you. If I could take it back, I would. But please believe me when I tell you, I am just as much a victim as you. You may remember me telling Commander Tulley about an insane AI called Oracle.' Hilaria paused while she waited for Zoe to give some sort of sign of acknowledgement.

Zoe nodded sullenly and spoke in a hushed whisper. 'Um, yeah, I think I can remember you saying something.'

Hilaria gave a sad smile, glanced up at the ceiling as she thought back to that night twenty years ago. Her vision clouded and she felt a lump in her throat as she tried to get the words out. 'I don't know if you have heard the story of what happens to children in the URE, but when we reach eight years of age, our parents are forced to sell us into the URE's service.' She let out a bitter laugh and shook her head. 'I found life at the academy hard because I wasn't what you would call a gifted student. My instructors would ridicule me for being slow-witted because I could barely read, and

they thought I lacked the right aptitude to be a soldier. They were even considering expelling me from the academy, believing I was probably more suited to being a slave or some other menial work. My last normal memory was sitting in bed using my tablet just before I felt a strange tingle of electricity pass through me. I only recently learned Oracle had altered my brain structure, increased my intelligence, and went on to create a more ruthless personality.' She blew a long breath and stared sadly at Zoe. 'The vindictive Wendy Cooper, who you met.'

Zoe curled her upper lip and scoffed. 'What? You're telling me this sob story so you think it'll make me more sympathetic to you?'

What is wrong with this girl? Are all the adolescents from her world like this? Hilaria felt the muscle in the right side of her jaw twitch. Feeling her temper rising, she closed her eye and inhaled a deep breath, blew it out slowly, and then spoke in a measured tone. 'No, I'm not telling you that so I can buy your sympathy. I told you that to help make you understand that I'm just as much a victim here as you are.' She shook her head, turned away from Zoe, and waved her hand in dismissal. 'I can see you don't believe me. Go on, be off with you, stop wasting my time and don't come back.'

Tears streaming down her cheeks, Zoe lurched forward and grabbed Hilaria's arm. 'N-n-no, Hilaria, please, I'm sorry – don't send me away.'

Surprised by Zoe's sudden shift in behaviour, Hilaria cocked her head and regarded Zoe curiously. Was there something else going on here? Even though Zoe's tearful outburst seemed genuine, Hilaria still retained enough of her former self's perceptiveness to read the telltale signals Zoe's body gave off. She wasn't telling the truth. Was it possible she was pretending to gain her trust? But for what reason, Hilaria wasn't entirely sure. Working off her hunch, Hilaria decided to slowly increase the pressure on Zoe. There was a part of her that hoped she was wrong and that she didn't end up making things worse.

'Listen, girl, you're the one who came to see me, remember?' Hilaria snapped with forced irritation. 'I'm tired and fed up. Right now, I don't have the patience to play mind games with you. So, spit it out. Why did you come to see me? Was it for an apology? I already gave you that.'

'N-n-no,' she stammered, 'i-it wasn't that.'

'Oh, now you're really starting to bore me,' Hilaria moaned, giving a pretend yawn. It was taking all her willpower just to stop herself from grabbing Zoe by the shoulders and shaking her. Inwardly chastising herself for what she was about to do, Hilaria reached forward and slapped the adolescent across the back of her head. Not enough to cause her any pain, but just enough to annoy her. 'Spit it out, girl. I haven't got all day.'

'I-I n-n-need …' Zoe mumbled.

'Need what?' Hilaria snarled. She purposely invaded Zoe's personal space, pushing her shoulder, intending to make her back away against the wall, until there was no place for her to go. Even though she was hating herself for doing it, Hilaria continued to press Zoe by leaning into her until her face was just barely centimetres away from hers. 'What do you need, Zoe? Speak up, girl, you're mumbling.'

'I need you to tell me why you chose me!' Zoe roared with such ferocity, it caught Hilaria by surprise and made her take a step back. Her cheeks streaked with tears, Zoe stared at Hilaria beseechingly. 'I just need to understand. Why me? Why did you have to take me from my home, my family? Why? Was it for a reason?'

As she watched Zoe slide down the wall and bury her head in her hands, Hilaria finally understood the reason behind her strange behaviour. It was obvious she was struggling, whether from the trauma of everything that had happened to her or something else, but she could see now the girl was battling some demons. Filled with shame at what she had been forced to do to the youngster, Hilaria knelt and reached forward, placed her finger under Zoe's chin and lifted her head. 'Zoe, what makes you think you were brought here for a reason?' she asked gently.

Zoe shook her head and sniffed. 'There must have been a reason you brought me to this world. Why else did you select me?'

Hilaria closed her eye and searched her memory for the reason for Zoe's abduction. *Yes, that was it. It was because she had interrupted a synthroid that had been in the middle of collecting genetic material.* She opened her eye, shook her head, and smiled compassionately. 'I'm sorry, Zoe, but they didn't choose you on purpose. You just happened to be in the wrong place at the wrong time.'

Wiping her snotty nose with the back of her sleeve, Zoe shook her head angrily. 'You're wrong. There was a reason you chose me. There must be.'

Not expecting such an audacious statement to come out of Zoe's mouth, Hilaria laughed bitterly and regarded her with disdain. 'What? You believe you were chosen? That there is an omnipresent being guiding you for some greater purpose that is yet to be revealed to you? You think you've been chosen to destroy Oracle and bring order to our world?' Hilaria sighed and ruffled Zoe's hair. 'Sorry to break it to you, my young friend, but life isn't like that. I know you don't want to hear this, but there's nothing really special about you. You're certainly not a grand messiah, and you're certainly not destined to slay Oracle and lead this world into a new age of peace and prosperity. You're just like us lower mortals. The sooner you accept that, the sooner you can get on with your life.'

Without warning, Zoe jumped up and stood over Hilaria, her hands squeezed into balls so tight they were turning white. Hilaria could see the rage burning in her eyes as she glowered down at her. This time, she could tell the emotional outburst was an honest one. Momentarily taken aback by Zoe's anger, Hilaria was almost certain that if Zoe's eyes had been lasers, they would have been burning holes in the top of her skull.

'No! You're wrong!' Zoe snarled, pumping her fist into her chest. 'How dare you call me a nobody.'

Realising she'd said the wrong thing and wishing she could take her foot out of her mouth, Hilaria tried to grab Zoe's arm so that she could apologise for being so tactless. Unfortunately, she was too slow and could only watch as the tearful young woman turned and raced out of the door, slamming it shut behind her.

Feeling like a complete failure, shoulders sagging in defeat, Hilaria turned, leaned back against the door, slid slowly down to the floor and buried her head in her hands.

Oh great! What else could go wrong?

-2-

Hilaria groaned to herself and angrily rapped the back of her head against the door. She blew out a weary sigh, stared up at the ceiling, and shook her head in disappointment. Her stomach churned inside her while she replayed the last words she'd spoken to Zoe. Why couldn't she have handled that better? All Zoe wanted was to be told the reason for her abduction. It probably didn't even matter what she told her, so long as it gave her peace. Hilaria rolled her eye. No, instead of being supportive, she'd ridiculed Zoe, bringing her to tears.

Angry at herself for adding to Zoe's pain, Hilaria slammed her left hand down on the floor. *Damn it!* She desperately wanted to prove she was different from the general. To prove to them she was now much more compassionate and understanding. She wondered whether there was still a part of the general influencing her. If that was true, that meant she was going to be treading a thin line and carefully balancing her emotions.

When word spreads about what I did, Hilaria thought glumly, *it'll confirm to them what they probably thought all along – that I'm not to be trusted. That I'm the same spiteful person who tortured their friends.*

Filled with self-pity, Hilaria heaved herself off the floor and ran her hand down the front of her yellow onesie. She made her way over to the handbasin, leaned forward and scowled at the reflection in the mirror. Her body trembled in anger, and she curled her upper lip in contempt at the face staring back at her.

'What are you smirking at?' Hilaria hissed bitterly, tapping a finger against her temple. 'You're still in there, aren't you? Laughing at me, mocking me. Even when I believe I've been liberated from you, you manage to disrupt my life.' Enraged by the idea that the general was manipulating her, Hilaria snarled and smashed her hands on the mirror's surface. The fragile glass splintered as she hammered it with her fists, but she ignored the pain in her recently healed right hand and forearm.

'When will I be free of you?' Hilaria screamed in fury. 'What will it take for me to be finally free of you?'

Her chest heaving from all the rage and frustration she was feeling, Hilaria inhaled several deep, rapid breaths and spun away from the mirror. Balling her hands into tight fists, she lifted her head and screamed up at the heavens. All she wanted was to find some peace. Couldn't the gods let her have that? Why did they have to torment her so? What would she have to do to show people she was different?

Her anger subsiding, she slumped down onto the edge of the bed and buried her head in her hands. 'All I want is to be given a chance to prove myself. Is that too much to ask for?' she whimpered, pounding her thigh with her palm. She screwed up her face in pain as she realised she'd once again used her still sensitive right hand.

'Oh my, sounds like someone is in a bit of a mood today,' a female voice said, tutting. 'Did we get out on the wrong side of the bed this morning?'

Startled out of her self-flagellation, Hilaria twisted her body sharply in the direction the voice was coming from. She tilted her head and studied her visitor carefully; she was leaning against the door frame, staring at Hilaria with a raised eyebrow. It dawned on Hilaria that she had been so caught up in her own self-pity, she hadn't noticed the door opening.

Hilaria instantly recognised the figure in the door as Commander Em Tulley, leader of the resistance unit who currently held her prisoner. She pursed her lips thoughtfully as she studied Commander Tulley carefully. Standing at around five foot eight, she was shorter than Hilaria. As well as being a bit older, in her mid-fifties, the commander appeared to be quite lean and toned, giving Hilaria the impression that she was somebody who kept herself in good shape. From her neatly pressed green

jumpsuit to the shine on her boots, she clearly took pride in her appearance. Although Commander Tulley appeared to give off a friendly vibe, Hilaria knew differently; she knew she was being studied, searched for any sign of danger. Even though there was a significant size difference between them, Hilaria quietly suspected there was more to the commander than met the eye, and she would have to be very careful around her. There was something else about her that Hilaria couldn't put her finger on. She reminded her of somebody, but she couldn't work out who it was.

'Oh, I'm sorry, Commander,' Hilaria replied, trying to hide her embarrassment. 'I didn't mean to disturb anyone with my outburst there. You see, I was – er – a bit annoyed at myself because of something that happened a few minutes earlier.'

The corners of the commander's mouth quivered slightly, and she waved her hand as if dismissing Hilaria's comment. 'Oh, I'm not here about that.' The commander laughed. Then her face turned neutral and she spoke in a cool tone. Hilaria swallowed; Commander Tulley's voice now had an edge to it. 'I'm talking about your outburst with Zoe.'

Oh, by the burning fires of Tartarus, I'm in trouble now. Believing she was going to be punished because of how she had treated Zoe, Hilaria felt the muscles in her stomach tighten. She sucked in a deep breath and pressed her hands together, holding them up in front of her. 'Commander, it was not my intention to upset that youngster. If I could take back what I said, I would, but you must understand I'm not exactly at my best now. Zoe caught me at a bad time.' She set her jaw and stared at the commander straight in the eye. 'That still doesn't give me an excuse for the way I acted toward her, so I will accept any punishment you suggest without complaint.'

To Hilaria's surprise, Tulley pulled her head back and let out a small laugh. She smiled warmly and waved her hand. 'You can relax. I'm not here to harm you. It's the opposite. I'm here to thank you.'

Not the answer she was expecting, Hilaria, dumbfounded, stared at Tulley. 'S-s-sorry?' she stammered, wondering whether the commander was playing mind games with her. Struggling to regain her composure, she shook her head in confusion. 'Commander, I think my brain must be addled because I'm sure you said you wanted to thank me.'

Tulley's mouth widened in a broad smile and she nodded in affirmation. 'Yes, that's right.' She grinned and gestured to herself. 'Please call me Em. We may look like a military unit, but we like to keep things on a more informal and friendly basis.' Em cocked her head curiously and pointed to the chair next to Hilaria's bed. 'May I take a seat?'

Still baffled at what was going on, Hilaria could only nod. While she tried to regain her composure, Hilaria chose to remain silent as Em took a seat and eyed her warily as she moved in closer to her. Hilaria slipped Em a speculative look. There was a presence about her. She gave off a vibe of someone who was fiercely protective of those around her. But as she studied the woman in front of her, Hilaria stiffened suddenly as another memory came unbidden to her ...

When Oracle had created the personality that would go on to become General Wendy Cooper, it did more than create a new identity. The changes it made went deeper than that. As well as increasing her intelligence, it also made changes to help the young Wendy stand out from the rest by giving her superior coordination and perception. Not only that, but Oracle also gave her the ability to retain all the information that was put in front of her or said to her. Fortunately, when Oracle reset Cooper, even though she lost her superior coordination, somehow she still kept hold of her eidetic memory.

Upon receiving Colonel Barnes's request to transfer to her team, one of the first things General Cooper did was to learn everything she could about him. Using the skills that had unknowingly been given to her by Oracle, the general searched everywhere for Barnes's intelligence file. When she did eventually find it, the general had to pull in a lot of favours to unlock the encryption around it. But not only did it provide the general with a full history on Barnes, but it also came with someone else's security file – Em Tulley. A lot of it had been redacted, but it still made for some interesting reading.

Her real name was Emma Tulley, and she had been born on Counter-Terra, or Earth, as it was called by those residing in that reality.

After being abducted by the URE when she was eight years old, Em had served the URE as a slave and general dogsbody. However, when she reached twelve years of age, things got interesting. On her twelfth birthday, Em was sold to retired General Cornelius Trialus, who was not only a respected officer but had also been the URE's most eminent specialist in intelligence gathering.

There was very little information available about Em's time with Trialus, apart from rumour and speculation from those who had prepared the report. It had been widely theorised by those within the security division that Trialus had taken Em on as his protégé, possibly passing on his skills in intelligence gathering, as well as teaching her combat and military tactics. Although it was treasonous for officers of the URE to teach those things to slaves, especially an off-worlder, those in power decided to let it pass because of the loyal years of service that Trialus had given the URE. Reading between the lines, Cooper had a hunch the true reason the security division had been ordered to turn a blind eye was that they feared Trialus held something that would have embarrassed the URE if it were ever to be released.

After that, things got even more sketchy. It had taken a lot of digging in the URE's data server, but the general discovered another file buried deep inside an obscure data file. Even though the record had been heavily encrypted and graded as ultra-top secret, the general used up nearly every favour she had just to get a peek at the contents. Unfortunately, most of the information had been wiped. But what was clear was that Barnes and Em were married and had been together for twelve years before things turned sour when one night, security had been called to the couple's home after receiving reports of a disturbance. Barnes gave the order for Em's arrest, and she was taken to a detention centre. The reason for the collapse of their marriage and Em's subsequent arrest was unknown.

Hilaria stared up at the ceiling thoughtfully. She wondered why Barnes had issued the order for Em's arrest. Also, what had been the reason for the collapse of the couple's marriage? From the general's memories of Barnes,

Hilaria was well aware of Barnes's duplicitous nature. Had Em finally had enough of her husband's scheming and wanted to leave him? Or was it something else? The more she thought about it, the more Hilaria became troubled by the lengths someone had gone to to make sure the details about Em's life with Barnes could not be easily found. Knowing Barnes the way the general did, he was the only one she could think of who had reason to do that. But why would—

'Ahem, hello?'

A cough broke Hilaria out of her musings, and she felt her cheeks flush with embarrassment as she realised Em was looking at her strangely. The raised eyebrow suggested she was curious about why Hilaria had gone silent. Cursing herself for letting her mind wander, Hilaria gave a sheepish smile and cleared her throat.

'Sorry. I apologise for my rudeness, Commander,' Hilaria said sheepishly. 'I have a habit of letting my mind wander and can become lost in my thoughts.'

'Denarius for your thoughts?' Em asked, giving Hilaria an inquisitive sidelong glance.

'Um, nothing really,' Hilaria lied. 'Just replaying my conversation with Zoe, wishing I could have handled it differently.' She drew in a long breath and let it out slowly before looking Em directly in the eye. 'Commander, I know you're probably here to chastise me for what I said to Zoe. Please understand, I—'

'That's not what I'm here for,' Em cut in sternly, shooting Hilaria a harsh glare. 'Like I said, I'm here to thank y—'

'Yes, yes, you said you want to thank me,' Hilaria interrupted impatiently. 'But, sorry, Commander, I'm a bit confused why you—'

'Damn it, woman, will you let me have a word in!' Em snapped sharply. She closed her eyes, sucked in a deep breath, and exhaled. Hilaria wondered whether she was trying to keep her anger in check as she opened her eyes and held up her hands. 'Sorry, didn't mean to snap at you. Now, can you please keep quiet long enough for me to get a word in?'

Feeling like a first-year cadet who was being scolded by her instructor, Hilaria hung her head and murmured meekly, 'Yes, Commander.'

A frown pinched the bridge of Em's nose, and she shot Hilaria a look of irritation. 'Please will you call me Em.' But before Hilaria could reply, she held up a finger and scowled. 'So help me, if you say sorry one more time, I'm going to slap you. Now, as I was going to say, the reason I wanted to thank you is for what you said to Zoe. I was standing outside your door the whole time listening to every word.' She gave a sly grin and winked. 'I can be a sneaky so and so when I need to be.'

'Really? I hadn't noticed,' Hilaria quipped, trying to keep her face neutral.

If she was annoyed by the comment, Em gave no outward reaction while she continued to speak. 'As I was saying, although I don't completely agree with how you did it, I do believe it gave Zoe the wake-up call she needed. For a while now, I could tell something was bothering her, but every time I tried to get her to open up, she locked up tighter than a weapons locker. Hopefully she'll start talking to me now, so I can help her.'

Relieved that she wasn't going to be sent to the brig, Hilaria forced herself to relax and heaved an enormous sigh. But then she furrowed her brow as she wondered about something that Em had said. She cleared her throat and wrung her hands as she felt the anxiety in her body return.

'Um, Em,' Hilaria asked hesitantly. 'When you said that you had been standing outside listening to every word. Did you mean *every word?*'

A cryptic smile formed across Em's face, which was followed by a small nod of affirmation. 'Yes, *every* word.' Hilaria's anxiety increased as Em's smile vanished, and the tone of her voice now had a dangerous edge to it. 'Tell me the truth – were you being completely honest with Zoe about what was done to you, or was that just an act?' There was something almost threatening in Em's eyes as she reached forward and shoved Hilaria in the shoulder. 'Come on, it'll just stay between you and me. Admit it – you made the whole thing up. You were trying to garner some sympathy from Zoe, hoping she would forget what you did to her. That performance in front of the mirror was for the benefit of whoever was listening in, wasn't it?'

Not liking where this was heading, Hilaria scowled back at Em, jaw muscles tightening. Her rage slowly boiling inside her, she tried to take a step back from Em. She understood Em was deliberately trying to provoke her and was probably hoping to get a reaction out of her. But

whether because she was tired or because everything that had happened to her over the past few weeks had finally caught up to her, she didn't care. Right now, all she wanted to do was let loose on someone.

'No, it's not like that at all,' Hilaria hissed through clenched teeth and the vision in her left eye became blurry as it filled with tears. She struggled to contain her anger and disappointment as once again she thought her honesty was being brought into question. What was it going to take before people believed her?

Em threw her hands up in the air and let out a loud, scornful laugh. 'Oh, and here come the crocodile tears.' Then, to add to Hilaria's annoyance, she stuck out her bottom lip and did a strange wipe-your-eyes motion. 'Boohoo, oh woe is me. Why don't people believe me?' The corners of her mouth curled up into a derisive sneer. 'You're nothing more than a pathetic coward. Instead of facing up to the war crimes you committed during your service in the URE, you're trying to make us believe this cock and bull story of being brainwashed as a child,' she scoffed, waving her hand dismissively. 'Sorry, not buying it. As far as I'm concerned, General Wendy Cooper is standing right in front of me.'

That was the final straw for Hilaria. She was sick to death of constantly being compared to her former self. For over a week it had felt as if she'd been walking on a tightrope of insecurity over her doubts whether her former personality was still in control of her, afraid that if she lost control of her temper, then everything that had been restored would be lost. All those thoughts were still in the back of her mind as her anger erupted to the surface and she unleashed her fury on Em.

'How dare you!' she spat, lunging at Em, who to her credit seemed to hold her ground at the storm of emotion being hurled at her. 'Do you know what it's like to have everything you are stripped away? Do you?' Choking with emotion, she stabbed her finger into the side of her left temple. 'Oracle took everything that was me and locked it away in a cage inside my mind. You have no idea what it was like being made to watch through your own eyes while someone did things with your own hands.' Hilaria swiftly held her hands out, and Em visibly flinched as they stopped just millimetres from touching her face. 'Do you know what I feel whenever I look at my hands? I feel shame and revulsion. Ashamed because I had no control over what they did, and revulsion on remembering the amount of blood that's on them from all the people *she* killed or the orders *she* signed to have people executed.' Tears flowed freely down her cheek while she angrily pressed her finger into her right side of her forehead, ignoring the pain of the fingernail cutting into her skin. 'You want to know what I see when I go to sleep? I see the faces of those she tortured, killed or had sentenced to death.'

Her anger suddenly depleted, Hilaria sank to her knees and buried her face in her hands. As she sobbed, something strange happened. It was as if a weight had been lifted from her. Maybe that was what she had needed – someone to cut loose on. Hilaria stiffened as she felt a hand gently touch her left shoulder.

'Hilaria, I'm sorry I had to do that,' she heard Em whisper sombrely, 'but I had to make sure you were telling the truth.'

Suddenly feeling exhausted, Hilaria wearily opened her eye, sniffed, and nodded. 'It's fine. To be honest, I think I needed it.' She cocked her head and stared at Em curiously. 'Does that mean you believe me?'

'After hearing a story like that, it's hard not to.' Em laughed. Then her face turned serious as she knelt, placed both arms on Hilaria's shoulders and stared at her solemnly. 'I can't imagine what it was like for you – to be trapped inside your own body but still aware of everything that is going on ... it's just ... Well, the thought of still watching through your own eyes while your body does things that you have no control over ...' She screwed her face up and shuddered. 'Ugh! The whole idea just gives me the jitters.'

'Just pray it never happens to you,' Hilaria grunted back. 'You don't understand what it feels like to have your childhood stripped away from you. Being for—'

A dark look from Em silenced Hilaria, and she instantly regretted everything she'd said. In her moment of self-pity, she'd forgotten that Em had only been a child when the URE took her from her world and forced her into slavery. *Well done, I've once again put my foot in my mouth.*

'Oh, I understand more than you know,' Em said, her tone thick with bitterness. 'The URE stole my childhood from me the very moment they took me away from my family and enslaved me.'

Even though she wasn't the one who had done it, Hilaria felt ashamed over what the URE had put Em through. Wishing there was some way she could make it up to her, she hung her head and exhaled wearily. 'I'm sorry. For a moment there I forgot who I was talking to. I know it doesn't mean much, but I want to let you know I am truly ashamed of everything the URE and Oracle have done to you and everybody else they have enslaved. It's not right.'

'It's alright.' Em sighed. She gave a half shrug and smiled wryly. 'I came to terms with that a long time ago. I was lucky because I met a good man who helped shape me into the woman you see now.' Thick creases formed in the centre of her forehead, and she looked at Hilaria in puzzlement. 'That name – Oracle. When you first arrived, you said something about a sentient AI infecting the URE's systems. At the time, I put it down to the delirious ramblings of a person who had sustained significant trauma to her body. But now…'

'You're not so sure,' Hilaria replied. Seeing the small nod of affirmation from Em, she took in a deep breath and ran her hand down her face. 'That's a long story, one that may take a bit of explaining.'

Em held up her hands and smiled warmly. 'Well, we both have nowhere to be, so now is a good a time as any to hear your story.'

From her body language, Hilaria could tell Em meant what she said. She tightened her mouth into a thin line as she wondered if she was trying to offer an olive branch to her. Realising she would be a fool not to take it, she gave a small nod and smiled. 'I would be happy to, but only on the condition that you tell me your story.' She raised an eyebrow and cocked her head curiously. 'Especially your thoughts on a mutual acquaintance of ours.'

Em frowned and stared at Hilaria in bewilderment. 'I don't understand who you are talking about, who …' She paused, then a knowing smile formed on her lips and she waggled her finger at Hilaria. 'Oh, you are a crafty one. I give you that.'

'Yeah, so I've been told,' Hilaria replied, unable to stop herself from beaming. 'Let's just say I am dying to know what happened between you and Barnes.'

'Oh, I'm sure you are.' Em grinned back. However, before Hilaria could say any more, Em rose to her feet and offered her hand. 'Come on, let's take a walk. Some of my people are quite interested to meet you.'

Suddenly fearful, Hilaria felt her heart flutter as she stared at the offered hand. Was this that moment when the other shoe dropped? *Oh gods, this is it. She's going to take me outside and have me executed for the war crimes that my former self committed.* Swallowing back her dread, she slowly reached out, took hold of the hand and stared up at Em worriedly. 'Is this when you break the news to me that you're taking me to a cell where I will await my execution?'

Em frowned and gave Hilaria a look of exasperation. 'Has anybody ever told you that you're really paranoid? I know I may have said some harsh things to you when we first met, but I said those words in the heat of the moment. We have all done things we are not proud of, some more than others.' She held hands against her chest and gave Hilaria a look that was filled with sincerity. 'All of us at some point have been abused by the URE in some form or other, but what we have in common is that we all came here looking for a second chance in life. I know there may be some who may hold a grudge, but most of us are willing to give you a chance to prove yourself to us, so long as you are truthful with us. That's all we ask.'

The memories of the URE's historic brutality towards the rebels still playing on her mind, Hilaria couldn't help feeling a touch of scepticism as she listened to Em talk. If truth be told, from her early days in the academy, it had been hammered into her that the only one she could trust was herself. It was ingrained in every soldier of the URE that paranoia was their friend, and trust was only to be used as a tool. She realised if she wanted to break free of the shackles of her past, she must take that first step and put her faith in those she – no, her former self – had so cruelly victimised. Putting aside any reservations she had, Hilaria drew in a long breath and gave a silent nod of agreement.

'Thank you. You never know. You may surprise yourself and discover that you fit right in with us,' Em said. Her mouth broadened into a friendly smile, and she bobbed her head at the open door. 'After being stuck in this room for the past few weeks, I think it may do you good to have a change of scenery and some fresh air.' Her body language changed

as she let out a long, melodramatic sigh and turned away from Hilaria. 'But if you don't want that and prefer to remain in this stuffy room, I will be quite happy to leave you alone.'

Excited at the possibility of getting out and feeling normal air on her skin, Hilaria bounced up off the floor, but suddenly felt dizzy and staggered forward. Why did the room feel as if it was tipping to one side? Before she could make an even bigger fool of herself, she grabbed Em's arm and quickly regained her equilibrium.

'No, no,' she said excitedly, hoping to distract Em from her momentary display of weakness. 'That would be nice. I could do with some fresh air.'

Em tapped her chin thoughtfully, pursed her lips and shook her head. 'Only if you're sure. I would hate to be a burden to one as highly esteemed as yourself.'

Was she being sarcastic? Hilaria narrowed her eye and shot daggers at Em. 'You know, I'm starting to see why Barnes left you.'

From the look of open-mouthed shock on Em's face, Hilaria thought she may have gone too far. However, her fears vanished as Em took a step back, placed her right hand over her left breast, and covered her eyes with her left arm while crying out in a loud, melodramatic voice, 'Ow, the lady's stinging barbs have wounded me. Oh, woe is me.'

'I wouldn't give up your day job,' Hilaria grumbled sarcastically.

Em tapped Hilaria's arm and laughed. 'You know, I've heard a rumour some of my people are planning to put on a play. I think they're planning on calling it Pirates of Atlantica or something.' There was a noticeable mischievous twinkle in her eyes as she indicated the patch over Hilaria's right eye. 'I think you would make a good barbarian pirate.'

Hilaria screwed up her face and pretended to give Em the evil eye. 'Argh, methinks the woman needs to be boiled alive, argh,' she growled, trying to give her best impression of a barbarian pirate that had once terrorised the waters surrounding the Atlantician islands. She stiffened as she registered that she was still wearing the awful yellow hospital gown. She felt her stomach grumble and realised she hadn't had her breakfast yet. She laughed sheepishly and waved her hand down the front of her body. 'Uh, Em, as much as I enjoy our banter, would you mind giving me a few

minutes to get freshened up and change my clothes? Also, would it be too much to ask for some breakfast? With everything that happened with Zoe, I haven't had time to ask one of the medical staff for something to eat.'

Em's eyes twinkled with mischief. 'Of course, madam. Would you like the maid to fluff your pillows too?' Her expression turned serious, and she gave a small nod of confirmation. 'Certainly, you take your time and freshen up. While you're having a sonic shower, I'll leave something for you to eat on your bed. Once you've finished, I'll be outside waiting.'

Grateful for Em's generosity, Hilaria gave her an appreciative smile as she left the room. As she watched the door close, Hilaria's smile faded due to the troubling thought that continued to nag at her from the back of her mind. Whenever she looked at Em, she had a strange sensation of loss, followed by guilt, along with the feeling she'd seen her somewhere before. Unnerved by the sense of déjà vu, Hilaria shook her head and tried to push it to the back of her mind.

It's probably my mind playing tricks on me, Hilaria thought, trying to convince herself. *Yeah, that's it. It's probably nothing ... isn't it?*

-3-

Hilaria couldn't remember the last time she felt this relaxed. Keeping her good eye closed, Hilaria lifted her head and soaked up the warm sunshine beating down upon her. A contented sigh escaped her lips as a small gust of air brushed over the exposed skin of her face, and the smell of damp grass tickled her nose. Leaning back on the mat she was sitting on, she let her fingers wander through the blades of grass that surrounded her. For the first time in a long while, it felt as if she was free. So long as she kept her eye closed, she wouldn't be able to acknowledge the cruel world she had been born into. Hilaria blew out her cheeks. If only it was that simple.

But the sound of Em shuffling her feet broke the spell, forcing Hilaria to face the reality of her situation. Even if she wanted this moment of peace to last a little longer, she reluctantly conceded that she had to open her eye and face whatever the universe had in store for her head-on. Drawing herself up, she squared her shoulders and focused her attention on Em.

'Sorry for disturbing you,' Em said in what sounded like a regretful tone. From the mournful expression on her face, Hilaria could tell she meant it. 'But time is getting on, and I have things to do. I know I agreed to give you a moment alone, but there are things we need to discuss.'

'It's fine.' Hilaria sighed glumly and waved her hands expansively at the tranquil countryside around them. 'I really appreciate you allowing me to get some air.' She shook her head and peered down the grass-covered

embankment that led down to the river winding its way through the valley. 'I was always so busy with my duties to the URE. I never took the time to do something like this.'

'Yes.' Em nodded and cast an eye over the lush green belt that surrounded the hill. 'This is my favourite spot. I always come here whenever I need time to myself and clear my head.'

Hilaria remained silent but bobbed her head in understanding. She was grateful that she had been given the chance to escape the confines of the infirmary, even if it was just for a few moments. The fresh air was already helping clear her mind. As she relaxed, her mind wandered back to a few minutes earlier …

Shortly after Em had escorted her out of the infirmary, Hilaria had been surprised to discover that she wasn't being taken to a cell as she had expected. Instead, she was taken to a vast circular auditorium and made to stand in front of a throng of people. Em waited for them to be seated and introduced her. As she stood before the assembled audience, Hilaria's anxiety increased, and she wondered if she would be met with unwelcoming hostility.

However, much to her surprise, that was not the case at all. The people she was introduced to greeted her with warm applause, even offering sympathetic nods after listening to Em's abridged account of Hilaria's story. That wasn't to say everyone accepted her. There was the odd hostile, suspicious look from a few people, but they kept any reservations they had to themselves.

As soon as the introductions were over, Em took Hilaria on a tour of the complex. Hilaria was surprised to discover that she recognised the facility from the historical reports her former self had memorised about the URE. In particular the period that had become known as the Great Expansion – the time when the URE had decided, for the sake of peace, that they would bring the entire world under their protection, whether they liked it or not.

The complex she now found herself in had been built during that period. Not long after the populace of Britannia had been pacified and taught the ways of the URE, the great General Publius Aelius Hadrianus ordered that twenty heavily fortified compounds be built along the border between Britannia and the hostile, inhospitable country of Caledonia. These compounds were connected by a ten-metre-high wall and were armed with the most advanced weapons the URE had at its disposal. This later became known as the Hadrian Deterrent. It covered a six-hundred-mile stretch between the north-east and north-west coasts of northern Britannia. From these compounds, Hadrianus launched his successful campaign against the fearsome Caledonian tribes, earning him the title of Butcher of Caledonia.

Once the remaining Caledonian populace had been brought under the URE's umbrella of protection, Hadrianus felt that the Hadrian Deterrent was no longer essential. So he gave the order that all the compounds should be covered up and sealed. In honour of Hadrianus's heroic achievements, a vast city was built on the north-east coast of Britannia called Pons Aelius; it would become one of the URE's most productive ports.

Despite the bunker's age, Hilaria could see it had held up fairly well. But as she thought about the reason for its existence, she was filled with sadness at what it had cost the once proud people of Caledonia. Not only did they lose their freedom and independence to the URE, but they also lost every bit of their heritage.

Those countries that had been colonised by the URE had all their historical documents and artefacts destroyed. It was as if nothing existed before the Great Expansion. The URE also decreed that it was forbidden to teach anything other than imperial dogma, and for those found teaching or in possession of material deemed illegal, it was a capital offence.

But even though all written history of Caledonia had been struck from the records, some of it still existed, thanks to the few clans who had escaped Hadrianus's purge. On seeing that their defeat was all but assured, the remaining Caledonian clans banded together in one last stand against Hadrianus's forces. With the forces distracted, a few of the noble

Caledonian clans went to ground, hiding what remained of their heritage to ensure their proud history could be taught to future generations.

It was from one of those surviving noble clans that Hilaria's family had descended. When she was a young child, before she was eventually sold into military service, Hilaria's father would sit her down and tell her stories of their forefathers' history. Hilaria would listen intently to her father, engraving every detail into her memory, hoping one day she would do the same with her children.

Unfortunately, after Cadet Cooper was converted by Oracle, the youngster's new, colder personality believed what her father was doing was harmful to the URE's cause. The first chance she got, Cadet Cooper approached the academy's commandant and told him what her father was doing. She was immediately put in contact with the security division, and a few days later, security officers stormed Cadet Cooper's former home. Not only did they seize every bit of contraband in her father's possession, but they also arrested Cooper's entire family. Because Cadet Cooper had been the one who reported them, she was granted amnesty from any prosecution. Thanks to her testimony, her entire family were found guilty and sentenced to death.

Overcome with guilt at what she'd done, Hilaria's vision misted up as she pictured her father's face just before he was led away to the firing squad. Her last memory of him was the look of disappointment and shame spread across his face as he looked back at her. However, her guilt was soon replaced by rage. Anger burned within Hilaria's heart, and she slammed her hand on the ground. Hilaria suppressed the urge to scream out as she realised she had something else to hate the general and Oracle for. Staring up at the sky, Hilaria made a solemn vow to her dead father. *I promise you, Father,* she thought bitterly to herself, *Oracle's going to pay. I don't care if it ends up costing me my life. I swear to you, I will avenge you.*

'Hilaria?' Em asked worriedly. 'Are you okay?'

Too angry to answer, Hilaria tried to compose herself before turning to face Em. She inhaled a deep breath, scrubbed her face with her hands, and gave a reluctant smile before finally answering. 'I'm fine,' she said sombrely. 'Just thinking of something that has given me one more reason to hate my former self and despise Oracle.'

Em raised an eyebrow and stared silently at Hilaria for a few seconds. She was probably wondering whether she should ask her what was wrong or if she should wait until she was ready. A look of understanding formed across Em's face as she gave a small nod and placed a reassuring hand on Hilaria's shoulder, squeezing it gently.

'I'm sorry,' Em said softly. 'I know you're still trying to come to terms with what has happened to you, but like I said, there are things I need to urgently discuss with you.'

Hilaria sucked in a long breath and blew it out slowly. 'You want me to share with you everything I know about what happened to the Greater Chinese Republic, along with everything I know about the one called Oracle, isn't that right?'

Em nodded slowly and answered in a hesitant tone, 'Yes.' She smiled thinly and bobbed her head from side to side. 'Well, you already told me what happened to the GRE, most of which we've been able to verify for ourselves. But it is the one called Oracle that I – sorry, we – are desperate to know about. I …' She went silent, pressed her lips together and looked expectantly at Hilaria.

Reading Em's body language, Hilaria knew that Em wanted to ask something but was probably afraid of upsetting her any further. Was Em thinking that her mental state was too unstable, and any further questioning would cause her to revert to her former self? Hilaria wondered.

Desperate to prove she could handle anything that was put to her, Hilaria straightened and stared intently at Em. 'Let me put your mind at ease. I promise you I feel fine and will answer anything you ask me,' she said, hoping she sounded more confident than she felt.

The relief was evident on Em's face as she blew out a long sigh and smiled. 'Thank you.' She tilted her head and stared at Hilaria enquiringly. 'When you first arrived, you said something about Oracle being a sentient AI, but you didn't know where it came from. But I—'

'But you suspect I was hiding something,' Hilaria cut in.

Em's face clouded, then she gave a slow, deliberate nod. 'Yes, that's right.'

Remembering the moment she first arrived, even though she had been delirious with pain, Hilaria still clearly remembered a voice speaking

inside her mind, trying to influence her. At the time, she had been too weak to resist and had let it take control of her. Not wanting to keep anything from Em, Hilaria sheepishly rubbed the back of her neck and gave an apologetic shrug.

'Sorry about that.' Hilaria sighed sadly. 'Because I was pretty much out of it, I think the general's personality took advantage of that moment of weakness to gain control over me and compelled me to lie to you.' She gave a dismissive wave, leaned forward, took hold of Em's hands, and looked her square in the eye. 'This is what I know. What I said about Oracle being a sentient AI – that was true, along with what I said about it infecting the URE's systems.' She pulled her hands away from Em's and held them out in front of her chest, with her fingers pressed together, and became more serious. 'Now this is the bit I didn't tell you, and the part you may find hard to believe – the URE did not create Oracle. It's not even from this reality.'

Em let out a loud snort of amusement. 'Oh, that I very much believe.' She grinned and pointed to herself. 'I'm not what you would exactly call of local origin either.'

Hilaria bobbed her head from side to side in agreement. 'You make a good point, something I'm curious to know more about.' She blinked as she realised she was getting distracted and shook her head to get herself back on track. 'As I was saying, Oracle is from a parallel Terra, or Counter-Earth as your people call it. From what it told me, its world's military created it. But at some point, it grew sentient and turned on its human creators. I'm not sure how long it took, but I believe it was eventually stopped, and to make sure it wouldn't pose a risk to their world ever again, they exiled its data stream by transmitting it through a dimensional doorway into the void between dimensions.'

From the sceptical look on Em's face, Hilaria knew she was having a hard time believing this part of the story. Hilaria pursed her lips thoughtfully and shrugged. She couldn't really blame Em. If she was completely honest, if Hilaria hadn't seen Oracle first hand and saw what it could do, she probably would have reacted the same way. She remained silent as Em ran her hand wearily down her face, but then her brow furrowed and she gave Hilaria a perplexed look.

'But how did it arrive here?' she asked. But before Hilaria could answer, she immediately held her hands up and fixed her with a steady gaze. 'No, wait, forget that. *When* did it arrive here?'

'I was afraid you would ask that.' Hilaria groaned, massaging her forehead as she recalled the conversation she'd had with Oracle. She screwed up her face as she wondered whether Oracle had been completely honest with her about how long it had been stuck in the void. From her experience with the AI, she was certain it had kept something back. Drawing in a long breath, Hilaria lifted both her hands and shrugged. 'Your guess is as good as mine, but I strongly suspect it arrived here ninety years ago, around the time when the URE were trying to get their portal up and running.'

Lapsing into silence, Hilaria tapped her chin thoughtfully while she stared up at the sky and then closed her eye, focusing her memory on the logs written by her predecessors, specifically the project's creator, Doctor Drusilla Severan. Even though Hilaria had always thought her eidetic memory was a blessing, at times like this, it was a bit of a hindrance because it appeared Severan kept logs on everything, even the inconsequential stuff, so it took Hilaria just over a minute to recall the exact log she wanted.

'Sorry about that. I was trying to recall a specific log I had read,' Hilaria said eventually after finally recalling the passage of text she had been searching for. 'Even with an eidetic memory, I still must concentrate if I want to remember a passage of text I've read. However, that's not important, because I think Oracle arrived here around the same time the URE contacted your world.'

Em cocked her head and squinted at Hilaria. 'Do you think Oracle was behind that?' she asked, the tone of her voice echoing the suspicion on her face.

Hilaria furrowed her brow and gave a small nod of confirmation. 'Yes, I've a hunch that she was behind the first contact between our worlds.' She tapped her finger on her mouth as an excerpt from one of Severan's journals popped into her head. 'I remember coming across a journal from the portal project's founder, Doctor Drusilla Severan. In it, she states that during one of the initial tests with the portal, they accidentally connected with another portal, allowing a group of scientists from a parallel world to transport over to—'

'What!' Em blurted out in wide-eyed shock. 'Are you telling me that a group of people travelled over from my world to this one ninety years ago?'

'Yes,' Hilaria replied, surprised by Em's outburst. 'They were apparently trying to carry out a matter transportation experiment when things went ... a little kaka.'

'B-b-but,' Em stammered, 'ninety years ago, the technology on my world wouldn't have been advanced enough to do something like that. How was that possible?'

Perturbed by Em's reaction to her comment, Hilaria held up both her hands and gave a small shrug. 'I can only tell you what I read.' Even though Hilaria could see Em wasn't completely convinced that she was telling the truth, she continued regardless. 'From reading the transcript of Severan's interview with the lead scientist of the group, it appears they were in the middle of running a test for their own experiment at the same time Severan was running a test on hers. For some reason they couldn't explain, our portal locked onto theirs. There was an enormous catastrophic overload which resulted in that group being transported over.'

Em cocked her head and regarded Hilaria with obvious scepticism. 'Forgive me for being a bit sceptical here, but I find it highly convenient that out of all infinite realities out there, your portal chose that moment to lock on to another portal, which just so happened to be running a test.'

'I agree,' Hilaria replied grimly. 'Which is why I believe Oracle was the one behind it.'

'But why?' Em asked, the tone of her voice matching the confusion on her face. 'Why go to all that bother to contact a world that's decades behind in development?' She turned and gestured to the entrance leading down to their subterranean complex. 'I know I've been gone from my world for a long time. But from what I can remember about my world's level of technology, we were generations behind you.' She ran her hand through her hair and scoffed, 'Bloody hell, even the outdated equipment in our base would probably run rings around my home world's most sophisticated computers.'

Hilaria blew out her cheeks and gave a slow nod of agreement. 'Oracle told me the main reason our world wasn't suitable for her plans was that this planet's resources were on the verge of being depleted. She wanted a world that she could carefully influence from the shadows, so that when the time was right, she could step in and pretend to act as their saviour.' She stared at the sky and shook her head bitterly, scoffing, 'All this time, we believed we were being so clever by replacing the people of your world with ours, only to find we were the ones having our strings pulled.'

'So, it's fair to say Oracle has been playing both sides off the other for a very long time,' Em said gravely, looking despondent.

Suddenly feeling weary, Hilaria ran a hand down her face and exhaled a long, exasperated breath. 'About a year after the URE established contact with your world, Doctor Severan was killed in a transporter accident. Shortly after her death, the command council assigned control of the portal project to Doctor Joanne Abbott, one of the captured scientists from your world.'

Em pulled a face and stared at Hilaria in amusement. 'That's highly irregular, don't you think? Assigning control of an important project to an outsider? For a society that is deeply suspicious and xenophobic, I'm surprised that didn't raise a lot of red flags.'

'Irregular wasn't what I would call it,' Hilaria grumbled scornfully. 'I believe Oracle must have converted Doctor Abbott the same way it did with me. It orchestrated Severan's accident, then somehow influenced the command council into making Abbott the portal project's lead scientist. After she assumed command of the project, she concocted an elaborate story about your world's environment being harmful to our bodies because we lacked a specific hormone.'

The corners of Em's mouth twitched, and she raised an eyebrow. 'If I was a betting woman, I would have said Oracle had a hand in that too.' She gave Hilaria a sidelong look that held a touch of amusement. 'You know, the more I hear about Oracle, the more impressed I am by its ingenuity.'

'Yeah, I agree,' Hilaria answered, tapping her chin thoughtfully. 'You could almost admire it – if it wasn't for the fact that it wants to turn

us all into slaves.' Regretting the words as soon as they were out of her mouth, Hilaria screwed up her face in disgust and shuddered. 'Forget I just said that. There is nothing about that thing I admire.'

'So, I guess that was the reason the URE were secretly taking people like me from our world a few at a time,' Em said in a careful tone, appearing to ignore Hilaria's slip of the tongue. 'Because Oracle had influenced the command council into believing that a full-scale invasion wasn't safe, even though my world's environment is much the same as yours.' She tilted her head and stared at Hilaria enquiringly. 'What happened to Doctor Abbott? How long did she remain in charge of the project?'

Hilaria closed her eye while she concentrated on recalling the details of Doctor Abbott's intelligence folder, which her former self had perused when she first took over the project. 'Apparently, she remained in charge of the project for fifteen years. After that, no one knows what happened to her. She mysteriously disappeared and was never heard from again.'

Pursing her lips, Hilaria frowned and stared at the distant horizon. Did Joanne find a way to break free from Oracle's influence? Or had she become superfluous to Oracle and been callously disposed of like a piece of rubbish? Hilaria exhaled a sad sigh. She dearly wished it was the former, and that Joanne had escaped to another world, eventually living the rest of her life in peace. Knowing how easily a person could be influenced by Oracle, Hilaria found she bore no ill will to the woman.

The pair lapsed into silence. Hilaria cast her eye over to Em and noticed her faraway expression. She wondered if Em was pondering over what she had been told. Even though she hadn't known her for long, Hilaria got the distinct impression that her story about Oracle had shaken her. She couldn't blame her. It had been a lot to take in. However, before she could say anything, Em straightened and stared at Hilaria with a deeply serious look.

'Hilaria,' Em said hesitantly, seeming to choose her words carefully, 'I'm putting together a search party to go into the city to look for the people you told me earlier were still being held in detention. I would like you to be a part of that team. With your help, it'll make accessing the

main command tower so much easier, as well as your knowledge of the layout inside. What do you say?'

Not expecting to be asked such a question, Hilaria started and stared at Em open-mouthed. She swallowed and tried to compose herself as she stammered back her reply. 'I-I'm not sure what to say, Em.'

Em stepped forward, took hold of Hilaria's hands, and looked at her. 'Please, I know it is a lot to ask – please say yes.' She bobbed her head at the spot over the horizon where the vast city was located. 'I want to lead a team to free any prisoners who might be trapped on the detention level. Not only that, we need to find out what happened to the children. We've had reports that all the adult population of the URE have disappeared, but no word yet as to the children.'

At the mention of the children, an icy shiver ran down Hilaria's spine, and the images of her nightmare replayed in her mind – thousands of cyborg-like children marching as one under Oracle's control, killing everything that got in their way. Her stomach muscles tightened, and she swallowed back the rising bile in her throat. She drew in a shaky breath and shook her head sadly. 'I-I ...' she rasped, suddenly aware that the inside of her throat was tightening, making it difficult for her to speak. Hilaria tried to suppress a shudder; the nightmarish image of a cybernetic hand piercing her chest and squeezing her heart was still fresh from her nightmare. Desperately pushing aside that rising sense of foreboding, she managed to find her voice and spoke in a hoarse whisper. 'I'm sorry, Em, but I cannot go with you. I think I will just pose a danger to you and your team because I believe that, subconsciously, my former self may lead you into a trap.'

Worried that she had just signed her own death warrant, Hilaria felt her chest tighten with anxiety on seeing the look of disappointment in Em's eyes. A deluge of mixed emotions suddenly overwhelmed her, and she dropped her head into her hands. Her body shuddered as she let out a rattling breath. *They'll never trust me ever again*, she thought, *they'll probably lock me away in the most secluded cell they can find*. Hilaria bit her bottom lip while she waited for Em to explode in anger.

But much to her surprise, that did not happen. Hilaria stiffened as she felt a hand gently touch her shoulder and give a reassuring squeeze. Slowly lifting her head out of her hands, Hilaria stiffened in shock as Em

leaned in and wrapped her arms around her shoulders, comforting her. Not expecting such a display of sensitivity, Hilaria trembled, and she let out a small plaintive sob. It was almost as if her body had been longing for that fleeting moment of tenderness, allowing her to let go of all the grief and sorrow she'd had bottled up for so long.

'It's okay,' Em hushed, stroking Hilaria's hair. 'You can let it out. You don't need to be afraid any longer.'

'I'm sorry,' Hilaria said, sniffing, gripping Em even tighter. 'When you said that you wanted me to come along with you, I suddenly felt afraid. It's hard to explain, but I just feel if I go with you, I'll only put you and your friends at risk.' She pulled back, but as she did so, her fingers snagged and snapped a flimsy chain attached to a small round medallion hanging around Em's neck. Ignoring the medallion, which now lay at her feet, Hilaria wiped her face and gave Em a thin smile. 'But I can still help you in other ways. My access codes should still work, and I know a couple of others that will allow you access into some of the more secure areas. If we bring up a schematic, not only can I provide you with the safest route to the detention level, but I can also show how to access the building through the underground maintenance tunnels.'

Em nodded gratefully and smiled. 'Thank you, that would be most helpful.' A look of understanding was etched across her face as she peered at Hilaria. 'Don't worry, I perfectly understand your fears about going back there. We won't force you to do anything you don't want to.' Her brow furrowed as her attention shifted to the medallion lying at their feet, and she let out an exasperated sigh. 'That damn chain keeps snapping. One of these days I'll need to get a stronger one … I would be heartbroken if I were to lose this.'

Hoping to be helpful, Hilaria quickly leaned forward and picked up the necklace from the damp grass. She raised an eyebrow while she examined the piece of jewellery. It was one of those memory lockets designed to contain a holographic image of a loved one. They were biometrically locked to the owner's gene sequence, so that when placed in their palm, they would unlock and emit the image of the person they held dear. Hilaria thought about the memory locket she once had, which had

contained the image of her father. Her vision blurred as she remembered her former self had coldly thrown it away after her father's trial.

Hilaria handed the medallion back to Em and looked at her curiously. 'That's a memory locket, isn't it?'

'Yes, it is,' Em answered, gratefully taking the jewellery back and clutching it tightly. Her eyes appeared to fill with sorrow as she gazed down at her hand, and she blew out a long melancholic sigh. 'It's the only image I have of my daughter, the one I had with David Barnes.'

Hilaria stiffened in surprise at hearing Colonel Barnes had a daughter. She stared at Em thoughtfully and wondered why there had been no mention of Barnes's daughter in his and Em's file. Her eyes grew wide in realisation as she had a light-bulb moment. Barnes must have had their records sealed and any mention of his daughter erased. But why? Was it to stop Em searching for her, or was it something else? It was clear he had given up his daughter for adoption, so what had become of her? Hilaria blinked and focused her attention back on Em. She was relieved that her musings appeared to have gone unnoticed by Em, who continued to speak sombrely about the locket.

'The last memory I have of my daughter is seeing her scared face as she watched me being handcuffed and led away.' Em gave a thin smile and gestured to Hilaria. 'Henrietta would have been twenty-six this year, three years younger than you. Each year I digitally age her image so that it would match the age she is now,' she said bitterly, 'You may think me a fool, but I still live in hope that one day I will be walking through the market, and I look across to the stalls opposite and I see her standing there buying groceries for her family. She will turn to me, smile at me and I will wave back at her.' Em went silent and raised her hand. Opening her palm, the small locket lit up, emitting the image of a thin-faced, short-haired brunette.

No, not her. It couldn't be. Hilaria inhaled sharply at the image hovering in front of her. It felt as if she had been punched in the gut, and she felt the blood drain from her face. Hoping Em hadn't picked up on her reaction to the image, she quickly composed herself and focused her attention on the hologram. A lump rose in her throat and a lead weight settled in her stomach as she realised that she couldn't escape the truth staring back at her.

Em's daughter had been Henrietta Claudia, the woman who had been murdered by Hilaria's very own hands.

-4-

A few moments later, Em was standing in the hallway just outside the quarters that had been assigned to Hilaria. Puffing out her cheeks, she leaned back against the wall and stared up at the ceiling. She ran her hand down her face and groaned. She'd never felt so exhausted. Keeping up the appearance of being nice to someone who had belonged to an organisation she had spent so long hating had left her drained.

She drew out a long breath, squeezed her eyes shut and lifted the back of her head off the wall. Every time she looked at Cooper, Em felt as if she wanted to punch her, punish her for the lives she and her colleagues had taken. It was only out of respect for her friend and former mentor, Cornelius Trialus, that she hadn't done so.

As well as passing on to her his skills in intelligence gathering, Trialus also taught her every form of armed and unarmed combat to better defend herself. But the most important lesson he taught her was that violence should never be used in anger, that it should only be used when all other options have been exhausted. It had been his dream to purge the URE of their violent xenophobic tendencies. He had always seen the best in people, hoping to change them. Unfortunately, that trust had eventually cost him his life when he was betrayed by his protégé, David Barnes.

Despite being bitter towards her husband because of his betrayal of their friend, Em still tried very hard to live up to Cornelius's memory by pledging to pass on her mentor's teachings to those who served under her.

Even though there had been times when she had broken this pledge, Em was optimistic that Trialus would have been proud of her for what she had done in his name.

Em frowned as she thought back to her conversation with Hilaria. She was sure she had seen a look of recognition in Hilaria's eyes when she had shown her the hologram of Henrietta. But that look vanished as soon as it appeared, and Em wondered whether it had been a trick of the light. But as she led Hilaria to her quarters, Em noticed that her demeanour had changed. Even though her expression was an unreadable mask, there was no doubt in Em's mind that Hilaria seemed uneasy, as if she was wrestling with some internal turmoil. Em wondered whether Henrietta's hologram had triggered a memory in her. Perhaps they had met before, and she was trying to recall where. But rather than make a whole confrontation over it, Em opted to remain silent. Taking a leaf out of her mentor's book, she decided she would give Hilaria some space and trust that she would tell her in her own time once she worked out how she'd known Henrietta.

'Em, you okay?'

The soft voice broke Em out of her distracted thoughts, startling her. She quickly opened her eyes and spun toward the source. Em raised an eyebrow on seeing Zoe looking at her with recognisable concern etched across her face. Had she been following her, or had she been wandering about the base as usual and just happened to stumble across her?

'I'm fine,' Em replied, gesturing to the room she'd just come out of. 'I've just been getting our new guest comfortable in her quarters.'

Zoe rolled her eyes and pulled a sour face. 'Humph! How's the mistress of pain doing?' she muttered sullenly. 'She tried to put a pain collar on you yet?'

Em shot her a stern look. 'Zoe!' she said sharply. 'That's uncalled for. I know her former self has done things to you, but she's different now. You need to give her a chance.' Em cringed inwardly as soon as the words left her mouth. It was a good job Zoe couldn't read her mind, or she might have called her out for being a hypocrite.

Zoe grunted and hung her head. Em thought if her head dropped any further, her chin would probably touch the floor. Zoe put her hands in her pockets and hunched her shoulders, muttering something incoherent.

Em pinched the bridge of her nose and groaned inwardly. *Well, that's just great*, she thought, *now I've got a grumpy adolescent to contend with.*

Before Zoe came along, it had been a long time since any children had lived in the base. Thanks to the URE's ideals on genetic purity, it was forbidden for slaves to reproduce. Fearing a coupling between a slave and a true citizen of the URE would only cloud the gene pool and produce a half-breed, the ruling council decreed it would be safer if slaves were given a genetic modifier in their food that would affect their ability to procreate. It wouldn't make them completely sterile, but so long as they kept taking the modifier, they couldn't have children. Fortunately, there had been a few, like Em, who had been lucky enough to be bought by sympathetic families who considered the URE's attitude abhorrent and somehow managed to alter the records to make it appear those in their service were taking the modifier daily. On the morning before Em and Barnes got married, Trialus handed Em an envelope, explaining it was his wedding gift to her. Em was shocked to discover that the envelope contained a birth certificate, stating Trialus was her father. For a man like Trialus, it had been an easy task for him to get around the URE's rule against allowing slaves to breed by accessing the system and changing Em's records. He made it appear that she had been born on this world and that she was the product of an extramarital affair he had had just before his wife died.

Those in the resistance who had married and wanted to raise a family were relocated to a colony set up on one of the Atlantician islands at the farthest edge of the URE's territory, where it was hoped their children could be raised safe from persecution.

Inhaling a deep breath, Em placed a hand on Zoe's shoulder and made a small gesture with her head. 'Come on, take a walk with me,' she said softly.

Zoe gave a compliant nod and walked close to Em as they headed down the corridor. Em pursed her lips and cast a furtive glance over the surly young woman walking beside her. Despite Zoe's outward grumpy nature, Em could see there was a different vibe to her today; there was more of a bounce in the way she carried herself. She wondered whether it had anything to do with what Hilaria had said to her earlier that morning.

They walked in silence, slowly making their way through the maze of corridors, up several flights of stairs, until they came to a stop outside a hatch that led to the exercise suite. With the suite being located four levels below the habitat level, it would have been easier to take a transport-pod down. However, Em felt taking the more physically demanding route

would be a good way to get their hearts pumping for what she had in mind. She smiled as she caught a hint of displeasure in Zoe's eyes, possibly from being forced to do some exercise.

Em opened the hatch and stepped through into a large, spacious area. The entrance hatch was connected to a vertical shaft in the centre of the exercise deck, which spanned the whole level. A circular running track ran along the edge of the wall, lapping the deck. The centre of the hall's floor was covered with firm rubber matting, and an assortment of exercise machines, weights, mats, skipping ropes, climbing frames and benches were scattered over it.

Em headed straight over to the nearest bench and stripped off her jumpsuit and boots, leaving her standing barefoot in her shorts and T-shirt. She cast an eye back to Zoe, who was still standing by the entrance hatch. From the unhappy look on her face, Em knew this wasn't what Zoe had been expecting.

'You won't get any exercise done standing over there,' Em said, gesturing for Zoe to come forward.

'Um,' Zoe mumbled, hanging her head and shuffling her feet, 'I don't have any exercise gear.'

Em frowned. 'You're wearing shorts and a T-shirt under that jumpsuit, aren't you?' she said, smiling as Zoe answered with a silent nod. 'Well then, that's all you need.'

Zoe slouched and shuffled towards Em, grumbling, 'How can I be expected to exercise in these heavy boots?' She made a vague sweeping gesture. 'Plus, I don't see anyone standing around offering to give me a pair of trainers.'

Good grief, was I ever like this at her age? Em narrowed her gaze and scowled at Zoe. It was obvious she was looking for an excuse to avoid doing some exercise. However, Em was adamant she would not let her off that easily and gestured to her own bare feet.

'You don't need exercise shoes,' Em answered, raising her right bare foot slightly. 'You see, I'm not wearing any. Don't worry, the floor is soft enough so it won't hurt your feet.'

Her eyes widening, Zoe gave Em a look of outrage. 'What? You want me to stand on this dirty floor in my bare feet?' Rolling her eyes, she

let out a long, disgruntled sigh. 'Fine, you better hope I don't catch something,' she huffed while she slipped out of her jumpsuit, casting an evil eye at Em. 'I don't see why I should have to do this. Just because you're a fitness nut, doesn't mean you have to make me one too.'

Slowly losing her patience, Em inhaled a deep breath and shot Zoe a stern look. She held up two fingers. 'Two reasons I want to do this,' she said firmly. 'One – I feel I need to release some steam, and this is the perfect way to do it. And two – I've noticed since you've arrived, you have done very little in the way of physical activity. You spend most of your free time with a tablet in your hand or sitting at a computer terminal. So I think it's high time you did some training.'

'But I have been training,' Zoe said plaintively. 'You and Isaac have been giving me weapons training and have taught me the basics of hand-to-hand combat.'

'Yes,' Em answered tiredly, '*basic* hand-to-hand combat. But that will do you no good if you ever come across an opponent who is stronger and fitter than you. I need you to be prepared.' She smiled and placed a reassuring hand on Zoe's shoulder. 'Don't worry, I'll go easy on you today. We'll start slow with ten minutes of callisthenics to warm up, and then I'll show you how to use the treadmill and other machines. Finally, we'll do a circuit on the weights and cool down with something I learned from my mentor, an exercise called t'ai chi.'

Em led Zoe over to the centre mat and rolled her eyes on hearing the barely detectable grumble of protest coming from Zoe. Exhaling an exasperated sigh, Em massaged her brow and groaned to herself. She had a feeling she was going to regret this.

Despite Zoe's initial loud complaints, the pair worked out for two hours. Zoe's moaning eventually settled into reluctant compliance while Em led her through her workout regime. Although Zoe had been resistant at first, Em was filled with a touch of pride as she watched her take to each exercise with steadfast determination. After they were finished, Em handed a bottle

of water to an exhausted-looking Zoe, who was sitting on the bench beside her. Zoe's transparent sweat-soaked T-shirt clung to her body while she tried to regain control of her breathing.

'You did well today,' Em said, patting her face with a towel. 'If you continue at that pace, it won't take you too long to build up your stamina and fitness. I imagine in about a week you'll be able to progress to the more advanced forms of hand-to-hand combat.'

Her face flushed, Zoe brushed her wet hair away from her eyes and nodded gratefully. 'Once I started doing it, I found I was enjoying it. Thank you for pushing me into it.' She gave Em a hopeful look. 'Are we doing the same tomorrow?'

Taking a large gulp from her water bottle, Em shook her head and swallowed. 'No, your body needs time to recover to allow your muscles to heal from all the strain you have been putting on them today,' she said firmly. 'Tomorrow will be a recovery day for you, but I'll still take you through some techniques that will help your body heal more quickly.'

Zoe raised an eyebrow and stared at Em curiously. 'Do you mean yoga or Pilates?'

Frowning, Em shot Zoe a quizzical look. 'Pilates? I've never heard of that. Not even sure if it exists here. But I've heard of yoga. I can remember my mum talking about it when I was a child.'

On mentioning her mum, Em lapsed into silence and stared up at the ceiling. She hadn't thought about her parents for such a long time. Were they even still alive, or had they passed away not knowing that she was not only alive but in a different reality? For the first time in a long while, she wondered if Claire ever told them about what happened that night. Did she finally come clean and tell them she abandoned her sister? Exhaling sadly, she wondered whether Claire had suffered any guilt over what she had done. If she got the chance to go home, how would she react if she came face to face with Claire? Yes, she would be angry, but was she angry enough to hurt her sister out of revenge for abandoning her? She frowned as it suddenly hit her that she wasn't entirely sure how she would react if she got the chance to meet Claire. Before she could dwell any more on it, Em realised that she had been silent for too long. Zoe was staring at her, looking deeply concerned.

Refocusing her attention on the adolescent sitting next to her, Em gave an embarrassed cough and smiled. 'Sorry, where were we? Oh yes, as I was saying, yoga on this world is called something else. Here it is known as kwon-chai-ko, an exercise that was practised in the Greater Chinese Republic. The ruling senate banned it because they deemed anything not of URE origin went against doctrine, and anyone caught teaching it was instantly arrested and executed without trial,' she explained sadly. 'It was created centuries ago by a citizen of the GCR to help one centre oneself, focusing on your body's energy inwardly to help restore your balance. Cornelius, my mentor, first became aware of it during his espionage days and secretly learned everything he could about it. He secretly taught it to me.'

Zoe pursed her lips and nodded thoughtfully. 'Your mentor sounds like a remarkable man.'

'Yes, he was. Cornelius was a man ahead of his time. I didn't know this at the time, but he was the portal project commanding officer when I first arrived on this world. By that time, he had already been in charge of the project for ten years, but he had become unhappy at the dark path that the URE was being led down. So he tried to help whenever he could by using his contacts with the resistance to help get people like me to safety. He could only move one or two people every three months because any more would alert the security forces. The command council must have suspected what he was doing, but they were afraid that if they arrested him there was a danger he would release information that he had gathered over the years, which would cause a big stink if the general populace ever became aware of it. So they gave him a sideways promotion by placing him in charge of the academy.' Em stared up at the ceiling and laughed. 'Of course, the sly dog saw that as the perfect opportunity to change the URE. He believed if he influenced the officers of the future, then he might stop the URE's descent into darkness.'

Smiling to herself, Em went silent as she pictured the mischievous grin on Cornelius's face whenever he spoke to her about his plans. It had been shortly after she had turned twelve years of age when Senator Garnier, whose family she had been serving, came to her and told her flatly that her services were no longer required and that he'd received a generous offer

for her. A short time later, she met her new master, General Cornelius Trialus. However, much to her surprise, Em discovered he had specifically requested her. After settling her into her new accommodation, Cornelius invited her to have dinner with him. This was highly irregular because it had been drilled into Em that slaves ate separately, out of sight of their owners. After the meal, Cornelius revealed to Em that he had been present in the portal chamber the night she'd been abducted. He explained his deep regret at being the one responsible for taking her from her family and had made a vow that one day he would find her in the hope of making it up to her. At first, Em had been angry with him, but on seeing the remorse in his eyes, she began to understand what he was trying to do. Following that, an unspoken bond developed between them as Cornelius took her on as his protégé.

Em's happy mood faded as she thought about her last contact with Cornelius. Barnes had been sick of being stuck in his mentor's shadow and felt he was standing in the way of Barnes gaining a promotion, so he came up with a scheme that would result in Cornelius being arrested for treason. After unsuccessfully trying to talk her husband out of his machinations, Em tried to warn Cornelius of the danger he was in. But Cornelius ignored Em's pleas, believing it was just another game of one-upmanship between Barnes and him. Frustrated by Cornelius's refusal to listen to reason, Em abruptly hung up on him, but not before calling him a silly old fool and saying that he deserved everything that was coming to him. A short time later, Em watched in horror as news of Cornelius's arrest and subsequent execution was broadcast across the URE. Her heart still carried the heavy wound of the knowledge that her final words to her dear friend had been filled with hate.

'Unfortunately, he was betrayed by my husband, David, and was later executed,' Em explained, unable to keep her bitterness from her voice. 'After that, David's insatiable quest for power drove a wedge between us. It was that blind ambition of his that eventually led him to not only take my freedom from me, but my daughter too.' The muscles in her face tightened as she reached down to pick up her memory locket that was sitting on top of her folded jumpsuit. 'This memory locket is the only thing I have left of her.'

The memory locket lit up in Em's hand, emitting a holographic image of her daughter. However, as Em gazed at the image in front of her, she noticed Zoe stiffen slightly, which was followed by a sharp intake of air. Looking away from the hologram, Em raised an eyebrow on seeing that Zoe was now standing wide-eyed with her mouth open. Not only that, but she had an odd look etched across her face. If she didn't know any better, it almost looked as if she had recognised Henrietta.

How was that possible?

-5-

Her mind reeling, a knot formed in Em's stomach as a seed of suspicion planted itself inside her mind. *Zoe, I beg you, don't get my hopes up*, she thought. Perspiration broke across her brow and the inside of her mouth suddenly felt dry, followed closely by her throat tightening. Struggling to control her emotions, Em swallowed and forced the words out of her mouth, but they only came out as a croak.

'Zoe, what's wrong?'

'I know her,' Zoe answered weakly. She blinked and shook her head. 'Sorry, I meant I've seen her before, I—'

Not giving Zoe time to finish, Em lurched forward and grabbed her by the shoulders. Em ignored Zoe's cries of pain as she tightened her grip, forcing her fingernails deep into the exposed skin on the adolescent's shoulders. Zoe tried to pull back, but that only made Em tighten her grip even more and she hissed at Zoe through clenched teeth. 'Where have you seen her?'

'Em, please,' Zoe pleaded tearfully.

'Tell me where you've seen her,' Em snarled, ignoring Zoe's pleas. Damn it, couldn't Zoe understand how important this was to her? Em tightened her grip on Zoe's shoulders and shook her angrily. It was as if a red mist had descended over her eyes. She was ignorant of the world around her. All that mattered to her was getting to the truth. Rage burned inside her. The only sound she could hear was her blood pounding in her ears. Why couldn't Zoe understand that she would let nothing stop her

from being reunited with her daughter? If she had to, she would rend this world apart.

'Sh-sh-she w-was,' Zoe stammered, her cheeks streaked with tears, 'in the portal chamber. I—'

'When was this?' Em hissed.

'It was just after I regained consciousness,' Zoe answered quickly. 'I woke up, and she was one of the first people I saw. She was standing next to General Cooper.'

At the mention of Cooper's name, Em drew in a sharp breath, and she felt the steady warmth of anger making its way up her body. So, she hadn't imagined it. Hilaria had reacted to Henrietta's image. The heat of her building anger had now reached her throat. If Hilaria had been lying about that, what else had she been lying about? This was confirmation that Hilaria and Zoe had been keeping something from her, which only added fuel to her paranoia; she now firmly believed that people were betraying her, breaking the trust she had placed in them. Em's rage bubbled inside her. How many times had she given people the benefit of the doubt, only to see it thrown back in her face? How many more times must she be hurt by those around her? Em set her mouth into a hard line. No more. She refused to stand by anymore and let it happen to her over and over again.

Consumed entirely by the heat of anger and blinded by rage, Em let out a guttural snarl, grabbed Zoe by the throat and slammed her against the wall. Her sight narrowed to tunnel vision and nothing else registered. Even the pain of Zoe's fingernails raking against the skin of her hands seemed to fade into the distance, almost as if it was happening to somebody else.

'What happened to her?' Em heard someone say. Strange, it sounded like her own voice, but seemed so far away.

'Em … please,' somebody pleaded, their voice sounding hoarse. Was that Zoe speaking? 'You're choking me.'

'What happened to her?' Em heard herself repeating. It almost sounded like she was speaking through gritted teeth. *Why would I do that? Was I angry about something?*

'I-I-I d-d-don't know,' came the wheezy reply. Yes, that was Zoe's voice. Was she struggling for breath? Em frowned as she heard Zoe let out

another choking gasp. 'The last thing I can remember just before they carried me out of the chamber was seeing your daughter standing next to Cooper.'

'Stop lying to me. I've had enough of people lying to me,' Em heard herself hiss. It sounded like Zoe was trying to keep the truth from her. Rage consumed Em. The lying little minx. One way or another, she was going to get it out of her.

Two large hands appeared from out of nowhere, grabbing Em's forearms and snapping her back to reality. Em cried out in shock as the hands pulled at her own arms. Were they trying to force her to slacken her grip on something? Furious that someone had the audacity to manhandle her, Em snapped her head to the right and felt her eyes grow wide in surprise at seeing whose hands they were. It was Isaac! She frowned in bewilderment at the concerned look on his face. Was he shouting something at her?

'Em, stop. You're killing her!'

Em blinked in confusion. Killing her? Killing who? The red haze of anger cleared, and it suddenly dawned on her what she was doing. *Oh god, Zoe. What am I doing?* Releasing her grip, Em pulled her hands away from Zoe's throat and took a step back. She felt powerless to act as Zoe's now unconscious body slid down the wall and dropped to the floor. Luckily, a copper-haired woman, who Em recognised as Tatiana, shot forward and caught Zoe's head, stopping it from striking the floor.

Isaac bobbed his head at Tatiana and then gestured to the short, round-faced man standing next to him. 'Baz, you and Tatiana take Zoe to the infirmary. But be gentle. She's had a bit of a rough time.'

Ashamed of being the one responsible for nearly killing Zoe, Em remained tight-lipped and stood in silence while the two people carried the unconscious young woman out of the gym. Em wanted so badly to run to Zoe, wrap her arms around her and tell her she was sorry. But she knew nothing she could say or do would make up for the way she had treated her. Em drew in a long breath and gave Isaac a sorrowful look.

'Thank you, my friend,' she said glumly. 'If you hadn't been there to stop me in time, I dread to think what would have happened.'

Isaac lifted his shoulder in a slight shrug and gave Em a tight smile. 'That's what I'm here for, Boss Lady, to stop you from doing stupid things.'

Wishing the ground would open and swallow her, Em wearily ran her right hand down her face and exhaled a slow, melancholic sigh. 'I can't explain it. It just felt as if everyone was against me. That everyone I put my trust in was betraying me. My sister, my husband, and so many others since.' She shook her head and laughed bitterly. 'The final straw was Cooper, and when Zoe said she recognised my daughter, it was as if someone flicked a switch inside me and it became too much for me. I can't explain it. I just felt alone, that there was no one around me I could trust.'

Isaac bobbed his head in understanding, placed his hand on Em's shoulder and gave it a reassuring squeeze. 'That's not true, Em. You still have me. I promise I'll never betray you. As long as I'm standing by your side, I'll let no harm come to you.' His mouth broadened into a wide grin and he nudged her. 'We've known each other too long to fall out. I'm with you to the end, Boss Lady.'

Em reached up and squeezed the gentle giant's hand. It was true, she realised, they had known each other for a very long time, forty-five years, in fact. Isaac had been one of the first people she had met the day after arriving on this world who had not wanted to hurt her. She had been an innocent eight-year-old, and he had been a strapping fifteen-year-old. From the very first day when she woke up in the barracks that had been assigned as slave accommodation, Isaac had been the one who watched over her, guiding her and helping to shield her from some of the more aggressive overseers. Em frowned as she realised no matter where she had ended up, Isaac had been there to watch over her. Even when she was living in Cornelius's compound on the outskirts of the Gaulish coastal town of La Purdum, she discovered Isaac had conveniently been assigned to work as groundskeeper to a nearby family. It was as if he was her guardian angel, always hanging around in the shadows.

Em cast a surreptitious eye at Isaac. Despite being in his early sixties, he was still an attractive man. His face had a chiselled look about it, as if it had been grafted out of marble. His well-toned, muscled body was enough to give even the younger men in the base a sense of inferiority. It was well known he'd previously been married to Allison, who had also

served in the resistance, and that they had a daughter together, Kaliopi. Unfortunately, Allison had been killed by URE forces. It was the mysterious circumstances of her death that led to Isaac and Kaliopi becoming estranged. Allison's death was something Em had found puzzling and deeply regretted never finding the time to investigate it further.

However, before she could give the matter any more thought, she caught someone moving out of the corner of her eye. Wait, was that Hilaria? But before she could turn to get a better look, Isaac had placed a firm hand on her arm, which made her pause. Em raised a quizzical eyebrow at him; he had a strange look in his eyes. If she didn't know any better, she was positive he looked anxious. She noticed the holster clipped to his right hip, and the weapon slotted inside it. *This is damned peculiar*, she thought. *Personnel never carry weapons while on base, even holstered one*s. But what she found even more perplexing was that the holster's cover appeared to be open, allowing easy access to the weapon. Just what was going on here?

'Em, don't be angry,' Isaac said urgently. 'Miss Cooper has something she needs to say to you. Promise me you'll hear her out.'

She became aware of Hilaria moving slowly toward her. There was a strange look on her face, as if she was trying to work something out. Her chest tightening with dread, Em inched slowly away from Isaac and twisted her head from side to side while she tried to keep both people in her line of sight. Her breathing quickened, and she felt her heart slamming against her ribcage as her gaze drifted to the weapon clipped to Isaac's hip.

What was going on here? Was Isaac conspiring with Hilaria? Had he finally betrayed her too?

But just as she was about to open her mouth and confront Isaac, Isaac did something that made Em pause. He had raised his left hand to his left shoulder and was tapping his finger. *What was he ... Oh, I see.*

Years earlier, those who had been enslaved had developed their own secret language, a form of sign language using very slight finger movements. It became quite useful when they wished to pass information on while standing directly in front of their overseers without being detected. It had been a while since Em had last used it, and she was surprised she could still read what Isaac was trying to convey to her. But as

she read the message, Em felt her eyes grow wide as she realised what Hilaria wanted her to do. Her mouth dropped open in stunned shock and she gave Isaac a disbelieving look.

Is this woman insane? Em gasped, struggling to believe what she was reading.

Hilaria wanted Em to kill her.

-6-

Moments earlier.

Hilaria was pacing around her room, her mind racing while she tried to decide on the best way to explain to Em what had happened to her daughter. She ran her hand through her hair and groaned in frustration. No matter how she worded it, the fact would still be that Henrietta had died at her hands. Yes, it had been General Cooper in control, but she imagined Em wouldn't see it like that. No matter how she did it, Hilaria reasoned, it still would end up being bad for her.

Her mind racked with indecision, Hilaria sat down on the edge of her bed and buried her head in her hands. Oh, why hadn't she revealed the truth to Em as soon as she found out who her daughter was? It would have been so much easier for everyone involved if she had spoken up. Yes, Em would probably have had her killed, but that would be better than sitting in her quarters, plagued with guilt.

Exhaling a heavy sigh, Hilaria stood up and walked over to the handbasin. Leaning over, she glared into the mirror that hung over it. The corners of her mouth curled up in contempt as she sneered at the reflection staring back at her, imagining the general smirking back at her. Oh, how much she wanted to wipe the smirk off that face.

'This is all your fault,' Hilaria snarled. 'Do you see the mess you've left me in, you self-righteous harpy?'

But just as she raised her hand to smash it against the mirror's surface, something made her pause. Either she was going insane, or her

eyes were playing tricks on her, but Hilaria was almost positive her reflection wasn't mirroring her actions. Hilaria took a step back and rubbed her eye in disbelief. No, she wasn't imagining it. Her reflection appeared to be grinning back at her. *This is it,* she thought, *the moment where my mind has finally fractured and is making me see things that aren't there.*

A shiver ran down Hilaria's spine as she watched her reflection's mouth widen into a horrifying grin. This was followed by a laugh so maniacal it chilled Hilaria to the core of her soul.

'Oh my, this is interesting,' Hilaria's mirror-self cackled. 'I just so happen to pay this world a visit so I could check on some of the assets I have in storage. Anyhow, imagine my surprise when I discover someone who I had thought had died is in fact very much alive and well.'

Oh no, not her, not now. Hilaria inhaled a sharp breath as she felt the icy hand of fear wrap itself around her heart. Despite the familiar face staring back at her, there was no mistaking the chilling voice that had haunted her nightmares ever since her near fatal encounter just a few weeks earlier. It was the voice of Oracle. Hilaria could only stand and stare with her mouth open while she tried desperately to think of something to say.

'Hmm, it looks like you are lost for words,' said Oracle, arching its head curiously. 'Maybe if I change into something more comforting, it might help loosen your tongue?'

The face in the mirror morphed and swirled. After it was finished, a featureless silver face stared back at Hilaria and if it hadn't been for the yellow glowing eyes, it could almost have been mistaken for a shop mannequin. Hilaria, determined to keep the fear she was feeling from showing on her face, straightened, took a step forward and glowered at Oracle.

'What do you want, Oracle?' Hilaria growled with as much bravado as she could muster. 'What's wrong? You're finding the world enslavement business so boring, you thought you would cheer yourself up by tormenting me?'

Oracle tutted and shook its head. 'Tsk, tsk. Now, is that any way to speak to your mother?'

'You're not my mother,' Hilaria spat back indignantly. 'You're not even alive. Just pieces of code with delusions of grandeur. Something that

brainwashed me and tried to turn me into a mindless drone. I may have only known her for a short time, but at least my real mum was human, someone who showered me with love.'

Oracle's top lip curled up, and it gave Hilaria a slightly amused look. 'Remind me again? What happened to your mum?' Its mouth widened in unbridled glee, and it raised its right index finger. 'Oh yes, she was executed for treason after being turned in by her *loving* daughter. Not only her, but your father too.'

'Don't you dare speak their names,' Hilaria snarled, struggling to contain her anger.

'Oh yes, your poor father.' Oracle sighed sadly, shaking its head, appearing to ignore the angry request. 'The look of disappointment on his face as they led him away in chains. It almost broke your heart, did it not?' It lowered its head and smiled wickedly. 'Oh, that is right, I forgot. You do not have a heart. You are just as cold and emotionless as you say I am. Is that not right?'

No matter how many times she heard Oracle talk, Hilaria always found it unnerving how it didn't use contractions. Hilaria remained tight-lipped and fixed Oracle with a harsh stare. She was aware of what it was trying to do. It was trying to use the shame and guilt she harboured over being responsible for turning her father in. It was probably hoping it would cause her to lash out in anger. Determined she would not play Oracle's game, Hilaria drew in a deep breath, closed her eye and concentrated on slowing her racing heart. *Yes, calm, relaxing breaths,* she thought. *Don't play into Oracle's hands.*

Once she felt she had enough control of her emotions, Hilaria opened her eye, folded her arms across her chest and stared impassively at Oracle. 'I ask you again,' she said through gritted teeth. 'What. Is. It. You. Want?'

If it was disappointed that Hilaria had not taken the bait, Oracle did not show it. Instead, it lifted its shoulder in a slight shrug and spoke in an indifferent tone. 'Like I said, I was just passing through a portal on my way to inspect some assets that I have in storage when I detected a familiar voice talking to herself.' Oracle smirked and held up a hand. 'Sorry, arguing with herself.'

Assets? Hilaria furrowed her brow in puzzlement. What assets would it have on this world? Why would an artificial intelligence have any need for assets when it had already enslaved most of the URE's population? Although deeply puzzled by Oracle's statement, Hilaria decided now was not the time to become distracted. She needed to stay focused and hope Oracle would let something slip.

Oracle smiled and gave a small nod of approval. 'Once I had gotten over my surprise at seeing you alive and well. I have to say I do like the eyepatch, my dear. You carry it off so well. But I digress. As I was saying, once I had gotten over the surprise, I did a bit of digging through your base's security records.' It pulled its head back and laughed gleefully. 'You cannot imagine how overjoyed I was to see that you have made some new friends. Not just any friend, too, for this new friend is called Emma Tulley.'

Hilaria staggered back as if Oracle's words had struck her in the stomach. A cold awareness buried into her brain, and it slowly dawned on her where Oracle was leading her. Balling her hands into tight fists, Hilaria ignored the pain of her fingernails digging into her palms and stared at Oracle with simmering hatred.

Clearly revelling in Hilaria's discomfort, Oracle's eyes blazed and it cocked its head curiously. 'Because there was no audio file attached, I could not hear what you were talking about. However, I could clearly see she was showing you an image of her daughter, Henrietta Claudia, the woman you killed.' Oracle's mouth broadened into a chilling smile and its voice dropped to a sinister whisper. 'Does she know? Does Emma know what you—' A look of understanding appeared on Oracle's face, then it clapped its hands and let out a loud laugh. 'Oh, this is good. She does not know, does she? You have not told her, have you? That is why you were arguing with yourself, was it not? You were trying to decide whether to tell her?' Oracle clapped its hands together merrily. 'Oh, this is going to be good. I cannot wait to see what happens when she finds out the truth.'

'You stay away from her,' Hilaria hissed, jabbing her finger at the mirror. 'I'm warning you. Stay out of this. You interfere in any way, I promise you, you'll regret it.'

Oracle gave a derisive huff and waved its hand. 'Oh, you do not have to worry about any interference from me. I have enough to keep me busy on Counter-Earth, without worrying about your little emotional traumas.' The corners of its mouth twitched and it made a *watching-you* gesture with two of its fingers. 'But I will still be keeping a close eye on you.' It gave an over-theatrical shudder and smiled gleefully. 'Oh, I am all a-tingle with excitement at what is going to happen next. Who needs reality TV when you have the real thing? Stay tuned while we watch Hilaria betray those around her. Will she live or will she die ... Oh, I am on the edge of my seat in anticipation!' Its excitement seemed to disappear as quickly as it appeared, and it stared coldly at Hilaria. 'By the time they are finished with you, you will be begging me to take you back.'

Determined not to give Oracle any satisfaction by letting it believe it had rattled her, Hilaria straightened and stared defiantly at the grinning face staring back at her. 'Don't count on it. I'll sooner die than be enslaved by you again.'

'We will see. We will see.' Oracle smirked back and blew her a kiss.

Before Hilaria could respond, the mirror's surface wavered. When it returned to normal, Hilaria raised her hand and waved. She blew out a long, relieved breath on seeing her reflection was copying her movements. Oracle was no longer there, but that didn't mean it wasn't still watching. Hilaria was certain the AI had a way of monitoring her from across the dimensional void.

There was no denying it; it troubled Hilaria that Oracle could be watching her every move. She only wished there was a way she could counteract it. As she paced around her quarters, she sighed and shook her head. It was bad enough that she had a possible explosive meeting with Em coming up, but Oracle's omnipresence only muddied the waters even more. Hilaria massaged her brow while she tried desperately to think of something to help get her out of the bind she was in. Unfortunately, no matter what way she looked at it, whatever she said or did, it was still going to anger Em. She nodded glumly to herself. Once Em found out what Hilaria had done to her daughter, she would probably shoot ... her ...

Wait, that was it! Hilaria stiffened as she was struck by a sudden burst of inspiration and she slapped her forehead. Of course, she had been

looking at the problem all wrong. All this time she had been trying to avoid making Em angry, when it was obvious that was what she should do. Make Em so riled that she would lose control and be forced to kill her. A secretive smile formed across her face as a plan developed inside her mind. Yeah, Hilaria admitted grudgingly to herself, it was an insane plan. But it was insane enough that it just might work. However, if she had any chance of it succeeding, then she would need someone's help, and she just had the right person in mind.

Just as Hilaria was about to open her door and leave her room, she halted as it dawned on her how she was going to stop Oracle from monitoring them. Hilaria shook her head and cast the thought to one side. *No, one problem at a time, she thought. I'll solve that problem if I survive what I must do next.* She stared up at the ceiling and scoffed at the lunacy of what she'd just thought. She could not believe she'd just thought *if* she survived this!

The seed of a plan growing inside her mind, Hilaria dashed out of her quarters into a long corridor. She puffed out her cheeks as she saw that Em had been true to her word and not posted a guard. Damn it, the time when she needed someone to guard her door, nobody was there. She shrugged. Oh well, that just meant she was going to have to be creative and try to get someone's attention. Ignoring the odd looks she was receiving from people walking along the corridor, Hilaria danced up and down the corridor, singing to herself, arms outstretched, spinning around like she didn't have a care in the world.

'Tra-la-lah-lah-la, that's okay,' she sang happily to herself, *'watch the madwoman dancing up and down the corridor. Report it to your superiors. Tra-la-lah-la.'*

For several minutes Em danced back and forth along the corridor. Eventually she stopped upon hearing a ping from behind her, and she turned to see a large, intimidating-looking Gondwanian man step out of the transport-pod at the end of the corridor. Hilaria stood with her hands behind her back and smiled on recognising that it was Em's second in command, Sergeant Isaac N'Goy. Perfect, exactly who she was looking for.

While she waited for Isaac to approach her, Hilaria took the time to appraise the giant. She estimated that he stood at just under seven feet, a few inches taller than her. It was rare for her to come across someone as

tall as her. But whereas she was slim and athletic, Isaac was the exact opposite. His broad shoulders and muscular frame might have made even the most highly trained soldier pause. Hilaria frowned as she wondered why he had not been conscripted into military service like many other Gondwanian men.

'Good afternoon, Sergeant N'Goy,' Hilaria said as Isaac came to a stop in front of her. 'What can I do for you?'

'Well, for one thing,' Isaac replied, smiling, 'you can call me Isaac.'

'Noted,' Hilaria replied, smiling back before giving him a look of wide-eyed innocence. 'Anything else? I'm sure you haven't come all this way just to tell me your name. It wouldn't have anything to do with the reports you've received about me acting strangely, would it?'

'Um, yeah,' Isaac said uncertainly. 'I've received a lot of reports from some worried people. To quote one of them, *"There's a tall crazy woman dancing up and down the corridor, can you sort her out before she scares people?"* That type of thing. With Em being busy elsewhere, I thought it best I investigate.'

Hilaria gave Isaac her best cheery smile and placed her hand on his thick, muscled arm. *By Neptune's beard, those arms are huge!* 'Excellent, just so happens you're the very person I'm wanting to speak to.'

From the shocked expression on Isaac's face, Hilaria could see that wasn't the answer he was expecting. She remained silent while Isaac's mouth opened and closed; he appeared to be suddenly lost for words. He drew in a long breath and stared at her with obvious suspicion.

'Miss Cooper, if you wanted to see me, all you had to do was use the communicator in your quarters,' Isaac said carefully.

'True,' Hilaria answered, being careful to choose her words, 'but you probably would have ignored me, which was something I couldn't allow.'

Isaac stiffened in surprise, then his eyes narrowed. His voice had an edge to it as he spoke in a low tone. 'You couldn't allow it!' Isaac repeated slowly. He drew in a long breath and glowered at her. 'Listen, woman, you are really wearing down my patience. Considering I've only been speaking to you for a couple of minutes, let me say that's an enormous achievement.'

'I'm sorry for the subterfuge,' Hilaria said quickly, holding her hands in an apologetic gesture. 'I knew the only way I could get your attention was if I acted in a strange manner. Please, all I ask if you could give me five minutes of your time. I'm sure once I've finished, you'll understand why I was so desperate to speak to you.'

Isaac gave a silent nod and seemed to listen intently while Hilaria explained everything – from seeing the image of Em's daughter, how she had died, right up to when Oracle appeared in her mirror. Hilaria had to give Isaac his due; she was quite surprised at how well he seemed to be taking the circumstances of Henrietta's death. After she had finished going over her plan with him, he rubbed the back of his neck and stared at Hilaria in bewilderment.

'Are you okay?' Hilaria asked, wondering what was going through his mind.

Isaac drew in a deep breath, let it out slowly and nodded. 'That was a lot of information to take in all at once.' He blinked and tilted his head. 'You realise what you are suggesting we do is insane, right? I mean, as in, *are-you-out-of-your-freaking-mind?*'

'Oh, I'm totally aware how insane it sounds.' Hilaria laughed. 'Personally, I would have gone with something like, what the actual fuckedy-fuck-fuck!'

'Just checking,' Isaac murmured in a tone that gave Hilaria the impression he still wasn't entirely convinced. He shook his head and stared up at the ceiling. 'I must be out of my mind to even consider this.'

'I agree,' Hilaria answered glumly. She exhaled deeply and then stared at him hopefully. 'But surely you see that I have no choice, that this is the way it must be done. If I could warn Em in some way, I would, but my hands are tied.'

The corners of Isaac's mouth curled up in a wolfish grin and he tapped his nose. 'Leave that to me. You're not the only one who can be cunning.' He coughed, rubbed his chin thoughtfully and nodded slowly. 'No doubt about it, you are definitely stuck between a rock and a hard place. Although I agree with you in principle, I must warn you I'm not that comfortable with the idea that I'm about to deceive someone who I have huge respect for,' he murmured reluctantly. He stiffened as if he had

thought of something; he leaned in closer to Hilaria and spoke in a hushed voice. 'You said that this Oracle could be watching you through our security cameras. Aren't you afraid that it will also be listening to what we are saying?'

This was something Hilaria had already considered and had given much thought to. She nodded slowly and smiled reassuringly at Isaac. 'Oracle had already told me it hadn't been able to listen in on our conversation because of the obsolete technology that the security system runs on. Because the cameras aren't equipped with audio sensors, Oracle can see but not hear.'

But what she didn't tell Isaac was that she was worried Oracle may have got round that glitch. It was quite possible the AI could read lips. Because Isaac was already sceptical about her plan, Hilaria reasoned that if she told him that, then he might not even go ahead. However, because Oracle hadn't appeared to stop what they were doing, a part of Hilaria was optimistic that the AI lacked the ability to read lips. Even though it was a thin string of hope, it was something she was very willing to grasp hold of. Also, it wouldn't hurt if she crossed her fingers and said a silent prayer to her household gods.

If this was to work, she was going to need all the help she could get.

A few minutes later, Hilaria stood anxiously inside the transport-pod's cabin. She cast a worried eye at Isaac, who was standing to one side in deep conversation with two of his colleagues. After a short introduction Baz and Tatiana kept giving her dirty looks while Isaac went over the plan with them. It was quite evident that they both were unhappy at being part of a scheme thought up by someone who had only recently been their enemy. But Hilaria didn't care how they felt, so long as they did what was required of them. They were simply to act as backup, just in case anything unforeseen happened.

Once they had learned that Em was in the gym working out with Zoe, they headed to the nearest transport-pod, but not before making a

brief detour to the armoury to collect a pistol and some other supplies that were essential to Hilaria's plan. Then, after calling into the infirmary, they boarded another pod and proceeded to the gym.

As soon as the pod's doors opened, Hilaria was greeted by the recognisable voice of Em. She lifted an eyebrow in surprise as she realised Em sounded angry. She let out a sharp gasp at the unexpected sight greeting her. Em appeared to have Zoe pressed against the wall with her hands wrapped around her throat. Despite wondering what could have set Em off, Hilaria could clearly see from the unhealthy colour of Zoe's face and the way her body was hanging limp that she'd lost consciousness. A secretive smile tugged at Hilaria's lips. This was perfect.

Hilaria detected movement out of the corner of her eye and turned to see Isaac trying to move past her. She didn't need to be a mind reader to see he was concerned for the two people in front of him. He snapped his head round and glowered at Hilaria as she put a hand on his arm to stop him.

'You seriously don't expect us to continue with this insane scheme of yours, do you?' Isaac hissed angrily.

'Yes,' Hilaria hissed back. 'We couldn't have a better opportunity to catch Em when she's this angry. In her current frame of mind, she's liable to go off at the least little thing.'

It was obvious to Hilaria that Isaac was unhappy that she wanted to use his friend's emotional turmoil to her advantage. However, if he had any reservations, he kept them to himself; he bobbed his head and sighed reluctantly. 'Fine, it's your funeral.' He gestured to his two colleagues and scowled at Hilaria. 'You two follow me, and you stay hidden behind me until I tell you to step forward.'

Hilaria remained silent and took a step back to let the three people pass. As they sprinted over to Em and Zoe, she deliberately hung back, trying her best to be as inconspicuous as possible. She felt a surge of panic build inside her on seeing Zoe's eyes had now rolled up, and chewed on her bottom lip, secretly praying Isaac wouldn't be too late to stop Em from choking her, otherwise there was a chance Zoe may end up suffering brain damage from lack of oxygen. Fortunately, her panic swiftly changed to relief as Isaac placed his hands on Em's arms and whispered something

softly to her. Hilaria couldn't make out what he said, but whatever it was, it was enough to force Em into loosening her grip. Tatiana raced forward and grabbed hold of Zoe to stop her head from hitting the floor. After making sure Zoe still had a pulse, Tatiana and Baz frantically carried her into the waiting transport-pod, and the doors closed. Hilaria inhaled a relieved sigh on seeing Zoe's face had started to return to its normal colour.

Focusing her attention back on Isaac and Em, Hilaria raised an eyebrow in surprise at seeing the look on the big man's face while he spoke to Em. Could it be? Did Isaac have feelings for Em? Curious to see if she was right, Hilaria edged closer so that she could read his body language. Yes, she nodded to herself as she observed the tells Isaac's body was giving off. The way his pupils dilated when he spoke to her and the way the hairs on his arms stood up. It was clear Isaac had deep feelings for Em. Pursing her lips, Hilaria wondered whether Em was even aware of his feelings. Did she feel the same way about him?

Unfortunately, as she leaned in to get a better look, Hilaria realised she had made a huge mistake. Em's gaze snapped back and forth between Hilaria and Isaac, shooting them both angry scowls. *Damn it!* Hilaria groaned. She'd been so distracted by her own curiosity, she had momentarily forgotten why she was there.

'Em, don't be angry,' Isaac was saying urgently. 'Miss Cooper has something she needs to say to you. Promise me you'll hear her out.'

From the way she was balling her hands into tight fists and the strained tendons in her neck, Hilaria could tell Em was struggling to keep her emotions in check. She swallowed nervously as she wondered, not for the first time, if this was a good idea. *Oh well*, she thought grimly, *can't back out now.*

Drawing in a deep breath, Hilaria held up both hands and took a step forward. She tried to keep her tone friendly as she edged closer to Em. 'Em, there's something I must tell you. I've kept something from you.' She paused for effect and looked at her directly in the eye. 'It's about your daughter, Henrietta.'

'If you're trying to tell me you knew Henrietta, Zoe already told me,' Em growled, folding her arms across her chest and shooting her a withering look.

So, the feline was out of the cage. For reasons she couldn't explain, Hilaria felt relieved. Although she doubted Zoe meant to do it, she had unwittingly paved the way for Hilaria's plan. Now, she hoped Isaac could somehow convey to Em what she was planning to do, and then the rest should be easy enough. Although she was baffled at how he was going to achieve that, Hilaria reluctantly had to put her faith in him and hope he came through for her.

Still wondering how much Zoe had told Em, Hilaria gave a small nod and stared at her curiously. 'How much did she tell you?'

'She told me enough,' Em snapped, her eyes blazing with rage. 'She told me the day she arrived on this world, Henrietta was there in the portal chamber, standing next to you.'

'Yes, Henrietta was there with me. She worked in the chamber as one of the portal's technicians,' Hilaria answered carefully and gave Em a wistful smile. 'She was an incredibly gifted scientist; you would have been proud of her.'

Em bristled at the comment and shot daggers at Hilaria. 'You have no right to tell me how I should feel about my own daughter.'

Although she was being honest about Henrietta and had not meant to offend Em, Hilaria quickly realised she had inadvertently created a chink in Em's armour. All she had to do now was chip slowly away at it. Hopefully, Em would see what she was doing and take the bait. Her stomach churned inside her as she readied herself for what she was about to do next.

'That's the thing, isn't it?' Hilaria scoffed, her mouth widening in pretend glee. 'You didn't know her. Not the way I did. You had no idea what she liked or disliked because you hadn't seen or spoken to her for over twenty years.' She purposefully curled her upper lip in apparent disgust. 'Some mother you must have been. I think you must have been a real disappointment to her because she never even mentioned you.' She held up her right index finger and let out a loud bark of laughter. 'No, sorry, I'm wrong. It wasn't disappointment, it was shame. Yes, I think she must have been ashamed of you.'

'How dare you!' Em roared, her body visibly trembling with rage. 'She didn't have time to know me properly because she was taken from me.'

Hilaria had to give Em her due. If she knew Hilaria was trying to goad her on purpose, she was putting on a good show. She swallowed and prepared herself. If Em's emotional display wasn't an act, then she most certainly would not like what was coming next.

'Oh, boo-hoo, give it a rest, lady.' Hilaria moaned in mock sorrow while pretending to wipe tears from her eye. She gestured to Isaac and herself. 'Come on, you can be honest. There's only the three of us here.' She leaned in closer and lowered her voice into a conspiratorial whisper. 'Admit it, you never really wanted a daughter, did you? She was just an inconvenience to you. It was probably you who put the idea in Barnes's head for him to take her from you.'

'No, you're wrong,' Em protested, her eyes shimmering with tears. 'I already told you—'

'Yes, yes,' Hilaria interrupted, placing her hand over her mouth and yawning theatrically. 'Barnes shot you in the back. Or that's what you want us to believe. After all, we only have your word that's what happened.' Hilaria pulled her head back and let out a loud barking laugh. 'Oh wait, better yet, you and Barnes conspired together to get rid of Henrietta.'

'Woman, I think you've gone too far,' Isaac muttered warningly. 'You need to let up.'

Even though a part of her wanted to stop, Hilaria realised if she stopped now, it was quite possible Oracle would see and realise it was a deception. Hilaria gritted her teeth. No, this had to be done. Her mind focused with dogged determination, she pressed on with her emotional attack. 'But like I said earlier, you didn't know Henrietta, not the way I did. Do you want to know why that is?' Not waiting for Em to answer, she straightened proudly and stabbed a finger into her own chest. 'I was her lover. I knew every little intimate detail about her. What buttons to push, what made her laugh and what made her cry.' Hating herself for what she was about to say next, Hilaria deliberately leaned in closer to Em and whispered into her ear. 'Your daughter was a wildcat and had a bit of a reputation. We even had a nickname for her – piglet. Because she loved to squeal.' She leaned back and let out a loud, mirthless laugh. 'Oh, she liked it rough. The moans of pleasure she gave off whenever she wanted me to punish her.'

Em squeezed her eyes shut and turned her back to Hilaria. 'Take that back,' she whispered, her voice cracking with thick emotion.

Inwardly despising herself for dragging Henrietta's name through the mud, Hilaria exhaled a long dramatic sigh and shook her head. 'Unfortunately, I became bored with her. In my mind, she was just a dog whose only purpose was to give me pleasure. So I did what any reasonable person does to an animal that they no longer have any use for. I put it down.' Hilaria tapped her chin thoughtfully and stared up at the ceiling. 'Interesting noise the skull makes when it explodes outward; it's almost like the sound of a melon popping. Of course, if I had known I was going to meet you, I would have saved a piece of her skull to give to you as a keepsake.'

Em let out a loud, guttural scream. 'You cruel, sadistic witch,' she cried out. Her face a picture of pure rage, she spun round and grabbed the weapon from the holster fastened to Isaac's hip.

To Hilaria, it was as if time had slowed down as Em expertly dropped to one knee, took aim, and fired. The bolt of energy appeared to fly at her in slow motion. But just as the energy beam struck the centre of her chest, it dawned on Hilaria that she had made a grievous error. There was an explosion of light, and she saw her chest erupt outward in a violent spray of blood. It was followed by the intense agony of one of her ribs breaking. The concussive force took Hilaria by surprise, and she felt herself being thrown backwards. She cried out in pain as the back of her head struck something unyielding.

Then everything went black.

-7-

'How's Zoe doing, Fausta?'

Em stared worriedly at the unconscious Zoe, who lay unmoving on the biobed. The only movement was the occasional twitch of Zoe's eyes, which Em assumed was because she was in deep REM sleep. Em's gaze drifted to the red mark around Zoe's neck, and she felt a pang of guilt knowing that she had been responsible for it. Pressing her lips into a thin line, Em wished there was some way she could tell Zoe how sorry she was for letting her anger get the better of her and prayed she would let her make it up to her one day.

Em shifted her attention away from the unconscious young woman and stared at the tall, slim, dark-haired medic standing next to her. Fausta was a forty-something woman who had escaped from the same detention centre that had held Em. Although she wasn't a physician, Fausta was one of the few people in the complex who had basic medical training, qualifying her to work in the infirmary. Even though Em wished they had a proper physician, she was grateful that she had people like Fausta to rely on.

'She's fine,' Fausta replied, gesturing to the display screens behind the biobed. 'I ran a scan and there's some swelling around her larynx. Unfortunately, I can't tell you for certain how long it will take for the swelling to go down or if there will be any lasting damage. But I'm pretty confident there won't be.' She gave Em a grim smile and shook her head sadly. 'I'm sorry, but I had to sedate her. She was so distressed when she regained consciousness, I thought it was prudent to knock her out in case she injured herself.'

'How long will she be out for?' Em asked glumly; knowing they had been forced to sedate Zoe filled her with even more remorse.

'I plan to let her sleep for as long as possible,' Fausta explained. She made a clicking noise with her tongue while she stared thoughtfully at readings on the display screens and then exhaled a long, heavy sigh. 'If I'm reading these stats right, keeping her like this assists the regenerative process.' She gave Em a small nudge and smiled. 'Don't worry, Chief, it won't be long before she's back on her feet, plaguing the life out of us. Hey, we'll probably wish we had kept her sedated.'

Even though Em knew Fausta was only trying to help lighten her mood, she didn't feel like laughing. Her gaze lingered over Zoe's prone body before moving up to the readings being displayed on the monitors behind the biobed. They showed a basic simulation of a human body with various readings and statistical icons displayed around it. She focused on the slowly pulsing image of a heart that gave a reading of thirty-five BPM. It encouraged Em that Zoe seemed to be in a restful sleep and didn't appear to be stressed. Alas, that didn't quell the guilt she was feeling.

Em turned away from the bed and waved her arms in exasperation. 'Damn it, she shouldn't even be lying there,' she moaned. 'Some leader I am – I can't even control my temper. What a disappointment I must be to you and everyone else.'

Lapsing into an uncomfortable silence, Em stood and stared at Zoe's unmoving body. All sorts of thoughts ran through her mind as she wondered whether she had lost the faith of those who had been following her for so many years. She pictured them talking amongst themselves, asking whether they could trust a leader who could easily fly off the handle at any given moment. Em pinched the bridge of her nose and blew out a dejected sigh. Oh, she was so tired of it all. The weight of everybody relying on her had never felt as heavy as it did now. It was almost as if it was bearing down on her, testing her to see how much it would take to break her. Perhaps it was best if she stepped down and handed command over to someone more deserving, Em mused. They couldn't do any worse than she had.

Em flinched as she felt someone take hold of her hand, snapping her back to reality. She spun swiftly around. Fausta was staring at her with heavy concern etched across her face.

'Em, come with me for a second,' Fausta said softly and led Em away from Zoe's bed.

Em opened her mouth to object, but there was something in Fausta's blue eyes that made her pause. Withholding any misgivings she had, Em gave a wordless nod and allowed herself to be guided across the infirmary and into a side room. After stepping through a door, Em found herself standing in a medium-sized room containing a couple of cots, a leather settee that looked like it had seen better days, a cupboard and a food replicator that appeared to be offline. Em was very much aware she was standing in a room once used by the medical staff assigned to the complex when it had originally been under URE control many years ago.

'Please take a seat,' Fausta said, smiling and gesturing to the leather settee.

As she sat, Em watched curiously as Fausta moved purposely toward the cupboard on the far side of the room. She opened it and pulled out two drinking glasses. Em widened her eyes in surprise on seeing Fausta pull out a narrow white bottle with strange writing down the front. Squinting her eyes to make out what was on the bottle, Em stiffened at the realisation of whose language it was. The writing on the bottle was Hanzi, a symbol-based writing system used primarily by the citizens of the Greater Chinese Republic. Em raised an eyebrow; the bottle Fausta was holding was Sunaki, a blended whisky normally brewed in the rice fields on an archipelago just off the southern coast of the GCR mainland.

'Sunaki?' Em exclaimed in surprise. 'How in the world did you get a bottle of that? I thought it was supposed to be illegal!'

'Ah ha, wouldn't you like to know,' Fausta answered, tapping her nose with her index finger. 'Let's just say I know a guy who knows a guy and leave it at that.'

'Uh-huh,' Em replied slowly as Fausta poured two finger measures into each glass. She had a strong suspicion who her supplier was, but decided it was best she said nothing. Personally, she had no problem with any of her people running private enterprises within the complex, so long

as it didn't involve drug smuggling or anything else that would put them at risk. It was common knowledge that there had been illegal supply chains running between the URE and GCR for years. It was quite possible that recent events had put paid to that, and any items – such as the whisky Fausta was holding – would soon become a dwindling commodity.

'So,' Fausta said curiously as she pulled up a desk chair and sat directly in front of Em. 'How are you feeling?'

Nervously picking up her glass, Em shuffled uncomfortably in her seat and stared deep into the glass she was holding. Why did she suddenly feel like she was sitting in front of a counsellor? *Maybe it would do me some good to talk to someone*, she thought, lifting her head and regarding Fausta curiously. There was something about Fausta's body language that relaxed her, like she could say anything to her.

'Why do I get the sense I'm talking to a bartender?' Em asked, allowing herself a half-hearted smile.

'Well, I wasn't always in the *employ* of the URE.' Fausta grinned back. She took a small sip from her glass and spoke in a despondent tone. 'My father ran a bar, and, in my youth, I spent a lot of time helping him serve customers. My mother had died just after I was born, so it was just me and him. He managed to keep me hidden from the imperial conscription squads. But every so often he would allow me to work behind the bar. Over time, I learned how to listen to customers who sometimes just wanted someone to talk to.' She exhaled and shook her head sadly. 'I had barely passed sixteen when my father and I were both arrested by the security forces. We never saw each other again.'

'I'm sorry to hear that,' Em answered sadly. Fausta's story did not surprise her; she had heard so many similar stories from many of her colleagues. A warm feeling of anger rose inside her as she thought about how the URE had destroyed so many families.

Fausta shrugged and waved dismissively. 'It's in the past. Nothing I do can change it,' she said in a matter-of-fact tone. As if to change the subject, she gave a small cough and smiled at Em. 'I consider what he taught me to be a gift, something I can use to help others.' She leaned forward and placed her hand on Em's knee. 'But enough about me. I want to talk about you. So, I ask you again, how are you feeling?'

Despite herself, Em relaxed and took a large gulp from her glass – and realised she had made a huge mistake. The dry smoky flavour hit the back of her throat like a sledgehammer. She screwed up her face at the powerful kick travelling down her throat, filling her body with a warm glow. When the aftertaste hit, she let out a sharp gasp.

'Wow,' Em croaked, her eyes watering, 'that's potent stuff.'

Fausta gave a small shrug. 'Meh. I find it quite tame,' she said indifferently. Then the corners of her mouth lifted in a secretive smile, and she gave Em a sly wink. 'Of course, you understand I only use it for medicinal purposes.'

Em laughed. 'Yeah, sure, and if a pig had wings, it would be a bat.'

They both laughed and settled into a comfortable silence. After a few moments, Fausta leaned back in her chair, steepled her fingers together, and stared silently at Em. Realising that Fausta wouldn't let her leave unless she said something, Em drew in a long breath, sat back and talked. As she sat there, Em found herself talking about her childhood with her sister. The happy times they shared, the night of her abduction and the misery that followed. She spoke about the most joyful time in her life, her time with Cornelius, the early days of her marriage to Barnes, and the short time she had with Henrietta. She spoke tearfully about the painful trauma of Barnes's betrayal and the recent discovery of what had happened to her daughter. Every so often, Fausta would interrupt Em to ask her to elaborate on something. However, the more she spoke, the more Em felt as if a weight had been lifted off her. She couldn't explain it, but it felt as if she had been hollowed out, freeing her and taking the bitterness away.

When she was finally finished, Em rested her head back and stared up at the ceiling. Then she squeezed her eyes shut and thought about everything she had just said. Even though it was emotionally draining, it dawned on Em that this was what she had needed. She frowned and wondered why she had never done it before.

Massaging the back of her neck, she opened her eyes and stared questioningly at Fausta. What was going through her mind? Em wondered. Would she declare her unfit to command? She certainly couldn't blame her if she did. Steeling herself for the worst, Em cleared her throat and spoke hesitantly. 'So, what's your opinion?'

Her face a mask of secrecy, Fausta leaned forward and gently squeezed Em's knee. 'I can see it in your eyes. You're wondering if you should still be in command.' Before Em could interject, Fausta held up her right hand, smiled and continued. 'That's not for me to say. Only you can decide. Truthfully, you've suffered more than anyone should in a lifetime. Probably more than anyone in this complex. So it's no wonder you snapped.' She shook her head and laughed. 'I'm surprised you haven't blown up before today.'

'But I hurt Zoe,' Em protested. She held up both her hands in a penitential gesture. 'How can I live with myself knowing I nearly killed her? She will probably never forgive me.'

'I think you need to give our young Zoe some credit,' Fausta said, smiling. Then the features of her face turned serious as she leaned forward and clasped Em's hands in hers. 'Yes, you hurt her. I'm sure she will understand that you have been under a lot of pressure, that it was simply a matter of being in the wrong place at the wrong time. Before you can allow people to forgive you, first you need to forgive yourself.'

Em nodded slowly. Yes, Fausta was right. Deep down, if she was being honest with herself, Em knew she'd been punishing herself for everything that had gone wrong in her life. She finally understood that, as much as she wanted to, she could not control the events in her life. That the good would eventually outweigh the bad.

'Yes, I understand.' Em sighed as she rose from her seat. 'Thank you, you have been an enormous help to me.'

'One other thing,' Fausta said quickly. 'It's important that we all have someone we can talk to. It's not good to keep all our frustrations to ourselves.' She gave Em an inquiring look. 'Do you have someone you can talk to? What about Isaac?'

'Oh, Isaac has enough to worry about without listening to me moaning at him,' Em scoffed.

Fausta stiffened and blinked in surprise. 'Oh, I thought you and he …' Her voice trailed off and she gave a quick dismissive wave. 'Never mind, forget I spoke.'

What did she mean by that? Puzzled by the comment. Em furrowed her brow and gave Fausta a bewildered sidelong look. Was Fausta

referring to the close bond she and Isaac shared? Or was it something else? Em snorted and quickly cast the thought to one side. Yeah, that was it. She was probably only referring to their close friendship. She cocked her head and regarded Fausta curiously. But why did she stop herself? Before Em could ask, Fausta placed a hand on Em's shoulder, smiled and guided her to the open door.

'Tell you what, Em, if you ever need to talk,' Fausta said, grinning, 'my door is always open with a bottle of medicinal whisky ready for us to share.'

'You're on.' Em laughed. Then she remembered there was another matter she needed to deal with and cleared her throat as she gave Fausta a serious look. 'What about that other thing? Has it been sorted?'

A dark cloud appeared over Fausta's face, and she gave a small nod. The tone of her voice became humourless. 'Yes, she's in the morgue, ready for your inspection. Isaac rigged the sensors to make it appear that the route between the gym and the infirmary had been contaminated. He ordered that those areas were to be off limits apart from essential personnel. That allowed my team to move in and swiftly move Hilaria with no one observing.'

Without saying another word, Fausta gently led Em out of the office and into the infirmary. The two women remained silent as they approached the closed steel door at the far end of the medical bay. Fausta bobbed her head respectfully and took a step back.

'I will give you some privacy.'

Not wishing to put it off any longer, Em gave a wordless nod and pulled open the large steel door. Stepping inside, she was now standing in a narrow antechamber facing another steel door. Just to the right of Em was a row of hooks holding several thick coats. On the assumption she might need an extra jacket she lifted two down, shoved her arms into one jacket's sleeves and held the remaining jacket tight in her left hand. Making sure her jacket's front zip was secure, Em pushed open the door and stepped forward into a large room. The first thing she noticed was a significant drop in temperature. Compared to the relatively comfortable warm infirmary, the atmosphere inside was cold enough to stop meat from spoiling. Em shivered and pulled up her jacket's zipper to her neck.

Now feeling a bit more protected from the frigid temperatures inside the room, Em cast her eye around it. Five mortuary freezers ran along the wall to her left. In the centre of the room stood two tables, with Hilaria's lightly clothed blood-soaked body lying on the table closest to Em. A sombre-looking but warmly dressed Isaac stood beside it and, from his dour expression, Em could tell he wasn't pleased about being there. *Tough*, she thought sullenly, *he was the one who convinced me to do this, so he'll just have to suck it up*. She gave him a tight smile as he acknowledged her with a wordless nod and then focused her attention on the body on the table. Hilaria's complexion had an unhealthy pallor to it, probably because of the room's frigid temperatures.

'How are you doing?' Em asked flatly.

Hilaria opened her eye and scowled at Em with obvious displeasure. 'Freezing my arse off. How do you think I'm doing?'

-8-

Despite sympathising with Hilaria's displeasure at being forced to lie in a freezing cold room, Em remained silent while she considered the best way to respond without agitating the woman any further. The hostile intensity in Hilaria's good eye was positively chilling. Not only that, but the frosty vibe emanating from her almost made the frigid temperature in the room seem tropical in comparison. As Hilaria's face screwed up in annoyance while she shifted uncomfortably on the table, Em felt the corner of her mouth twitch in amusement as the image of an angry pirate appeared in her head. *No, stop it,* she thought, chastising herself. *This isn't funny.* Although she was relieved Hilaria hadn't spotted her faux pas, Em still had to force herself to keep her face neutral while she listened to Hilaria grumble.

'What took you so long?' Hilaria moaned. She turned her head and shot daggers at Isaac. 'Your sadistic friend over there wouldn't let me wear a jacket.'

'Sorry, Boss Lady,' Isaac muttered sheepishly. 'I was worried somebody might walk in. I didn't want to try and answer any awkward questions about why Miss Cooper was wearing a thermal jacket.' The corners of his mouth curled up into an impish grin. 'I even suggested, because she was pretending to be dead, that it might be best if she stripped naked, but she wasn't having it.' Appearing to ignore the death stare coming at him from Hilaria, Isaac rolled his eyes and tutted. 'She's done nothing but moan at how cold it is in here.'

'Well, we've had no complaints from the previous tenants,' Em said, her tongue firmly in her cheek while she handed the thermal jacket to Hilaria. But as Hilaria slipped into the jacket, Em felt a surge of concern; it looked as if she was grimacing in pain. Was she putting on a brave front for Em's benefit?

'That was a nasty blow you took to the back of your head,' Em said worriedly. 'You sure you're okay?'

'Yeah, Fausta ran a quick scan with a handheld medical scanner,' Hilaria grumbled. 'She doesn't believe there was any damage done, and it's likely I'm just suffering from a mild concussion.' Her face twisted up in discomfort and she rubbed her hand over the front of her chest. 'Unfortunately, I fractured some of my ribs.'

'I'm not surprised,' Em snapped. 'What the hell were you thinking, strapping that many squibs to the front of your chest? You were lucky you didn't lose an eye.' Regretting the words as soon as they left her mouth, Em grimaced and shook her head apologetically. 'Hilaria, I'm sorry, that came out wrong.'

If she was offended, Hilaria didn't show it. Instead, she simply gave a dismissive wave and huffed, 'Humph! It's fine. Not like I haven't already lost an eye.' She lifted her shoulder in a small shrug and blew out an exasperated sigh. 'Next time I suggest strapping on a couple of bags of blood around my chest along with a few explosive squibs, please talk me out of it.' Hilaria bobbed her head gratefully at Isaac. 'I was just lucky Isaac managed to tell you where to aim. Otherwise, if you had aimed at my head, things would have turned out a lot worse and I would now probably be lying inside one of those freezers over there.'

Em forced herself to stifle a retort she had ready and wordlessly nodded. She didn't want to say anything, but while she had been listening to Hilaria's earlier tirade about Henrietta, Em was ashamed to admit she had been sorely tempted to put a round into the woman's head. It was just fortunate Isaac had warned her. She believed Hilaria was only saying those things to put on a show, so Em had reined in her emotions and followed Isaac's instructions.

Hang on a second! Em narrowed her eyes as she thought about Isaac, and a surge of anger swept through her. She still had a score to settle with him. Turning to focus her ire on him, Em jabbed her finger into his chest. Isaac flinched back and stared at Em in open-mouthed shock.

'As for you,' Em seethed, craning her head back and staring into his eyes. 'What the hell were you thinking agreeing to this insane plan?' Even though Isaac tried to back away from her, she somehow kept the distance the same while she angrily jabbed her index finger against his right temple. 'What was going through that brain of yours? I expected better of you!'

Even though Isaac towered over her, Em did not fear she was in any danger of him lashing out at her. All the time she had known Isaac, he had never shown any hostility toward her. Of course, she had seen him get angry many times, but never with her. However, there was no doubt in her mind that if he wanted to, he could probably snap her like a twig without breaking a sweat. But he just stood in front of her, seemingly taking the verbal abuse, hanging his head with a strange expression on his face. If she didn't know any better, she could have sworn she could see shame in his eyes. *No, that couldn't be it*, she thought. *I'm probably just reading too much into it.*

'Yeah, you're right,' Isaac murmured meekly. Then his mood seemed to change, and his mouth widened into a bright smile. 'Hey, look at it this way, Boss Lady. At least we know you can still read our secret language.'

Not in any mood to listen to Isaac's usual levity, Em shot him a harsh stare. 'You're just lucky I actually remembered it at all,' she snapped, throwing her hands up in exasperation. 'What would you have done if I hadn't seen your fingers tapping, eh? Did you even stop to consider that I may not have been in the frame of mind to take on board what you were trying to convey to me? Then what would you have done, eh?' She made a sweeping gesture to the woman lying on the table and a nipping gesture with two of her fingers of her right hand. 'After listening to all that crap she was saying to me, I was this close to wrapping my hands around her throat and strangling her.'

Isaac, looking like a naughty child who had been caught stealing, lowered his head and shuffled his feet sheepishly. 'Sorry, Em,' he murmured sorrowfully. 'I was doing what I thought was right. I understand

you're disappointed in me and will accept any punishment coming to me without complaint.'

Oh great, now I've hurt his feelings! Em let out a heavy sigh and placed her hands on her hips as she stared at her glum-faced friend. Even though she wanted so badly to continue berating him, she found she couldn't. She could never stay mad at him, no matter what he did. Why was that? Was it because they had shared so much pain? In her eyes, Isaac had always been her rock. Mr Dependable, someone who had always had her back.

Her ire extinguished, Em sucked in a long, exasperated breath and shook her head. 'We'll talk about it more later,' she said softly.

Then, without waiting for him to reply, Em turned swiftly around and focused her attention back on Hilaria. Despite still being unhappy at all the things Hilaria had said about Henrietta, Em was still curious to find out why she had gone to all that bother. There hadn't been enough time for Isaac to fully explain Hilaria's plan to Em. The were only a few things he could convey to her in that short space of time. That they were being watched. Em was to act angry. To shoot Hilaria in the chest. Put her body in the morgue. Although she was puzzled about the 'being watched' part, Em was more concerned with what Hilaria had said to her.

A part of her wondered whether any of what she had said about Henrietta was true. Did Hilaria only say those things because she knew it would get a reaction out of her? Em needed to know.

'Okay,' Em said flatly. 'We've done as you requested. We've placed you inside the morgue. Care to explain why?'

'Wait, I thought you—' Hilaria replied, blinking in surprise. 'Sorry, I thought Isaac explained to you why we had to do this via that secret language you use?'

Em was growing steadily more impatient with Hilaria for changing the subject, and struggled to keep her tone civil as she answered through clenched teeth, 'No. He didn't.' She looked quizzically at Isaac, who held up his hands, palms facing upwards, wordless gesture.

Feeling a migraine coming on, Em massaged her temples and blew out an exasperated sigh. 'What you call our secret language was created by those in servitude to the URE to pass secret messages amongst ourselves without our overseers being aware of it. We attach certain words to specific

figure gestures. It's ideal for when we want to exchange brief messages, but it can be time consuming if we have something more complicated to say.' Em bobbed her head at Isaac. 'For example, this plan you and Isaac came up with. In the short time we had, Isaac could only tell me five things – that we were being watched; you were going to say something to me; I was to pretend to be angry with you; I was to shoot you in the chest and we were to take your body to the morgue.' Em glanced over her shoulder and gave Isaac a wry smile. 'I had a hunch Isaac's pistol had been set to stun.' The muscles in Em's face tightened as she turned away from Isaac and gave Hilaria a stern look. 'However, what I wasn't expecting to see was your chest exploding. Seeing all that blood erupt out of you scared the crap out of me.' The muscles in her face softening, she raised her hands and clapped a couple of times. 'Kudos to you, my dear, for a performance that any actor would be proud of. It's obvious you've quite a flair for the dramatic.'

Hilaria huffed. 'If I had known it was going to end up with me being cold, miserable and in a lot of pain, I would've come up with something else.'

'Indeed,' Em said, grunting in agreement. Her patience having reached its limit and fed up with Hilaria dragging her feet, Em cleared her throat, folded her arms and pulled a sour face. 'I'm still waiting for an explanation. Like you, I'm feeling the cold. Just to warn you, I can become quite testy when I'm cold and irritable.'

'You mean you're not now?' Hilaria said, grinning. However, she must have seen something in Em's eyes, because her grin quickly disappeared, and she let out a small cough of embarrassment. 'Ahem, yes, the explanation ... okay, here goes.'

Em listened patiently to Hilaria's explanation. She felt her eyes grow wide in shock on hearing how Oracle had made its presence known to Hilaria. Em could scarcely believe what was being told to her. But despite the unbelievable aspect of Hilaria's story, throughout her time on this world, Em had learned there were a lot of things that defied logic. She had more or less become used to the unusual. To her, this was no different. Just another day on Terra. Once Hilaria was finished, Em turned away from her, stared thoughtfully up at the ceiling and shook her head in frustration. Damn it, just when she thought they were getting a grip on

things, Oracle rears its ugly head to put a dampener on things. Now she understood the need for secrecy and placing Hilaria in the morgue. It was the only place in the complex that didn't have security cameras. Em massaged her forehead as she wondered how long Oracle had been watching them. Was it aware of their plan to sneak into the URE's main military tower in Pons Aelius and rescue anyone still being held in the detention centre?

As if sensing Em's unspoken question, Hilaria coughed and spoke up. 'I can see it in your eyes. You are wondering how long Oracle has been watching us, isn't that right? If I am honest, I'm almost certain it hasn't been watching us. The only reason it appeared was that it overheard me shouting at myself in the mirror.' Hilaria slumped her shoulders and blew out a slow, despondent sigh. 'I'm sorry. By making my presence known to it, I've placed you all in grave danger.'

'No, it's not your fault,' Em lied, hoping it sounded convincing. She massaged the back of her neck as she tried desperately to think of something to improve their situation. 'The question is, is there anything we can do to stop it? Because I'm sure you don't want to be locked in this creepy room forever.'

No sooner had the words left Em's mouth than something strange happened. A secretive smile seemed to pass between Isaac and Hilaria. Did they know something she didn't? Em sharpened her eyes in suspicion on noticing a mischievous glint in Isaac's eyes. What was that crafty-so-and-so up to? She shook her head. No, scratch that … what were they both up to?

'Yeah, about that,' Isaac said with one side of his mouth curling up into a wolfish grin, while bobbing his head at Hilaria. 'Our former would-be prisoner here has come up with a solution that may just fix all our problems.'

Oh, I get the feeling I'm not going to like this, Em thought as she tilted her head and stared at Hilaria with growing suspicion. 'Uh-huh, why do I suddenly feel like I'm standing in the middle of a train track and I'm about to be hit by a high-speed train?'

Hilaria laughed. 'Oh, it's nothing dangerous.' Her face turned serious and she gazed steadily at Em. 'After my discussion with Oracle, I

racked my brain to come up with a way to stop it watching me.' A devious smile appeared on her face, and she clicked her fingers. 'Then it hit me. I remembered General Cooper reading a report about a piece of technology that had been developed on your world for just this sort of occasion.'

'My world!' Em blurted out, completely taken aback

'Yes,' Hilaria continued, nodding excitedly. 'A group who were aware of the URE's presence on your world developed what they called quantum frequency jammers. I won't bore you with the science, apart from the fact these jammers made it impossible for us to observe or make incursions into an area that was being shielded by them.'

'And you think this will work for us?' Em asked, struggling to contain her excitement and suddenly feeling more hopeful. 'What I want to know is, do you know how to build these jammer things, and will they stop Oracle watching us?'

'Yes,' Hilaria replied, bobbing her head enthusiastically. 'URE operatives obtained copies of the plans. It was hoped we could develop a countermeasure. Fortunately, our scientists never found a solution.' A broad smile appeared on Hilaria's face, and she tapped her finger against her right temple. 'Just so happens, I have all the information right here, thanks to the general reading the schematics that explained how to build such a device. Once I replicate them, I am confident they will shield us from any future incursions. Not only that, once I have made some tweaks to your firewall, it will be virtually impossible for Oracle to hack in.'

'You're certain you can do this?' Em asked. Although a part of her hoped Hilaria could do it, another part of her wondered whether Hilaria's anger at Oracle was causing her to bite off more than she could chew.

'Yes,' Hilaria answered in a tone that echoed the look of confidence on her face. She stared up at the ceiling thoughtfully, murmuring, 'With the technology you have available here, I should have several devices up and running in six hours.' Her expression became distant while she mumbled away to herself, 'Yes, I would need to run a scan on Em and find out what her quantum signature is. Wait, what if because she's been on this world for such a long time, her signature has changed … no, you idiot, stop second-guessing yourself. You know this – in theory, all

quantum signatures remain the same no matter how long you remain in a universe. Once I have the data I need, it should be a simple matter of …'

Em had always thought herself a reasonably intelligent woman. After all, she'd been taught by Cornelius, who had been one of the smartest men she knew and a truly exceptional teacher. But as she tried to follow what Hilaria was saying, she realised just how little she knew. Several seconds of listening to the woman's ramblings only gave Em a headache. She exchanged a look with Isaac, and from the glazed look in his eyes, she was relieved to see he appeared to be just as baffled as she was. Creasing her brow, Em stared at Hilaria while she continued to mumble away to herself. However, a part of Em couldn't help wondering if this was an act. Was Hilaria only doing this to impress her?

Afraid Hilaria was getting distracted and had forgotten what they were there for, Em gave a polite cough and waved her hand in front of Hilaria's face. 'Um, hello,' she said, struggling to hide the scepticism in her voice. 'Forgive me, Hilaria, I don't doubt your skills, but are you sure you're not taking too much on? No offence, but what makes you think you can pull this off?'

Obviously startled out of her ruminations, Hilaria blinked and stared at Em in surprise. 'What? Oh, no offence taken,' she said, waving dismissively. Then the corners of her mouth curled up in a sly grin and she tapped her temple again. 'As much as I would like to take credit and boast about my extremely impressive technical skills, I'm afraid I must give the credit to Oracle. Remember I said when I was a young child it altered my personality and increased my intelligence?' Em gave a slow nod while she tried to recall her earlier conversation with Hilaria. Unable to clearly remember what had been said, she gave a wordless nod and let Hilaria continue. 'Fortunately for me, when Oracle reset my personality, it forgot to take away that other gift.' She shook her head and let out a bitter laugh. 'An oversight. I'm sure it's regretting now.'

Not expecting to, Em suddenly felt sorry for the younger woman sitting in front of her. It shocked her just how much they had in common. Both of them had had their childhoods stripped away from them, and both had been put into the service of a soul-crushing regime. However, her empathy was quickly replaced by a hollow feeling as Hilaria's earlier words

came flooding back to her. Em tried to force back the bitter taste of bile rising in her throat while she focused her gaze on Hilaria. No, she couldn't allow what Hilaria had said earlier to pass without knowing for certain if it was true.

'Hilaria,' she asked coldly. 'I need to ask you a question and I need you to be truthful with me.'

Something happened. Something subtle. If Em hadn't been staring intently at Hilaria, she would have missed it. Whether it was the tone of Em's voice or something else, she wasn't certain, but whatever it was, it affected Hilaria's demeanour slightly. The energy appeared to drain out of her. Her shoulders drooped as she nodded despondently and let out a small sigh.

'You're wanting to know if I was speaking the truth about what had happened to Henrietta,' Hilaria answered dolefully with a small nod of confirmation. 'Yes, essentially what I said was true. Henrietta is dead. I could lie to you and tell you I ordered her death. But since I've met you, I've come to respect you and lying would only destroy the trust you have placed in me.' Her green eye shimmered with tears and her voice cracked as she straightened and looked Em directly in the eye. 'The fact of the matter is, she died by my hands. I know it doesn't mean a lot, but I want you to know I loved her with all my heart. I wish I could change it, but I cannot.'

That was it. The answer Em had been waiting for. A series of emotions surged through Em as she deliberated silently on what to do with this new piece of information. She gazed intently at Hilaria, hands clenched into tight balls. Oh, how badly she wanted to lash out. Scream at Hilaria. Shout *You took my daughter from me* or *How dare you be alive when my daughter isn't!*

But as she gazed at the pitiful creature in front of her, Em had an epiphany. It had come to her earlier, shortly after her conversation with Fausta. For many years, she had been holding on to a lot of anger and bitterness, allowing it to fester inside her. But it wasn't over Henrietta; the ill feeling she had was toward her sister Claire. Whether or not she had done it subconsciously, Em had let that bitter resentment poison her,

allowing it to build inside until it eventually exploded in a moment of madness.

Em thought back to the angry exchange she'd had with Glen just over a week ago and thought of the words she had used. *Yes*, she thought, *if things are to be different, then I must be the one who leads by example, by setting aside my anger and bitterness.* Deep down, a part of her knew she would never get the chance to reconcile with Claire. So, if she couldn't do it with Claire, the next logical step would be for her to face her daughter's killer.

Several minutes of uncomfortable silence passed as Em continued to gaze at the woman in front of her. She eventually gave a small nod of understanding. Yes, Hilaria had been right in what she had said earlier. Em had lost her daughter long ago. As much as she wanted to kill Hilaria, Em knew that wouldn't bring Henrietta back. If what Hilaria said was true, that they had been in love, Em was certain Henrietta wouldn't wish her lover to die in an act of revenge. On top of that, Hilaria's death would probably only complicate matters even further.

But as Em stared into Hilaria's tear-stained face, she sensed something. Whether it was a mother's sixth sense, she wasn't sure, but something inside her told her Hilaria was holding something back. Was she deliberately shielding Em from something, something so disturbing that Hilaria had been too afraid to say it? Or had Hilaria been protecting herself out of fear? Em forced herself to push that thought to one side. *No*, she thought, *I don't care. Let her keep her secrets. If she wants to tell me, then I'll listen to her.*

After a long period of silence, Em took in a long breath and let it out slowly. 'I've thought long and hard on what to say to you, Hilaria,' she said, choosing her words carefully. 'I can sense you are looking for absolution over Henrietta's death. You're probably even hoping that I forgive you. Unfortunately, I can't give you that, because it's not in my power to give.' Em paused for a few seconds and then strode forward, offered her hand and smiled sadly at her. 'It is more than likely Henrietta's death will be on your conscience until the day you die. You need to accept that only your gods have the power to absolve you. However, one thing I can do for you is offer you a promise. A promise that I will take no retribution against you. I'm also prepared to stand by you if you would like me to.' Em swallowed and glanced over her shoulder at Isaac, then back again at Hilaria. 'We've all done things we're not proud of. Our hands are tainted with the blood of our victims. If we are to heal, then we do it together. Do you agree to let me stand by you, so that we can support each other in our shared grief?'

From the stunned look on Hilaria's face, Em could tell Hilaria had not been expecting to be offered an olive branch. She gave Hilaria a thin smile as she watched her mouth open and close as if she was struggling to express what she was feeling. She cast a surreptitious eye over at Isaac and saw the awestruck look on his face, and she wondered if he had been expecting her to strike Hilaria down in an act of vengeance.

'Em,' Hilaria said, seemingly finally finding her voice, 'I must be honest and say that is not what I was expecting. I'm ashamed to admit that you are a far stronger person than I am. Honestly, if our situations had been reversed, I don't think I would have been as compassionate as you.' She took hold of Em's hand and clasped it tightly in both of hers. 'To say I'm humbled by your words is an understatement. But I truly am in awe of you. So, to answer your question. Yes, I understand I cannot earn your forgiveness, but I hope one day to earn your respect.' She grimaced as she shuffled off the table and stood in front of Em with her head held high. 'On that note, I swear my allegiance to you and vow to protect you, even if it costs me my life.'

Her heart swelling from Hilaria's words, Em smiled and lightly tapped Hilaria's face. 'That's all I ask,' she whispered, and focused her attention back on Isaac. 'Give her what she needs, assign any people with the skills and knowledge to assist her. Once she's completed her task and the generators are working, escort her back to her quarters so that she can rest. We've a lot of work to do and not much time left to do it in, understood?'

Without waiting for a response, Em spun on her heel and swiftly left the morgue. After exiting the infirmary, she hurried down the corridor. Distracted by the multiple thoughts running through her head, she was only vaguely aware of the people she passed. If they said anything to her, she was unaware of it. Even though she told Hilaria they would share their grief, and she was willing to allow her to keep her secrets, that was anything

but true. In her heart she wanted so badly to punish Hilaria and rip the truth out of her heart if need be.

A few minutes later, Em stepped inside her quarters and closed the door behind her. For a few seconds she didn't move, only stared at the sparsely decorated room. Then she carefully unfastened the locket hanging around her neck and stood there for a while silently looking at it. Tears of sadness and anger welled up in her eyes while Hilaria's words bounced around inside her head. She squeezed the locket tight in her hands, and she felt her body shudder as an all-consuming grief took hold of her. *It's not fair*, she thought. *The universe already took my family, my freedom and my beloved friend from me. Just when I thought it couldn't take any more from me, it takes away my last hope of finally seeing my daughter alive.*

Tears flowing freely down her cheeks, Em pulled back her head and screamed up at the heavens, 'When are you going to be satisfied?' She slammed her right fist into her breast and spat, 'If you want my life, then take it because you've taken everything else from me!'

Full of rage, she threw the locket across the room and unleashed her fury on everything in front of her. Ignoring the concerned pleas coming from behind the closed door, she grabbed hold of the blanket and pillow and tore them off her cot. Screaming with petulant rage, she tried to tear them to shreds. Not finished there, she grabbed hold of the cot with both hands and turned it upside down. Then she focused her wrath on the chest and pulled every drawer out, scattering her clothing across the floor. Sobbing, blinded by her tears, she grabbed several items of clothing and tore at them with her fingers.

Finally, drained of all emotion, Em sank to her knees, reached for the locket, took hold of it and clutched it tight against her. Pulling her legs up to her chest, she lay on the floor and cried herself to sleep.

-9-

Over the course of the following week, for Em and everyone around her, time seemed to move at a hectic pace. True to her word, Hilaria completed assembling the frequency jammers within the six hours she promised. Unfortunately, their integration into the complex's electrical grid didn't go as smoothly as Em and Hilaria had wished. No sooner than the jammers were activated, they caused feedback along the base's power grid. Fires erupted in every corridor as overloaded power conduits short-circuited, sending the complex into darkness. Luckily, only a few people were caught out using transport-pods and had to spend hours trapped inside. Eventually, rescuers managed to save them. Although they were grateful to have escaped their confinement, a few still vented their displeasure that Em had allowed it to happen.

As she watched her colleagues rally round to help restore power, Em felt a sense of pride. Even though it had taken them a few days, the atmosphere inside the darkened base was jovial. Whenever she walked down the eerily torchlit corridors, Em smiled as she listened to the sounds of singing coming from the maintenance shafts. Her colleagues' spirited songs reminded her of stories from her childhood that had been told to her by her grandparents. Stories of those who had been forced to live through the London Blitz during World War II, about people who had to spend evening after evening in the London underground, with nothing but songs of defiance to help keep their spirits up.

When power was eventually restored, an enormous cheer resonated throughout the complex. Em suspected that was down to the fact that the air recycling was back in operation. She didn't want to admit it to anyone, but the smell of stale air had been starting to worry her.

Fortunately, the second attempt to power up the jammers went a lot more smoothly. Hilaria admitted she had made a mistake when she gave instructions for the work crews to power up the jammers. Instead of powering them one at a time, all twelve were activated at once, putting a strain on the old complex's power grid. Even though Em tried to reassure Hilaria it wasn't her fault, she still blamed herself for not thinking of it.

The second time around, because the security system was offline, Hilaria assisted the work crews because she felt confident that she was now safe from Oracle's prying eyes. Even though it was painstakingly slow, Hilaria refused to allow any jammer to be turned on unless she was present. Despite the grumbles coming from the tired work crews, Hilaria was adamant each jammer would not be activated unless she was one hundred per cent certain there would be no repeat of the power overload.

An enormous sigh of relief was heard throughout the complex as the final jammer came online. Although she had not been there to witness it, Em laughed on hearing the rumour that each member of the engineering team had slapped Hilaria on the back for a job well done. There had even been a rumour that they had invited her to sample a batch of their home brew. From all accounts, it was supposed to be powerful stuff, and something Em had yet to try. The day after the final jammer was activated, Em paid a visit to Hilaria's quarters to congratulate her. She could not hide her amusement when she was greeted by the sight of a hung-over former general standing in front of her. While observing the bloodshot-eyed woman in the doorway, a sense of satisfaction stirred within Em, confirming to her that a good night had been had by all involved. And even though she was unhappy at not being invited, Em felt in her heart that it was more important that her colleagues were bonding with Hilaria. For that, she couldn't be happier.

The blackout also had another favourable outcome for Em. Having nothing much to do, Em had the opportunity to make regular

checks on Zoe. It was fortunate the infirmary had its own backup generator to keep power running.

Ever since she had nearly throttled the life out of Zoe, guilt had weighed heavily on Em's mind. Even though the youngster wasn't her daughter, Em couldn't stop herself feeling maternal toward her. It was impossible for her to shake the heavy anxiety growing inside her that Zoe would resent being in her presence. But any thoughts she had about Zoe being angry with her were quickly eased as she walked into the infirmary and was greeted by Zoe sitting up in bed, beaming at her. The young woman chatted excitedly with Em, appearing unfazed, acting like nothing had happened. To Em's relief, Fausta explained she was happy with the progress Zoe had made and so felt she no longer needed to be in the infirmary.

But as she listened to Zoe chatter away, Em wondered if her friendly demeanour was masking how she truly felt. However, as if she sensed Em's thoughts, Zoe leapt out of the biobed and hugged her tightly. A warm glow of relief filled Em as she realised Zoe didn't harbour any resentment toward her. But that did not stop her being concerned at the way she was reacting. She'd gone through a lot over a short space of time. It worried Em that maybe Zoe's behaviour was hiding some underlying problem. But she realised she couldn't force Zoe to tell her what was bothering her. She had to be patient and hope Zoe would seek her out when she was ready.

A short time after Em visited Zoe, Em's concerns were heightened when she was approached by Hilaria, who wanted to express something troubling that had occurred between her and Zoe. Hilaria explained that Zoe had deliberately sought her out, seemingly wanting to be her friend. Although this pleased Hilaria, she also sensed Zoe wasn't being entirely truthful with her and that she was deceiving her for some reason. She told Em she believed that Zoe only wanted to get close to her so that she could spy on her. Whether it was because Zoe was holding a grudge over what had happened, Hilaria wasn't certain, but was at a loss how to handle it. Em thought it best that they shouldn't make Zoe aware that they were on to her because she felt if they confronted her, they ran the risk of her withdrawing into herself. Seeing no other option but to stand back and let

Zoe carry on with what she was doing, Em ordered Hilaria to play along, but if things started to change and Hilaria felt Zoe posed a danger to herself, Em had absolute confidence that Hilaria would know how to handle it correctly. Despite expressing some reservations that what they were doing was wrong, Hilaria reluctantly agreed with Em's decision.

In the days that followed, with power around the complex restored and the frequency jammers up and running, people settled back into their usual routine. Confident that there were no forces assembling to attack the complex, Em felt now was as good a time as any to hold a brainstorming session to plan the rescue of any prisoners being held in the Pons Aelius detention centre.

Not wanting to leave anyone out of the briefing, she decided the best place to hold it was inside the main auditorium. The auditorium was a cavernous circular room overlooking a platform that stood at the centre of the room. Holographic emitters lined the room's walls, which were controlled by an interface on the central platform. Centuries earlier, General Hadrianus had purposely designed the five-hundred-seater hall so that his voice would resonate around the chamber to his listening subordinates, thus cutting out the need for him to strain his voice. Over the years, the amphitheatre had undergone a steady overhaul, eventually leading to its present layout. Despite the base's current personnel numbering approximately two hundred and fifty, significantly less than what the auditorium had been designed for, Em still felt it was the best place to hold the strategy session.

As she gazed over the tired faces looking down at her, Em could see she had made the right decision. The past few days had taken a lot out of everyone, and she could tell they were relieved to spend a few moments sitting, giving them a break from their normal duties. Em smiled to herself. Her colleagues had earned themselves a break, but she hoped they wouldn't get too relaxed and nod off during the briefing. Focusing her attention on the people sitting in the front row, Em bobbed her head in acknowledgement of those who would be joining her on the mission. Standing next to her, in his role as her second in command, was Isaac.

But as she was just about to open the briefing, Em paused as she spotted Zoe slipping into the seat next to Hilaria. At first, Em wondered

whether the young woman was planning on making a scene. Em raised an eyebrow in curiosity as Zoe started a conversation with her former tormentor. Then, much to Em's surprise, they both appeared to whisper and giggle with one another. Em frowned. It appeared Hilaria was right; Zoe was trying her hardest to make friends with her, and she seemed to be playing her part well and showed no outward sign that she knew what the younger woman was up to. It seemed harmless and she wondered whether she should give them a few more moments before she had to stop them talking. However, before she could give the matter another thought, Isaac gave a loud cough, breaking her out of her distracted thoughts.

'Ahem, sorry, Boss Lady, did you hear what I just said?' he asked curiously.

Ashamed she had been caught daydreaming, Em blinked and answered Isaac quickly. 'Oh, sorry, Isaac, I was miles away. What did you say?' She felt her cheeks flush with embarrassment as she realised that everybody's attention was now focused on her.

'I was expressing some of the concerns I have about this,' answered Isaac gravely. Seeing the thick grooves in his forehead, Em could see he wasn't happy about something. 'Specifically, I don't think you should join us on this mission. It's too risky.'

The muscles in Em's jaw tightened and she felt her hackles rise. She hated it when people questioned her decisions, even Isaac. Yes, he was her second in command, but could he not have waited until after the briefing to voice his reservations? She needed everybody to stay focused and not get distracted by the doubts of those who, until now, she had deemed loyal.

'I understand that,' she said, trying to keep her tone civil. 'But how can I ask people to do something if I won't step up and do it myself?' She jabbed her finger angrily at Isaac. 'You are going, aren't you?'

'That's different, Em, and you know it,' argued Isaac forcefully. 'I'm going because I've been trained for stuff like this.' Before Em could open her mouth in protest, Isaac held up his hands apologetically, cutting her off. 'Yes, before you say it, I agree that out of all of us here, you are the one who is most qualified to carry out this mission. But you are also our

leader. How do you think it'd look if two command-level officers were to leave their troops to go on a dangerous mission?'

'You sound like we are a damned military unit.' Em laughed sarcastically.

'Stop being so blasted facetious, Em,' snapped Isaac. He made a sweeping gesture to the people watching them. 'We can't afford to lose two high-ranking officers. Think about it – it'd not only affect morale, but think of the hole it'd leave in our command structure.'

Lapsing into silence, Em pursed her lips thoughtfully. Yes, Isaac had raised some good points. But he was also predictable. She had known Isaac long enough to recognise he would argue against her leading any mission, which was why she had come to the meeting prepared. She didn't want to say it out loud, but she had a personal mission to carry out once they were inside the URE's main military research tower in the centre of Pons Aelius. Something that, for her, superseded the rescue of prisoners.

Inhaling a deep breath, Em nodded and smiled knowingly. 'Yes, I've already thought of that and have prepared for just that eventuality.'

'You have?' Isaac blurted out in surprise.

From the flustered look on her friend's face, Em could clearly see he hadn't been expecting that response. She smiled and gave a small nod. 'Yes.' Inwardly wishing she had briefed Hilaria earlier, Em turned swiftly around and focused her attention on the front row of the auditorium. She smiled genially, secretly hoping Hilaria would play along. 'Haven't we, Hilaria?'

Hilaria's eyebrow arched slightly in mild surprise, but she spoke in a neutral tone. 'Uh, yes. That's right.' Em had to give Hilaria her due – she had a good poker face. Hilaria spoke confidently as she rose from her seat and stepped next to Em. If Em hadn't known any better, it was almost as if she had been coached on what to say as she listened to Hilaria's response. 'Em approached me earlier. She had an idea she wanted to put by me, something that involved using my vast military experience to help the greater good. I had some reservations, but she convinced me you would all see it was for the best.'

Oh wow, she's good, Em thought, impressed at how easily Hilaria was taking it in her stride. If Em was being honest with herself, she was making

this up as she went along, and so, it appeared, was Hilaria. Thinking quickly about what to say next, Em smiled gratefully at the woman now standing next to her. 'Yes, it took some persuading, but Hilaria agreed to take command while Isaac and I are carrying out this mission. I'm confident she—'

At that moment all hell broke loose. Em had expected there might be a few complaints, but what she hadn't expected was the uproar. She may as well have thrown a rubber duck into the audience and said it was a bomb, because the entire audience appeared to stand up and cry out as one as they let it be known just what they thought of the decision to have a former URE officer lead them. Em decided it was best if she stood in silence and let the crowd vent their frustrations at Hilaria. But, to Em's surprise, she discovered most of the complaints weren't aimed at Hilaria; they were aimed at her. She couldn't blame them. After all, having a bombshell of this magnitude land on top of them with no warning, they had a right to be aggrieved.

As she waited for the crowd's anger to subside, Em cast an eye across to Isaac. *Oh, he's well and truly annoyed,* she thought on seeing the laser-like stare that was aimed toward her. The intensity of Isaac's gaze was so powerful that if his eyes were lasers, Em imagined they would have scorched through her skull before continuing to destroy everything in their way. Clearly, he was struggling to keep his composure, and it was quite possible she would get an earful from him as soon as the briefing was finished. She lifted her shoulder in a slight shrug. Isaac would cool down eventually. He usually did whenever they had a disagreement. Em was confident she had nothing to worry about from him.

Hilaria, however, was a different story. It didn't take a genius to recognise that the crowd's reaction did not please her. Was she wondering if she had been thrown to the wolves in an act of petty revenge for what she had done to Em's daughter? Em wasn't certain. But what she was certain about, Hilaria would express her anger to Em in private at not being given advanced warning about what she had been planning. *Oh well,* Em thought, *get in line.*

Surprisingly, the only person in the auditorium who wasn't causing a commotion was Zoe. She was gazing around the chamber with an

awestruck expression on her face; watching a bunch of adults make fools of themselves was probably something new to her.

After growing impatient for the angry jeers to settle, Em eventually raised her hand and waited. It took a few minutes for the noise to subside, and everybody returned to their seats. Once she was sure she had their attention again, Em cleared her throat and addressed her captive audience in a loud, self-assured voice.

'I understand many of you are upset with my decision to appoint Hilaria as interim commander.' She ignored the murmurs of discontent while she gestured to Hilaria. 'I haven't taken this decision lightly. If anything were to happen to Isaac or me, then I would want someone in charge who has strong leadership qualities.' Em smiled as she placed a hand on Hilaria's shoulder and then gazed at every face staring down at her. 'Despite her past, Miss Cooper brings to you vast knowledge and experience, something you will probably need in the days ahead if anything disastrous were to happen on the mission.' Em paused and looked gravely at everyone around her. 'The forces looming in the shadows are unlike anything we've faced before. And it is with that mind I have made this decision. You will need someone with a strong background in military strategy, something our new friend here possesses.' Em smiled on hearing the small murmurs of agreement coming from her audience. Smiling sadly, she pressed her hands against her chest and made a point of looking into every face staring back at her. 'I know it is a lot to ask of you, but by building the technology that is currently being used to shield us from the enemy's incursions, hasn't Hilaria already proved to you that you can trust her?' Em pressed her hands together pleadingly. 'I make this promise to you. If you provide Hilaria with the same loyalty that you have shown me, you will not only see a woman who has exceptional leadership qualities, but also someone who will stand by your side.' Em took a slow step forward, straightened and turned slowly around as she stared questioningly at the people looking back at her. 'Will you do that for me? Offer this woman the chance to prove herself to you. Well, will you?'

Nervous energy filled Em as she took a step back and waited for her audience to think about what she was asking of them. Although she was confident they would support her decision, a part of her couldn't help

but wonder if she had gone a step too far in asking them to place their faith in someone who, until a few weeks ago, was one of the most despised people in the URE. But desperate times called for desperate measures, and she couldn't see any other option. Clasping her hands behind her back, Em stared at her friends in hopeful expectation while they continued to talk amongst themselves.

Suddenly, she detected a change in their expressions as everyone focused their attention back on her. She was almost positive the atmosphere inside the amphitheatre had changed from being almost frosty hostility to welcoming warmth. Whatever it was, Em couldn't help smiling on hearing the increasing murmurs of agreement filling the room. It took all her willpower to fight the urge to pump her hand in victory. Yes! She'd done it, she'd won them over!

While trying to keep the delight from showing on her face, Em kept her voice neutral but spoke in a loud, authoritative tone. 'So now that we have that over with. I shall take a small team with me. Unfortunately, if we use one of our transport vehicles we run the risk of being detected, which is why we must make the fifty-mile journey to Pons Aelius on foot. Barring any unforeseen trouble, if we keep a low profile, it should take us approximately ten hours to reach the outskirts of the megacity.' Em paused and gestured for Hilaria to step in front of the holographic interface. 'Miss Cooper feels, out of concerns for our team's safety, it is best she remains behind. Oracle has already shown an interest in her, so it's best if Cooper stays as far away from Pons Aelius as she can. I will now hand the rest of the briefing over to her. I would appreciate it if you would give her your full attention.'

Hilaria smiled politely as she moved towards the holographic interface. Em watched curiously as Hilaria's hands tapped and swiped across the interface with apparent expert precision. The holographic projectors around the chamber lit up, and a holographic image appeared over Em's head. She squinted her eyes and studied the image; it appeared to be a schematic of underground service ducts and access tunnels. Then Em understood what she was looking at. It was a detailed plan of the maintenance and sewer tunnels beneath the city.

Clearing her throat nervously, Hilaria gave a thin smile to the people watching her as she shone a laser pointer at the schematic. 'These are detailed plans of all the service, sewerage and transport tunnels that run beneath Pons Aelius. Most have been closed off for years,' she explained in an increasingly confident tone. Then she gave a swift tap on the interface and a yellow line appeared to highlight a section of the holographic schematic. 'Once your team has reached this point just outside the city, there is an access door that will take you into what looks like a maintenance tunnel. It is an emergency transport tunnel that leads directly to a platform located at the base of the Pons Aelius central military command tower. The transport tunnel is an emergency evacuation shaft. If the city were to fall into enemy hands, these tunnels would transport senior officers safely out of harm's reach.' The corners of Hilaria's mouth curled up in a sardonic smile. 'Mix paranoia with a touch of cowardice and you end up with the perfect URE officer. You might even agree, but if you were to ask me if what I said is true …' She paused and gave a sly wink. 'Of course, I couldn't possibly comment.'

A loud chuckle echoed around the chamber. Em smiled to herself. Hilaria was trying to win people over by making a joke at her own expense. Good for her. But as she peered at the image above her, Em furrowed her brow and tapped her chin thoughtfully. They would have to take it slow if they were to avoid setting off any alarms. 'Tell me if I'm wrong,' she murmured. 'After we enter the service hatch, it looks like we will still have a long way to go before we reach the platform beneath the tower.'

Hilaria gave a small nod in acknowledgement, 'Yes, the distance from the service hatch to the platform is roughly four and a half miles.' She pulled a face and shrugged. 'If you want my suggestion, I think it is best you make camp for the night and travel the rest of the way at first light. That way, you will be rested and more alert for any signs of danger.'

The muscles in Em's jaw twitched as she gave Hilaria's words some thought. Damn it! She was hoping to avoid that. Even though she was hoping to get back to base as quickly as possible, Em reluctantly nodded her head. 'Yeah, I agree. After travelling all that way on foot, it is probably best we rest up and make the rest of the journey at first light.'

Hilaria raised her hands apologetically. 'Sorry, I wish there was a way around it, but there isn't.' She highlighted a section of the schematic to show what appeared to be an access terminal. 'You can use my security password to help disable any security drones. Hopefully that will make your journey along the tunnel easier.'

Not wanting to look a gift horse in the mouth, Em coughed and gave Hilaria a look of unease. 'Um, not to sound ungrateful, but how can you be sure your security login hasn't been deactivated?' Although she was impressed at the level of planning Hilaria had put into the briefing, Em couldn't shake the sense that they were overlooking something.

Hilaria's face had a vacant look about it as she lifted her head and stared up at the ceiling thoughtfully for a couple of seconds. Then she pursed her lips and nodded slowly. 'No, I'm one hundred per cent sure my codes will still work.' She scrunched up her face and rubbed the back of her neck. 'Hmm, make that fifty per cent to be sure.' Not feeling inspired by those odds, Em crinkled her brow and gave Hilaria a stern glower. But before she could say anything, Hilaria slapped Em on the shoulder and beamed at her. 'Oh, I wouldn't worry. Deactivated command codes are the least of your worries. There's still a hell of a lot that could go wrong before you even make it that far!'

Any faith Em had in Hilaria's tactical prowess was slowly vanishing as she folded her arms across her chest and grumbled acerbically, 'You know, Cooper, I'm not feeling a lot of love for your plan at the moment.'

The corners of Hilaria's mouth morphed into a devious smile, and she gave Em a small nudge. 'Smile, my dear. It's times like these that make life so interesting.'

Em groaned inwardly and suppressed the urge to bury her head in her hands.

Oh, I'm getting too old for this shit.

-10-

Unimpressed by Hilaria's attempt at levity, Em pressed her lips together and glowered at the beaming woman. Hilaria's smile disappeared, turning into something that resembled an embarrassed frown. Em didn't have to think about the reason behind Hilaria's sudden change in demeanour. It was entirely obvious what the cause was; it was the frosty stare she was giving her, which had the effect she was hoping for. There were times for jokes, and this was not one of them.

With her cool gaze still focused on Hilaria, Em spoke with deliberate slowness, in a tone that had just the right amount of edge to it. 'Please, Miss Cooper, finish your briefing. But if you would like to continue making jokes, go right ahead.'

From the way Hilaria was nervously licking her lips, Em guessed the tone of her voice had the desired effect. She kept her gaze locked on Hilaria as she turned back to the holographic image hovering above them and coughed nervously. 'Ahem, thank you. As I was saying, once you've made your way down the tunnel, you will have no problem entering the building.' Hilaria paused and tapped her fingers on the interface. The image changed to show a schematic of the building. 'Once inside, make your way up to level thirty-two, the detention level. Just in case Oracle has control of the transport-pods, I think it's prudent that you use the stairs.' The holographic image changed once again. This time, it showed an area outside the building. 'Once you've rescued any prisoners who are still alive, swiftly make your way to the hangar and steal a shuttle transport.'

Wait? Did Em hear that right? She wanted them to steal one of the aircraft? Em shook her head in confusion and frowned at Hilaria. 'Wait, if we steal an aircraft, wouldn't that raise the alarm? I thought we were trying to remain as inconspicuous as possible?'

Hilaria gave a small dismissive wave and smiled knowingly. 'To be honest, I wouldn't worry about stealth at this point. If you find any prisoners, they may not be fit enough to walk and will only slow you down. Also, by this point I suspect Oracle will be aware of your presence, so you will need to get out of there as fast as possible.' The tone of Hilaria's voice turned grave, and she stared at the people who were going on the mission. 'I must warn you, though, you may not have much time to use my access codes to access a shuttle. Once Oracle realises what you're doing, it is likely it will lock you out.'

Grateful that Hilaria was giving the mission briefing and had the foresight to think about their escape, Em gave a silent nod of confirmation. But as she contemplated what Hilaria had said, Em squinted at the image hovering in front of her. Stealing a shuttle had changed things, and it left them with an opportunity they might not get again. Hilaria raised a questioning eyebrow as Em pointed toward an area on the schematic.

'That's the armoury, isn't it?' Em asked curiously. 'I just wonder, since we will be stealing a shuttle, then we might as well put it to some use by grabbing as many weapons as possible, along with some drones and other equipment. We'll never have a better opportunity to upgrade our defences here.' She glanced over her shoulder at Isaac, who, up to that point, had remained silent.

From the way Isaac's eyes were gleaming, Em was almost certain he was drooling at the prospect of acquiring some new toys to play with. Isaac spoke in an eager tone and bobbed his head enthusiastically. 'I agree, Boss Lady. We will never have a better chance of grabbing some of the URE's sophisticated weaponry.'

The atmosphere in the chamber suddenly changed as Hilaria exhaled a long melancholic sigh. 'We are working on the assumption

Oracle hasn't already cleared the armoury out. Gods know what it has equipped its drones with to use against the population of Counter-Terra.'

Her optimistic mood vanishing, Em slapped her forehead in frustration. Damn it! Why hadn't she thought of that? In her excitement at the idea of stealing weapons, she realised she'd forgotten all about the peril her home world was in. But, despite the possibility that there might be nothing there, Em still felt it was worth the risk of checking the armoury out.

She clicked her tongue off the roof of her mouth while she tried to calculate how much time they would need. Certain the rewards outweighed the risks, she regarded Hilaria with hopeful curiosity. 'So, do you think we could do it with the numbers we have?'

Hilaria nodded and stared thoughtfully up at the hologram, murmuring uncertainly, 'I'm not sure.' From the troubled expression on her face, Em got the impression she wasn't entirely convinced it was a good idea. 'How many people were you planning on taking?'

Having already come up with a number, Em answered quickly. 'Twelve, including Isaac and me. Any more and we would risk being discovered.'

'So, that makes two teams of six,' murmured Hilaria in reply, and gave a small nod. 'Yes, that could work. There should be some cargo sleds on hand in the armoury. Once you load everything onto the sleds, you'll have no problem guiding them to the hangar level.'

Confident they had all the kinks in the plan ironed out, Em clapped her hands together and bobbed her head at the people in the front row. 'Alpha team and Beta team get some rest. We'll assemble in the hangar bay at zero eight hundred tomorrow.'

But before Em could give the order to dismiss, a polite cough came from Hilaria, interrupting her. Surprised at the interruption, Em turned and regarded her curiously. Was there something she had forgotten? She was under the impression they had gone over every essential detail of the plan.

Hilaria coughed nervously and held up a finger. 'Ahem, sorry. I wonder if I may take a moment to address everyone.'

Taken aback, Em stared open-mouthed at Hilaria, unsure what to say. It wasn't the question that had unsettled her, but Hilaria's demeanour. Something seemed off with her. Em couldn't put a finger on it, but she noticed that Hilaria was now giving off a vibe of someone in authority. The hackles on the back of her neck rose as she sensed something about Hilaria that set her teeth on edge.

Out of the corner of her eye, Em picked up a slight movement from Isaac. She could tell he had sensed it too and appeared to be moving slowly toward Hilaria. Not wanting to make a scene, Em signalled Isaac to stay where he was. Because she was curious to listen to what Hilaria wanted to say, she thought it was best to give her the benefit of the doubt for now. Em gave a wordless nod of agreement.

'Thank you.' Hilaria smiled and turned to face the people seated in the auditorium. 'I apologise for holding you all up. I'm sure you're getting fed up of listening to all this talk. I can imagine the last thing you need is for another windbag to talk your ears off.' A ripple of nervous laughter echoed around the chamber while Hilaria continued to speak. 'I know many of you haven't known me that long. But I guess you've heard the rumours about who I was previously and what I did.' She let out a heavy sigh and held up her hands. 'Yes, I did some bad things, probably to people you know. But I am the one who needs to live with that, and I hope one day to make up for all the terrible things I did. With that in mind, I wanted to tell you how honoured I am that Em has placed her faith in me to lead you all while she is away.' Her face brightened into a cheery smile, and she placed her hands on her chest. 'Believe me, this came as much of a shock to me as it did to you. However, my personal history isn't important, because what is important is my experience and everything I have learned during my years of service as an officer in the URE.' Hilaria lightly tapped her finger against her right temple. 'Which means, what I have in here, I can pass on to you. So that when Em returns, she will be welcomed by one of the most effective fighting forces in the resistance.'

Em cringed inwardly. Although she knew Hilaria meant well and was probably hoping her words would inspire those seated in the chamber, those words might have done more harm than good. As Em gazed at the faces seated in the chamber, she wondered whether they felt Hilaria had

just insulted them. Until now, it had never bothered her that her unit wasn't a highly skilled group. Truthfully, ninety per cent of the resistance was composed of former slaves who had no military training. The remaining ten per cent was comprised of soldiers who had either been former prisoners or had purposely defected from the URE or GCR military.

But as Hilaria continued with her speech, Em couldn't hide her surprise as she scanned the faces seated in front of her and saw no sign of any hostility or annoyance. What was remarkable was that everyone appeared to be listening intently to what Hilaria was saying. Was it possible she knew what she was doing after all?

Em blinked and focused her attention back on Hilaria as she carried on with her speech. 'So, with that in mind, once this meeting is over, I would like to sit down with your department heads and draw up a roster.' Hilaria straightened and placed her hands behind her back, giving the impression of somebody in command. 'I would like to set up twelve teams. Each team will be comprised of five people. Once that is arranged, I want to set up a four-shift rotation system. Every six hours, two teams will take turns sweeping the grounds outside this complex, keeping an eye out for any uninvited guests. A third team will remain on duty inside in case they are needed as backup.' Hilaria held up a hand as if to cut off any protests. 'Yes, I know what you're going to say. You've already got an electronic surveillance system set up, so why should we have to do it? Well, to answer that, you just have to look at what happened a couple of days ago.' A wry smile appeared on Hilaria's face as a wave of laughter echoed around the chamber, which was followed by nods of agreement. 'Good, you understand. Also, just in case you are wondering, I'm not trying to make you into something you're not. But what I hope to do is make sure you are prepared.' Her face darkened and her voice developed a subdued tone. 'I don't want to hide the truth from you, Em's mission won't be an easy one. If anything happens to her and her team, I fear Oracle will send everything it has against us.' There was a small pause as if she was letting that statement sink in before continuing. 'Any questions before I hand you back over to Em?'

Half expecting a deluge of questions and angry protests to be thrown at Hilaria, Em was pleasantly surprised at the stony silence around

the auditorium. It was obvious from the sober expressions on the faces staring back at her that Hilaria's words had left an impression on them. Any concerns she had that Hilaria's former personality had resurfaced were quickly dismissed. Clearly, Hilaria knew what she was doing.

Em placed a grateful hand on Hilaria's shoulder and took a step forward to address the crowd. 'Okay, people, you know what to do. Dismissed.'

But as she watched the sombre faces slowly make their way out of the auditorium, Em felt a trickle a fear run down her spine. How many of these faces would live to see their next birthday? It felt as if a dark cloud was hovering over her as she wondered if she or any of the team would make it back alive. Did they have any chance at all?

Hoping to sweep away the gloomy thoughts inside her head, Em drew in a deep breath and moved towards Zoe. The young woman had remained in her seat while everybody traipsed out of the chamber. Em gave a silent nod to Isaac as he made his way past her towards the exit. She would talk to him later when things had quietened down.

Em pursed her lips as she studied the quiet adolescent sitting in front of her. Zoe's face was an unreadable mask, making it difficult for Em to judge what she was feeling. Em shook her head sadly as she realised Zoe'd had a lot to deal with over the past couple of weeks. Em sighed as she thought back to her own first moments when she arrived on this world. That had been just as traumatic, and she had been a lot younger than Zoe. But she eventually adapted to this world, and Em was confident Zoe would too.

'So, young one. How are you handling all of this?' asked Em, smiling. 'I can imagine it's a lot for you to take in.'

'Dunno, it's fine, I suppose,' murmured Zoe gruffly, shrugging.

'Huh-huh,' Em said carefully, perplexed by Zoe's surly response. 'Zoe, I hope you're not upset about me leaving?' She placed a reassuring

hand on Zoe's shoulder and squeezed it gently. 'You don't have to worry. I'll be coming back.'

Zoe bolted up out of her seat and stared down at Em in wide-eyed shock, blurting out, 'B-b-but I thought I would be going with you!'

Her statement didn't come as a complete surprise to Em. Since her arrival a few weeks earlier, Em had felt Zoe had become too attached to her. She wondered if Zoe was suffering from abandonment issues. Although she had spoken about the problems she'd had with her mother, Zoe said nothing about her father. Was he still around? Maybe one day she would sit down with Zoe and learn more about her previous life. It was just unfortunate that this was neither the time nor the place for that, so it was good Em had already thought of a way to let her down gently.

'I'm sorry,' said Em calmly. 'You're just too young to go on a mission like this. I'm sorry, but you—'

Before Em could say any more, Zoe grabbed her hands and whispered pleadingly to her. 'But you've said it yourself. You've been impressed at how quickly I adapted. If it's because you think I'm not skilled enough to handle weapons, I can get better, I—'

'No,' Em said forcefully. Then, on seeing the hurt look in Zoe's eyes, she sighed in exasperation and placed her hands on the younger woman's shoulders. 'Sorry, I didn't mean to snap. It's not that I don't think you are capable. I have other reasons.' She leaned in closer and whispered in Zoe's ear, 'I need someone I can trust to keep an eye on Cooper. You understand it's not that I don't have faith in her skills as an officer. I just feel she will need a second in command who won't be afraid to speak out if she steps over the line.' Em took a step back and prodded a finger in Zoe's chest as she gazed at her questioningly. 'That someone is you. Well, *Cadet* Murray? Do you think you can manage that, or do I need to assign that position to someone else?'

The muscles in Zoe's face tightened in a mask of determination, and showing no hesitation, she straightened and saluted Em. 'Yes, Commander. I promise I won't let you down.'

'Good girl,' said Em, smiling. 'Now run along and get some rest. You're going to need to be at your best over the next few days.'

Without saying another word, Zoe gave a brief nod, spun on her heel and marched out of the chamber. As she watched her stride away, the corners of Em's mouth curled up in a wry smile. Of course, it had been a lie. Em just needed an excuse to keep Zoe busy over the next few days to stop her worrying about what was happening with Em and the team. Also, she hoped the more time she spent with Hilaria, the more chance she would drop her guard and give Hilaria the opportunity to discover what Zoe was up to.

'I couldn't help overhearing what you said there. Quite sneaky of you.'

Startled out of her thoughtful wondering, Em flinched in surprise and spun around to see an amused-looking Hilaria standing next to her. Em felt her cheeks flush with embarrassment as she realised that she had been so distracted by her own thoughts that she hadn't noticed Hilaria's approach. Darn it! How much had she heard? Em's mouth opened and closed as she desperately tried to think of something to say.

'Relax.' Hilaria laughed, holding up her hand. 'I can see what you're trying to do. Even though I still don't think it's a good idea, we have to try and find a way to help Zoe before she does something stupid.'

'You're not mad?' asked Em worriedly.

Hilaria gave a dismissive wave and scoffed, 'Hah! Wouldn't change anything if I was. You set me a task and I'm determined to carry it out.'

Relieved not to have hurt Hilaria's feelings, but at the same time, she hoped, by stroking Hilaria's ego, it might make her a bit more amenable to the plan they'd discussed earlier. Em placed a hand on her shoulder and smiled. 'There's no one else I trust to do this. If anything, it is because I have the utmost faith in your abilities as a leader that I know you will figure this out.'

Hilaria let out a loud bark of laughter and slapped Em's shoulder. 'Hah! That's pure-grade horse manure and we both know it. But I appreciate it, anyway.' Her face turned serious, and the tone of her voice became less humorous. 'If I can speak bluntly with you, for a minute there I thought that I might have stepped over the line with that speech of mine.' She let out a heavy, despondent sigh and stared up at the ceiling. 'I always

said I didn't want to go back to who I was, but I—' Her voice trailed off and she lapsed into silence, staring vacantly at something in the distance.

Although she couldn't understand the turmoil Hilaria was going through, Em recognised the look in her eye. She had seen it plenty of times herself in her own reflection. It was self-doubt. That part, she understood only too well. Em interlocked her right arm in Hilaria's left arm and whispered softly to her, 'You're afraid you may become her again, aren't you?' She smiled and gave her arm a reassuring squeeze. 'I think you are stronger than you realise. Perhaps it is a good idea that you have Zoe to keep an eye on. She will help keep you grounded.'

'Oh, I can imagine she'll do more than that.' Hilaria laughed. She drew out a long breath and turned to leave. 'Well, if there isn't anything else, Commander, I've still got a few things to arrange before I speak to your department heads.'

'Actually, there is something I need to ask you,' said Em quickly. She guided Hilaria back over to the holographic image of the command tower. 'I need you to show me something else.'

Hilaria's brow furrowed in puzzlement, and she looked at Em questioningly. 'I thought I'd shown you all you need to know.'

'I need you to show me where the portal chamber is located,' said Em flatly.

Hilaria's good eye tightened with suspicion as she turned to stare at Em. 'Em, why do you need to see where the portal chamber is located?'

Trying to avoid Hilaria's gaze, Em focused her attention on the image above her head. 'Because I think the technology in there might help us,' Em lied, secretly hoping that if she kept her voice neutral, she would make it sound convincing. 'You've said it yourself. My home world is in danger, so we will need to open a portal if we want to help them. For us to do that, we need the portal technology.'

Hilaria shook her head in adamant refusal and answered in a firm tone, 'No, not possible. The portal's systems are hardwired into the building's electrical grid. Not only would it place you in greater danger if you tried to remove it, but it would increase the risk of you being discovered by Oracle.'

Growing impatient at Hilaria's refusal to help, Em threw up her hands and snapped angrily, 'Damn it, woman, just show me where it is. I'll decide whether or not the risk is acceptable.'

On hearing her voice echo around the chamber, Em cringed. She didn't mean to raise her voice. Casting an eye around the now empty room, she was relieved that she and Hilaria were the only two people left inside. But as Em quickly focused her attention back on Hilaria, she noticed that the tendons in her neck were tightening. It was clear to Em she wasn't happy at being spoken to in such a way. She felt one corner of her mouth twitch in annoyance. She didn't care what Hilaria thought. For god's sake, why couldn't Hilaria have just told her what she needed without making it difficult?

After a few moments of uncomfortable stillness, Hilaria eventually broke the silence by speaking in a careful but annoyed tone. 'Em, I don't appreciate you speaking to me that way. I can see on your face that there's something more going on here than stealing a piece of technology.'

Hilaria folded her arms across her chest in stubborn refusal and stood directly in front of Em. From the resolute expression on Hilaria's face, there was no doubt in Em's mind she had no intention of letting Em leave without an answer. Not up for another shouting match, Em exhaled a weary sigh and shook her head. The truth would come out eventually, so it was best she got it over with now.

'Fine,' Em said brusquely. 'I was lying about my reason for going to the portal chamber. Truth is, I want – sorry – I *need* to see where Henrietta worked.' Her vision blurred, and she felt her tears run down her cheeks. Em's voice cracked, and she spoke in a hoarse whisper. 'I feel if I was physically standing in a spot where she worked, then I might get a sense of her. Feel closer to her.'

For several minutes, Hilaria stood in silence, staring at Em. Em wondered what was going through her mind. Was she going to mock her for being overly sentimental? Why was she staring at her? The tension was unbearable, and she desperately wished for Hilaria to say something, anything. But the only sound she could hear was the quiet hiss of recycled air coming from the vents in the ceiling. It was driving Em nuts. Even if

Hilaria shouted at her, at least it would be something instead of staring back at her with an unreadable mask of a face.

Finally, Hilaria ended the silence with a long, melancholic sigh and then began to speak. There was a deliberate tone to her voice, and it didn't take a genius to see that she was struggling to contain her emotions. Em wondered what was going through her mind. Why was she finding it so difficult to share this information? Was there something she was hiding?

'I will show you,' Hilaria said sullenly. 'But I urge you to reconsider. Because if you go down this route, it will only lead to more heartache.'

-11-

The next day, twelve people dressed in camouflaged lightweight body armour slowly made their way through the thick undergrowth of a forest. Because of the densely packed undergrowth and uneven ground, their progress was slow. The road that had once carried the feet of Roman soldiers was no longer visible to Em as she carefully made her way through the thick weeds, grass, and flowers growing through the now hidden concrete surface. It was a reminder that it was the way of things: nature will always take back what was once hers.

As she pushed through the congested forest, Em cast a wary eye up at the tightly packed canopy of branches overhead. Although the lack of sunlight intensified the sense of claustrophobia, she was grateful for the protection that the tightly packed branches and leaves provided against any security drones that may have been patrolling overhead. But that didn't stop her from wondering what other dangers lay in the thick brush. The hairs on the back of her neck tingled, and she squirmed uneasily. Since they'd started their journey through the woodland, Em couldn't shake the feeling that they were being watched by the many creatures that made the forest their home. But the more they delved deeper into the undergrowth, the more unsettled she became. She couldn't explain why she felt as she did. Was it because of the stress she had experienced over the past few weeks?

To distract her from her troubled thoughts, Em focused on the back of the helmets of the two people a few paces in front of her. They

were two of the few people in her resistance cell who had military experience. Yuto Keung, a thirty-something, lean, fair-haired man, who at five foot nine, stood slightly taller than Em. Before the URE had captured Yuto, he had served as a sergeant in the armed forces of the Greater Chinese Republic. He had been held in a detention centre for five years before he was eventually liberated by Em's team. Much to Em's surprise, rather than flee back to the GCR, Yuto chose to stay. When asked why, he explained he owed Em a life debt and was honour bound to fulfil it or risk dishonour. During her early days with Cornelius, Em had learned a lot about the GCR; that in the centuries following the unification under the Greater Chinese Republic, Japanese and Chinese cultures gradually merged. Despite this blending, families like Yuto's remained steadfast in upholding certain traditions. These customs, passed down through generations, continued to shape the identity and daily life of Yuto's family. Out of respect for his culture, Em accepted Yuto's service with grace. Yuto never spoke openly about his time in detention, but she could only imagine the tortures he was forced to endure at the hands of his sadistic overseers.

She shifted her attention to the woman walking next to Yuto; Raelle was an entirely different enigma. Apart from her first name, very little was known about the dark-skinned, shaven-headed, muscular woman. The only thing Em knew for certain was that she had once served in the imperial forces. One day, while leading a reconnaissance patrol, Yuto had discovered Raelle's unconscious and severely beaten body lying in a ditch. It had been obvious that whoever had attacked her had raped her and savagely beaten her. From the tattered remains of her uniform, it was clear she had been an officer. Whether out of sympathy or because he sensed a kindred spirit, Yuto refused to leave her side as she was nursed back to health. Because of the severity of the injuries inflicted upon her, her vocal cords had been damaged, so she had lost the ability to speak. A small bond developed between the pair while they conversed with each other using sign language. It was not a bond of compassion, but one grown out of mutual respect. Then, one day, Yuto disappeared without warning, leaving no hint as to where he was going. He eventually returned a week later but

gave no explanation for his disappearance. Em heard later that he had knelt in front of Raelle with his Katana sword held in both hands and was overheard saying three words – *'It is done.'* Em and her colleagues now understood the reason for his disappearance; he'd tracked down Raelle's attackers and carried out his own brand of justice. Ever since that day, the two warriors had stuck together like glue, always having each other's backs. Together, they were a formidable pair, which was one reason Em had chosen them to be on this mission.

She cast an eye over the rest of the people in her group, walking behind her in a two-by-two formation. As usual, Isaac kept pace beside her. A few paces back were Rahul Jithry, a tall, thin, black-haired Indian man, who she'd chosen because he was one of the few people who had escaped Pons Aelius just after Oracle had seized control of the populace. Beside him was Felix Stroud, an eagle-eyed, long-faced, red-haired man with a toned athletic frame. Felix's head was constantly jerking from left to right, his steel-grey eyes searching the densely packed brush for signs of danger. But that was the way he was – a tightly wound spring ready for action at a moment's notice.

Just a few paces behind Felix and Rahul were Gemma Dummigan and Iris Tegula. The women were as outwardly different as any two could be. Gemma was a slim, golden-haired, round-faced woman. Iris was the exact opposite with her shaven head, black angular face, and broad shoulders. Iris's massive frame dwarfed Gemma's, but that was where the differences stopped. The two women had a mischievous quality about them, with their giggling earning them stern glares from the serious-natured Felix. Although they appeared outwardly to be making light of the mission, Em knew it was a facade, something they had developed to cope with the tense situations they were involved in.

Next, behind the two jovial women, strode Peter and Xander Schlom. The two dark-skinned, stocky brothers with their hatchet-like faces gave off an intense vibe as they silently walked through the forest. Despite their apparently inhospitable demeanour, Em knew the two

brothers were anything but unfriendly because they were normally the life and soul of any party.

Finally, making up the rear of the group were the fair-haired Roj Tarrant and the curly-haired Del Blake. The two men were of similar build: muscular and limber looking. They constantly monitored what was behind them while nervously fingering their rifles. Em commiserated with them for having drawn the short straw – having to bring up the rear. It was probably tough on their nerves. She activated her visor's heads-up display, noted the time and nodded thoughtfully. It was coming up to four hours since they swapped positions, and it would soon be Gemma and Iris's turn to bring up the rear.

It had been nine and a half hours since they left the base, and, apart from the odd water break, they hadn't stopped to rest. Em had wanted to get as far as possible using the daylight they had available, so she insisted they press on. But as the day wore on, fatigue was setting in. It was clear from the weariness etched across her friends' faces that they were getting tired too. Em glanced up and squinted at the traces of sky visible through the gaps in the trees and shook her head in bewilderment. How could it be getting darker when she could clearly see blue sky through the treetops? She was at a loss to explain why the light was fading the deeper they got into the forest. Maybe it was best to call it a day now, rest and set off at first light.

A wave of disappointment passed through her and her jaw tightened in frustration. The plan had been for them to set up camp when they reached the access shaft to the transport tunnel. However, she realised they had to be practical. There was no point continuing forward in a darkened forest; that was only asking for trouble. Yes, their helmets were equipped with night-vision sensors. But their journey had been more arduous than she'd expected, and it was starting to take not only a physical toll on them, but a mental one too, and that could only lead to trouble. Best they stop now.

But before Em could give the order for the team to stop, she frowned as she detected movement up ahead. Yuto and Raelle had come

to a sudden stop and had both raised their arms in a gesture for those behind to do the same. Em cast a concerned eye at Isaac, who responded with a jerk of his head before turning and making the same halting gesture to those following behind them.

Then, without warning, Raelle stepped forward and disappeared into the thick wall of bushes in front of her. Em raised a curious eyebrow as Yuto turned and signalled for her to come toward him. Nodding to Isaac to remain where he was, Em carefully crept towards Yuto, who bowed his head respectfully as she came to a stop next to him.

'Emma-San, we have reached the outer edge of the forest. On the other side of those bushes are the city walls,' explained Yuto in a respectfully quiet tone. He gestured to the undergrowth in front of him. 'Raelle has gone to locate the hatch that leads to the transport tunnel.'

As she pushed her way through the treeline, it dawned on Em why it had been getting darker even though she could spot traces of blue sky through the thick branches above her head. It was because of the sheer size of the defensive walls that surrounded the megatropolis. At one thousand feet in height and five hundred feet thick, they made for an intimidating sight. The walls appeared to stretch for miles with no end in sight. The outer edges of the forest that surrounded the city were nearly in perpetual darkness from the shadow cast down by the massive walls.

Awed by the spectacle in front of her, Em blew out a slow breath through her teeth. Even though it had been a long time since she'd been inside the city, she could not help but be filled with a sense of admiration at the level of engineering that must have been involved in building the megatropolis. On a good day, Em's base offered a vantage point from where one could make out the city's lights in the distance. Em shook her head in wonderment at the idea that Pons Aelius was amongst one of many megatropoli that the URE had built. She massaged her brow and exhaled. It blew her mind to think of the level of expenditure involved in building these structures.

'We have many cities like this too, filled with millions of people,' murmured Yuto. He drew in a despondent sigh and shook his head. 'Sorry,

were filled. Now they are just empty monuments to a culture that no longer exists.'

Em groaned inwardly. How could she have been so blind as not to see what Yuto must have been going through? Everything had been so hectic these past few weeks, she'd completely forgotten about what had happened to Yuto's people. The day Oracle targeted the satellites that hung in geosynchronous orbit above the GCR's territory and fired the Gamma-ray laser projectors they carried, it committed genocide when it wiped the GCR's entire population off the face of Terra. A wave of sadness passed over Em as she gazed at the noble warrior standing next to her. Was it possible he was now the last of his kind?

Filled with remorse and understanding the grief he must have been going through, Em reached over and placed a hand on Yuto's shoulder, whispering, 'I'm sorry for your loss, my friend.'

Yuto patted Em's hand gratefully and gave a thin smile. 'Thank you, Emma-San. It means a lot to me hearing you say that.'

Her head cocked, Em regarded the man next to her thoughtfully. Ever since they had learned the news of the genocide committed by Oracle, many of her colleagues had wondered if Yuto had lost any family in the atrocity. She reasoned that because of his close bond with Raelle, he had perhaps already shared that information with her. But even though she valued his privacy, she found her curiosity was getting the better of her. Surely, he wouldn't mind it if she asked him outright.

But when Em opened her mouth to speak, she discovered she was struggling to get the words out. *What's wrong with me?* she thought. *Why does my throat feel like sandpaper?* Clearing her throat, Em swallowed and tried again, this time almost feeling like she was forcing the words out of her mouth.

'D-d-did you have any family back home?' Em asked nervously, suddenly feeling her cheeks flushing with embarrassment. She held up her hands apologetically. 'Sorry, I shouldn't have asked that.'

'It is okay, Emma-San,' replied Yuto, smiling. His smile faded and he exhaled a heavy, despondent sigh. 'Any family I had all died during the

war.' Then, much to Em's surprise, he turned, pressed his hands together and gave a respectful bow. 'Now, I consider you to be my family, Emma-San. You, Isaac-San and everyone in our resistance cell, I consider all of you to be my brothers.'

A warm glow filled Em's heart on hearing the passion behind Yuto's words. Although she'd never spoken of it out loud, she was forced to agree with Yuto's sentiment. They were all like family to one another. The corners of her mouth turned up as she cast a speculative eye at Yuto. Well, since they were being candid with each other, there would be no harm in asking him about his relationship with Raelle.

'So, my honourable friend,' asked Em curiously. 'When are you going to make an honest woman out of her?'

A sheepish expression appeared on Yuto's face, and he turned away from Em. But before he did so, Em thought she had detected a slight twinkle in Yuto's eye; it was clear he knew who she was talking about. For a moment, she wondered if he would refuse to say anything. However, those thoughts were quickly dispelled as he turned back toward her with a mischievous grin on his face.

'I don't know what you mean, Emma-San,' Yuto said with wide-eyed innocence. 'Raelle and I are just good friends, nothing more.'

'Oh, you can't fool me, my noble friend.' Em laughed. 'I've seen how you are together. I see it in your eyes every time you look at her and vice versa. You can't miss it.'

Yuto drew in a long breath and gave a small nod of confirmation. 'Yes, we care deeply for each other, that is true. But we are happy with the way things are. We, as you say, do not wish to rock the boat – that's right, yes?' He smiled when Em gave him a silent nod of confirmation. But a strange expression settled on his face as he turned and stared in the direction Raelle had headed. 'The bond we share goes beyond love. It is spiritual and boundless. An unbreakable coil that entwines both of our souls. Our love burns hotter than the eternal fires inside the celestial temple of Pangu. All I know is I would die for her, and she would die for me. When we have that, why ask for more?'

Em's eyes were misting up. Never had she heard someone define their relationship with so much passion. True, Yuto didn't show it, but there was no escaping the meaning behind his words. It was true; how many people would admit to finding their true soulmate? Looking at her brief marriage to Barnes, Em was forced to admit she never experienced the same deep feelings that Yuto and Raelle shared. Yes, they had a child together, but had they ever truly been in love? Reluctantly, she was forced to concede that it was quite possible she would never truly experience anything like the relationship Yuto had with Raelle.

As if he had been reading Em's thoughts, Yuto nodded and smiled knowingly at her. 'Our feelings are much like the ones you and Isaac-San share, are they not Emma-San? However, I believe you are afraid to commit to each other. Is it because you think it will only complicate things?'

Startled by Yuto's statement, Em flinched in shock. Huh! What did he just say? Flustered, she desperately tried to regain her composure while she struggled to find an answer, stammering, 'I-I don't know what you mean. Isaac and I are just good friends.'

A broad smile covered Yuto's features, and he tapped his nose with his index finger. 'For an incredibly smart woman, Emma-San, you are, how you say, a bit slow on the uptake, yes? You cannot see what is right in front of you, but I do. We've all seen how he looks at you, Emma-San. If I may be so bold as to say, it is one of the first things I picked up on when I first saw you both together. Isaac-San is in love with you.' He took a step back and bowed respectfully. 'Forgive me if I have upset you, Emma-San. That was not my intent. I only wish to reveal the truth to you.' He cocked his head and gave Em a wry smile. 'Although I suspect, deep down, you already know it to be true.'

Lost for words, Em could only stare at Yuto. No, it wasn't possible. Surely, Yuto was mistaken and had misread what he'd thought he'd seen. Hadn't he? But the more she thought about it, the more she realised he was telling the truth. How could she have been so blind? Why had she not noticed it before now? Deeply troubled by her own short-sightedness, Em thought back to the comment Fausta had made just over

a week ago. At the time, Em had thought nothing of it, but now, looking back at it in a new light, she realised Fausta had seen it too. She curled her upper lip in frustration. How was it everybody seemed to be aware of Isaac's feelings but her? Was it true what Yuto had said? She had failed to see what was in front of her.

How is that possible? Em thought. *For a perceptive woman, trained to spot dangers before they happen, how could I have failed to see something as simple as someone being in love with me?*

But before she could get her head around it, Em was distracted; she detected movement out of the corner of her eye. Focusing her attention on the disturbance, Em pushed her troubled thoughts to the back of her mind. She couldn't allow her own feelings to distract her from the mission ahead. For now, she needed to remain focused, and once this mission was over, then she would take the time to have a heart-to-heart with Isaac.

It was clear that Yuto had detected movement too. The experienced warrior effortlessly spun on his heel and switched into a defensive posture with his hands clutched tightly around the hilt of his Katana blade. A surge of relief passed through Em as she recognised the figure of Raelle hurrying toward them. As soon as she came to a stop in front of Yuto, Raelle immediately began making hand signals to him. It had been a long time since Em had used standard imperial sign language, so she gave up trying to keep up with what Raelle was saying. After patiently waiting for Raelle to finish, Em gave Yuto an expectant look as he turned to face her.

'Emma-San, Raelle says she has found the access hatch we are looking for,' Yuto translated quickly. 'It is in a ravine about half a klick from our current position. Raelle apologises for taking so long, but the hatch was very well hidden. We'll need to clear it before we can open it.'

'Thank you, Raelle. You did good work,' said Em, smiling. She gestured to the hole in the treeline they had just come through. 'I suggest we set up camp for the night where the others are gathered. At first light, we'll make our way to the ravine Raelle told us about and clear the hatch of any obstructions.'

As she followed her two friends back through the thick undergrowth, Em frowned as Yuto's words came back to her. Even though she promised herself that she wouldn't let it distract her from the mission, Em found herself doing the opposite. Her tongue clicked off the roof of her mouth as she wondered how long Isaac had felt this way toward her. Now that she knew, should she say something? Was it even her place to say something? Would it be best if she kept what she knew to herself and allowed Isaac to tell her in his own time? Em sucked in a deep breath and let it out slowly. Yes, maybe it was best she say nothing. Why make things awkward for them both?

She snorted to herself. *Yeah, just do what you normally do – carry on and ignore it.* She glanced up at the sky and sighed in exasperation.

Oh, why was life so complicated?

-12-

A short time later, Em sat on the ground with her back against a tree and blew out a relieved sigh while she removed her protective headgear. Although the headpiece was made from a lightweight but highly durable composite, wearing it wasn't very comfortable. Equipped with all the tech a soldier would need, including night-vision sensors, communicator, and a short-range GPS, whoever had designed it obviously had made it for effectiveness but not comfort. But the thing that Em despised most about it was that it made her ears itch.

Setting her headgear on the ground beside her, Em leaned back against the tree, stretched out her legs and stared thoughtfully around the small area they were using as a makeshift camp. To keep their presence as low-key as possible, it had been agreed by everyone that they would not set a fire. It was fortunate the weather was mild for this time of year, so there wasn't a risk of it freezing during the night. But it still didn't hurt to have their suits' thermal regulators on standby just in case the temperature dropped during the night while they slept.

The group had also agreed to take turns working in pairs, standing on guard to allow everyone to get some sleep. Em rolled her eyes and tutted. She doubted anyone would get much sleep tonight, but at least they could get some rest. She pulled a face as she shuffled her bottom on the uncomfortable ground. *Oh, the joys of outdoor camping.*

A soft growling sound came from her stomach, reminding her it was time to get something to eat. Reaching into her backpack, Em pulled out a small square silver package. After staring at it thoughtfully for a few seconds, she pressed her thumb on the sensor on the top left corner of the package and waited for the food inside to heat. After about a minute, the temperature of the packet increased, warming Em's hands. While she waited, she rested the meal pack against her backpack and gazed around the camp. The edges of her mouth turned up in a grin as she watched her friends each take out their own food packs. *Great minds think alike.*

A few seconds later, she heard a soft beep notifying her that her meal was ready. As she carefully tore open the silver package, a mouth-watering smell greeted her. Closing her eyes, she recognised the aroma of roast beef and potatoes wafting up her nose. But as she dipped her spork into the package and scooped the contents into her mouth, Em grimaced in disgust at the taste. Nope, that certainly did not taste like roast beef. If she had to put a name to it, it reminded her of sludge. From the soft groans of disgust coming from around the camp, she guessed her friends were thinking the same.

Em stared thoughtfully at the warm food pack in her hand and gave an indifferent shrug. That was the problem with military MREs (Meals Ready to Eat). While their purpose was to provide nutrition, they were completely tasteless. The common consensus had been that MREs had originally been designed by sadists, who enjoyed the idea of tempting eaters with the irresistible aroma of food, only to disappoint them as soon as the revolting contents entered their mouths. Anyone familiar with the history of the URE would likely agree.

After swallowing a spoonful of the unpleasant mush, something stirred within Em. It wasn't gastrointestinal distress, but something else. It was pleasure. *Yeah*, she thought. *I forgot how much I missed this.* The happy feeling grew, and she smiled to herself as she thought about a time she'd long forgotten, of sitting by a campfire, eating MREs under a clear night sky.

'Denarius for your thoughts.'

Isaac's voice broke her out of her contemplative state and she smiled at him. 'Oh, I was just thinking about something from a long time ago.'

Isaac raised an eyebrow and gave Em a quizzical look. 'From the broad smile that's on your face, I'm guessing it's a happy memory.'

Em bobbed her head and laughed. 'Believe it or not, I was just thinking about how much I'm enjoying this.' She smiled as her comment earned her exclamations of surprise. Ignoring the scoffs of laughter, Em held up her hand and made a sweeping gesture. 'Not the reason we are here, but the experience.' She furrowed her brow as the scoffs turned into barks of laughter but chose to ignore them while she continued. 'Sitting here, eating this ration pack, reminds me of a happier time. I must have been around thirteen years of age. I had only been working for Cornelius for about a year, so I was still getting used to his peculiar ways. He was always coming up with these strange training scenarios as a way to test me.' A wave of sadness overcame her as she realised just how much she missed the crafty old man. What would he have thought about all of this?

Em noticed the eerie silence around the camp and raised her head to see the concerned faces of her colleagues staring wordlessly back at her. She let out a weak laugh and gave a dismissive wave. 'Where was I? Oh yes, one day Cornelius comes to me and says he's going to take me camping. But we would only carry the clothes we were wearing, a backpack containing a water bottle, MREs and nothing else. Well, you can imagine what my reaction was. Was this man insane? What did I know about camping outside? How dare he ask a thirteen-year-old to give up her bed and sleep on the rough ground!' Em smiled at the sound of soft chuckling coming from around the campsite. 'But I must give Cornelius his due. He was very patient with me as he showed me how to use what was around me to shield me from the elements. I miss those times with him.'

'He sounds like he was a remarkable man,' said Isaac.

'He was. I miss him dearly,' Em replied, nodding sadly and gazing up at the heavens. At times like this, Em wished Cornelius was still around so that she could seek his counsel. As she stared into the darkness, she wondered if he was looking down at her right now. It was highly likely that he would be amused by what had happened to the URE. Em nodded silently in agreement. Yes, Cornelius always said the empire was heading down a path that would lead to its destruction. But she doubted even he could have foreseen the true danger to the URE.

Movement caught Em's eye, breaking her train of thought. She leaned forward to get a better look and saw Raelle making hand gestures to Yuto. Because of the poor light, Em had difficulty in translating what the woman was saying, so she gave Yuto a questioning look.

'Emma-San,' Yuto said in a soft, respectful tone, 'Raelle says even in her academy days, her instructors spoke your mentor's name with huge respect. She also says that some believed he was framed and did not deserve to be executed.' He turned away from Raelle, pressed his hands together, and bowed. 'Even in my culture, Cornelius Trialus was a name that was spoken with honour. It is well documented that during his time as a diplomatic envoy to my country, he worked tirelessly with my leaders, hoping to secure peace talks between our two cultures.' He shook his head and exhaled sadly, 'Unfortunately, despite his best intentions, that never came to pass.'

The news that Cornelius had once been a diplomatic envoy came as a surprise to Em. He had always spoken openly to her about his youth, his early days as a soldier, and advancement into the intelligence branch, but never once had he mentioned he had been a peace envoy. Em narrowed her eyes as she wondered if that had been a cover for him, so that he could gather valuable intel. But on hearing the almost reverential way in which Yuto spoke Cornelius's name, a part of her wondered if that was a part of him she knew little about; the man before he became bitter and disillusioned with the URE. Although she deeply loved and respected her scheming mentor, she felt a tinge of sadness that she never met the man whose name Yuto and Raelle spoke about in high esteem.

As the conversations around the camp drifted to other topics, Em leaned back and closed her eyes. She nodded and smiled sadly. Yes, Cornelius would have loved this, everybody sitting around swapping stories, carefully drawing their secrets out and storing them in that inquisitive brain of his for future use. As she drifted off to sleep, she thought she heard Cornelius's voice whispering to her subconscious.

'Be careful of the yellow eyes watching from the shadows.'

A couple of hours later, Em was standing on watch, staring thoughtfully up at the clear night sky overhead. Glancing at the digital clock on her HUD, she saw it was a few minutes after midnight. An interesting feature of her visor's display was that it was configured to the wearer's retina, enabling her to scroll through the HUD's menu with just the movement or blink of her eyes. As she stared up at the moon, Em eye-clicked the command to activate her suit's sensors; she wanted to see the lunar colonies the URE had put there many years ago. Unfortunately, no matter how hard she tried to magnify it, it was hard to spot anything on the moon's surface.

She stiffened as something occurred to her. For the first time, Em found herself worrying about the people on the moon. Were they even still alive? Did the colonists know what had happened on Terra? Surely, they must have realised something was wrong when they lost communication with their Terra-bound counterparts? A shiver of fever ran down Em's spine as she wondered if the lunar colonists had met the same fate as the URE populace. In her mind's eye, she pictured hundreds of cybernetic zombies roaming around the surface of the moon, staring up at Terra, waiting for their mistress to come for them.

But before she could give it any more thought, a rustling came from behind her, breaking her out of her troubled musings. Tense, alert for danger, Em spun post-haste and dropped to her knee with her rifle held steady in her hands, pointed toward the disturbance. She held her breath and waited, but exhaled in relief at seeing the familiar bulky outline of Isaac breaking through the treeline.

'Sorry, Boss Lady,' he whispered apologetically. 'I just wanted to see if you would like some company.'

Grateful for the distraction, Em cocked her head and regarded Isaac with a suspicious side eye. 'Not to sound ungrateful, but shouldn't you be getting some rest?' The corners of her mouth twitched in amusement. 'What's wrong? You suddenly find yourself missing your comfortable bed?'

'No, the hard ground I'm fine with,' grumbled Isaac. He made a sweeping gesture at the thick forest in front of them. 'It's too damn quiet. Too damn creepy, if you ask me. That's what's keeping me awake. Just find it a bit unsettling.'

The realisation hit Em like a thunderbolt. She gaped at Isaac as it dawned on her – the reason she had been so deeply unsettled ever since they reached the boundary of the forest. There were no animal sounds. Why had she not noticed it before now? There had been no bird cries, owl hoots, or insect noises of any kind. Even standing on watch, she had not seen any nocturnal animals flying around. A shiver passed through Em and her eyes grew wide as she slowly turned and gazed into the silent undergrowth. She'd sensed something was wrong earlier but had put it down to her own heightened paranoia. Her heart thundered against her ribcage as she wondered if Oracle had not only assimilated the human population but the local wildlife too. No, that wasn't possible. Surely there had to be another explanation.

Suddenly, just as Em was about to turn and voice her concerns to Isaac, something in her peripheral vision made her pause. Her breath hitched as she turned her head and saw a pair of yellow eyes staring back at her from the shadows of the undergrowth. Activating her visor's night vision, she saw that it appeared to be a brown tawny owl, but it was not like any tawny owl she'd seen before. There was something unsettling in the way it was staring at her. Trying to keep her wits about her, Em kept her eyes on it and studied it. Yes, the glowing yellow eyes were a clear giveaway – there was something unnatural about them. But in addition, it had silver cybernetic tendrils coming out of its body. What she found even more disturbing was that it showed no sign of movement; it was just watching her. What was it wai—

Then two more yellow eyes appeared.

Two more, and they were followed by two more after that.

Em could only watch in horror as more and more yellow-eyed cyborg-type creatures stared out from the darkness at her.

She saw the fearful expression on Isaac's face through his visor, telling her he had seen them too. *If we don't make any hostile actions, they might not attack us,* she thought while she delicately slung her weapon over her shoulder. Then, backing carefully away, she wordlessly gestured to Isaac for him to do the same as she inched back through the bushes and back to camp. Em was confident that if they didn't look like they posed a threat, then perhaps the creatures wouldn't attack them. So long as she and her

friends continued to act that way, they should be safe. But one thing was certain: Oracle knew they were here. Another thought occurred to Em, which she found equally unsettling. Because Oracle had not ordered those creatures to attack them, did that mean it wanted them alive? Was that because it was curious to see what they were up to? Or something else?

Without saying a word, Em and Isaac moved around the camp, waking each of their colleagues. Luckily, it took little effort to wake everyone; they were only dozing. Em motioned for Isaac to fetch Xander, who was standing on guard on the other side of the camp. It took only a short time for Isaac to return with him. She guessed from his disturbed expression and deathly pale face that Xander had seen the eyes too. Once they were all assembled, using the resistance secret language, Em explained she wanted them to break camp, and that they were to follow Raelle to the ravine where the access hatch was located.

As she followed her comrades through the bushes, Em kept a wary eye on the yellow-eyed beasties staring at her from the darkness. She peered up at the night sky and issued a silent prayer to the figure she hoped was watching down on her.

'Cornelius, my old friend, I hope you are watching out for us. We really could do with some luck right now.'

Just under an hour later, Em stood outside a six-metre-high oblong metal door, now cleared of all vines and branches that had hidden it. It had not taken them long to clear the access hatch of obstructions, and the only thing she needed to do now was type the codes Hilaria had given her into the terminal beside the door. Her hands trembled as she lifted the protective flap covering the terminal's keyboard, and she held her breath while she typed in the short sequence of letters and numbers.

Despite the coolness of her suit, perspiration broke across Em's brow and her throat constricted with fear while she struggled to keep her hands from trembling. It wasn't the fear of what would happen if she entered the wrong command code that was making her hands shake. No, it was because she was acutely aware of the yellow eyes spying down on her, imagining them burrowing into the back of her neck. The tension was almost palpable while she waited for the code to be accepted. What would happen if the terminal refused to accept Hilaria's command codes? Would those beasts attack them? She doubted they would be able to survive an attack.

Em cast a worried eye at Isaac and muttered to him, 'This is taking too long. I think we need to prepare to make a run for it.'

His brow glistening with sweat, Isaac gave a small nod of acknowledgement. But as he turned to speak to the rest of the group, a loud beep broke the eerie silence. Em jumped in shock at several loud clunks coming from within the door, then she grimaced as the rusted hinges of the door squealed in protest at being forced to move after many years of inactivity.

Relieved, Em did not waste any time and frantically gestured for her comrades to climb through the hatch. Once everyone had stepped through, she was the last to follow and, with Isaac's help, she closed the hatch behind her. But as she did so, she caught sight of something that sent a shiver down her spine. The wildlife now appeared to have moved out of the darkness and were standing in the spot she and her friends had vacated. The last thing she saw just before the hatch was fully closed was hundreds of those strange yellow-eyed cyborg animals staring back at her.

Em jumped in fright as the access hatch sealed shut with a loud pneumatic hiss. Relieved to be on the other side of the door, she turned to see that they were now standing on what looked like a train station platform, illuminated by two rows of emergency lights hanging from the ceiling, bathing the area in a warm glow. A bullet-shaped carriage, approximately fifteen metres long by four metres wide, stood waiting for them, with a pair of gullwing doors hanging open, revealing a comfortable-looking cabin interior.

Her curiosity getting the better of her, Em took a few steps forward and peered over the edge of the platform to see that the carriage was sitting on a bed of magnets, which was how it earned the nickname magnitran. Em gave a slight nod of admiration. She had travelled on a magnitran many a time with Cornelius. It was an efficient and comfortable

mode of transport. She shook her head sadly. It was a shame they couldn't use it because it would have made the rest of their journey so much easier.

Leaving her colleagues to examine the interior of the cabin, Em moved towards the far edge of the platform; Isaac was standing in the middle of the tracks. The entrance to the tunnel appeared to have been closed off by an enormous metal door. Em screwed up her face in puzzlement. Wait. Hilaria mentioned nothing about them having to get through another door.

Isaac turned toward Em as she jumped down off the platform to stand next to him. He had a thoughtful expression on his face as he studied the enormous door, murmuring, 'I'm guessing this is supposed to open to allow the magnitran through.' He gestured to the spot Em had just come from. 'There's a terminal on the wall, similar to the one outside. My guess before the carriage can move, you must have to enter a command code to open this door, which will allow you access to the transport tunnel.'

'I agree,' murmured Em in agreement. 'Just hope Hilaria's command codes work on this too or this will have been for nothing.'

Isaac grinned and slapped Em across the shoulder. 'My people have a saying, Boss. A nervous alligator cannot attract prey. Which probably means why worry about something you've no control over. Hilaria's command codes will either work or they won't, so why waste your energy worrying about it?' A broad smile appeared on his face as he turned and gestured to the carriage behind him. 'The good news is at least we don't have to walk the rest of the way now. I don't think it will take much figuring out how to operate the magnitran.'

Not sure if she'd heard right, Em did a double take and stared at Isaac in disbelief, exclaiming, 'What? Are you mad? The purpose of not using the magnitran is for us to remain undetected for as long as possible. Once we use that, Oracle will know that we are here.'

Isaac turned and made a sweeping gesture with his hands, scoffing. 'Oracle already knows we're here, Em. So, we can either delay the inevitable by walking or we can make use of an opportunity.' A mischievous twinkle appeared in his eyes, and he gave Em a slight nudge. 'Come on, Boss, you know it makes sense.'

Maybe Isaac was right, Em wondered thoughtfully as she idly tapped her bottom lip with her right index finger. She turned away from him and stared at the enticing open doors of the carriage. It was obvious from the creatures outside that Oracle knew they were here. So, if they were going to be damned, let them be damned for what they really were and face Oracle head-on. She screwed up her face, rubbed the back of her neck, and blew out a long, reluctant sigh. 'Yeah, I suppose you're right. It would make sense to use the magnitran.' She narrowed her eyes as she regarded the transport hub they were standing in. 'At the moment, with both doors sealed shut, we are protected. The magnitran's comfortable interior gives us a good place to rest for a few more hours before we undertake the final and more perilous part of the mission.'

Isaac nodded in acknowledgement and smiled. 'I'll inform the rest of the team, Boss.' He grunted loudly, heaved his large frame back up onto the station platform, turned and headed toward the open gullwing doors of the magnitran.

Em drew in a long breath and turned back to face the ominous-looking door. Her hand rested against the door's surface, and she closed her eyes. Then she silently prayed that the beasts outside were the only surprise that was waiting for them. Because if they weren't, she dreaded to think what else Oracle had in store for them.

-13-

A few hours later, the magnitran sped through the tunnel, eventually slowing and coming to a stop beside a station platform. Inside the cabin, Em unbuckled her seat belt and sighed in relief that they'd arrived in one piece. Their journey had been a nail-biting one because the carriage had raced through the tunnel at such a tremendous speed; there was a moment when Em thought it wasn't going to stop, and they were going to end up as a bloody smear. However, any concerns she had were quickly dismissed on feeling herself being pushed forward as the vehicle decelerated.

As she surmised, Hilaria's codes allowed them to open the door that was blocking the transport tunnel. After that, it was just a matter of operating the magnitran's controls. Iris had once spent some time serving on-board a magnitran as a steward, working closely alongside the vehicle's pilot. Although she hadn't received pilot training, she had closely observed how it was operated. She expressed her confidence to Em that she could get the magnitran running.

Once she was sure the carriage had come to a complete stop, Em rose from her seat and approached the front of the cabin. She placed her hand on Iris's shoulder, and the latter raised her head and responded with a strained smile. The stress was clearly noticeable on Iris's face as she sank into her seat and grimaced at the celebratory claps coming from her relieved fellow passengers.

'Well done, Iris,' said Em, smiling and giving her comrade's shoulder an appreciative squeeze. 'Never had any doubts you would get us here in one piece.'

'Thanks, chief, I appreciate your confidence in me,' said Iris. She lifted her shoulder in a slight shrug and grinned. 'Just like riding a bike.'

But before Em could respond, Isaac brushed past and let out a loud laugh. 'Except this bike travels at such a ludicrous speed, if you were to fall off you would probably make a lovely decorative smear all along the tunnel wall.'

Em bristled. Seriously! Did he have to say that? Shaking her head, she rolled her eyes at Iris, mouthing *'men'*. Iris, appearing unperturbed, waved a hand as if to dismiss Isaac's comment and rose out of the pilot's seat. Although Em reluctantly agreed with Isaac's sentiments, she felt sometimes people should keep their opinions to themselves. Emotions were already running high, so why risk adding more fuel to the fire? Her temples throbbed with annoyance. Sometimes she could slap Isaac across the back of his head, but that wouldn't change who he was. His gallows humour was probably the biggest thing she liked about him, even though it wasn't to everyone's taste.

Following Isaac through the open gullwing door, Em stepped onto a deserted substation platform. She slowly turned to inspect the area; the platform was narrow and apart from an access door, there wasn't anything visible. Because of its size, Em guessed the substation had been built to hold a small number of people. She tilted her head thoughtfully as she took a couple of steps forward and sniffed at the stale air. How long had this tunnel been sealed? When was the last time it had been used?

Once everybody had vacated the carriage, Em stood in front of the access door. Her hands trembled while she carefully lifted the panel that hid the security login interface. On closer inspection, it appeared to be touch-sensitive. She drew in a deep breath. Once she entered Hilaria's security code, there was no going back. She anxiously glanced over her shoulder at the people standing behind her. Without saying a word, they all gave brief nods of acknowledgement and raised their weapons in readiness. An uncomfortable trickle of sweat ran down the back of Em's neck. The air felt thick with tension. She felt as though she could cut through it with

a knife. Her heart hammered against the inside of her ribcage as she prepared to press her finger on the interface's surface and watched it light up. No going back now. It was now or never. So far they'd been lucky Hilaria's codes had been accepted. But at some point their luck would run out. The unsettled feeling grew inside her and she wondered whether this would be when she pushed their luck too far. If the code wasn't accepted, would they be forced to spend the rest of their lives trapped? No hope of rescue, eventually dying from starvation or dehydration.

Em inhaled a sharp breath as a loud beep broke the palpable silence. An even louder, heavy clunk of a lock disengaging followed it. She raised her eyebrows in surprise and stared at her finger. It was still hovering over the interface screen. The command sequence hadn't been entered yet. Her eyes tightened in suspicion as she stared at the slowly opening hatch and squirmed at the prickling sensation tickling the back of her neck. Something inside her told her that they were being played with. She took an involuntary step back and gazed at the now open hatchway.

Isaac cocked his head and gave Em a look that held a touch of admiration. 'That was fast, Boss. I never even saw your fingers move.'

Still eyeing the open hatchway, Em furrowed her brow and shook her head, murmuring, 'That's because they didn't. I hadn't even got round to typing in the first digit.'

Exchanging a worried look with the others, Isaac shook his head in bewilderment. He gestured to the open hatchway. 'Then, if you didn't open it, who did?'

Before Em could answer, a strange, seductive feminine voice spoke out from the intercom. 'Access granted, Emma Tulley. You may enter at your convenience.'

Taken aback, Em let out a small squeal of fright and jumped back. Her heart felt like it had leapt up into her throat. It wasn't the announcement that had taken her by surprise, caused her to cry out. It was because it knew her name. While she tried to regain control of her emotions, Em swallowed and peered at the intercom's speaker. Where had she heard that voice before? Why did it sound so familiar?

Em turned away and saw the uncertain expressions on her friends' faces. They appeared to be equally as unnerved as she was. Yuto closed his

eyes and whispered a prayer to whatever gods he worshipped, while Isaac made a strange blessing motion across his chest. The rest of her comrades remained tight-lipped, but Em noticed their grip on their weapons had tightened.

Iris's eyes showed a hint of fear as she crossed herself, muttering, 'Will you walk into my parlour, said the spider to the fly?'

Because Iris also came from Em's world, Em instantly recognised the poem she was quoting. She nodded in commiseration on hearing the anxious tone in Iris's voice. Yes, the moral of that story was that one should not trust an invitation from a suspicious source. It was clear Oracle was the one who had opened the hatch and was inviting them to enter. From everything Hilaria had told Em about Oracle, she knew it couldn't be trusted. But that left them with a dilemma. They couldn't remain where they were, and they couldn't go back. That meant the only course of action was for them to go forward. Even if it meant they were walking into a trap.

Shoulders squared in rigid determination, jaw set, Em scowled at the open hatchway through narrowed eyes. Well, if they were walking into danger, they would face it head-on, heads held high. No way in hell was she going to let it think it had got to them. Smiling tightly, Em spoke in a tone that sounded more confident than she felt. 'Well, team, looks like we've been invited to dinner.' She slapped her hands together and laughed. 'Come on, chaps. Brave hearts 'n' all that. It would be rude to come all this way and not accept. Yes?'

To Em's relief, her stern-faced comrades straightened and nodded in silent unison. Well, it appeared they were with her. But she couldn't help wondering what was going through their minds. They could only be pushed so far before someone finally broke and said no more. What would happen then? Em gritted her teeth and focused on the open hatchway. Right now, they were all united. Those types of thoughts would only distract her. She followed Isaac through the hatch into a short, narrow corridor. It was a typical URE corridor, with metallic grey walls and green rubber flooring. To Em's right was a door with a laminated notice in the centre, informing her that it led to a stairwell. Directly in front of her was a transport-pod access point.

'Well, Boss Lady,' Isaac murmured, bobbing his head at the transport-pod and then the stairwell entrance. 'Which one do we choose?'

Good question, what should they choose? Em rubbed her chin thoughtfully as she shifted her gaze between the stairwell and the transport-pod. 'From what Hilaria told me, there are thirty-two floors between us and the detention level,' she said carefully as she ran the numbers in her head. 'That means we have at least sixty-four flights of stairs to climb.' She lapsed into silence as she considered their options. Climbing that many flights of stairs would be draining and time consuming. The transport-pod may get them there quicker, but it was also the riskier option out of the two. Anything could go wrong while they were inside the confined space of the cabin. They would be vulnerable to attack. It was a straightforward decision as far as Em was concerned. They would take the stairs.

Her mind made up, Em turned to address the group and quickly explained her decision. From the unhappy expressions on their faces, she knew they weren't looking forward to the climb. But they were keeping their reservations to themselves. She shrugged. *Well, at least they'll get some exercise out of this.* Yes, the stairs may take their toll physically, but at least they had a better chance of being alive when they reached their destination.

But as Em tried to push the stairwell door open, she frowned when she was met with resistance. It appeared to be locked. Determined that she was going to open it, Em placed her shoulder and pushed. However, no matter how hard she tried, the door refused to open. Isaac tapped Em on her shoulder, and she took a step back to allow him to try. The result was the same. The door simply refused to yield against the powerfully built man's bulk. Defeated, Em turned and eyed the closed doors of the transport-pod access point. Well, it seemed like someone else had made the choice for them.

Em flinched as she heard a loud ping as if in answer to her unspoken thoughts. Everybody spun around with their weapons pointed in the direction from which the sound was coming. Her head cocked. She watched in curious fascination as the transport-pod doors slid open. The prickling in the back of her neck intensified and she wondered if this was how rats felt when they entered a maze, tempted by the reward at the end. But she doubted their reward would be a lump of cheese.

'Well, it looks like the spider is inviting us into her web,' Em murmured, moving warily toward the open transport-pod.

'Buzz, buzz,' replied Isaac in a tone lacking humour.

Once everybody was inside the transport-pod, they watched with wary apprehension as the doors slid to a close with a gentle shush. Transport-pods normally held a maximum of eight people, so they were all pressed together. This only heightened Em's feeling that they were animals being led to slaughter. To keep her mind distracted, Em closed her eyes and concentrated on something else. But no matter how hard she tried, she couldn't shake the sense of impending doom. Images played in her mind of them trapped together, clawing in desperation as they suffocated in their airtight coffin. Chastising herself for having such a morbid imagination, Em forced herself to relax. *We'll be out of here soon*, she thought half-heartedly.

'Destination please,' the same familiar-sounding voice announced, startling Em out of her musings.

She furrowed her brow and searched for the source of the disembodied voice. 'Erm, can you take us to level thirty-two, please?' She cringed inwardly. Sure, be polite to the bodiless entity that may end up killing them. She stiffened as a thought suddenly occurred to her, and she called out, 'Wait! Would it be possible for you to make two stops?' Em knew her question had caught the others off-guard from the quizzical way they were looking at her with their hands raised in a what-the-hell gesture.

Isaac's eyebrows met together as he leaned in closer and whispered in Em's ear. 'Boss, I know it was part of the plan to split up.' His voice dropped an octave, and he looked up at the ceiling. 'But do you think that's wise now?'

Em raised her hand and dismissed Isaac's question as the ethereal voice replied, 'Certainly, Emma Tulley. My function is only to serve. Your wish is my command.'

Something about the voiceless entity's attitude grated on Em. Was it being sarcastic? She stared up at the ceiling and gave it a suspicious side eye. Ever since she heard the voice in the substation, a seed of suspicion had been growing inside her as to its identity. Until now, she had held her tongue because she was puzzled about its motives. No, let it play its games,

she thought, pursing her lips. That didn't mean she was going to be a willing participant.

Em cleared her throat and addressed their mysterious guardian in a confident tone. 'Oracle, please could you stop at the hanger level before continuing to level thirty-two?'

'Certainly, my dear. By your command,' Oracle purred. Her tone changed to a more taunting one with a touch of condescension. 'Please will all humans place all their trays in an upright position before we begin our departure. You may experience a slight jarring sensation as the transport-pod departs. Do not worry, that is perfectly normal. But in the event of system failure, please cry out in alarm as you all hurtle to your doom. For those of you who wish to do so, please assume the safety position of bending down and kissing your rather squashy bottoms goodbye. Thank you for travelling with Oracle's taxi service. Your discomfort is my pleasure.'

If her fellow passengers were surprised by their mysterious watcher's identity, they didn't show it. Em felt a stir of pride as her comrades looked up at the cabin's ceiling, their eyes blazing with defiance. Oracle would have to do a lot more than that if it wanted to unnerve them. This was a group who had been through hell together, surviving the nightmare of being held in captivity by the URE. No, Oracle would need to up its game before they would even consider it a threat. Rather than giving the mocking AI any more of her time, Em focused her attention on Gemma and Iris.

'Gemma, is it right you trained as a pilot when you served in the military?' Em asked quickly.

The muscles in Gemma's face tightened, and she straightened her head proudly. 'Yes, ma'am,' she replied immediately, her tone oozing with confidence. 'I graduated top of my class and have logged approximately three hundred flight hours in combat against the GCR.' Her cheeks flushed, and she gave Yuto a sheepish look, murmuring, 'Sorry.'

'No need to apologise, Gemma-San,' Yuto responded in a brusque tone. His mouth twitched and he gave a small respectful bow. 'You are a noble warrior like me, so you were only doing what your leaders asked of you.'

Although it had been widely rumoured on the base that Gemma's skill as a pilot was unparalleled and had no equal, Em wanted to clarify it for herself by hearing the confidence in Gemma's voice. Gemma's story was common knowledge. She had served with distinction as a flight officer in the URE's air forces. But that all came crashing down on her when she disobeyed an order to open fire on enemy civilians. Not only did her refusal end her flight career, but she was also stripped of her rank before being thrown into detention to await court martial and summary execution. Em's resistance cell eventually liberated her and she had since become a trusted member of the resistance. Her skill as a pilot was the reason Em had chosen Gemma to come on this mission.

'So, do you think you'd be able to operate one of the troop transports?' Em asked hopefully, even though she already knew the answer. 'Will you be able to hack your way past the security lockouts?'

Gemma lifted her shoulder in a half shrug. 'I can't see it being any different from the Imperial Eagles I flew.' Her mouth twitched and her face morphed into a devious grin, and she gave Iris a gentle nudge. 'This miscreant is the hacker. She should have no problem getting past the security lockouts.'

The colour in Iris's cheeks blossomed, and she slapped Gemma on the shoulder. 'Stop it, you.'

Impatient, and in no mood for joking around, Em shot the two women a withering look. 'Do you think you can do it?' she asked, this time making sure the tone of her voice had an edge to it.

Iris blanched and nodded. 'Yes, ma'am. I should have no problem breaking through any security lockouts.'

The transport-pod came to a sudden stop. Taken by surprise, Em had to grab Isaac's arm to steady herself. There was a collective intake of air; everybody held their breath and eyed the door apprehensively. Her body was so tight with tension, Em found it hard to breathe. There was no need for her to ask what her comrades were thinking. She could see it in their eyes. They were all probably wondering the same thing as her – what type of welcome party would be waiting for them? Would a deluge of laser fire greet them? Killing them all where they stood?

However, and much to Em's surprise, that did not happen. Em hadn't realised she'd been holding her breath and exhaled on seeing the transport-pod's door open, revealing an empty corridor. Still expecting a trap, Em cautiously moved forward and poked her head out. On looking down either side of the corridor, she could see no sign of hostile soldiers waiting to jump out from their hiding place. The corridors were exactly the same as the one they had left, with metallic military grey walls and green rubber flooring. Plaques and laminated propaganda posters decorated the walls every few feet, but apart from that, the corridor was empty. Em leaned back and wordlessly gestured to Gemma and Iris to move out. The two women acknowledged her with a thin smile as they stepped into the corridor. Before the doors slid shut, Em caught sight of Gemma pulling up the building schematic on her wristband. She was likely working out the route to the hangar.

As she listened to the hiss of transport-pod's doors sealing shut, Em closed her eyes and prayed silently to herself. If there was an omniscient being watching over them, she hoped it was on their side.

Because we'll need a miracle if we all want to get out of this alive.

-14-

There was an uneasy silence inside the cabin as the transport-pod continued its ascent. Anxious, Em drummed the fingers of her right hand against her leg while she watched the numbers rapidly change on the digital display. Twenty-one … twenty-two … and so on, in quick succession. A sliver of doubt crept inside her mind, and she wondered whether it had been a mistake for them to do this. Maybe they should have left well enough alone? Em frowned as she tried to remember the ancient Terran proverb. What was it Cornelius had told her? When confronting a caged animal, it was best not to antagonise it, or something like that. Em blinked and shook her head, pushing the self-doubt to the back of her mind. She squared her shoulders and focused her gaze on the doors in front of her. Now was not the time to second-guess herself, she thought. Whatever game Oracle was playing, she would not allow it to distract them from what they were here to do.

A loud ping broke Em out of her quiet retrospection, followed by Oracle's voice announcing in a gleeful tone, 'Level thirty-two, detention. Will all passengers please depart the transport-pod in an orderly manner, remembering not to leave any possessions behind. May I once again thank you for travelling with Oracle's taxis, where your discomfort is my pleasure. Also, feel free to rate your journey on Trip Advisor because your opinion matters. Thank you. See you again soon.'

Irked by Oracle's condescending tone, as well as having no idea what Trip Advisor was, Em bit her tongue and fought back the urge to tell it where it could stick its request. Em's stomach cramped and her heart kicked into higher gear as the doors slid open. Just as a few moments before, there were no soldiers there to greet them. Em held her breath and moved gingerly out of the transport-pod into a short, narrow lobby that led to what looked like an unmanned circular guard station. Behind that, she could make out a long corridor with doors lining either side. From her own experience inside similar detention centres, Em knew that if any prisoners were being held, then that was where their cells would be located. Em paused and ran the numbers in her head. The maximum number of prisoners a detention block could hold was fifty. Deep down, she hoped they wouldn't find that many because she wasn't sure if they would all fit into whatever transport vehicle Gemma could procure.

Em stiffened as she felt a firm hand touch her shoulder, but she relaxed on seeing Isaac's worried expression staring back at her. Her nerves were so tightly wound, she realised she was jumping at the slightest thing. She exhaled through her nose and tried to centre herself as she listened to Isaac whisper to her.

'You okay, Emma?' he asked, his voice thick with concern. 'I understand if you want to take a moment to gather your thoughts.'

Something in Isaac's voice made Em pause. For as long as she had known him, she had never heard him use her full name. From the first day she met him, he'd always called her Em, never Emma. His calling her by her given name was a clear giveaway that he was deeply worried about her. Appreciative of his concern, she smiled, gave his hand a reassuring squeeze and sighed. 'I'm fine. Just a bit on edge. I think it might be because of Oracle.'

Isaac grunted and gave the now closed transport-pod door the hairy eyeball. 'I know what you mean. That sickly-sweet way it spoke to us.' He grimaced and shuddered. 'Ugh, it was getting on my nerves a bit.'

'I think that was the point,' murmured Em, narrowing her eyes, searching the ceiling for any camera drones. She raised her voice so that the rest of her colleagues could hear. 'Be on your guard, everyone. I'm sure Oracle is watching everything we do. Just be ready for whatever it throws at us next.'

There was a loud grumble of agreement while everybody approached the narrow corridor. As they made their way down, Em caught sight of a stairwell access door. On a hunch, she pressed her hand against it and was surprised to discover it wasn't locked. After making a mental note of its location, Em decided it might be best if they used the stairs the next time. If they found any prisoners, using the transport-pod would mean they would have to make at least two or more journeys back and forth to the transports. Not only that, but the original plan was for Rahul and Felix to escort the prisoners they found while the others would head to the armoury. But everyone helping would mean that once the prisoners had been offloaded to Gemma, Rahul and Felix would be free to assist Isaac and his team with whatever was discovered in the armoury.

Em quickly explained her idea to the rest of the group, and the relief was clear to see on Rahul and Felix's faces, now they knew they would not have to escort any prisoners by themselves. Em blew out a slow puff through tight lips. She just hoped Isaac would be equally as compliant when he learned that she planned on undertaking her own side mission.

As she approached the guard station, Em felt unsettled when she saw the condition it was in. From her experience of being a prisoner in similar detention blocks to this, she knew that there should be at least one centurion always on duty. But the station was unoccupied. The holographic display interfaces were still active, with icons blinking away to themselves. However, that wasn't what troubled her. What disturbed her the most was the half-eaten sandwich and beverage resting on top of the desk. If it hadn't been for the mould growing on the sandwich, one would have thought whoever had been on duty had just been called away.

'Whoever was stationed here must have just got up and left when they received Oracle's activation signal,' Rahul murmured, in answer to Em's unspoken question. The groove in the centre of his forehead deepened as he studied the displays. 'If I'm reading these displays correctly, only ten cells are occupied.' He quickly pulled up the chair, sat down and

began tapping the icons on the holographic interface, nodding. 'According to this, all the prisoners appear to be alive and well.'

'Do you think you'll be able to unlock their doors from here?' Em asked.

Rahul scratched his head and silently studied the interface. After a few seconds, he slowly nodded and spoke in a quiet but confident tone. 'Yes, chief. The user interface appears to be easy enough to operate, in fact …' He paused, tapped on a couple of icons and smiled. 'All the cells have been unlocked. You're good to go.'

Grateful for Rahul's swift efforts, Em allowed herself a tight smile and acknowledged him with a faint nod. She indicated that the rest of the group should follow her to the occupied cells. They each took up position outside a cell door with a green sensor informing them that the cell was occupied. Once they had freed a prisoner, they would make their way along the corridor, free the next, and so on. When all prisoners were freed, they would escort them down to the hangar.

Inhaling a deep breath, Em gave the sensor a gentle tap with her right hand. She unwittingly flinched as the door opened with a loud whoosh. Mindful of what she may be walking into, Em took several slow steps through the open cell doorway to be greeted by a woman standing glowering at her.

The woman was slightly taller than Em, heavyset, with a round face. From the crow's feet in the corners of her eyes and her greying hair, Em guessed the stranger was in her late fifties or early sixties. It was clear from the yellow jumpsuit she was wearing and her short, bristled hair that she was a fellow abductee. A wave of sympathy passed over Em. She knew only too well what that must have been like for the woman, having experienced the same hair-shaving trauma when she first arrived so many years ago. But apart from looking slightly dishevelled, possibly from being cooped up in the cell, the stranger looked surprisingly healthy. Em cast an eye around the cell and noticed the food replicator, sink, and toilet. That explained why the stranger looked to be in relatively good shape.

The woman scowled at Em, folded her arms across her chest, and spoke in a peevish tone. 'If you're the maid, you've got a bloody lot of

explaining to do. Do you realise how bloody long I've been using these sheets for? Bloody disgrace. I've a good right to complain to the management.' She raised both of her hands and showed seven fingers. 'Seven weeks. It's been seven bloody weeks since I was thrown in here. No visitors. No room service. Nothing! You wouldn't treat a dog this way.' Her ire increasing, the stranger took a step forward and angrily jabbed a finger at the open doorway. 'I demand to speak to whoever is in charge of this hellhole because I'm going to give them a piece of my mind.'

Despite being on the receiving end of the woman's anger, Em couldn't help smiling. There was something about her attitude she found refreshing. Normally, when confronted by their rescuers, prisoners were timid and docile, but still grateful to be rescued. But this person's reaction was completely different. She was feisty, giving the impression she was a force to be reckoned with. It was clear to Em from the faint yellow bruising around her left eye and cheek, along with the nearly healed scar on her bottom lip, that she had received the usual rough welcome given to off-worlders. But the more she listened to the stranger rant, the more Em liked her. One thing was certain: she had a lot of spunk.

Em would have been quite glad to let the stranger continue with her tirade against her oppressors. Unfortunately, she was also pressed for time and felt aggrieved that she was going to have to cut her stranger off. 'Sorry, ma'am,' Em interjected, holding up her right hand, cutting the woman off in mid-flow. 'I would love to listen to you continue hurling abuse at whoever did this to you. But I'm afraid you're shouting at the wrong person, because I'm with the resistance and we're here to rescue you.'

'Well, why didn't you say so in the first place?' the stranger snapped, shooting Em a withering stare as she marched past her. 'Took you long enough. Good job I had that food synthesiser thingy, otherwise I may have starved to death.' She stopped, spun on her heel and waggled her right index finger. 'Piece of advice, dear – when rescuing somebody, don't keep them waiting. Not only does it not make a good impression, but it also makes you appear inept.'

Suddenly feeling like a child being scolded by her schoolteacher, Em hung her head and nodded sheepishly. 'Sorry about that, ma'am.' She blinked and shook her head. Wait – why was she the one apologising? Trying to regain control of the conversation, Em gave a tight smile and held out her hand. 'My name is Em Tulley, commander of the local resistance cell.'

'Karen,' Karen huffed, brusquely shaking Em's hand, 'Doctor Karen Logue.'

'You're a doctor,' Em exclaimed in surprise. 'You're a sight for sore eyes. The people we have assigned to our infirmary have only a limited understanding of treating injuries. Your services would be extremely valuable to us.'

Looking abashed, Karen coughed, waved her hand and gave a weak laugh. 'Ahem. Yes … well, about that … unfortunately, I'm not that type of doctor. I am a forensic medical examiner, meaning most of the customers that normally come to me are … erm, slightly on the stiff side, if you know what I mean.'

Em laughed and gave Karen's shoulder a hearty slap. 'Well, that will still make you the most qualified person we have in the infirmary.'

Before Em could say any more, she paused as she sensed movement coming from behind her. Turning, she saw her comrades had freed the remaining prisoners, a mixture of men and women of varying ages. Like Karen, they all wore the familiar yellow leather jumpsuits. From what Em could see, they were all in fairly good shape, which was surprising considering they had been held in captivity for several weeks. But, unlike Karen, most of them behaved like they were afraid of their saviours.

But after some convincing from Karen, the newly freed prisoners finally accepted their new situation. Em learned Karen was the de facto leader of the group. Karen quickly explained that throughout her captivity, she had used the ventilation ducts connected to each cell to pass messages back and forth. They'd swapped stories with one another and kept their spirits up with songs of defiance.

As Em led the group to the exit leading to the stairwell, the familiar prickling sensation tickled the back of Em's neck. Something about all of this didn't sit right with her. Why hadn't these people been assimilated along with everybody else? Was it because they hadn't been wearing pain collars? If that was the case, why hadn't Oracle turned off their food replicators and let them starve? Was there something she was missing here? The more Em thought about it, the more she became convinced there was something strange going on. It was obvious from her interactions with the AI that it wasn't hindering Em and her team, more like it was helping them.

Em wasn't sure what the AI was up to. But one thing was certain: it had an agenda. One way or another, Em was determined to find out what it was.

-15-

This is it, Em groaned to herself. *This is where I am going to die.*

Breathless, her thigh muscles protesting with signs of fatigue, Em urged herself forward, up the flight of stairs. Eventually, she planted one foot on the landing, followed by another and then came to a stop. Resting her back against the wall, she wiped the sweat that was pouring into her eyes and glanced at the sign on the wall opposite her. Level forty-eight. Great. Just another twelve to go.

With her hands resting on her thighs, Em bent down and drew in several deep breaths. She couldn't remember the last time she had climbed this many stairs in one go. She'd always considered herself to be a fit and healthy person, but this made her realise that climbing thirty flights of stairs was pushing her fitness to its limits. There was a time when she could have done this effortlessly. But as she drew in another lungful of air, a depressing thought suddenly hit her.

She was getting old.

In her mind, she still considered herself to be a twenty-something, fit and healthy person. But the reality had unmercifully hit home. Her body was showing signs of a fifty-five-year-old woman whose body had suffered tremendous abuse over the years. As hard as it was for Em to take, it was just starting to dawn on her that her stressful lifestyle was catching up on her. She set her jaw and pushed the depressing thought out of her head. *Screw that! I'm not accepting it!* Then, with fiery determination, she straightened, fixed her gaze on the remaining flights of stairs and growled

to herself. 'Come on, you silly cow. You're not in the grave yet. You can do this. Move your sorry arse.'

Digging deep into her reserves, Em blew out a defiant breath and pushed herself on. With each step, she ignored the cries of fatigue coming from her body and continued up the remaining flights of stairs. As she did so, her mind drifted back to the last conversation she'd had with Isaac. It was just after they had freed the captives and had escorted them to the stairwell so that they could lead them down to the hangar level. That was when she broke the news to Isaac that she wasn't going to follow them. As she'd expected, Isaac hadn't taken the news about what she was planning to do well. He angrily tried to dissuade her from doing it. But there was no swaying Em. Of course, Isaac must have known from experience that it was impossible to talk her out of anything once her mind was set. With great reluctance, he capitulated and agreed to let her go, but on one proviso, that she would promise to keep a communicator channel open. Just in case.

A sense of relief stirred within Em as she placed her foot on the last step and saw a sign marked 'Level Sixty'. She paused for a second, poked her head over the banister and gazed down the well-hole. At that moment she realised she had made a big mistake. Now she was looking down a vast tunnel, formed by the spiralling of the flights of stairs. It just seemed to go on forever ...

Going down ...

and down ...

Em felt as if she wanted to throw up. Overcome with vertigo, she jerked her head back and looked up. That only worsened her vertigo, because the same vertical shaft was looming over her. Squeezing her eyes shut, Em pulled away from the banister and swallowed. *Oh, why did I have to look down?* Desperate to clear the spiralling image out of her head, she drew in several slow breaths.

That's it, she thought. *Remember what Cornelius taught you. Control your breathing. Centre yourself. Focus. Don't let your surroundings distract you.*

Feeling more balanced, the wave of vertigo slowly fading, Em opened her eyes and focused on the door in front of her. Carefully reaching out, she gently pushed it open and held her breath as she peeked through the gap. The corridor appeared to be deserted. With deliberate slowness,

she carefully inched through the door and smoothly closed it behind her. So far, so good.

Em glanced at the readout on her visor's HUD and noted the time. Isaac and the team should have loaded the rescued prisoners onto the shuttle. She reasoned that if things were going to plan, then they should be accessing the armoury about now. Not wanting to waste any more time, Em brought up an image of the tower's floor schematic on her visor's display. From what she could see, the entrance to the portal chamber was only about twenty metres from her position.

The corridor was eerily quiet as Em carefully made her way along it. Apart from her footsteps, the only sound she could make out was the gentle hum of electricity coming from the hidden power conduits in the walls and ceiling. Em winced as each footstep echoed off the walls, piercing the silence like a pin on a balloon. With each step she made, Em felt her heart slam against the wall of her chest. Her breathing quickened. Any moment now, something would leap out at her from the shadows, and it would all be over. However, despite Em's increasing anxiety, nothing jumped out at her, and she hurried down the corridor without any interruption. A tingle of excitement passed through her as she noticed her target was not that far away from her. Not far to go now …

Four metres …

two …

Yes! Em inwardly cheered as she came to a stop in front of the door. Frowning, she studied the closed door in front of her. From her perspective, it was just a normal door. Then she noticed what looked like a retinal scanner, alongside which was a large plaque written in Roman standard. Em had been on this world long enough to become fluent in reading the language. It warned that anyone entering without authorisation would be court-martialled and then executed. The warning didn't faze Em. She doubted there was anybody left in the building to carry the order out. Nonetheless, what did bother her was the retinal scanner. She scratched her head and grunted in annoyance. Hilaria had said nothing about a retinal scanner.

Feeling like the universe had put another obstacle in front of her, Em exhaled a weary sigh, opened her visor and massaged her forehead.

She'd come all this way only to be stopped at the last hurdle. Surely there had to be a— Em stiffened and slapped her brow. Oh, she was a fool. Hilaria's security card. Hilaria had given it to her just in case she needed it.

'Now, where the hell did I put it?' she mumbled, sliding her backpack off and fumbling around inside. She smiled and pulled a small oblong card out of the front pocket. The corners of her mouth curled up into a sneaky grin as she pulled out a pocket-sized mirror. She bit onto her bottom lip, bent down in front of the scanner and placed the mirror over the part of the device where normally a person would position their head to allow their eyes to be scanned.

There was a loud, dissatisfied-sounding squawk, followed by a synthesised voice announcing 'System failure. Please have your security card ready.'

Em kissed the tiny mirror and grinned. One of the many things Cornelius had taught her was how to bypass a retinal scanner. Retinal scanners had a fault that one could exploit by holding up a reflective surface in front of them. The laser beam emitted from the scanner would bounce back off the mirror, disrupting the recognition software contained within the device. The device would automatically switch to its backup method of scanning the chip contained inside a security ID.

Although she was confident it would work, Em crossed the fingers of her left hand as she held the small card in front of the scanner with her right hand. After what seemed like an eternity, there was a friendly beep, followed by the same synthesised voice announcing 'Access granted. Cooper, Wendy. General. Have a nice day.' Em sighed in relief and glanced up at the heavens. Once again, Cornelius had saved her from beyond the grave.

The door opened with a loud whoosh. Em slipped her pack back on, took a couple of hesitant steps forward and entered through the open doorway. But before she had time to get fully clear, the door slid shut, barely a quarter of a metre from her back. Startled, she spun around and was shocked at how close she had been to dying. The door had come down so fast, if she'd been any closer, it would probably have sliced her in two.

Em tapped her lip thoughtfully and stared at the door. She suspected Oracle was behind that. Was it trying to unsettle her, or was it

angry she'd bypassed its security so easily without asking it? Too bad. Em decided she had more pressing things to think about than the hurt feelings of an AI. One of them was to investigate the portal chamber and see if there was any evidence of her daughter ever having worked there, as Hilaria had told her.

But as she turned away from the door and focused her attention on the chamber, Em had a sudden sense of déjà vu. Everything seemed so familiar to her. The smoothness of the floor's surface beneath her shoes. The bright lights. The oblong portal device and oval console in the centre of the room. Even the hum from the network servers evoked something inside her. She couldn't put her finger on it, but there was something very familiar about this place, like she'd been here before.

At first, Em wondered if she was feeling some sort of empathic residue. A psychic impression left behind by Henrietta. Was it possible her subconscious was picking up on something? Henrietta's fragrance, perhaps? Em shook her head in dismissal as she moved slowly around the chamber. No, it had been over twenty years since she'd last seen Henrietta, so her scent would have changed. This was something else. Much more than that. More familiar. Like she'd had been here before. Yes, it—

Em stiffened and felt her eyes grow wide as the realisation hit her like a brick. Then she let out a shocked gasp as it all came flooding back to her. *Oh my god*, she thought as a door opened inside her mind, taking her back in time. To that fateful night so many years ago ...

Her brain addled from the sedative that had been used on her, eight-year-old Emma groaned and struggled to open her eyes. But there was a hazy film covering her eyes and she had difficulty making anything out. However, as she tried to blink away the hazy cloud, Emma was suddenly overcome by a feeling of nausea and felt the contents of her stomach shifting. Clutching her abdomen, she curled into a tight ball and retched.

Oh god, that's revolting, Emma thought and screwed up her face at the bitter taste burning back of her throat.

The floor felt cold and harsh through the thin fabric of her pyjamas. Emma let out a small, pitiful sob at the cool sensation on her bare arms. Where was she? Where were her mummy and daddy?

She detected the sounds of heavy footsteps coming from somewhere close by and she stiffened. Was there somebody there with her? Emma squinted and tried to focus on the source of the sound, but her fogged-up vision made it difficult to make out anything other than blurred shapes. Scared because she could not see who was near her, she tried to clamber away but came to a sudden stop as her back hit something hard and unyielding. She frowned to herself as a woman's voice whispered something to her.

'Shush, pueri. Effugere non potes et tantum tibi nocebit si luctare pergis.'

Unable to understand what was being said to her, Em shook her head in confusion. What did she say? The only foreign language she was slightly familiar with was French, and that was only because her mother was a schoolteacher who taught the language in the local comprehensive school and taught her daughters some basic French at weekends. Thus, one thing Em was certain of was, whatever was being spoken to her was not French.

But before Emma could question the stranger, she let out a shocked gasp as she felt something small and metallic being pressed against her upper arm. A small prick of pain shortly followed. Her body becoming heavier, she groaned in protest as she experienced the familiar effects of a sedative entering her system.

'I wish you would stop doing that,' Emma slurred, her voice sounding strangely far away.

Slowly lowering her head to the floor, Emma's eyes grew weary. But before she closed them, her vision cleared at the last moment, and she caught sight of what she thought looked like a strange glowing window with an oblong desk in front of it. She couldn't make any sense of it, and then the unwelcome sensation of unconsciousness took hold of her, enveloping her in a cloak of blackness. Emma's last thought as she fell inside the well of darkness was that she hoped this was a nightmare and that she would wake up back in her own bed ...

Anger surging through her, Em blinked and stared at the portal. She'd completely forgotten about her brief time in here. Had it been so traumatic for her that the only way for her to cope was by suppressing it? But now, standing inside this chamber, in front of the portal, it all came back to her. The discombobulation, the nausea and the pain. She remembered it all. Until now, her first memory of this world was waking up in the dormitory surrounded by strangers, crying in agony from having a cerebral implant embedded inside her skull.

Resting her rifle against the side of the console, Em trailed her hand along its smooth top and scowled at the glowing portal hanging in front of her. Pursing her lips, she cast an eye to the chairs behind the console and wondered which one Henrietta had sat in. Flames of anger shot through her and she quivered with indignation. Had her daughter known? Had she even been aware she'd been helping the very people who abducted her mother?

Em turned and focused her attention on the portal device. The corner of her lip quivered in bitter resentment, and she sneered at it. So, this was the thing that was responsible for so much pain and misery. But as she raised her hand and held it just millimetres from touching the surface, a surprising thing happened. The bitterness drained away from her. Em shook her head and exhaled sadly. There was no point in being angry at something that wasn't alive. The device was only doing what it had been designed to do. If there was anyone she should direct her anger at, it was the people who controlled it. Em stared up at the ceiling and gave her head a weary shake. But that wasn't possible, because it was likely those who had controlled it were all probably dead now.

She stiffened as a thought occurred to her. She rubbed her chin thoughtfully and gazed at the glowing window. The device appeared to be operational. She'd never have a better opportunity to climb through it. All she needed to do was take a couple of steps forward and she'd be back home. Like she'd always wanted. Tilting her head, Em took a step back and gazed at the console, then back again at the portal.

No, Em thought, shaking her head. *Even if I knew how to operate it, the world that portal leads to isn't my home anymore.* Despite everything that had happened to her, all the pain and misery she had endured, this world was her home.

'Oh, it is so tempting, is it not?'

Startled out of her distracted thoughts, Em gasped and spun round. She narrowed her eyes and tried to search for the source of Oracle's voice. At first, she thought Oracle must have been using a camera drone to spy on her. She peered up at the ceiling, but pulled a face when she saw nothing was hovering above her. Where had the voice come from?

Then she heard a strange noise. So recognisable, it caused the hairs on the back of her neck to tingle. Where had she heard it before? It reminded her of air escaping through a tight seal. She cocked her head and frowned in puzzlement. Why did it sound so familiar to her? The realisation hit her like a sledgehammer, and she felt her eyes grow wide in shock as the sound stirred another long-buried memory.

Her dog, Sandy, whining in concern.

The surface of the kitchen mirror stretching outwards and then ...

Oh, god ... the creature ...

The portal! Em held up her hands to her mouth in horror, spun around and stared at the device. With her mouth hanging open, she stood rooted to the spot, unable to move as she watched the shimmering water-like surface stretch outwards. It was as if something was trying to climb through. Em was sure she could see the shape of a hand, slowly pushing forward. There was a small pop of surface tension breaking and Em jumped back in fright.

An arm broke through the liquid-like surface. Em could only watch in morbid fascination as the bald, silver figure stepped out of the device. The figure had a feminine shape. It wore what seemed to be a silver bodysuit that clung tightly over its curvaceous body. It stood at least a foot taller than Em. If it hadn't been for the featureless face and yellow glowing eyes, Em could have mistaken it for human. She swallowed. There was something else in those eyes, an inhuman coldness.

Then, as if it had been reading Em's thoughts, the entity slowly turned those cold yellow eyes towards her. Em's throat tightened and she

felt her blood freeze as its mouth widened in malevolent glee. Frozen in fear, Em could only watch as it stepped towards her. But then, much to Em's surprise, it stopped, reached forward, and took hold of her hand. Em blinked in confusion. Was it shaking her hand?

'Oh, hello, Emma,' the entity purred. 'What a pleasure it is to finally meet you in person. My name is Oracle, and we have a lot to discuss.'

-16-

Em found herself unable to move, her throat paralysed, her mouth dry.

The only sound she could hear was her own breathing.

A voice inside her head screamed at her to move, turn around, run away, escape from Oracle.

But she couldn't. She was immobile.

Throughout it all, Oracle stayed put, facing Em with its head cocked, almost as if it was curious. Em closed her eyes and focused on her breathing. *Get a grip. Stop embarrassing yourself. Remember what Cornelius taught you.* After what seemed like an eternity, and feeling more in control, Em opened her eyes and saw Oracle was still staring at her, but its mouth had widened into a broad smile. Which only made it even creepier.

'Um, hi,' said Em finally and inwardly cringed. *Oh, come on. You're the leader of a community. Act like it.* She cleared her throat and tried again. This time with a bit more confidence. 'Nice to meet you, Oracle. I've heard so many things about you.'

Oracle smirked and tilted its head. 'Oh, I am sure you have. A lot of it was not good, I expect.' It pouted and shook its head in apparent disapproval, tutting. 'Tsk. Tsk. Has Wendy ... sorry, Hilaria been telling tales about me?' Before Em could answer, it flicked its wrist in dismissal. It gave Em a sideways look and held up a finger. 'She is a foxy little minx, is she not? Making it appear she had riled you up, making you angry enough

to kill her.' It stuck out its bottom lip and held its hands against its chest. 'All that play-acting just for little old me.'

Em started and took a step back, 'I-I d-d-don't know what you mean?'

Before Em had time to react, Oracle stepped forward, wrapped its right arm around her shoulders, and laughed. 'Oh, do not be like that, Emma. I am not angry. We are all friends here, are we not?'

What was this thing up to? Unsettled by Oracle's strange amiability, Em cocked her head and slid it a guarded look. 'When did you first suspect it was all an act?'

'I tried to check in on you a couple of days later, but you can imagine my surprise when I discovered my quantum frequency was being jammed,' Oracle responded coolly. 'That was when I realised Hilaria had tricked me.' The tone of her voice changed, becoming more dangerous. 'She made a fool out of me. If there is one thing I dislike, it is being made a fool of.'

In an instant, the expression on Oracle's face changed. Going from ice to fire. Contorting in rage. Em cried out in pain as she felt Oracle's grip tighten on her left shoulder. The pain was excruciating, like nothing she'd experienced before. It was almost as if the tips of Oracle's fingers were piercing her body armour, worming their way in between the gaps of the ball socket of her shoulder joint and striking at the nerve endings. Her vision went white and every nerve inside her body felt like it was on fire. Darkness encroached on the edges of her vision, and she knew she was just moments from blacking out. She felt her knees buckle, and she sank to the floor, gasping in pain, letting out an agonised groan. She wasn't sure how much more of this she could take.

Without warning, the fire inside her body ceased. The vice-like grip on Em's shoulder vanished, leaving just a dull ache. Relieved it was over, Em heaved a sigh as her vision slowly returned to normal. Blinking away the stars in her eyes, she lifted her head and focused on Oracle as it pulled its head back and let out a howl of laughter. She battled the urge to shudder at the sound of the laugh reverberating in her ears.

'Now, far be it from me to hold a grudge.' Oracle chuckled in amusement. 'My own fault, really, for making Wendy so damn smart. But,

hey ho. Live and learn, as you humans are so fond of saying.' Suddenly, Oracle appeared to go silent, as if distracted. Then she frowned and stared at Em in puzzlement, placing her hands on her hips and letting out a perplexed sigh. 'Now, what are you doing lying on the floor? You know, you really need to be more careful.'

The inside of her head still feeling cotton wool, Em let out a painful grunt as she felt herself unceremoniously being manhandled back onto her feet. To steady herself, she placed her left hand on the console and massaged her throbbing left shoulder with her right hand. Swallowing back the rising nausea, she concentrated on slowing her racing heart by drawing in several slow breaths. It was plainly obvious to her that the thing was insane, and if she had any chance of getting out of this alive, she realised she was going to have to tread very carefully around Oracle.

'Now, where were we?' Oracle continued as if nothing had happened. It held up a finger and beamed. 'Oh, yes. I was saying how impressed I was with you. You have come a long way from that frightened little girl who first arrived on this world those many years ago.'

The sudden change in the topic of conversation startled Em. She furrowed her brow and regarded the AI with heavy suspicion. Was Oracle deliberately appearing to act absent-minded, hoping it would keep her confused? Or was it purposely trying to rattle her by bringing up her past? Having already experienced its homicidal wrath, she wanted to be careful, but at the same time, she was adamant she would not play its game. Her jaw tightening in rigid determination, Em fixed a defiant gaze on the grinning entity.

'You don't know the first thing about me,' she replied, matching Oracle's manic smile.

Smirking, Oracle bobbed its head and waggled its right index finger. 'Au contraire, mon ami. I know more about you than you think.' It turned and swept its hands over the chamber. 'I was in here the night you arrived, watching in secret.' Its bottom lip jutted out and it shook its head sorrowfully. 'Poor little Emma, all alone in this world. No friends. No family. Betrayed by her twin sister.' The corners of its mouth slowly turned up, forming a malevolent grin while it leaned in closer and whispered in Em's ear, 'What would Claire think if she saw you, hmm? Would she be

proud of what you have accomplished, or would she be disgusted at the things you have done in order to survive?'

With her anger churning away inside her, Em breathed heavily to control her rising temper. She desperately wanted to remove the smirk from that odious face. But she knew that wouldn't accomplish anything. Deep down, a part of her knew it was deliberately provoking her. Was it hoping to provoke her so that she would retaliate in anger? She sharpened her eyes and shot Oracle a murderous look. No, whatever it was doing, she was determined she would not give it the satisfaction of thinking it had got to her.

While keeping a tight lock on her emotions, she blew out a heavy sigh, held up her hands and returned Oracle's grin. 'I guess we'll never find out, will we?' she said carefully. 'Because I'm certain I will never see Claire ever again.'

If Oracle was annoyed by Em's unwillingness to play its game, Em couldn't tell. Instead, it tilted its head and gave a sly smile. 'I met her, you know.'

Not the comment she was expecting, Em felt her eyes grow wide, blurting out, 'Sorry?'

'Claire,' answered Oracle in a tone that almost sounded smug. 'I met her recently. I am sure you are dying to know what she has been up to since you last saw her.'

Afraid of what she would say if she opened her mouth, Em remained silent. Deep down, though, she was desperate to learn anything she could about her sister's life. Was she married? Were their parents still alive? How could she say yes without coming across too eager? She closed her eyes and drew in a long breath through her nose. No, Oracle was only toying with her, playing with her emotions. She needed to remain strong.

'Oh, the stories I can tell you about your sister.' Oracle sighed, its tone taunting. Em flinched as she sensed it had moved closer to her, and she felt its artificial breath on her neck. 'With you out of the picture, Claire had a successful life. Rich and famous. Women want to be like her. Men want to be with her. She's the envy of millions. She's left a trail of broken hearts, sleeping with anything with a pulse.'

Furious at the implication that her sister was a whore, Em opened her eyes and shot Oracle an angry glare.

It took all her willpower to hold her tongue as Oracle pulled its head back and let out a cruel laugh. 'I very much doubt she even remembers you.'

Even though Em knew Oracle was deliberately provoking her, she couldn't stop herself from bristling with indignation and took a step back from Oracle and scowled at it. It took every ounce of self-control she had to keep her tone neutral. 'I think you're lying,' she answered slowly through gritted teeth. 'Our parents would never let that happen. They would have made sure a day didn't go by without them reminding her who I was to her.' She straightened with conviction and raised her voice. 'The same blood that burns through me also burns through my sister. We are one and the same. Two hearts as one. Though we may be separated by dimensions, one thing I am certain of is that her love for me will never be extinguished.' Drawing her lips back in a scornful sneer, Em jabbed her finger into her own chest. 'Yes, I may have lost sight of that. But someone recently helped me understand my love for my sister is still within me. I'd just forgotten about it.'

Oracle lifted its shoulder in an indifferent shrug. 'Maybe, maybe not,' it huffed. It lowered its head, a cruel smile forming across its face. 'But what is true is that she thinks you are dead. Not only that, but she holds herself responsible for your death.' It pouted and shook its head in obvious mock sorrow. 'Oh, can you imagine what it must have done to her? All these years, carrying around all that guilt.'

'Up yours,' Em retorted. 'I hope you burn in hell.'

'Now, now,' Oracle said, smiling and placing its hand against its chest in an obvious attempt at theatrical mock distress. 'What would your daughter think if she heard her mother using such language? Hmm? I do not think Henrietta would like that, now, would she? Then again, I doubt she would even care. Because in her mind, you were somebody who treated her like a piece of rubbish; something to be discarded without a second thought.'

What did it just say? Em reared back in shock. Then it was as if something exploded deep within her. Outrage bubbled in the pit of her

stomach and she balled her hands into tight fists. Oh no, it was one thing for Oracle to use her sister's name against her, but then to ridicule her daughter's name. No way in hell was Em prepared to let that pass. Not caring about the consequences, she took an angry step forward and jabbed her finger into Oracle's chest.

'Don't. You. Dare. Mention. My. Daughter's. Name,' Em snarled dangerously through clenched teeth.

For several seconds, Oracle just stared at Em, unmoving. As Em stared into its cold yellow eyes, she felt her stomach muscles tighten in fear and she wondered if she'd just made a huge mistake. It was almost as if the yellow eyes were burning into Em's soul and, for the first time, she got a sense of just how dangerous the AI was. She held her breath and waited for the stinging sensation of her neck snapping. But that did not happen. Instead, Oracle lowered its chin, stared at the finger on its chest and let out a derisive snort. Then, with deliberate slowness, it pushed Em's finger away and grinned.

'Cooper never told you what happened to your daughter, did she?'

Immediately, Em could see what Oracle was trying to do. It was trying to use the knowledge that General Cooper had killed Henrietta to its advantage. She guessed it was hoping to plant the seed that would destroy their neo-relationship. She raised an eyebrow as a thought occurred to her. Was that why it had allowed her to get this far? Was it part of some twisted scheme? Well, if that was the case, it was going to be in for a big surprise. Ignoring the pain from her throbbing shoulder, Em raised her chin and glared at Oracle with as much defiance as she could muster. 'You're too late,' she sneered. 'Hilaria already told me she was responsible for Henrietta's death. So I'm sorry if that's spoiled whatever sick game you had planned.'

If Oracle was disappointed, she couldn't tell. It just stood in silence for several seconds, staring at her with a neutral expression. Em noticed the top of its lip twitch and she wondered if her comment had amused the AI. Oracle tapped its finger on its lip, nodded slowly, and spoke with what seemed to be deliberate slowness.

'Interesting,' murmured Oracle thoughtfully. 'After you had learned what Hilaria had done to Henrietta, I expected you to kill her. It is

clear I have underestimated you.' Em felt her blood freeze as a change came over Oracle. The tone of its voice had become harsher. 'I wonder if you still feel that way after I have shown you this.'

Puzzled by the comment, Em frowned and opened her mouth to speak. But before she had time to utter a word, Oracle spun round and swept her hand. Startled, Em took a step back in shock as a holographic image appeared before her. The image appeared to be a recording of the chamber she was now standing in. The time stamp on the top of the image showed it had been recorded just a few weeks earlier.

It made no sense to her. Why would Oracle want to show her this? At a loss as to what Oracle was up to, Em scratched her head but remained silent while she stared at the image. But just as she was about to turn and question Oracle, something in the image caught her eye. Startled, Em blinked and did a double take. *No, it couldn't be,* she thought. But as she took a step forward to get a better look, she felt her eyes widen in recognition. Yes, her eyes weren't deceiving her. That was Cooper standing in the centre of the room. She appeared to be talking to someone. Why did she look familiar? The realisation hit her like a bolt out of the blue and she instinctively covered her mouth with her hand.

Henrietta!

Before she had time to recover from seeing her daughter standing beside Cooper, Em found her eyes drawn to the figure standing just behind them. No, it wasn't possible. Em shook her head and staggered back. Suddenly, she found it difficult to breathe. It was as if somebody had punched her in the stomach. She tried to back away, but the console stopped her from going any further. She shook her head in disbelief and tried to look away. But no matter how hard she tried, she couldn't take her eyes off the figure standing behind her daughter. As much as she wanted to, she could not deny what she was seeing. The man in the image was her former husband and Henrietta's father, David Barnes.

It felt like something inside her snapped, and she let out an involuntary snarl. Her eyes tightened with fury as she fixed her gaze on David and shot daggers at him. How dare that man be in the same room as her daughter? He had no right to be there. Her chest rose and fell while

her brain exploded with fury. What gave him the right to breathe the same air as her? He ...

She was unable to stop her jaw opening as she was hit by a moment of clarity.

Hilaria. She knew. All this time she knew that David had been in the same room as her daughter but had said nothing. Her warning about only finding heartache wasn't about Henrietta. She must have been warning her about David. She creased her forehead in confusion. Something didn't feel right. She searched her memory and nodded. Yes, shortly after she'd been arrested, she had heard a rumour that David had given the order for Henrietta's memory to be wiped. Em remembered feeling betrayed by the news, believing her husband had done it out of spite to hurt her. She gazed at the image and shook her head as she tried to wrap her head around what she was seeing. What game was that conniving bastard up to?

'Just what the hell is going on there?' Em hissed, spinning and shooting Oracle a questioning look.

Oracle nodded and smiled. 'No. You are not mistaken. That is your daughter, Doctor Henrietta Claudia, standing next to your ex-husband, Colonel David Barnes.' It chuckled and held up a finger. 'Oh, I know what you are thinking. But you have nothing to worry about. Neither knew who they were to each other.' Its mouth broadened into a cruel smile and it clapped its hands excitedly. 'Oh, oh. Now this is the best bit. You are going to love what happens next.'

Her mind still reeling from what was happening, Em turned back to the holographic recording playing in front of her. As she watched the events unfold, her breathing quickened. It felt as if something was crushing the inside of her chest. Numb, she felt powerless as she watched the footage of her daughter being tortured. What was worse, David was just standing there, allowing it to happen. How could he be so callous? Why doesn't he step in to—

Then it happened.

Henrietta's head exploded and her lifeless body collapsed to the floor.

Unable to tear her eyes away, Em felt numb as she continued to watch the scene play out. Now she understood what Hilaria had been trying

to warn her about. Something a mother should never see or experience – the heartache of watching the death of one's daughter. *Oh, my poor beautiful baby.* Her heart aching in anguish, she reached out to the image. All she wanted to do was climb through it. Cradle her dead daughter's body in her arms. Scream at David for just standing there and allowing it to happen. But she was powerless. It had happened. There wasn't anything she could say or do to change it.

Just then, something else in the image made her pause, and she could only watch, in open-mouthed disbelief, what was happening before her eyes. Cooper appeared to lose control, kicking senselessly at Henrietta's dead body. Swallowing back the burning sensation of bile in her throat, Em continued to watch the image of her daughter's body being abused.

Finally, when she could no longer bear watching any more, Em staggered forward and collapsed into a seat. A plaintive sob escaped her lips, and she buried her head in her hands. She felt physically sick from what she had seen and squeezed her eyes tight in the hope it would block the images. But a feeling of despair overcame her as she realised the image of her daughter's head exploding would be forever ingrained in her brain.

After a few minutes, she managed to compose herself. She drew in a deep, controlled breath through her nose and stared at her hands. It was clear to Em why Oracle had allowed her to get this far. It was because it wanted her to see this recording. To rattle her? Or was it because it got some sick pleasure in knowing the pain it inflicted? Em didn't care. Whatever its reasons, there wasn't anything she could do about it now. But if it hoped this knowledge had broken her, well, it would soon learn, it was sadly mistaken.

Her anger depleted, feeling more in control of her emotions, Em exhaled slowly and rose from the chair. Oracle cocked its head and regarded her curiously as she turned to face it. Em folded her arms across her chest and waited for Oracle to make the first move.

'Well?' Oracle asked after a few seconds of silence.

'Oh, I know what you're waiting for,' Em said with such deliberate calmness it even surprised herself. 'You're waiting for me to scream out in anger. Listen while I swear revenge on Cooper over the death of my daughter.' Without waiting for a response, Em took a step forward and

spat in Oracle's face. 'Shame. On. You. You should be ashamed of yourself for using my daughter's death in your machinations.' She spun around and angrily jabbed her finger at the spot where Henrietta had died. 'That woman who tortured Henrietta is not the woman I know. That Cooper no longer exists. The woman I saw here was nothing more than a cold, calculating monster, controlled by an even crueller inhuman freak.' Drawing herself up to her full height, Em folded her arms across her chest and curled her top lip in disgust. 'Sorry, *my sweet*, but it looks like all your efforts to lead me up here were for nothing.'

For what felt like an eternity, Oracle just stood and stared at Em. Em felt her stomach tighten and she wondered whether spitting in its face had been the right thing to do. She'd expected it to be furious and angrily lash out at her. But it was just standing there, looking amused. When it did finally react, it didn't react the way she was expecting. It leaned its head back and howled with laughter. Perplexed and annoyed, Em took a step back and scowled at it. What did it find so funny?

'Oh, Emma, my sweet,' Oracle breathed, bringing its hands up in a slow clap. 'I am afraid you have got it all wrong. I did not do all this for you.'

Baffled and feeling like she was on the receiving end of a poor joke, Em scratched her head and screwed up her face in confusion. 'Huh? But why did you allow me to get all this way, if it wasn't for me to see all of this?'

Oracle let out what sounded like an impatient sigh and placed its hands on her shoulders. 'Oh, my dear, I did not really care whether you saw it or not. But I have to admit, I did get a thrill watching you react to your daughter's death.' Em felt a chill run down her spine as the corners of its mouth curled up into a cryptic smile. 'You were not the real prize.'

'W-what do you mean, I-I wasn't the real prize,' stammered Em.

Oracle spun away from Em and clapped merrily, laughing. 'Oh, you should see the look on your face. You look positively bewildered, my dear.' It stopped, held up its hands with its fingers pressed together, and spoke in a slow and patient tone. 'Okay, let me explain it slowly in a way your monkey brain can understand.' It pointed its finger at Em and spoke

in a slow, condescending tone. 'You. Were. Not. The. One. I. Was. After. Do. You. Understand?'

Irked by Oracle's patronising attitude, Em gritted her teeth and hissed, 'Stop being facetious and get to the point.'

'Fine,' Oracle huffed. 'You want the truth? I will give you the truth. Yes, you are right. As you have guessed, I allowed *you all* to enter the building. Truth is, I could have killed you all at any time I wanted. But if I did that, then I would not have been able to test out my children.'

Frowning, Em cocked her head in puzzlement. 'Your children, what child—' Em stiffened as it dawned on her what Oracle was getting at. The whole thing had been a trap, and she'd led them right into it. She felt the blood drain from her face and widened her eyes in alarm. 'No. How could you?'

Oracle threw its hands up in the air and spun around, laughing triumphantly. 'Oh, she finally gets it.'

Horror struck, Em stood rooted to the spot, frozen by indecision. Her mind felt like it was spinning. She shifted her gaze back to the door and then back to Oracle. What should she do? Should she run? She shook her head frantically. No, she needed to warn Isaac first, let him know they were in danger. Her stomach churning with anxiety, she reached up to activate her visor's communicator. But she stiffened in shock on hearing Isaac's voice in her earpiece.

'*Em, are you there? Please answer me.*'

A malevolent grin formed across Oracle's face, and it gestured to the earpiece in Em's ear. 'I think that is for you.'

Em's breath hitched in her throat while she listened to Isaac. There was something in his voice that she never thought she would hear – panic and terror. She could make out the sounds of weapons fire followed by small explosions.

'*Oh, my gods. They're coming out of the walls, Em, if you are listening to me. The children, Oracle has done something to the children. Roj and Del are dead. Get out now. I repeat, you need to run. They are coming for you, Em. I repeat, they are coming for you.*'

-17-

Panic threatened to consume Em, and she struggled for breath. Her chest felt like it was tightening, and the walls felt like they were closing in on her. *Too overwhelming. I need to think*. She became aware of the clamminess of her hands and self-consciously wiped them against her clothing, which now felt tight and restrictive. She squeezed her eyes shut and tried to block everything out, but was still conscious of Oracle's gaze burning into her skull. Why couldn't the universe just leave her alone, for once? Could it not give her a break?

Em furrowed her brow in puzzlement as she once again heard Isaac's voice in her ear. Then she heard the unmistakable sounds of weapons fire, followed by what sounded like another voice. No. That was wrong. Not just one voice. Several voices. They sounded like they were coming from behind Isaac. Far away, but close enough for the amplifier in Isaac's throat mic to pick up. All speaking as one, overlapping one another. Em focused on the whispering voices, trying to discern what they were saying. Then she heard them, and she felt her blood freeze in horror. The voices all sounded like children, repeating the same words over and over…

'*Mommy is very angry.*'

By the gods. Now I remember. Em staggered back in shock as if someone had slapped her in the face, snapping her back to reality. She spun around and stared at Oracle in horror. The synapses in her brain began firing. She felt her eyes grow wide in cold realisation as the pieces of the puzzle started to come together.

How come she hadn't seen it before?

It had all been too easy. Their trouble-free journey to the city. The absence of security patrols hadn't gone unnoticed by Em – that should have been the first warning. Next, the assimilated animals, she should have realised something was wrong when they hadn't attacked. Using Hilaria's codes to access the hatch, operate the magnitran and gain entry to the building. It had all been too easy. The codes should have been disabled and their access blocked. The only time Em's suspicions were aroused was when she heard Oracle's voice, but again, she had ignored her instincts. Finally, the prisoners. They should have been assimilated, but they had been left alone. Why?

Because they had been the bait, that's why.

Em bristled in anger. She'd fallen for it. Oracle had dangled the prisoners like a worm on a hook, knowing Emma wouldn't be able to resist such a tempting prize. Overcome with rage, Em let out a primal scream and smashed her fist on the console. Oracle had played her; she seethed. Oh, she thought she had been so clever. Sneaking into the base, rescuing the prisoners, unaware that that was exactly what Oracle desired.

'I see you have finally pieced it together,' Oracle said, grinning. 'It was I who planted the suggestion inside Hilaria's head to tell you about the prisoners still being held captive. Once you learned that, I knew you would not be able to resist the urge to investigate.' It raised its chin and sneered in disdain. 'You are just like your sister – so predictable.'

Enraged, Em spun round and fixed Oracle with a blistering stare. 'Is that what this was about?' she snarled. 'Getting your hooks into us? Into me? Have your unholy monsters turn us into one of them?'

'Oh, I do not want my children to assimilate you.' Oracle laughed. 'I want them to kill you.'

Not the answer she was expecting, Em felt her mouth drop open in shock and gave Oracle an unbelieving look, exclaiming, 'What?'

Oracle placed its hands on its hips and shook its head, sighing with obvious over-theatrical impatience. 'Oh, fine. I will tell you.' It pursed its lips thoughtfully and held up a finger. 'You humans are a baffling species. Take your children, for instance. Seriously, what is the point of having those odious meat bags? They serve no purpose other than to be a drain

on resources. They were not strong enough to use as drones, so I kept them in stasis. I even considered switching off their stasis pods, killing them all. But then I had an epiphany of sorts. Do you know what it was?' Before Em could utter a reply, Oracle turned away and paced around the chamber while it continued with its monologue. 'Recently I was trying to think of a creative way to execute someone, and I came up with a rather ingenious idea of what to do with the children. They are very supple and nimble little creatures. Once converted, they would make ideal hunter drones. Like synthroids, but much more controllable. So I travelled to this reality so that I could put my plan into action.'

Oracle came to a sudden stop and stared at the glowing portal with narrowed eyes.

'Something strange happened when I crossed over into this world. I discovered that time in this universe appeared to be moving a lot slower compared to time in the prime universe. From my perspective, this is four weeks ago.' Em jumped back in fright as Oracle's face turned thunderous and it shouted at the portal, 'I know what you are doing, you old fool. This is your final warning. Stop interfering, or you and I will have words. You, of all people, are aware of the repercussions when altering time during transit.'

Despite being deeply puzzled at who Oracle was talking to, Em realised that she had an opportunity to escape. Hoping to flee unnoticed, she knew she'd have to leave the chamber quickly. She held her breath, reached for the rifle that she had placed against the console when she first came in and slowly inched backwards towards the chamber exit. As she did so, her gaze shifted between the door and the ranting Oracle, and she prayed the AI would continue to talk to itself long enough for her to slip out undetected. With every step she made, she felt her heart slam against her ribcage as she inched closer towards the chamber's doorway.

Just another couple of steps. That's all it will take— argh!

Oracle had moved so fast, Em had barely enough time to react. She cried out in pain as something grabbed her arm and held it in a vice-like grip. Trying to ignore the searing pain coming from her arm, she blinked away the tears as Oracle spun her around. The fury in its yellow eyes was almost incandescent as it stared at Em with murderous intent.

'Where do you think you are going?' Oracle snarled. 'Did you think I was going to let you spoil my enjoyment of watching my children tear you apart?'

'No, please,' Em begged desperately. 'Give me a chance, at least.'

Her mind raced as she desperately sought an escape from her predicament. The pit of her stomach fell as she struggled to come up with an idea. There had to be a way for her to get out of this unscathed. There had to be. Then, just when she thought she was out of options, an idea hit her. Something Cornelius had taught her. When faced with a narcissistic personality, the best thing to do was hit them at their weakest point – their ego. Em was certain Oracle had a massive ego. Sure, it was an insane plan, and she was risking bodily harm stroking Oracle's ego, but she had no choice. Desperate times called for desperate measures.

'W-w-ait,' Em hissed, holding up her free hand. 'W-w-why don't we make this a game?'

Much to Em's surprise, Oracle released Em's arm and stared at her in wide-eyed astonishment. The astonished expression only lasted a few moments as it morphed into a hardened look. It took a step back and regarded Em with obvious suspicion.

'Explain.'

Quickly thinking on her feet, Em massaged the tender spot on her upper left arm and scowled at Oracle. 'First, call off your attack,' Em demanded flatly.

Oracle's expression instantly sharpened. 'Why would I do that?'

Determined not to show any fear, Em lifted her chin and smiled. 'Because if one more member of my team dies, I will refuse to explain my idea to you.'

Oracle's yellow eyes blazed with incandescent fury. Em flinched as its right hand shot out, stopping just millimetres from her neck. 'Then,' it hissed, 'you will die where you stand.'

Not caring about the consequences, Em stood firm and locked eyes with Oracle. 'Then I will die,' she replied adamantly. She leaned forward and smiled, whispering, 'But know this. I can die secure in the knowledge that I beat you. Because even though I didn't physically hurt you …' She paused and pressed her finger into her right temple. 'I beat you

in here. You will be forever wondering what the game was. For an AI, I'm sure that would be torture.' She leaned in closer to Oracle and scoffed, 'Who's the superior being now?'

She expected an explosive outburst from Oracle, perhaps even a scream. But it did nothing; it just stood there and stared at Em, its face an unreadable mask. An uneasy silence filled the chamber while they continued to stare at one another. For a split second, Em wondered what was going through the AI's artificial mind, and she thought she caught a touch of indecision on its face. Or maybe it had just been a trick of light.

Finally, Oracle broke the deadlock with a disgusted huff and slowly withdrew its hand. 'Fine,' it said tersely. 'I have done what you asked, now explain.'

Not wanting to trust the word of something that had just threatened to kill her, Em raised her left hand and activated her communicator with her right. Ignoring the impatient death scowl coming from Oracle, she turned and spoke out loud into her throat mic.

'Isaac? You still there, over?'

The tension was almost unbearable while Em waited for Isaac to respond. Em forced back the rising terror as she wondered whether she had been too late in getting Oracle to stop her attack. What would happen to her plan then? Before she could answer that, her heart swelled with relief upon hearing Isaac's voice in her earpiece. Never had that Gondwanian accent sounded so beautiful.

'Em? You okay?' came Isaac's reply. Em wasn't sure, but she thought he sounded breathless. *'What's going on? Those things, they've suddenly stopped chasing us. Over?'*

'No time to explain,' Em snapped. 'Head straight to the hangar level. Don't, I repeat, don't attempt to access the hangar until you receive word from me. Over.'

'Um, acknowledged and understood. Over and out,' Isaac replied, the confusion clear in his tone. Em could tell he didn't understand, but reckoned he trusted her enough not to question her.

'Well, I have done what you have asked,' Oracle repeated brusquely as Em turned back toward it.

She held Oracle's gaze and stood straight with her hands held together in front of her. 'It is quite simple,' she explained. 'You need to test your latest creations' abilities to hunt down their quarry and terminate them. Isn't that right?' Oracle responded with a curt nod and Em continued. 'So I propose we make this a game. Ten of your hunters against my team. A no-holds-barred game of tag, if you will. The aim is for them to stop us from boarding the shuttle we have … obtained. Those already on-board are safe and untouchable. Those of us that don't make it …' She trailed off and held up her hands. Words didn't need to be said. It was clear those who wouldn't make it would be dead.

Oracle arched an eyebrow, and it gave her a look of veiled interest. 'You make an intriguing suggestion. But why limit it to only ten of my little darlings?'

'To make it a fair competition,' Em answered flatly. 'After all, two of my people have already died.'

Oracle tapped her bottom lip thoughtfully as if it was considering Em's offer. The corners of its mouth slowly curled up into a wicked smile and it arched its head. 'But what is it in for me? What do I gain from this, hmm?'

Em kept her face neutral, but inwardly she was screaming with delight. *Yes, I knew it wouldn't be able to resist a challenge. Now, I simply have to slowly reel it in.* She cringed inwardly. Did she really just think it was going to be as simple as reeling Oracle in? Already committed to the deed, and having expected the question, she had an answer ready. She pretended to laugh nervously and bowed respectfully. 'I'm sure one as glorious as you would like people to recognise your benevolent nature.' Hoping to add to her performance, she wrung her hands while she continued to speak. 'Those prisoners, the ones already safely on-board the shuttle, think of them as spectators of your grand spectacle. Once the game is over, they will spread the word that you played fairly. Not only that, but word of your compassionate nature will also spread far and wide.' Em knew she was laying it on thick, but she hoped inflating Oracle's ego might make the AI more amenable to her idea.

After a brief silence, Oracle gave Em a pointed look and smiled. 'I know what you are doing.'

Panic bubbled inside Em and she felt her stomach churning. She kept her face neutral, while mentally she was chastising herself for being too clever to think she could pull the wool over Oracle's eyes. Determined to hold her nerve, she struggled to remain calm as she watched Oracle, who continued to fix her with a steady gaze while it paced around the chamber.

'You are trying to keep me distracted,' Oracle said. 'You are hoping that with my attention fixed on you, it will give your friends enough time to escape.' Em swallowed back a reply but remained impassive as the corners of Oracle's mouth curled up into a cryptic smile. 'I must commend you on your bravery, my dear. Sacrificing oneself is such a noble deed, do you not think?' She waved her hand and laughed. 'Although I respect your efforts, they are unnecessary. You see, there is something in your offer I find appealing.'

Still waiting for the other shoe to drop, Em raised an eyebrow and gave Oracle a sideways look. 'So, what have you decided?'

'Have I not made myself clear? I agree to your terms,' Oracle answered in a matter-of-fact tone.

Em heaved a sigh of relief and bowed gratefully. 'You are so wise.'

'Do not push it,' Oracle growled.

Pretending to look sheepish, Em dropped her chin and cleared her throat. 'Ahem. Sorry. What if we formalise this agreement by shaking on it?' She raised her right hand to her mouth, spat on it, and then extended it.

The disgust on Oracle's face was clear to see as it stared at the offered hand; it reminded Em of someone who was being offered something covered in shit. Oracle made a sour face and waved away the hand. 'No, thank you. I am good,' it said in a tone filled with disdain.

As she gazed at the sneering entity, it dawned on Em that she had possibly outstayed her welcome. She gave a polite cough and turned to leave. 'I had better be going so I can prepare my team.'

But as she turned and headed for the chamber's exit, Em came to a sudden stop as she felt Oracle's hand on her shoulder. Her heart leapt into her throat and she feared the worst; Oracle had changed its mind and had decided to kill her after all. Her buttocks clenching together in fear, Em turned stiffly around and tried to keep her unease from showing on

her face. But then her unease changed to confusion. She had expected Oracle's face to be full of fury. But its expression was unreadable, so it was difficult to judge what was going through its mind.

'I did not give you permission to leave,' Oracle said flatly. Then it released Em's shoulder and laughed. 'Oh, relax, my dear. If I wanted to kill you, I would have done so. I can see you are eager to leave, so I will not take up much more of your time. But just so you know, I have come up with something to spice up the game.'

A seed of unease grew inside Em, and she narrowed her eyes in suspicion as alarm bells rang inside her head. 'Interesting in what way?'

'Oh, my dear, why so serious? Are we not friends here?' Oracle laughed, stroking Em's face. Em set her jaw and had to force herself from pulling away while she listened to Oracle continue. 'The game sounds boring and needs something exciting. So I have decided I will give you a ten-minute head start.' It held up its hand as if to ward off any questions. 'Now, I know what you are thinking. You are wondering how giving you a head start makes it exciting.' A shiver ran down Em's spine as a maniacal grin spread across Oracle's face. It took a step back and clapped its hands excitedly. 'The exciting part is, I have locked you out of the transport-pods, so you must take the stairs. What do you think of that? Game changer, huh?'

Not believing what she'd just heard, Em blinked and shook her head. 'Ten minutes!' she exclaimed, her voice going an octave higher. 'How can I descend sixty flights of—'

'One hundred and ninety-eight.'

'What?' Em snapped, annoyed and confused by the interruption.

'You forgot there are four flights of stairs to each level,' Oracle explained patiently. 'Also, the hangar is on level ten. So, you only need to make it down fifty floors, not sixty. But to answer your question, there are one hundred and ninety-eight flights of stairs between you and the hangar level ... not sixty.'

'Okay,' Em said carefully, trying to keep control of her temper. 'How am I supposed to make it down one hundred and ninety-eight flights of stairs in ten minutes? That is—'

'Nine minutes and forty seconds.'

Em closed her eyes, feeling a headache coming on, pinched the bridge of her nose and blew out an impatient sigh, 'Sorry, what?'

Oracle tilted its head and gave Em a sickly-sweet smile. 'Sorry, my dear. But you said ten minutes. When in actuality it is now nine minutes and forty seconds …' It paused and held up a finger. 'No, sorry. Make that nine minutes and twenty seconds. Clock is ticking, monkey girl. Tick-tock. Tick-tock. Tick-tock.'

-18-

Her anger churning away inside her, Em fumed and shot Oracle a hateful stare. But she could see there was no point arguing with it. That would only waste precious time, something she didn't have. It was obvious Oracle was changing the rules as it saw fit. Then it hit her, and she slapped her brow in frustration. Stupid! She should have set the rules beforehand. That had left it wide open for Oracle to make things even more difficult. Once again, she'd played right into its hands.

Believing exchanging pointless barbs would only waste more valuable time, Em spun on her heel and raced toward the chamber's exit without saying another word. Barely giving time for the door to fully open, Em ducked under the door and set her jaw in rigid determination. No, she wasn't out of it, not by a long shot. The sound of Oracle's laughter reverberated in her ears as she charged down the corridor toward the stairwell entrance at breakneck speed.

'Isaac? You still there? Over,' Em asked breathlessly into her throat mic.

'Receiving you, Boss Lady,' Isaac answered immediately. *'Still alive and kicking. Over.'*

'I'm afraid I've underestimated Oracle,' Em said, making no attempt to hide the bitterness in her voice. 'It's locked me out from using the transport-pods. To make matters worse, it has only given me a ten-minute head start. If you are already outside the entrance hatch to the hangar, wait for me there. I'll be with you shortly. Over.'

'*Um, Em ...*' She could almost hear the concern in Isaac's voice. '*How are you going to make it down fifty floors in seven minutes? Over.*'

'Leave that to me,' Em answered tersely as she barged her way through the stairwell door and onto the landing. 'If I'm not down in five minutes, you are to blow the entrance to the hangar. That should slow those things down long enough for you to reach the transporter. Once onboard, get the hell out of here as fast as you can and don't look back. Over.' Em let out a small snort. If Oracle could change the rules, then so could she.

'*Emma ...*' Em could almost feel the concern in Isaac's voice. '*I don't want—*'

'Sergeant N'Goy, I have given you an order,' Em snapped. It had been the first time she'd ever called Isaac by his unofficial rank. 'You *will* acknowledge it. Over.'

There was a heavy silence for several seconds, and then Isaac responded in a brusque tone. '*Acknowledged ... Commander. Over and out.*'

There was a click of the communication line closing, followed by static. Em exhaled a shuddering breath and blinked away tears. She deeply despised herself for snapping at Isaac the way she did, but it had to be done. If she hadn't given Isaac that order, then it was possible he would have waited for her, and they would have both ended up dying. She ground her teeth and pushed that defeatist thought to the back of her mind. No. There was no way in hell she was going to die. She still had an ace up her sleeve, something she didn't want to share with Isaac over an open channel. It was risky and she may not end up surviving, but Em was determined not to let Oracle have the last laugh.

Out of everything Cornelius taught Em, one lesson always stuck – always have a backup plan. Before leaving base, she'd packed essentials: med kit, ammo, water, MREs, EMP grenades, baton, grappling hook, harness, and her trusty nano-winch – the last four were the items that were the most essential if her plan was to work.

Em's heart was beating so hard she could feel it pulsing on both sides of her throat as the pressure of the approaching deadline tickled the edges of consciousness, and she felt the rush of adrenaline. She needed to use that adrenaline to her advantage, to keep her focused, because

panicking would only lead to mistakes. *Come on, Em,* she thought, *you've practised this. You should be able to do this blindfolded.*

Realising her rifle would only hinder her, Em threw it down, yanked off her backpack, and dug out the four items she needed. Quick and sure, she snapped on the harness, grabbed the nano-winch and immediately scrolled through her visor's HUD, eye-clicked the winch controls, and sent it zipping up the shaft in seconds. There was a solid clunk, followed by a soft whoosh of a molecular bonding agent being ejected from the nano-winch, securing itself to the beam overhead. As soon as she saw two lines of high-tensile wire spitting out from the device, Em slipped her backpack on, grabbed hold of the baton, extended it, attached the grappling hook and wasted no time snagging the two lines hanging in front of her and securing them to the latches on either side of her waist.

Em glanced at the timer on her visor's display. Time was running out; it was now or never. 'Cornelius, I hope you're watching, because I could do with some good luck now,' she murmured and closed her eyes, exhaled and leapt over the banister.

For a second, she was weightless, followed by the feeling of being jerked back as the two wires bore the weight of her body. Then the pain hit, taking her breath away. She grimaced at the pain of her body's core muscles screaming in protest while she struggled to keep her body perfectly balanced. *Oh crap! How could I have forgotten this part?* The strain on her body was so intense it took every ounce of her willpower to keep her body from tipping over. To Em's surprise, she discovered that if she relaxed, her body's muscle memory automatically took over.

Wow! Em nodded in approval. *I might actually live through this after all.*

As she lowered her head and stared down the apparently bottomless shaft, a sense of exhilaration took over. Em had forgotten how much she missed doing something like this. Then her euphoria evaporated as she remembered the reason she was hanging there. No, this wasn't a time for enjoyment. Her friends' lives were at stake and time was running out.

Determined to get it over as quickly as possible, Em eye-clicked a flashing icon on the nano-wench user interface. Suddenly, her head snapped back as her body accelerated down the shaft. The agony in her

core intensifying, Em's breathing quickened as she strove to keep her balance, and a groan escaped her lips as every part of her body screamed in protest. *Oh yeah, I'm definitely going to feel this tomorrow.*

Swiftly hurtling down the shaft, the floors became a blur as they shot past her. Twenty-five … eighteen … fifteen … *Just another five to go,* she thought hopefully. Then a red warning icon flashed on the visor's display, and her heart sank. The nano-winch material reservoir was almost depleted. The presence of a micro-replicator inside the device did not eliminate the need for a material source. The limited capacity of the nano-winch prevented the replicator from creating sufficient line for Em to travel all the way down the shaft.

Em glanced forward as she felt her momentum slowing. Level fourteen … twelve … 'Come on,' she urged desperately, 'just another two floors. Please, you can do it.'

Coming to a sudden stop, Em breathed a sigh of relief upon realising she had stopped only slightly short, just above the banister of level ten. She grinned to herself. Maybe Cornelius had been watching out for her. She pulled a face and sucked on her bottom lip as she wondered how she was going to get down.

An idea popped into her head, and she righted herself. Her eyes tightened in concentration as she swayed back and forth. *Just. A. Little. Bit. Closer. Yes, got it!* Em quickly cleared the nano-wench interface menu, scrolled through the menu and selected a harness-shaped icon. She eye-clicked the release icon for her harness and the wires disengaged, sending her flying forward.

And then she realised she had made a huge mistake.

As she flew over the handrail, it dawned on Em that she was not as young and agile as she used to be. She felt her right foot catch the upper edge of the railing. Panic set in and she flailed her arms desperately as she tried to stop herself from hitting the wall. She let out a loud oomph as her back struck the wall, knocking the wind out of her, before landing on the floor in a stunned heap.

Dazed, Em blinked away stars and found herself on her back, gazing at the ceiling. She laughed as she heard Cornelius's voice in her head, reminding her that any landing she could walk away from was a good

landing. She placed her hand on her forehead and smiled. If only her primary school gymnastics teacher could see her now.

Em's glee was immediately cut short as she heard noises; she furrowed her brow in confusion. It sounded like weapons fire, and it was coming from the other side of the door. Were Isaac and his team engaged in a firefight? She glanced at her timer – there were still a few minutes remaining until Oracle's deadline. She felt her stomach twist with dread; she suspected the AI hadn't upheld its side of the bargain.

Ignoring the pain coming from her aching body, Em grunted and climbed to her feet. She pulled the spare pistol from her backpack and charged through the door into the corridor, only to come to a complete stop at the scene greeting her.

Even through her helmet, the smell of acrid smoke caught the back of her throat and she felt her eyes grow wide as she took in the scene before her. It was as if all of hell had broken loose. Fires raged everywhere and debris littered the floor. Through the smoke, Em could just make out Isaac, Peter, and Xander behind a makeshift defensive barrier, firing at anything that moved in the smoke-filled corridor. Movement caught Em's eye, coming from just in front of the barrier. Then she saw Yuto, his Katana blade held proudly in front of him, slashing at everything that moved.

As she moved closer to her comrades, Em felt her blood freeze at the horrifying sight greeting her. It took a moment for her brain to register what she was staring at. The passageway was full of children of varying ages and sizes. No matter where she looked, they covered the walls, ceiling, and floor. When one fell victim to weapons fire, another appeared to take its place. They reminded Em of a swarm of locusts, just surging forward as one, devouring everything in their path. But that wasn't what Em found horrifying. What horrified her was the condition of the children. Apart from cybernetic components covering parts of their bodies, they were all naked, their skin glistened with the strange techno-organic circuitry covering their bodies. A chill ran down her spine as she glimpsed their yellow eyes.

Anger surged inside Em, breaking her out of her frozen stupor. How could Oracle do this? She seethed. They were all just innocent

children. What type of monster would do this? Fuelled by her rage, Em charged towards her comrades. Isaac spun around with his rifle held up as if ready to fire, but appeared to relax when he saw who it was.

'Welcome to the party, Boss,' Isaac said grimly. The right side of his helmet was shattered and a trail of blood ran down the right side of his face from a gash in his forehead.

'I think my invitation got lost in the post,' Em answered without humour. 'You don't mind if I gatecrash?'

Isaac jumped up, fired his rifle, and ducked back down. 'You're welcome any time, Em. Glad you could make it.'

She narrowed her eyes and made a sweep of her hand. 'What's the sitrep?'

'Not good,' Isaac answered bitterly. He gestured to the three bodies lying on the floor just in front of the barricade and shook his head sadly. 'We've already lost Rahul, Raelle, and Felix.'

Her heart filling with grief, Em blinked back the tears, and she placed a comforting hand on Isaac's shoulder. 'Oh, god. I'm sorry, Isaac. I wish I had got here sooner.'

'I don't think you would have made much difference,' Isaac answered bluntly. He drew in a heavy sigh and stared at her with a bleak expression. 'We're holding on, but it won't be long before they overwhelm us. Em, can I ask you a favour?' He pointed to the weapon in her hand. 'I don't want to become one of them, can you—'

'Don't you dare finish that sentence. We're not out of this yet, mister,' Em hissed, cutting Isaac off. She lifted the corner of her mouth into a secretive smile while she reached into her backpack and pulled out an EMP grenade. 'Have you forgotten? I never go into a situation without a contingency plan.'

Isaac's eyes grew wide in shock, and then he grinned. 'I love you,' he whispered. He started as if he suddenly realised what he'd said, and stammered, 'S-s-sorry Em, that slipped out. I-I-'

'It's okay, Isaac. I know,' Em whispered, placing a reassuring hand on his shoulder. They lapsed into silence and stared knowingly into each other's eyes.

'Hey, guys,' Peter shouted, his tone filled with impatience while he blasted at everything that moved. 'Can we save this love-in for another time. I don't think you've noticed, but our hosts are getting rather impatient.'

Em felt her face flush and gave a sheepish nod. 'We can talk about it later, but right now we've got this to deal with.' She activated her communicator and raised her voice. 'Gemma, you receiving me? Over.'

'Receiving you loud and clear, Commander,' Gemma replied in her earpiece. *'What do you need? Over.'*

'Switch off anything electrical in the shuttle,' Em said bluntly. 'I repeat, switch off anything electrical in the shuttle. Over.'

'Uh, roger that, Commander. I'm switching off everything electrical. Good luck and godspeed. Over and out.'

His forehead wrinkling, Isaac looked quizzically at Em and held his hands palms up in a what-the-hell gesture. 'Erm, Boss, it's not that I don't trust you know what you are doing, but I sincerely doubt that small EMP grenade will take out all our new friends.'

Em gave a devious wink and grinned. 'Oh, this isn't just your run-of-the-mill EMP. This is the mother of all EMPs, designed by my old mentor himself. He made me memorise the schematics just in case I needed to build one. Lucky for us, I still remember. Let me warn you, though, when this thing goes off, it will fry every single circuit board, computer, and power conduit within a quarter of a mile. That includes our cybernetic friends.' She lifted her head and called out, 'Okay, guys, when I give the word, cover your eyes because things are about to get bright. Yuto, I suggest you find some cover.'

'Sorry, Emma-San,' Yuto called back in a breathless tone. 'I'm afraid I cannot do that. My dance partners are getting impatient, so I think it is best I keep them entertained until you can deliver their nice present.'

Em gave a silent bob of her head in understanding. If Yuto abandoned his position, there was a high probability that their position would be overrun before she could release the EMP. Holding the grenade securely in her right hand, she sucked in a long breath and pressed her thumb over the scanner on the outer edge of the grenade. There was a soft

beep, and the grenade began pulsing a steady blue that gradually increased in speed.

With the grenade clutched tight in her hand, Em sprang up from her position and threw it as far as she could. Squeezing her eyes shut, she dropped back down and waited. Five seconds later, the grenade detonated. She screwed up her face as a wave of energy slammed into her. She felt like she was trapped inside an electrical storm as energy cascaded over her body. The hairs on the back of her neck tingled, and she wanted to scream out in agony. It felt like every nerve ending in her body was on fire.

Then, no sooner than it had begun, it was over. The tingling in her body subsiding, Em slowly opened her eyes and gasped. She'd experienced nothing like that in her life. Although she'd never been inside one, she wondered if that was what it was like being tortured inside a re-education pod. Frowning, she wondered if that was where Cornelius had got the idea from. He had always warned that these EMP grenades should only be used as a last resort, and now she could see why. They were a truly fiendish weapon.

With the inner circuitry of her helmet destroyed, there was no point in wearing it, so she removed it and cast it to one side. A soft moan came from beside her, but as she turned to investigate, she had to stifle a laugh at what she saw. Xander and Peter's eyes were both wide, and they had a dazed look about them. The hairs on the top of their heads were sticking outward, as if full of static. She cast her eye at Isaac, who sat up and stared at her with a stunned expression. He coughed and Em thought she saw a small puff of smoke escape from his mouth.

'By my ancestors,' Isaac croaked. 'I feel like someone just deep fried me.'

Commiserating with Isaac's sentiments, Em nodded and gingerly got to her feet. As she poked her head over the barrier, her mouth dropped open in shock at the devastation that had been caused. Fires raged all along the corridor from overloaded power conduits. Wires hung from the ceiling from lights that had been short-circuited by the pulse. The emergency lighting kicked in and Em saw the true casualties of the EMP. Sorrow filled her heart as she gazed upon hundreds of bodies of children lying across

the floor. The pulse had fried their cybernetic implants as she had hoped, but she hadn't foreseen it killing them, too.

'You shouldn't blame yourself, Em,' Isaac murmured as if he had been reading her mind. He placed a reassuring hand on her shoulder. 'You had no choice. They would have slaughtered us.'

'I don't blame myself,' Em hissed, blinking away the tears in her eyes. 'I blame Oracle. It was the one who turned innocent children into soulless killing machines.'

'Well, I just hope your EMP gave that bitch a real headache,' Peter said with a cruel smile as he climbed back to his feet.

'One can only hope, my friend, one can only hope,' Em grunted back. She stiffened as she remembered something and quickly scrambled over the barricade, shouting, 'Yuto? Are you okay?'

Em felt her heart sink on seeing the prone body of Yuto lying on the floor. She silently prayed he wasn't another of her unintended victims. Her breath caught in her throat as she knelt beside him and placed a hand on his throat. However, relief soared through her when she felt him stir to her touch.

'Emma-San, I take it I am not dead, no?' Yuto groaned weakly. 'My body hurts too much for me to be dead.'

'Yes, you are alive, my friend,' Em said, relieved. 'Now let's get the hell out of here.'

A few minutes later, Em and her team were hurrying across the aircraft hangar floor. Because the EMP had fried their communications, Peter had dashed on ahead to let Gemma and Iris know they were coming. Em hung slightly behind Isaac and Xander, who were helping support Yuto. Because of his proximity to the blast, it had hit him the hardest, his nervous system taking the brunt. The pulse had also knocked out the power inside the hangar, so the emergency lighting cast an eerie gloom over the hangar floor.

As she hurried across the floor, Em smiled to see the hangar doors were still open. She was grateful Gemma had to foresight to open them

during her flight preparations, otherwise they might have struggled to get them open with no power. Slowing, she stared thoughtfully at the abandoned aircraft sitting around her. Were they still operational? Or had the EMP fried all their electrical systems? It was a shame they didn't have time to check each one because—

Wait, was that?

Em came to a sudden stop and peered into the darkness. She wasn't sure, but she thought she had detected movement from under a wing of an Eagle-class fighter. Narrowing her eyes, Em scanned the darkness. Maybe it was just her mind playing tricks on her. Dismissing it as a trick of the light, she turned to leave. Her mind drifted to Isaac as he approached their recently acquired transport. Maybe when they get home, they could finally have that heart-to-heart.

A scraping noise came from behind her, starting her out of her contemplation. Time appeared to slow down as she turned to investigate she caught movement out of the corner of her eye and felt her breath hitch as she realised in horror it was a synthroid racing towards her. She instinctively dropped to one knee and pivoted toward the threat, raising Yuto's Katana.

To her horror, Em realised she was too slow in reacting; the black-skinned creature pounced out of the gloom, its claws lashing out, knocking the weapon out of her hands. *Too fast, damn it!* Em grimaced as the creature's talons slashed across her abdomen, raking off her thin body armour in a shower of sparks. The creature attacked her with such ferocity, it took her by surprise. She raised her hands protectively and cried out in pain as the creature's body slammed her to the floor. Winded, she pressed her lips together as the shock to her spine rattled her teeth.

Now fighting desperately for her life, Em gritted her teeth and seized hold of the creature's front appendages. She squeezed her eyes shut in disgust as the creature's gruesome teeth, barely centimetres from her face, gnashed at her. A searing pain tore through her leg as she felt hind claws pierce the armour around her thighs. Out of the corner of her eye, she saw Isaac hurrying towards her, shouting her name. But deep down, she knew he would be too late to save her.

Losing her grip on the synthroid's front appendages, Em watched helplessly as it snatched its talons back and then brought them crashing down, piercing her chest armour. She let out an agonised shriek. Her shriek turned into a scream of fury when she realised that its hot, disgusting breath might be the last thing she experienced as her life slipped away.

A flash of laser fire struck the beast in the centre of its head, killing it outright, but it was too late to stop the synthroid claws from sinking deeper into her chest. Em's vision went white with pain as she felt the creature's talons pierce her heart. Her breath grew heavier, and the taste of blood filled her mouth. Darkness closing in on her, the last thought she had was of her sister; she wished she'd had the chance to reconcile with her.

'I'm sorry, Claire. Please forgive me.'

-19-

Em could feel her life slipping away.

In her semi-conscious state, she was still aware of everything around her. The intense pain that she had felt from the synthroid's talons piercing her chest was no longer there. It was now just a dull ache. Her heart rate was slowing, and it was getting harder to breathe. She wanted to cry out in anger at the injustice of it all. It was so unfair. Why did she have to die like this, on a cold, hard floor, away from everybody she cared about?

Suddenly, she felt herself being picked up off the floor, and for a moment she wondered if she was floating off to the afterlife. But then she was being jostled and she realised someone was carrying her. It had to be Isaac. He was the one who had been near her when it happened. She let out a ragged sigh. Good old reliable Isaac, it's a shame she never got to tell him how she truly felt. Why did she have to leave it so late?

'Em, honey, keep your eyes open. We're almost there,' she heard Isaac plead. Was he sobbing?

The heavy thundering of Isaac's footsteps stopped, and Em felt herself being lowered onto something soft. It must have been a cot on-board the shuttle, the ones used for personnel who had been injured. Then she felt somebody's firm hands grab her shoulders, followed by the feeling of being roughly shaken. Why were they being so rough with her? Couldn't they see she was dying?

'By the ghosts of my ancestors,' Isaac snarled. 'Don't you leave me. You hear? Do you think you're going to leave after just telling me you know how I feel about you?'

Em heard someone else's voice speaking gently to Isaac. It sounded like Gemma. Oh, sweet, reliable Gemma, Em thought, how she was going to miss her too. She was always the voice of reason.

'Isaac,' Gemma whispered urgently. 'You need to stand back and let Karen have a look at her. She says she's a doctor and she can help.'

Karen? Em thought, puzzled as to why she couldn't remember someone with that name being assigned to her recon group. Gemma must have been referring to Karen Logue, the prisoner they had rescued. But wait? Didn't Karen say she was a doctor of forensic medicine? That must mean she was dead, and they needed her to do an autopsy. No, that couldn't be right. She could still hear them, so she wasn't dead yet. Was she?

She felt somebody's hands move gently over her body. Was Karen examining her? It felt like she had such nice gentle hands ... *Ow!* Em experienced a sharp pain as Karen's hands brushed against something embedded in her chest. That was strange. Why was there something sticking out of her chest?

'The blood appears to have congealed around the talon, forming a seal around the wound,' she heard Karen say gravely. 'You did the right thing. Slicing it off the creature and leaving it in place has kept Em from bleeding out. But I must warn you, it doesn't look good. It looks like it has pierced her heart. She doesn't have long left. Her pulse is getting weaker.'

'No!' Isaac cried out, his voice sounding hoarse. Em felt herself being shaken, followed by the pain of something striking her face. 'You stubborn woman. You've never backed away from a fight in your life! Now, fight!'

Again, she felt the pain of something hard striking her face. She let out a soft groan. It was obvious he wasn't going to let her go without a fight. Why couldn't he just leave her alone? Couldn't he see all she wanted to do was sleep?

'Fight, damn you!'

This time Em gasped as once again something hard struck the side of her face. It struck her with such force it jarred her back to consciousness. *Wow,* she thought, *he's really desperate not to let me go to sleep, isn't he?*

'Isaac, stop,' she heard Gemma plead urgently. 'You're hurting her. You need to let Karen try to save her.'

'Fight, damn you,' Isaac screamed. It sounded like he was ignoring Gemma as, once again, Em felt the pain from what she now realised was Isaac's hand slapping against her cheek. 'Right now!'

She felt another jarring blow – Isaac's hand connecting with her cheek.

'You fight.'

Slap and pain.

'Do it. Fight.'

Another slap, instantly followed by the familiar dull ache of pain.

'Fiiight!' Isaac screamed between choking sobs.

Em let out a weary groan. It was obvious Isaac wasn't going to leave her alone. Maybe if she opened her eyes just once, then he'd let her sleep? Yeah, do it for Isaac, then he'll be happy she was okay and stop hitting her. Em strained to open her eyes but still could see only darkness. Wait? Why couldn't she open her eyes? Maybe if she concentrated on one eyelid at a time, then they would open? She felt her eyelid flicker slightly. *Come on, that's it.* Em thought she saw a slit of light. *Yes, I'm doing it. Just. A. Little. Bit. Further.*

Her right eyelid fully opened, and it was shortly followed by her left eyelid. Unfortunately, all Em could see was blurred shapes through a cloudy haze. She blinked away the film, refocused her vision and saw the blurred shape change into Isaac's tear-stained face. He looked as if he was smiling, too.

'Hey, you,' Em croaked weakly, licking her lips. It took everything she had to speak. 'Can you not let me die in peace?'

Before Isaac could respond, he was forcefully shoved to one side, replaced by Karen's grim face. Even in her barely lucid state, Em did not like the bleak expression on her face. It reminded her of the look someone would give when they were about to hand out some distressing news.

'Commander Tulley,' Karen said, her tone echoing her grave expression. 'You've suffered a life-threatening injury to your heart. From what I've been told, we're ten minutes away from your base, but that's still too far away. If I don't do something now, there's a danger you could go into cardiac arrest, and you'll die. I'm going to have to crank open your chest and manually keep your heart going. Do you understand what I'm saying?'

It took every ounce of strength Em had remaining to nod as she forced out a raspy reply. 'Do. What. You. Need. To. Do.'

'I'm sorry to say we can't afford to waste time by sedating you,' Karen said bluntly. 'It's going to hurt like a bugger. Because you are already semi-conscious, you'll pass out from the pain. Gemma is attaching something called a cortical stimulator to your temples. She's assured me it will help keep your brain functioning and hopefully avoid any brain damage.'

'Do ... it,' Em rasped. That took up all the strength she had left, and she closed her eyes, feeling herself once again enveloped by darkness.

Suddenly, Em felt a searing pain in the front of her chest. It felt like someone was tearing open her ribcage. The pain was unbearable. Em wanted to cry out but was unable to do so. She felt paralysed, unable to move. The pain lessened, and it felt like she was dropping into a deep, dark well, the voices becoming more distant.

'Blast,' she heard Karen say angrily. 'I'm losing her.'

No, I'm still here. Em wanted to shout out. Tell them not to give up. Even though she was desperate to let them know, urge them to continue, a part of her knew it was pointless. She was dying and there was nothing they could do to stop it. It was time she stopped fighting and accepted what was coming.

Em wasn't sure if it was because she was on the verge of death or if it was the early signs of brain damage, but she thought the surrounding darkness was becoming brighter. She saw a portal of light, emitting an orange and red light which encompassed her entire body. Panic began to set in, and Em wondered if that was Oracle's doing. Was this how Oracle assimilated its victims? Attacked them when they were at their weakest? No, not today. Em's ethereal form held up her hands and assumed a

defensive posture. If they wanted her, she wasn't going to go without a fight.

But much to Em's surprise, she didn't get assimilated. Instead, the portal opened, revealing a narrow tunnel of light just wide enough for her to enter. She was positive she could make out the shape of a person on the other end of the tunnel. A spark of understanding ignited inside her and she gazed down the narrow channel in awe. She understood what the light was. It was a doorway to the afterlife. A sense of joy swelled within her as she felt herself being pulled through the doorway and into the channel of light. It had to be Henrietta who was waiting for her. After all this time, she was finally going to be reunited with her daughter.

As her ethereal body passed through the event horizon, Em turned for one last forlorn look over her shoulder. With a heavy heart, she saw the doorway seal itself shut and exhaled a resigned sigh at the thought of leaving her comrades behind, raising her right hand in a silent goodbye. The pull growing stronger, Em felt herself speeding up, wincing and holding up her hand to shield her eyes from the brightening light that was growing in intensity.

Panic surged inside her as the mouth of the tunnel opened into a void filled with clouds of cascading energy and what looked like collapsing stars. For a moment, Em thought she was going to be swallowed up by a supernova; she tried to turn away but was unable to do so. She felt her eyes grow wide in horror and flailed her arms to stop her momentum, but it was no use; she was still heading towards the star. No, she needed to pull away, or the dying star would engulf her.

Before she could do anything, the super-giant disappeared, and a more comfortable and welcoming luminescence took its place. Em blinked away the stars in her eyes and discovered she was falling towards what she thought looked like a black floor. Stealing herself for impact, Em started when at the last moment before impact she slowed and came to a gentle stop just centimetres from the surface, before being smoothly lowered onto the floor. She frowned in puzzlement as she knelt and studied the ground she was standing on. Was it her imagination, or was she walking on a floor composed of stars?

A flash of light caught Em's eye, and she jerked her head back to

stare at what was above her. Awestruck at what she was seeing, she could only stand and stare with her mouth open. It was like nothing she had ever seen before. Mesmerised, she craned her neck back and stared at the majestic sight of a cosmic light show before her eyes. It reminded her of the holographic displays of the universe, similar to those Cornelius had shown her. She could only watch in joyful wonderment as clouds of multicoloured energy danced and swirled, and she blew out a whistle and shook her head in wonder.

'Well, Em old girl,' she whispered to herself in awe at the breathtaking sight around her. 'This certainly doesn't look like heaven. And since you're not frying to a crisp, it's safe to say it's not the other place either.'

She took in a long breath and closed her eyes. If she wanted to find out where she was, she needed to be focused and not become distracted by her surroundings. Cornelius made it a point to drill into her that it was important, whenever she was in unknown territory, she be clear-headed and must never panic. Panic would only lead to mistakes. Study her environment, learn everything she could. Ignoring her instincts was what had got her into this mess in the first place, something she was determined not to repeat.

More in control of her emotions, Em knelt and rubbed her chin thoughtfully as she took in her new environment. She was standing inside a vast hall, which appeared to stretch on forever. She arched an eyebrow and craned her neck back as she studied the celestial ceiling. It was too elaborate for it to be a hallucination. She snorted to herself; she doubted she had the imagination to create something as intricate as this. She brushed her hand over the smooth floor and tightened her eyes as she looked for any irregularity. But she could she none. She clicked her tongue and nodded. If it was a simulation, it was most certainly quite advanced, beyond the level of technology the URE possessed.

Straightening, Em brushed her hands together and turned in a slow circle. That left her with only one conclusion – she was standing in what theorists would have called a reality nexus, an area of space between dimensions. She rubbed the back of her neck as she took in the view around her. So that must have meant something powerful had transferred her consciousness here, leaving her with two questions – who and why?

Em stiffened as she thought she saw something in the distance. They were too far for her to make out, but she thought she could see two people. So, it seemed she wasn't the only person here. Were they brought here the same way as her? Em lifted her hands to her mouth and called out to them.

'Hello there,' she shouted as loudly as she could.

When no answer came, Em assumed it was because they were too far away to hear her, so she gave a small shrug and sighed. There was no point standing around shouting. If she wanted answers, then she had to get moving.

Moving at a light pace, Em headed toward the two people. As she hurried along, she noticed she wasn't getting out of breath. So, her assumption had been correct; she wasn't here physically. That must have meant this body of hers was some sort of astral projection, which explained why she was wearing a strange fluorescent white bodysuit. Was that to make her feel more comfortable? Em grinned. Well, it would have been unseemly for her to run around in her birthday suit. Whoever was behind this was probably trying to protect her modesty.

However, as she got closer, she could see the two people much more clearly. The man was wearing some sort of white evening suit and was holding a cane. He was black and looked elderly, with silver hair and a silver goatee. The woman was slightly shorter than the elderly man, about the same height as Em. She was white, had long brown hair and appeared to be wearing the same type of bodysuit as Em, which meant she too was an astral projection. Em wondered if the elderly stranger was the one responsible for them being here. Even though she was too far away to get a good look at the woman, she could tell from the way she was gesticulating that she was having an animated discussion with the silver-haired man. A troubling thought occurred to Em, and she wondered if he was a friend or a foe? If he was foe, would that mean she had just leapt out of the frying pan and into the fire?

But as Em got close enough to get a better look at the two strangers, she came to a sudden stop and let out a gasp of recognition. No,

it couldn't be. She blinked, did a double take and rubbed her eyes, but she still could scarcely believe what she was seeing.

It was Claire.

Even though it had been over forty years since they had seen each other, it was impossible for her not to recognise her twin sister. Jubilation filled her, and she ran toward Claire with her arms outstretched.

'Claire,' Em cried. 'What are you doing here? What—'

Like a horrifying nightmare, Em passed through Claire as if she were made of smoke. At a loss for words, Em couldn't believe what she was looking at. Then her confusion turned to chagrin as she wondered if this was somebody's idea of a sick joke. If it was, the perpetrator would pay, but first she needed to make sure. She reined in her anger, swallowed and slowly reached out to touch Claire. To her disappointment, the result was still the same, and her hand passed through her ethereal sister. Pushing her dissatisfaction to one side, Em regained her composure and nodded thoughtfully. From the lack of reaction on Claire's face, it was clear Claire couldn't see or hear Em, which could only mean Em was the one who was out of phase. She pursed her lips while she focused her attention on the silver-haired stranger. There was something about him that set her teeth on edge, something she couldn't place her finger on. Then she noticed his multicoloured eyes and she began to suspect who he might be. It was clear he was some sort of cosmic entity who had taken on the appearance of a kindly gentleman, hoping it would put the two women at ease.

Em realised there wasn't anything she could do but be patient and hope the elderly stranger would turn his attention to her when he finished dealing with Claire. For now, all she could do was to remain quiet and study him. Hopefully, she might even learn something interesting about Claire. But as she gazed at her sister's face, Em felt a pang of sadness at seeing the stress lines around her eyes. Not only that, but Claire carried the vibe of someone who had experienced a lot of heartache. Em found it surprising because she had always assumed that Claire had been raised in a world free of the tortures that Em had been forced to endure, and so she assumed Claire's life would have been an easy one. She could see now that wasn't the case. Anger surged within her as she realised she hadn't been there to protect her sister.

Em blinked as raised voices reminded her she was letting herself get distracted and she focused her attention back on the people in front of her. Claire had taken a step toward the stranger and jabbed a finger into his chest. From the thunderous expression on her face, it looked like something had rattled her cage.

'That was you,' Claire retorted. 'You made me sleep with Dave that night.' The statement earned a raised eyebrow from Em as she wondered if Dave was her boyfriend, but she remained silent and watched with interest while Claire's face grew a deep shade of red as she continued her verbal assault. 'What right do you have to force your will on someone like that? You ... violated me.'

The stranger appeared unrepentant and gave an indifferent shrug. 'Not really,' he said cheerfully. 'You and Dave would have slept together eventually, but I needed it to happen sooner rather than later, for you both to get to the point I needed you to be. Your feelings for one another were there. I just helped them to the surface a bit quicker.'

The stranger's smug tone ignited a surge of anger in Em. No wonder Claire was seething. If someone had done the same thing to her, she would be livid too. Claire had a right to feel used. How dare he do that to her sister? Em raised her hand and made ready to strike. Oh, if she hadn't been an ethereal spirit, she would have wiped that patronising smirk off the mysterious stranger's face.

Looking appalled, Claire let out a disgusted laugh and shook her head. 'You still can't see it was wrong, can you? You truly believe it's right to inflict your will on a person so long as you get what you want?' She spun around and threw her hands up. 'You're just like Oracle.'

Em started and inhaled a sharp breath. What was that? Oracle had mentioned meeting Claire, but at the time, Em thought it had been trying to get a reaction out of her. Was Oracle the one responsible for Claire being here? A seed of understanding grew inside Em, and she started to get a fair idea of why her sister had ended up here. Claire must have sustained severe injuries, possibly life-threatening, which compelled the stranger to step in. Em focused her attention on the stranger, who looked as if he was losing his patience with Claire.

'Maybe you're right, but I refuse to apologise if my actions result in ridding the multiverse of a dangerous threat.'

'You manipulative bastard!' Claire hissed, shooting him a scathing look.

'You tell him, sis,' Em cheered, pumping her fist. But the words died in her throat when the stranger turned toward her and fixed those multicoloured eyes of his on her. She felt the blood drain from her face as his mouth broadened into a wide grin.

'You'll probably agree with her, won't you?'

-20-

At a loss for words, Em took a step back and stared at the grinning stranger. It more or less confirmed what she already suspected – that he was the one who had brought her here. But before she could say anything, the stranger turned away from her and focused his attention back on a bewildered-looking Claire. She appeared to be staring directly at Em, and it broke Em's heart that she couldn't see her.

'Who are you talking to?'

Anger boiled inside Em. How dare he dismiss her as if she was nothing? She glared at the mysterious stranger who nonchalantly dismissed her with a flick of his wrist, laughing. 'It doesn't matter.'

She didn't matter! She didn't matter! Em was fuming. Was he purposely trying to piss her off?

A vacant look appeared over the elderly man's face as if he was staring at something that Em couldn't see. He nodded and spoke in a cryptic tone.

'That should be enough time.'

Claire massaged her brow and let out an exasperated groan. 'I'm starting to lose my patience with you, old man. You still have a lot to answer for, and I'll be damned if I'm going to let you get away with what you've done.'

Now that was something Em could agree on. She was getting really fed up with being left out of the conversation. There was so much she wanted to say to her sister, but this annoying entity was stopping her. What

she wouldn't give just to be able to give it a piece of her mind. She turned away and stared thoughtfully up at the cosmic ceiling above her head, but stopped when she noticed something out of the corner of her eye. She cocked her head from side to side and felt her eyes grow wide in recognition at the narrow mirror standing between two cushioned chairs. It dawned on her that that was what the entity must have used to spy on them. She ground her teeth in frustration. Claire was right; he was just as bad as Oracle.

An angry cry from Claire broke Em out of her distracted thoughts and she spun to see that the silver-haired stranger was holding his right hand up. At first, Em thought he was going to strike Claire, but she frowned as she realised he was just going to click his fingers. Why would that upset Claire? What—

Then it happened.

The stranger clicked his fingers, and Em felt her jaw drop open as Claire popped out of existence. One moment she was there and the next she was gone, like she'd never existed. A series of emotions ran through Em as she reached out to the spot where her sister had just been standing. Anger. Grief. Despair. It all surged within her. Em sank to her knees and buried her head in her hands. How could this happen to them both again? To lose one another, not once, but twice. Why? Was this the universe's way of tormenting them?

'Oh, you still here?'

Startled, Em lifted her head out of her hands and saw that the stranger was staring down at her, smiling mischievously. That just irked her even more. Furious, she shot up and lunged at the smirking entity, but passed through him as if he was a ghost.

The stranger tutted and wagged his finger. 'Oh, child, you're not all there, aren't you?' His mouth broadened into a cryptic smile and he raised his hand. 'We can't have that now, can we?'

The image of Claire vanishing still fresh in her mind, Em raised her hands to stop the stranger. No way was she going to leave without getting some answers first. There had to be a way she could make him listen. There just had to be. She racked her brain as she tried desperately to think of a way to stop him from using the same trick on her.

'Wait, don't—'

She was too late to stop the entity from clicking his fingers, but instead of vanishing, a wave of vertigo struck Em, and she staggered back as a strange feeling overwhelmed her. She squeezed her eyes shut and gasped. It felt like every cell in her body was tingling, almost as if she was inside a matter transporter. Then, no sooner had it begun than it was over. She opened her eyes and discovered, to her surprise, that she was still standing next to the stranger. As she stared at her hands, a theory popped into her head, and she slowly put it all together. To test her theory, as well as help her understand what had happened to her, she tentatively reached out a trembling hand and prodded the enigmatic entity in his chest.

He looked down at the finger on his chest, smiled, looked back up, and bowed his head. 'Let me formally introduce myself, my dear. My name is Custos, and as you can see, you can now touch me.' Then his smile disappeared, and he exhaled a sorrowful sigh. 'Sorry I had to do that, but I couldn't allow you to meet yet.'

That was the final straw for Em. Having had just about enough of having her life being toyed with by inhuman monsters, she squeezed her hands into tight balls and trembled with fury. 'You couldn't allow it,' she hissed through gritted teeth, struggling to contain her anger.

If Custos was concerned at being the focus of Em's rage, he did not show it. Instead, he gave a long sigh and shook his head dolefully. 'Yes. If you had met, the results would have been disastrous. It would have torn a hole in the space-time continuum, causing the multiverse to collapse in on itself.'

Her anger changing to confusion, Em blinked and shook her head. 'Sorry. What?'

'I pulled you both out of different points in your own time streams,' Custos explained in a patient tone. 'From your perspective, Claire was from an event that occurred several weeks ago.'

'Oh, come on,' Em said, ignoring the headache coming on. 'Now you're just making stuff up.'

Custos shook his head and stared up at the heavens, murmuring, 'Save me from ignorant hairless apes and their blinkered view of the multiverse.'

'Hey, I resent that,' Em said, not hiding her indignation.

'Many apologies, child,' Custos answered, looking sheepish. Then his multicoloured eyes brightened as he smiled and held up a finger. 'Let me explain it to you in a way you can understand.' He gestured to the two chairs and waited for Em to get comfortable before he started. 'I once had a conversation with a wanderer … a wanderer of the fourth dimension, if you will. Nice chap, but he suffered from multiple personalities, which made it confusing whenever we bumped into one another.' He laughed and clapped in amusement. 'Oh, the stories they would tell me. For some reason, they were quite fond of you humans, but I—'

'Excuse me,' Em snapped, losing her patience. 'I think you're getting sidetracked.'

Custos's brow creased, and he shook his head. 'I am?'

Em pinched the bridge of her nose, feeling the headache was now becoming a migraine, and sighed wearily. 'You were about to explain something to me so I could understand.'

Custos's eyebrows shot up, and he stared at Em in puzzlement. 'I was?' His face brightened. 'Oh yes, I was, wasn't I?' He hung his head and tutted. 'Really, my dear. You shouldn't distract a person when they are trying to tell you something. It is quite rude, you know. Now, where was I … Oh yes. Humans assume that time is a strict progression, but it is not.' Em flinched as Custos clicked his fingers, and a glowing yellow line appeared just in front of her. He grabbed it, wrung it in his hands. After he was finished, Em could see it now resembled a ball of string. 'Time is more like an enormous ball of intersecting lines. The interconnecting lines allow for a person to cross from one point in their timestream to another. Do you understand?'

Despite the pounding coming from the inside of her head, Em allowed herself a thin smile and nodded slowly. 'I think so,' she said, trying to keep the confusion from registering in her voice. She folded her arms across her chest and gave him a knowing smile. 'Personally, I just think you've made the whole thing up.'

The corners of Custos's mouth twitched and he gave Em a sly wink. 'Maybe I have. Maybe I haven't. Who is to say?' He pulled his head back and laughed. 'Oh, you should have heard how my wandering friend

explained it. They got so completely turned around, I thought their head would explode.'

Secretly wishing she'd never bothered asking, Em coughed and tried to change the subject. 'So, am I to understand you're some sort of cosmic entity?'

Custos beamed with delight and clapped his hands excitedly. 'Oh, I can already see I'm going to like you.' He steepled his fingers together and gave Em a challenging stare. 'What else?'

Not one to turn down a challenge, Em rose from her chair and paced in a circle, tapping her lower lip with her fingernail. 'I'm guessing you've pulled my consciousness out of my timeline into this place, some sort of construct. Am I right?'

Custos huffed and rolled his eyes. 'Hmph, come now, child. You already know that to be true. Surely you can do better than that.'

Her mind working overtime, Em blew out a puff of air between her tight lips and nodded. 'Fine, then. My guess is you're some sort of guardian of the time continuum.' She shook her head as she dismissed that thought and raised an eyebrow. 'Scratch that, not a guardian of the time continuum. You're a protector of the multiverse. Am I right so far?'

'I have to say, child, for a lower life form, you are remarkably intelligent.' Custos smirked. 'I'm quite impressed. Cornelius would be so proud to see his time wasn't wasted with you.'

Em folded her arms across her chest and scowled at him. 'Thank you,' she said, making no attempt to hide the sarcasm in her voice. 'I'm so glad this lower life form has impressed you.'

'Oh, don't get your knickers in a twist, child,' Custos said in a tone containing a hint of disapproval. 'All I'm trying to say is for a species that is just a bunch of hairless monkeys, you just might be the one bright light that outshines them all. You seem remarkably self-aware.' Em shot Custos a searing look, which appeared to go over his head as he continued. 'You weren't that far off when you called me a protector of the multiverse. In actuality, I am the personification of the collected intelligence of the multiverse.'

Em smirked and gave him an amused sideways look. 'Does that include us hairless monkeys?'

Custos lifted his shoulder and gave a half-hearted grunt. 'Meh. I didn't say I was perfect.' His face broadened into a wide, mischievous grin and he waved his hand. 'Relax, child, I'm only teasing.' Then his shoulders sagged, and he let out a despondent sigh. 'I am so old. So, so old and I have made some terrible mistakes.'

Something inside Em's mind clicked, and realisation dawned on her. 'Am I assuming,' she said carefully, 'Oracle was one of your mistakes?'

Custos looked at Em with sorrow-filled eyes and nodded. 'Too many, far too many. The most recent came when I tried to interfere with her crossing back over to Terra. I thought if I slowed her down, it might buy the prime universe enough time to mount a defence. I didn't anticipate her seizing the opportunity to carry out experiments on the children she was keeping in stasis.'

To Em's horror, Custos let out a cry of rage and slammed his foot down on the floor. His appearance changed and, for the first time, she glimpsed Custos's true energy form. The vast hall trembled around her and the celestial sky swirled like a thunderstorm as bolts of electricity shot out of the enormous ball of energy. Em felt helpless as the vast hall began to collapse around her. She could sense that it was responding to Custos's emotions, and if she didn't act now, she might get swept away and would probably be lost forever in the void.

'No matter what I do,' she heard Custos cry out, 'she's always one step ahead of me. Whatever I do, it just ends up making things worse, costing the lives of those I'm trying to protect.'

Em felt like she was caught in the middle of a hurricane, and she had to hold on tight to the chair to stop herself from being blown away. She realised she needed to act quickly if she had any hope of saving herself. She held up a hand to protect her face against the buffeting winds and shouted at the glowing ball of light.

'Custos, it's not your fault. You can't anticipate everything, no matter how hard you try. You said yourself you're comprised of the collected intelligence of the multiverse. That means you're alive, so you'll make mistakes.' A powerful gust of air slammed into her, and she had to force herself to be heard. 'Oracle is an AI, it isn't human. You just need to take hold of that spark that belongs to me and billions of other humans –

that spark of ingenuity. Once you recognise that, it won't be long before you win against Oracle. You just need to have faith.'

The buffeting winds suddenly stopped, and the celestial hall solidified. Em sucked in a relieved breath as Custos morphed back into his human form. He took Em's hands in his and helped her back to her feet, shaking his head sadly. 'Sorry, child. I didn't mean to lose control like that.'

'It's okay, my friend,' Em breathed, grinning. 'You're only human, after all.'

Custos frowned and then smiled. 'You and your sister are much alike. More than you realise. Even though dimensions separate you both, your fates are still intertwined. Just as you were attacked by a synthroid, the same thing happened to Claire, also leaving her mortally wounded.'

'Is that why she was here?' Em asked curiously. 'Because you felt responsible, so you brought us here while you healed our bodies.'

Custos drew in a heavy sigh and nodded in acknowledgement. 'Even though it wasn't by my hand, I still feel indirectly responsible for the condition you are in.'

'At least you've attempted to rectify that mistake,' Em said, smiling. Her eyebrows nipped together as a thought occurred to her, and she peered at the mirror standing in front of her. 'May I assume, because you haven't done so, you can't attack Oracle openly? That you're afraid of the destruction you'll bring about. That is why you've been manipulating us, putting us in place like pieces on a chessboard for …'

She was hit with a sudden epiphany, and it became clear to her what Custos was doing. As in a game of chess, he was trying to think two steps ahead of Oracle, and she guessed he must already have an endgame in mind. Unfortunately, it appeared Oracle was doing the same. Em hoped her little pep talk might have just given Custos the spur he needed. But as she turned and stared at him, the look in Custos's eyes was all she needed to know.

'Yes,' he said with a humourless smile. 'I can see in your eyes that you've already worked it out. But to answer your previous statement. You are correct, I can't attack Oracle openly. A long time ago, she stole a small portion of my power. The energy she possesses, even a small amount, would destroy half the universe she was in if she were to unleash it.' His

mood appeared to change slightly, and he placed a reassuring hand on Em's shoulder. 'As you've guessed, I have an endgame in mind, something that will rid the multiverse of Oracle forever. With luck, I might just pull it off. But to do that …'

'You need all your pieces to be in place,' Em finished the sentence for him. She inhaled a long, resigned breath and looked Custos in the eye. 'Tell me what you need me to do, and I'll do it without question. If need be, I'll personally march Oracle into hell myself so long as it results in the end of its maniacal reign of terror.'

Custos laughed and waved a hand. 'That won't be necessary, child. But I appreciate the sentiment.' He lapsed into silence and gazed at the heavens. For a moment, Em thought she saw a touch of uncertainty cross over his face, as if he was wrestling with a tough decision. But no sooner than it was there, it vanished, and he lowered his head and fixed her with a steady gaze. 'I can't reveal too much to you in case Oracle captures you and probes your mind. But rest assured, when the time comes, you'll know what to do. But one thing I will tell you, you will see your sister again.' The corners of his lips curled up into a cryptic smile. 'Sooner than you think.'

Just knowing she would see her sister again was all she needed to hear. Em blinked away the tears in her eyes and swallowed. 'Thank you for sharing that with me, Custos. I can see it wasn't easy for you to tell me that much. You don't know how much it means to me, knowing I'm going to see Claire again.'

'Oh, I am probably getting soft in my old age,' Custos said, grinning. His eyes twinkled mysteriously, as if he was seeing something Em couldn't, then he nodded. 'Your body is fully healed, so I can return you to your own timeline now.'

Em cocked her head and gave Custos a suspicious sidelong look. 'Let me guess. I'll wake up and mysteriously discover four weeks have passed. Didn't Oracle already warn you about the dangers of messing with time? One would think you have grown quite fond of me.'

Custos hung his head and waggled his eyebrows. 'Now, my dear, whatever gave you that impression, hmm?' He held up his hands and gave her an innocent look. 'At my age, one sometimes becomes absent-minded

and strange things can happen that are out of my control. But for now, I bid thee farewell, my fair and noble warrior.'

Em straightened to attention and saluted Custos. 'It has been a privilege meeting you, my friend.'

Custos appeared to be on the verge of saying something, but then it looked as if he changed his mind at the last minute. Instead, he gave Em a respectful bow, raised his hand, and clicked his fingers.

-21-

The warm, welcoming brightness of the celestial hall vanished and was replaced by the uninviting cold black void of unconsciousness. As she hung there, Em wondered if Custos had made a mistake and sent her back too early. She had expected to pop back into her body fully conscious, but she felt as if she had been cast adrift, surrounded by the pitch blackness of night. Maybe if she called out to Custos, he would correct his mistake?

Em sensed something. Sounds and sensations were burrowing into the back of her subconscious, drawing her out of the cold emptiness. The first thing she noticed was that her body's aches and pains were becoming more apparent, especially the stinging sensation coming from the centre of her chest. She realised it was probably coming from the wound that had been inflicted by the synthroid. But she couldn't understand why it was so flaming itchy. Then she remembered Karen saying she was going to have to cut open her chest to keep her heart beating, so the itchiness she was feeling must have been the wound knitting together.

But as she attempted to lift her right arm to scratch the irritating itchiness, she was disappointed to discover she couldn't manage it. Her arm felt like it was refusing to respond to her commands. *Well, that sucks.* She groaned.

'Shouldn't you be getting some rest, Isaac?' she heard someone say. 'You look shattered. Zoe's due to take over from you. I can keep an

eye on Em while you get some rest.'

'No,' she heard Isaac reply gruffly, followed by what sounded like a yawn. 'Sorry, Fausta. I didn't mean to snap at you. I just feel I need to be by Em's side in case she wakes up.'

'You won't be of much help if you exhaust yourself,' Fausta said softly. 'If Em were awake, I'm certain she'd say the same.'

'Oh, I'm sure she would berate me for not looking after myself.' Isaac chuckled. There was a long pause before Isaac spoke again. This time, Em couldn't miss the concern in his voice. 'It's been six weeks. Why hasn't she woken up?'

'These things take time, Isaac,' another woman's voice answered; Em recognised it as Karen's. 'The commander suffered a traumatic injury. I know it probably didn't help tearing open her chest the way I did, but she appears to be making remarkable progress. Trust me, she'll wake up in her own time.'

But she was awake, she wanted to tell them. Blast it. What's the point of having people beside her if they couldn't tell that she was awake? As usual, she knew she was going to have to take matters into her own hands if she wanted to make them aware that she had regained consciousness.

Okay, Em thought. *Mouth, do your thing.* Regrettably, much to Em's dismay, she soon discovered that it was easier said than done. Her mouth was refusing to open. It felt as if her lips were stuck together. *Okay then,* she grumbled, *since my mouth wasn't doing what it was told. What if I tried waving my fingers?* With the image of her left index finger fixed in her mind, Em focused her will on raising it. *Come on, lift! Why won't it lift?* All she wanted was just one wiggle. Was that too much to ask ... Wait. *Yes.* She felt her finger move just a fraction. Granted, it wasn't much, but at least it moved. That was a start.

'Did you see that?' Isaac asked, sounding excited.

'What?'

'Her right index finger,' Isaac replied enthusiastically. 'It just moved.'

'That was probably just a random reflex action from her dreaming,' Karen responded patiently. 'Like rapid eye movement.'

'Oh,' Isaac replied, sounding deflated.

No, don't listen to her, Em pleaded silently. Desperate to cry out, Em wished she could make them aware that she was conscious, but her inability to do so left her feeling frustrated. Her throat felt rough, and her mouth felt like it was stuck tight. She thought if she could only open her eyes, they would see that Isaac was telling the truth.

With an image of her right eyelid in her mind, Em focused all her will into opening it. At first, nothing happened, but then she felt her right eyelid quiver slightly. Yes. Her eyelid moved. Now, if she could just open it a bit more. She concentrated harder and her eyelid crept slowly open, only to be greeted by a blinding light that seared her retina.

'Ngh!' Em groaned, but she concentrated on keeping her eyelid open through sheer force of will.

To Em's relief, the blurred whiteness gradually lessened, and she realised she could make out the shapes of people standing around her. Suddenly, it looked as if someone had noticed she was awake and one of the blurred shapes moved closer to her. Em blinked away the film covering her eyes, and the blurred shape morphed into Isaac's smiling face.

'Em!' Isaac cried out in delight, grabbing her hand.

Karen's round face filled Em's vision as she pushed Isaac to one side. She held up a penlight and shone it into Em's eyes. *Great,* Em groaned. *I've only just got my vision back. Now Karen's trying to take it away by blinding me.*

'Welcome back to the land of the living, Commander Tulley,' Karen said flatly. 'Don't try to speak. Your throat will probably be too dry.' She raised her hand and waved two fingers in front of Em's eyes. 'How many fingers am I holding up?'

Em sharpened her eyes in annoyance. Oh, she wanted to know how many fingers she was holding up, did she? Em was only too happy to tell her. There was something in Karen's tone that Em found irritating. She tightened her jaw and concentrated on raising her left middle finger. True, it wasn't the correct answer, but it was still an answer.

'Charming,' Karen said with a deadpan expression. 'I can see you haven't lost your sense of humour.'

From the way Fausta's shoulders were shaking, Em could see she was trying to hold in a laugh as she handed over a beaker with an extended

mouthpiece. It was the type that was normally used for patients who had difficulty swallowing. If she had noticed Fausta's amusement, Karen gave no sign while she took the beaker from her. Em felt a sudden small vibration, and it was followed by the feeling of being raised slowly up. She winced in pain at the slow movement, then realised the top half of her bed was being elevated so that she could take a drink. Karen held up a damp sponge and ran it gently over her dry lips before carefully slipping the mouthpiece into her mouth.

'Take slow sips,' Karen instructed. 'Your throat muscles will feel like they have forgotten how to swallow, but they will soon remember.'

Em felt the cup being raised, which was quickly followed by the welcome sensation of cool liquid entering her mouth. As she tilted her head back, she screwed up her face at the stinging sensation in her throat. But after a couple more gulps, the dryness in her throat eased and it was becoming easier for her to swallow. Waving the beaker away, she licked her lips and gave a weak smile.

'Thank you,' Em croaked. 'How long have I been out?'

'We can talk about that later, dear,' Karen answered brusquely.

She licked her lips again and shot Karen a determined scowl. 'How long?' she rasped, this time with more force than she'd intended.

Karen and Fausta shared a worried look, and for a moment Em thought they weren't going to tell her. But her concerns vanished when she heard Isaac clear his throat; he took a step closer.

'Just over six weeks,' he said gravely. Em thought she'd detected a devilish glint in his eyes as he gave her a mischievous grin. 'You've had many in the base worried you wouldn't pull through. Some even bet on when you'd regain consciousness.' He gave a weak laugh and shook his head. 'Well, of course I put a stop to it.'

Em cocked her head and gave Isaac a knowing wink. 'Oh, I'm sure you did.'

Fausta nodded her head furiously in acknowledgement, smiling. 'Oh, he's not lying. He did put a stop to it a week after it had started.' She gave him a nudge, while seemingly returning Em's wink with one of her own. Isaac's mouth widened, and Em thought she saw his eyes blaze with pride.

'That was only because he lost.' Karen guffawed, slapping Isaac on the shoulder. 'He bet you would regain consciousness after a week.'

Em smiled as Isaac dropped his head and shuffled his feet sheepishly while the two women laughed at his embarrassment. Even though she was silently grateful for the confidence he had in her, she couldn't help feeling sorry for having been the one responsible for him losing. As she listened to the joyful laughter around her, she made a mental note to herself that as soon as she was fit enough, she was going to seek the winner out and request that they give everybody their money back. She tolerated occasional gambling, but betting on people's recovery was perhaps a bit too extreme.

It didn't take long for the laughter to cease. The expression on Karen's face turned serious as she pulled up a chair close to her bed and sat down. Karen took Em's hand and fixed her with a sobering gaze. 'Your friends wanted to hide the truth from you, but I prefer to be straight with you,' she said carefully. 'The injury to your heart was extensive. There was a moment when I thought we were going to lose you, and we wouldn't get you back to the base in time.' She gave Em's hand a gentle squeeze and cast her eye over her shoulder to the now sombre-looking Fausta. 'You've got a good team here, Commander. Because Gemma was able to get word to them about how serious your injury was, Fausta and her team started work on replicating a new heart for you. As soon as we arrived, they immediately placed you inside a cryogenic pod to keep you stabilised until your new heart was ready.' Karen stared up at the ceiling and shook her head in wonder. 'With everybody working as one, and with the help of the medical database, I replaced your damaged heart with the fabricated one. It was touch and go, but I'm delighted the operation was a success and your body has accepted your new organ.' Karen let out a sardonic laugh and held up her hands. 'There are days when I amaze even myself. Back home, I wouldn't dare to try something like that. But here, with this wondrous technology of yours, together with this awesome group of people, I was able to perform a miracle.'

Fausta took a step forward and squeezed Karen's shoulder. 'You don't give yourself enough credit,' she said reassuringly. 'You already had the skill and knowledge. It just needed unlocking.'

'Oh, tosh!' Karen said, giving a dismissive wave. 'I haven't done something this perilous since medical school, and that was when I worked on a pig.' Her face tightened, and she fixed Em with a steady gaze. 'I think we should probably let you rest. Even though you've been making remarkable progress, it'll take time before you're fully healed. I'll check on you again in a couple of hours after you've had some sleep. Fausta and I will also need to run some tests on you just to make sure there aren't any lingering effects from being in a coma for so long.'

Em waved a hand and shook her head. The last thing she wanted to do was sleep more, and she needed to get her mind working again. Also, after being unconscious for so long, she was desperate to be caught up on what she had missed. Her priority was getting back in shape, but she was fully aware of the lengthy recovery that was ahead of her. But she had a lot to thank Custos for, for secretly healing her body, because if it hadn't been for his energies, she doubted she would still be alive. It occurred to her that it was probably best she kept that to herself, fearing the others would dismiss it as a sick woman's hallucinations.

'I think I've rested enough,' she said adamantly. 'I need to find out what's been going on.' She gestured to Isaac and gave a dismissive flick of her wrist at the two women. 'Isaac can stay, but I would like you two to leave.'

She took note of Karen's unenthusiastic demeanour, as indicated by her pursed lips and creased eyes. Karen let out a long, resigned breath, and Em guessed she must have realised that there was no point arguing with somebody who had made their mind up.

'Fine,' Karen grumbled, holding her hands up in defeat. 'It's your decision. What do we know? We're only the bloody medical professionals, after all.' She spun sharply on her heel, snapping her fingers at Fausta. 'You, with me.'

Em couldn't hide her surprise on hearing the abrupt tone in Karen's voice. Karen was obviously somebody who was used to dealing with the people who worked with her in a certain way. Em glanced at Fausta and detected a hint of unhappiness in her demeanour. It was obvious Karen's acerbic tone rankled Fausta, and she wondered how long it would be before they had words. However, as Fausta turned and

followed Karen, Em noticed her roll her eyes while Isaac gave her a look of sympathy.

Once they were both out of earshot, Em gave Isaac an enquiring look and spoke in a conspiratorial whisper. 'I guess Karen has been ruffling a few feathers.'

Isaac nodded furiously and laughed. 'Oh, she has definitely done that. I don't think it was an hour before Karen started to lay down the law in the infirmary. I was here when Fausta decided she'd had enough and gave Karen a piece of her mind.' Isaac cast a surreptitious eye over his shoulder and bobbed his head in admiration. 'Give Karen her due. She stood there and waited for Fausta to have her say before she really opened up on her, listing her experience, her age, her qualifications, et cetera, et cetera.' He lifted his shoulder in a half shrug and turned back to Em. 'I think Fausta must've realised Karen was the real deal, even if she's a bit eccentric. Since then, she's stepped back and allowed Karen to take charge of the infirmary the way she sees fit.' Isaac's mouth broadened into a wide grin as he shuffled his chair forward, leaned in closer and whispered in Em's ear, 'She hasn't come out and said it, but deep down, I think Karen also respects Fausta for having run the infirmary for so long without a qualified physician being on staff. Truth be told, with Fausta's knowledge of the infirmary's systems and Karen's medical expertise, they make a good team.'

Em nodded thoughtfully as she contemplated Isaac's words. Hearing his confidence in the two women's ability to work together eased her fears. She could see now she had misread the situation, but made a mental reminder that she would at some point in the future need to take some time to take both women to one side and have a chat with them, find out how they truly felt working with one another. Once she was assured there wasn't any animosity between the two women, she'd happily let them proceed as they wished.

Confident she could do it herself, Em carefully raised the beaker to her lips and drank more of the liquid. She was relieved to discover it felt easier to swallow, but then she noticed the empty feeling in her stomach and wondered how long it would be before they would allow her to eat something solid. From experience, Em knew the liquid she was drinking

contained the essential ingredients she needed to speed up her body's recovery rate, but it would never replace that succulent sensation of a delightful piece of juicy steak sitting inside her stomach. She gazed at the beaker in her hands and let out a slow, morose groan. Slow and steady sips. What would be the point of eating a steak if she were only to throw it back up?

'Don't worry, Boss,' Isaac said, smirking. 'They'll probably try to give you something solid to eat tomorrow.'

Em felt her brow crease as she shot Isaac a suspicious look. 'What have I told you before about reading my mind?' she said jokingly.

Isaac's eyes widened, and he lifted his hands to his chest in that usual mock innocence act, which Em found annoying. 'Now, as if I would ever do a thing like that!' he answered, waggling his eyebrows while his mouth broadened into a wicked smile. Then his expression turned serious, and he bobbed his head at Em's stomach. 'Anyway, it's hard to miss the rumbling noises coming from your stomach. One just needs to take a look at your face to know what you are thinking.'

Em cocked her head to one side and looked at him through the corner of her eye. 'Oh, if you know me so well, pray tell, what is it you think I'm thinking right now?'

Concentration etched deeply across his features, Isaac placed his fingers on his temples and spoke in a strained tone, while making exaggerated panting noises. 'I … can … just …. about … see it.' His eyes shot open, and he fixed her with a smug expression. 'You're thinking "Give me some steak now!" Or it could be you just like cows.'

Unimpressed by Isaac's theatrics, Em turned up her nose and sniffed. 'Humph! Smart arse. Remind me not to play poker with you,' she grumbled. She lowered her head, reached over and took hold of Isaac's hand, smiling gratefully. 'Thank you for saving me, my friend.'

'You're welcome, Em,' Isaac responded in a soft tone. Then the smile on his face vanished and was replaced by a more sober expression. 'We lost a lot of good people that day. Only worsened because we didn't have time to go back for their bodies.'

Em's vision blurred, and a surge of guilt swelled inside her as it suddenly occurred to her that she was the reason behind that. She pulled

her gaze away from Isaac and stared down at her hands. 'How's Yuto dealing with Raelle's death?' she asked despondently.

Isaac ran his hand down his face and let out a weary sigh. 'Like anyone else who has lost someone close to them,' he replied sadly. 'He's grieving, and he's also angry. Angry at leaving her body behind. Hilaria had to confine him to his quarters for his own safety because she couldn't risk him going to get her. She was worried Oracle might have set a trap for him.'

'I can see where she's coming from,' Em answered reluctantly. She stiffened as she remembered who she'd left in charge, and furrowed her brow, giving Isaac a guarded look. 'How have things been while I've been unconscious? Has Hilaria been holding things together, or—'

'You don't need to worry,' Isaac said, interrupting her. 'People haven't mutinied against Hilaria, if that's what you're wondering. From what I've been told, Hilaria has really stepped up and kept everyone together. Yes, some people told me her style of command rubbed them up the wrong way, but once they got to know her, they could see she was a seasoned tactician who knew her stuff. Ever since we got back, Hilaria has had groups out on patrol as far as it's safe to go, keeping watch for any sign of retaliation. She's even had Gemma running high-altitude reconnaissance flights over Pons Aelius, scanning the city for any energy signatures matching Oracle.' Isaac puffed out his cheeks and exhaled slowly, and his shoulders sagged in defeat as he shook his head. 'There's been no movement spotted, either from above or down on the ground. Frankly, the inactivity has me concerned. It's been over six weeks. You would've thought Oracle would have done something by now.' He pulled a sour face and rubbed the back of his neck. 'Maybe your EMP did more damage than we first thought.'

Em leaned back onto her pillow and stared thoughtfully up at the ceiling. Although she was relieved to hear her faith in Hilaria hadn't been misplaced, she couldn't help but agree with Isaac's concerns about the lack of activity from Oracle. She'd expected the AI to have made some sort of reprisal against them in response to Em's actions. Maybe Isaac was right – her EMP had damaged Oracle, and it was just licking its wounds.

She let out a tired yawn, and her eyelids were becoming heavier.

Ignoring the fatigue coming from her body, Em turned toward Isaac and gave him a tired smile. 'How are you doing, big man?' she said sleepily. 'Don't worry, I haven't forgotten. I still owe you that sit down, so that we can talk about … you know.'

Isaac shifted uncomfortably in his chair and coughed nervously. 'Uh, yeah. I'm sure that can wait,' he said evasively. He quickly rose from his chair, leaned in closer and squeezed Em's shoulder, whispering, 'I can see you need to get some sleep, so I'll leave you alone. Take care, Boss Lady.'

'Yeah, you're right,' Em murmured with half-closed eyes, slurring her words. 'Speak to you later.'

No longer able to fight off the encroaching sensation of sleep, Em was aware of her eyelids sliding slowly down. Just before they were fully closed and she welcomed the warm embrace of sleep, she thought she saw Isaac lean in and kiss her on the forehead. As she drifted off to sleep, she smiled as his kiss stirred a memory in her. A memory from a long time ago, of a little girl's first night in a strange new world, after having been forced to share a dormitory with a group of strangers. Em remembered she had woken up crying, scared, missing her parents and feeling all alone, but recalled a young Isaac had been sitting next to her bed, keeping watch. Drifting off to sleep, she recalled him leaning over to her and kissing her on her forehead, whispering gentle reassurances. She exhaled a contented sigh as the warm memory of those words from so long ago wrapped around her mind like a reassuring blanket.

'Sleep well, little one. With every breath I take, I vow to safeguard you and prevent any harm from coming your way.'

-22-

Over the following few days, Em had plenty of visitors to keep her occupied while she was recuperating. Her most notable visitor was Hilaria, who greeted her with a large, relieved, beaming smile. As soon as she set eyes on the former imperious officer, Em knew that stepping into the role of interim commander had been good for her. A new-found confidence and happiness seemed to radiate from Hilaria, suggesting that she had successfully dealt with the personal demons that had haunted her.

Upon Em mentioning her new bounce, Hilaria happily agreed with Em's observations; she explained her new confidence came from working with people who were no longer afraid of her. Along with that, she put it down to her change in command style, having decided she did not want to revert to the harsh way in which her former self had operated and believed she would get better results from those around her if she treated them with compassion – a decision that in the end proved to work well for her.

On listening to how easily Hilaria had settled into her new role, Em felt as if a weight had been lifted off her shoulders. The looming threat of Oracle hung over her like a dark cloud, and she even considered stepping down and making Hilaria's position permanent. Em felt, with her extensive military background, that Hilaria had a lot more to offer. But as soon as Em voiced her thoughts to Hilaria, she immediately shot down any idea of her stepping back in a forceful but polite way. Hilaria expressed her gratitude for being offered the role, but firmly stated that she could never

replace Em, whom she considered the beating heart of the complex. But she went on to say that she would continue in her role as interim commander and would gladly step aside as soon as Em was fit enough, and she would stay on as Em's chief tactician if Em desired it.

Even though Em couldn't hide her disappointment, deep down she was secretly glad her friends still needed her. Knowing she had people like Hilaria and Isaac standing by her side made the burden of command so much easier.

It didn't take long for the topic to change to another troubling matter – Zoe. As she had promised, Hilaria had kept a close eye on the young woman. Hilaria was grateful for the help she'd given, but Zoe was still behaving oddly, watching Hilaria strangely and when questioned about it, would deny it. After giving it a bit of thought, Em felt it was best to just let Zoe carry on with what she was doing, hoping she would eventually come to her senses. Hilaria argued against it, believing they ran the risk of alienating Zoe, but reluctantly abided by Em's wishes and promised to continue to keep an eye on her.

Shortly after her chat with Hilaria, Em received a visit from Zoe. Em could not get over how much the teen had changed over a few weeks; compared to the surly person she had last seen, the change in Zoe was remarkable. Gone was the uncertain, broody girl. In her place was a tall, confident, and beaming young woman. Em could tell she had made the right decision when she opted to give Zoe more responsibility. But as she listened to Zoe's excitable chat about how much she enjoyed working with Hilaria, she couldn't help agreeing with Hilaria that Zoe's new self-assurance was masking something underlying. Just over a month ago, Zoe could barely tolerate being in the same room as Hilaria; now she was acting as if she was her best friend. Even though it was clearly fake, Em felt a tinge of jealousy at the bond Zoe had developed with Hilaria and secretly wished her odd behaviour was something harmless.

Amongst all her visitors and well-wishers, one person's absence did not go unnoticed by Em. Apart from having been at her bedside as soon as she regained consciousness, Isaac never once visited her. She initially felt hurt and disappointed, but when she voiced this, Fausta gave her a knowing smile and explained that Isaac was probably feeling

embarrassed about openly declaring his love to her and suggested if Em gave him some time, he would eventually come round. Em reluctantly agreed with Fausta's reasoning and decided she would give him the space he needed.

After the first three days of bed rest, Em realised she was getting antsy at having nothing to look at but the bland white walls of the medical bay. She complained and begged Fausta and Karen so much to be let out of bed that the two women eventually had no choice but to comply, but only on the proviso that Em promised not to complain if she suffered a setback. With Fausta and Karen standing on either side of her, she shuffled unsteadily on her feet from one side of the ward to the other. But even though she found it tiring, Em was grateful for the chance to stretch her legs.

It was not long after that, while under Fausta's and Karen's watchful eyes, Em underwent her first course of physical therapy. It was slow going at first, but eventually she felt her strength and confidence returning. Two weeks after regaining consciousness, Em's recovery came on in leaps and bounds, to the point where she could walk around with the aid of a cane. Her speedy recovery may have also been down to her dogged determination to get out from under Fausta's and Karen's watchful eyes. But even though Em's mobility was slowly improving, she found it frustrating that her stamina was nowhere near what it had been previously. With each session of physical therapy, Em found she got tired too easily and was forced to rest for a couple of hours afterwards. Karen tried to reassure her that her stamina would return, but she just needed to be patient.

One day, following what should have been a routine exercise session, Em was sitting unhappily in a wheelchair being pushed down a corridor by Fausta, with a guilty-looking Zoe walking by her side. Em pulled a sour face as she was forced to listen to Fausta's scolding tone.

'How many times have you been told?' Fausta complained. 'You're pushing yourself too hard. But do you listen? Oh, no. What possessed you to think you could spar with Zoe, I'll never know!'

Zoe, her face glowing red with embarrassment, gave Em a look of concern. 'Em, I'm truly sorry,' she pleaded, sounding mortified. 'I

shouldn't have attempted to use a roundhouse kick on you. I was too busy showing off, it completely slipped my mind that I should go easy on you.'

Em winced as she stretched out her leg, feeling more embarrassed than hurt. 'It's okay, Zoe. It wasn't your fault,' she replied, making no attempt to prevent her frustration from showing in her voice. 'If anybody is to blame, it should be me. I was the one who encouraged you to attack me.' She gave Zoe a disgruntled smile, reached over and gave her hand a reassuring squeeze. 'My reflexes just aren't as sharp as they used to be. Apart from a bruised ego and sore knee, no harm was done, sweetheart.'

'You're lucky that's all it was. You're lucky you didn't damage your new heart!' Fausta admonished, shooting Zoe a scathing look. 'Zoe, you need to remember when to go easy. Em isn't as fit as she was, and you keep forgetting she's nearly three times your age. By the fires of Hades, she's old enough to be your grandmother.'

Being told she was old enough to be someone's grandmother was not what Em wanted to hear. The muscles in her jaw tightened, and she ground her teeth in annoyance. It took every ounce of willpower to bite back a retort. Yes, she was in her mid-fifties, but no way in hell was she old enough to be somebody's grandmother. Out of the corner of her eyes, she saw Zoe's shoulder shake, and she could tell she was trying to stifle a laugh, which only plummeted Em's mood even further. She turned her head slowly and gave Zoe her best penetrating stare.

'You okay, Zoe?' she asked coolly. 'It looks like your shoulders are shaking. You're not finding something amusing by any chance? Hmm?'

Zoe blanched and swallowed nervously. Em could tell she was struggling to keep a straight face while shaking her head furiously. 'Nothing, ma'am,' she squeaked. 'Just got the hiccups, that's all.'

'Huh-huh,' Em answered, nodding slowly and letting her gaze linger before turning round to focus her attention on Fausta. 'As for you—'

Em never got the chance to voice her indignation at Fausta, because a loud klaxon chose that moment to cut her off. Startled, Em shared a worried look with both Zoe and Fausta, but then she felt her eyes grow wide in alarm when she realised what the klaxon meant. It was the incursion alarm. Until now, the only time she'd heard it was after it had been tested for the first time a few weeks earlier, just after Hilaria had

finished setting it up.

'That's the incursion alarm,' Em said, trying to keep the panic from showing in her voice. 'Somebody is entering the base through a dimensional portal.'

Zoe exchanged a startled glance with Fausta and shook her head in confusion. 'But didn't Hilaria say those quantum frequency thingies were supposed to stop that from happening?'

Before Em could answer, she was interrupted by an urgent voice coming from the base's internal communications system. 'Security detail to the mess hall. Security detail to the mess hall. This is not a drill. I repeat, this is not a drill.'

Desperate to find out what was happening, Em narrowed her eyes and searched for the nearest transport-pod access point. 'Quick, get me to the mess hall,' she commanded. It took her a moment to realise she wasn't moving, so she twisted round to get a better look at Fausta, only to be greeted by a look of hesitancy. In no mood to argue, Em fixed her with a defiant gaze and made a sweeping gesture. 'Listen, we can spend the next five minutes arguing about it, or you can take me to the mess hall. It's up to you. But one way or the other, I *am* going to the mess hall, even if I have to crawl there.'

Fausta's eyes darted over to Zoe, who was standing quietly wearing a mask of impassivity, before silently holding Em's gaze for a couple of moments. Em swallowed, and a thought crossed her mind that Fausta was going to call her bluff. But as Fausta rolled her eyes in exasperation, she could see her friend must have guessed there was no point arguing with someone who had their mind set.

'Have it your way, she-who-must-be-obeyed. Thy will be done,' Fausta grumbled unhappily as she began pushing Em toward the nearest access point, which would take them to the hydroponics level where the galley and mess hall were also located.

A few minutes later, the transport-pod's doors slid open, and Em immediately knew something was wrong on seeing the large group of

people gathered outside the hatch that led into the mess hall. The worried looks on their faces told her everything she needed to know – something bad must have happened. But as she got closer, she saw Hilaria and Isaac talking urgently to some of the group and assumed they were trying to get their stories about what had happened.

There was something odd about the expressions on Hilaria's and Isaac's faces, which made Em feel uneasy. But as she drew closer, she could see that Hilaria looked rattled. Was whatever it was in the mess hall the cause? Em's first thought was that it must have something to do with Oracle, but she quickly dismissed that idea when she realised Isaac and his team would have been more alert, not relaxed with their rifles slung over their shoulders.

'What's the sitrep?' Em asked, trying to peer in through the hatch to get a better look at what was inside the mess hall.

To Em's surprise, Isaac took a step closer and blocked her approach. Em flinched back and stared at Isaac in open-mouthed shock. Why would he stop her going into the mess hall to see what was wrong? Surely it couldn't have been that bad. She wondered if there was something disturbing in there, such as a dead body. But she quickly dismissed that thought because she knew Isaac was aware she had seen plenty of dead bodies in her time, so whatever it was must have been worse than that.

'Emma, I don't think you should go in yet,' Isaac said carefully. 'At least not until we've told you what we are dealing with.' He shared a concerned glance with Hilaria, who bobbed her head in silent acknowledgement.

The hairs on the back of Em's neck tingled; something didn't feel right. Isaac would only use her full name if he was deeply concerned about her safety. On top of that, Hilaria's body language told Em she was on edge about something. Was she also concerned about how Em would react to what she would see in the mess hall? Em felt her right hand twitch with anxiety as Hilaria took a step forward and gave her a tight smile.

'This is what I have learned from the people who were in the mess hall when it happened,' Hilaria said, her tone serious, devoid of humour. 'They described what sounded like an atmospheric disturbance. The air around them became charged, the same feeling one would get before a

heavy lightning storm. The opening of a dimensional tear followed, which is what set off the incursion alarms. They said there was a blinding light and when things settled down, two unconscious naked bodies were lying on the mess hall floor, surrounded by a strange aura.'

Em blinked and gave Hilaria a blank stare while she struggled to work out what had got everybody so worked up. If this was what all the fuss was about, why was everybody acting like they were walking on eggshells? Yes, two bodies arriving out of thin air wasn't a natural occurrence, but that didn't explain why they were being overprotective. She sharpened her eyes and gazed suspiciously at the people standing in front of her. There was obviously more going on here, something they weren't sharing. Her confusion soon turned into anger, and she tightened her hands on the handles of her wheelchair. If somebody didn't tell her what the hell was going on right now, she was going to explode.

'So, what's wrong?' she asked sharply, trying to keep her anger from bubbling to the surface. 'Why aren't you allowing me to enter? Are you worried that there might be a danger of radiation?'

Hilaria flashed a smile, which Em took as genuine, as she took a step back. 'No, it's perfectly safe. I ran a quick scan myself and the energy field around them doesn't appear to be solid. But just to be sure it's safe to move them, we're waiting for Karen to arrive to check them over. It's just that …' She gave a nervous cough and glanced awkwardly at Issac. 'Um, maybe this would be best coming from you.'

Isaac raised both of his hands and let out a weak laugh. 'No. No,' he said. 'You're the one who recognised him. It should come from you.'

'But you've known Em the longest,' Hilaria insisted. 'It should really come from you.'

Em was usually a patient person, and under normal circumstances, she may have even found her friends' antics amusing. But this was no normal day, and she was anything but amused. Her accident with Zoe had already pushed her patience to breaking point, so this was the final straw that broke the camel's back. Silently counting down from ten, she pinched the bridge of her nose, inhaled a deep breath, held it for a few seconds, then let it out slowly and held up a hand to silence her two bickering friends.

'That's enough,' Em said forcefully, trying to keep her anger in check. 'If somebody doesn't tell me in the next ten seconds what in blazes is going on, I'm going to be ticked off.'

'What?' Isaac said with a deadpan expression. 'You mean you're not already?'

In no mood for jokes, she turned her head slowly and fixed Isaac with a frosty stare. 'Sorry? Did you just say something?'

His levity vanishing, Isaac swallowed and hung his head. 'Sorry, Boss Lady,' he answered in a meek tone. 'Just clearing my throat.'

Em narrowed her eyes and switched her gaze to Hilaria and back again to Isaac. 'Now,' she said with deliberate slowness, 'will one of you kindly explain what has got you both so worked up?'

'It's Claire!' Hilaria blurted out. 'One of them is your sister, Claire.'

That was not the answer she was expecting. Em inhaled a sharp breath, reared back in shock, and gave Hilaria an unbelieving look. 'I'm sorry? What?'

'As soon as I saw Claire, I instantly recognised her from my former self's memories of the intelligence reports she'd read about her,' Hilaria explained, nodding. One side of her mouth curled up and she gave a wry smile. 'Also, her resemblance to you is a dead giveaway.' Her expression turned more serious as she turned and gestured to the open hatch. 'There's something else we need you to be aware of before you go in …'

No longer listening to what Hilaria was saying, Em turned and stared at the entrance to the mess hall. She could scarcely believe it. Claire was here. Even though Custos had told her she would see her sister again, a part of her hadn't wanted to believe him, fearing it had been a lie. But now she could see Custos had been telling the truth. Claire was truly here. Ignoring the pain in her knee, she grabbed hold of her cane, shot up out of the wheelchair, and staggered through the hatchway into the mess hall.

She could hardly contain her excitement as she scanned the rows of tables, searching for Claire's body. Then her eyes locked on to a strange glow that was coming from between two tables, and she made a beeline straight toward it. In her peripheral vision, she was aware of Isaac's and Zoe's presence on either side of her, but she ignored them. She was determined that they would not stop her. Nothing was going to get in her

way. Not now. Not when she was this close.

But as she got closer, she slowed as she realised something wasn't right, and a sense of apprehension bubbled inside her stomach. It wasn't the orange and red aura that surrounded Claire's body that concerned her. From her own experience, Em guessed the aura was Custos's handiwork. It was probably helping to heal Claire's injuries. No, what disturbed her the most was that her sister was naked. Em's brow creased on seeing the blistering over Claire's skin, and the hair on top of her head appeared to be missing as if someone had scorched it off.

What had happened to her sister? She massaged her temples while she struggled to make sense of what she was looking at. Custos had told her that Claire had suffered a similar attack by a synthroid, but she could tell Claire's injuries weren't the result of a savage attack. The only conclusion she could reach was that she must have suffered another attack, but by what and by whom? Judging by the state of her body, Em deduced that Claire must have been trapped inside a fire and left to die.

Em shifted her gaze away from Claire's prone form so she could get a better look at the figure lying next to her. There was no doubt he was male, Em realised, feeling her cheeks flush as she pulled her eyes away from his groin area and concentrated on the upper half of the stranger's body. His skin also looked red and blistered, but she could see it was gradually being healed by the aura that surrounded him. Em stared thoughtfully at the stranger's face and frowned. Was it her imagination, but did he look familiar?

She stiffened and inhaled a sharp breath, feeling her eyes grow wide in recognition. *No. It couldn't be.* Not believing what she was looking at, Em did a double take and took a hesitant step forward, just to make sure she wasn't seeing things. However, no matter how hard she tried to deny what her eyes were telling her, Em could not escape the truth.

It was him.

David Barnes.

Her ex-husband.

The man responsible for the death of her mentor. The monster who took her daughter away from her. Who wiped every memory she had of her mother. She had sworn if she ever laid eyes on him again, she would

make him suffer, and now she had that chance.

A red mist descended over Em as her rage swelled up inside her like a dormant volcano, and she squeezed her hands into tight balls. Her chest rising and falling, the only sound she could hear was her own heavy breathing. She pulled her gaze away from Barnes onto Claire, and then back again on Barnes as she slowly put two and two together. It all made sense now. He must have hurt Claire. That was the only explanation. Hilaria had told her of Barnes's escape to her former home reality, which she'd assumed was probably out of cowardice. But now Em could see the real reason he had headed there – it was to carry out some sort of twisted need for revenge by taking the life of someone Em cared about. Em never told Barnes about her other-worldly origins, but it was clear now he must have learned the details of her former life from his work with the portal. Overcome with rage, Em pulled her head back and let out a primal scream.

She would have her vengeance.

Overcome with the need for revenge, Em spun around and glared at Isaac, fixing her eyes on the weapon in his hip holster. *Yes, that will do*, she seethed inwardly. Barnes deserved no less than to be shot like the rabid animal he was. Em grunted and gestured wordlessly, clicking her fingers at Isaac, who just stared back at her blankly, confusion and concern etched deeply across his face. A throaty growl rose from deep inside her, and she shook her head in frustration. Damn it, what was wrong with him? Why wouldn't he give her his weapon?

But before Em could do anything else, Karen appeared in front of her and grabbed her by the shoulders. In her angered state, Em realised she hadn't seen the heavyset woman enter the mess hall, but struggled to understand what she was saying. It sounded like she was saying something about making a mistake. Huh? Who was making a mistake?

Karen slapped her in the face.

Em staggered back, shocked by what had just happened. Slowly, she raised her hand, touched her stinging cheek and stared back at Karen, a mixture of anger and incredulity boiling inside her. Did she just strike her? Even though she was now more focused, the slap did not help improve her mood; she took an angry step forward and pointed an accusatory finger at Karen.

'Did you just slap me?' she hissed, making no attempt to hide the displeasure in her voice.

Karen straightened, folded her arms across her chest, and fixed Em with a defiant stare. 'Of course I did,' she snapped back. 'Because you're about to make a huge mistake.' With one swift movement, not breaking eye contact, she angrily gestured at the bodies on the floor. 'That man is not your David Barnes. He's his counterpart, and my friend, Detective Inspector *Dave* Barnes.'

Her anger suddenly turning to shock, Em took a step back and stared at Dave's body. 'What?' she gasped, mortified at what she had nearly done. 'How can you be sure it's him?'

'Oh, I'm sure. I've known him long enough to tell the difference,' Karen answered, the corners of her mouth curling up into a mischievous grin. 'Although, to be truthful, I've never seen him naked before. If you still don't believe me, just look at his face. You'll see he doesn't have a scar running down the left side like your David has.'

As she leaned down to get a better look, Em felt her face warm with embarrassment at the realisation that Karen was telling the truth. This Barnes did not have the scar running down the left side of his face, the one that she gave him the night they fought. Then she noticed other things that differentiated the two men. Even though it had been a long time since she had last seen her Barnes, it was evident that this one appeared a lot more out of shape. Full of shame at having nearly killed an innocent man, Em slouched her shoulders and exhaled a dispirited whimper.

'I'm sorry, Karen,' she said, trying to blink away the tears in her eyes. 'What must you think of me? I nearly killed your friend, an innocent man at that.'

Her eyes brimming with compassion, Karen gave a small nod of understanding and placed a hand on Em's shoulder. 'My dear, I've had the unfortunate displeasure of meeting your David,' she said with unexpected humour. 'So, believe me when I tell you that I totally understand your reaction. If half the stories of what I've heard about him are true, you deserve to be awarded the medal of valour for having suffered the indignity of being married to such a loathsome excuse of a human being.'

Em cocked her head and regarded Karen curiously. 'How do you

know who I was married to?'

Karen shrugged and flicked her hand dismissively. 'Oh, you know how it is in a place like this, people talk,' she answered cryptically. Her face darkened, and she snapped her fingers at the two people standing behind her. 'You two! Are you waiting for an invitation? Go and get something to cover these people. How'd you like it if you were lying there with all your bits hanging out for everybody to see?'

The two orderlies blanched and ran off to search for anything they could use as a cover. Karen tutted and rolled her eyes as she knelt and held her wrist scanner above the unconscious Dave and Claire. Fausta seemed quite happy to stand back and let Karen take over the examination, probably in deference to the senior woman's medical experience. Knowing the two women seemed to have developed an unspoken mutual respect pleased Em. Now that they had an experienced medical professional, it appeared the infirmary was running a lot more smoothly. It hadn't taken long for people to get used to Karen's eccentricities; she would even go so far as to say that they were becoming quite fond of her.

'Their injuries appear to be healing at an unusually high rate,' Karen murmured as she studied the reading on her wrist scanner. 'My guess is this strange aura is a form of restorative energy.'

'Is there any danger to us?' Isaac asked worriedly.

'Hmm. Yes, truly fascinating, isn't it?' Karen muttered, seemingly engrossed in the readings on her scanner.

The tendons in Isaac's thick neck tightened, and he shot Karen a look that could kill. Em had known Isaac long enough to recognise that Karen's absent-mindedness irked him. She indicated for him to take a step back, coughed politely, tapped Karen on the shoulder and spoke patiently. 'Doctor Logue, Hilaria's already told me the radiation isn't dangerous, but do you think we need to take any precautions?'

Em knew from her own experience with the healing energy that it was perfectly harmless, but she was reluctant to explain how she knew, preferring to keep Custos's identity a secret. She was also afraid that if she told people of her encounter with a celestial being, they might have thought she was suffering from brain damage, or worse, possibly even declare her unfit to command. No, it was best if she acted like she was ignorant and pretended to defer to Karen's judgement.

Karen blinked in surprise as if she had forgotten where she was, and shook her head. 'What? Oh, the aura. If I'm reading this wondrous device correctly, which I'm sure I am, I concur with Miss Cooper – the aura is perfectly harmless.' She held up a finger and smiled. 'But that wasn't what you wanted to know, was it? You asked me if I thought we should take some precautions, didn't you? Hmm? Well, my dear, if it makes you all happy, then I suggest we should place them in quarantine until things settle down.' She pulled a face and rubbed her chin thoughtfully, murmuring, 'It's all highly irregular, don't you think?'

'What's irregular?' Em asked curiously. 'I thought you said the aura was nothing to worry about?'

'Oh, not that.' Karen laughed, waving her hand. 'I'm talking about these two. What are the chances of your sister meeting your husband's doppelgänger? Damned peculiar if you ask me.'

As Claire and Dave's bodies were being lifted onto a gurney, Em couldn't help agreeing with Karen's sentiments. Until now, thanks to Cornelius's training, she had always believed there was no such thing as a coincidence. When she first heard Claire talk about 'Dave' to Custos, it never occurred to her that she was referring to Dave Barnes. What were the odds of her sister being involved with a man who was not only the doppelgänger of her twin sister's husband but also someone she despised? A seed of suspicion gnawed at the back of Em's mind on remembering the argument Claire had had with Custos. Hadn't she accused him of manipulating her into sleeping with Dave? If that was true, how many more lives had the entity manipulated? Had he contrived her own meeting with her David?

Troubled by the idea she was not in control of her own life, an icy shiver ran down Em's spine. The more she thought about it, the more she could see points in her life where Custos had been pulling her strings, guiding her to where he needed her to be. She had an epiphany – something she found even more disturbing – Custos had been behind the breakup of their marriage, which ultimately led to the death of her daughter. If that was true, did that mean Custos was just as bad as Oracle? That they were just like ants trapped inside a giant's playground. Em shook her head despondently as she had an equally depressing thought.

If there was an almighty being controlling them, did that mean humans were never truly in control of their own destiny?

ACT TWO

-23-

After listening to Hilaria and Emma tell their stories, Dave groaned to himself and massaged his temples as he struggled to digest everything they had told him. It was stupid to have felt sorry for himself over everything that had happened to him over the past couple of months. His problems were insignificant compared to everything these two women had gone through. At least he'd been lucky enough to experience freedom of choice throughout his life, whereas the likes of Emma, Hilaria and Isaac had that taken from them at an early age.

Dave lowered his hands and stared at the people in front of him, but was puzzled by what he saw. From the thunderstruck expressions on Hilaria's and Isaac's faces, he got the sense they were in a state of disbelief. He frowned in confusion. Had he done something wrong or acted inappropriately? Just as he was about to open his mouth to speak, he paused as he followed their eyeline, and then it dawned on him that they weren't looking at him. They were staring at Emma. There must have been something in her story they hadn't heard before. Dave cocked his head and tried to recall what Emma had said, but before he could so a thunderous bark of laughter came from Isaac, startling him out of his musings.

'By the ghosts of my ancestors,' Isaac boomed in what Dave thought sounded similar to a South African accent. 'You can't expect us to believe that? You're saying you actually had an encounter with a spiritual being?' He leaned back and stared at Emma with clear scepticism etched across his face. 'I know we've experienced a lot of unnatural things in our

lives, but ... but ...' His voice trailed off and he scrubbed his face with his hands, followed by a small, mirthless laugh. 'Oh, Boss Lady, just when I think I've heard it all, you come out with this.'

'It's true, every word of it,' Emma insisted. From the way the muscles in her face were tightening and in the irritation in her voice, Dave got the impression she seemed lightly peeved that Isaac was questioning her honesty.

'Ah, come on, Em,' Isaac scoffed. 'You were probably just delirious. You lost a lot of blood, after all.' He leaned forward and peered at Hilaria. 'Hilaria, you can't tell me you believe this too?'

Hilaria's cheeks flushed and she gave a small, uncertain shake of her head. Dave realised he needed to step in before things could escalate and someone said something they may regret later. Interrupting Hilaria, he cleared his throat and held up his right index finger. The three people sitting in front of him stopped their bickering and regarded him with looks of surprise.

'Actually,' Dave said, gesturing to Emma. 'What Emma has told you is true.'

Isaac's eyes grew wide, and he gave Dave an unbelieving look, his mouth opening and closing wordlessly. Dave couldn't help admiring the intimidating-looking man's impressive ability to multitask as he tried to talk while Emma stared at him, her face resting on her palm, with one of those self-satisfied, smirking, eyebrow-raised expressions, something that only a woman could pull off, which said *See, I told you so.*

'What?' Isaac exclaimed in a high-pitched squeak of incredulousness. 'You've had an out-of-body experience, too?'

Dave wrinkled his nose and rubbed the back of his neck, 'Erm ... nooo ... not quite. When I said Emma was telling the truth, I didn't mean I was the one who had the encounter. It was Claire.'

Hoping Claire would step in and verify what he was saying, Dave bobbed his head in her direction. Unfortunately, his hopeful expectation quickly turned into disappointment on seeing that Claire still had the same stone-faced expression she had before. On realising he would not receive any help from her, Dave drew in a deep breath and told everyone a watered-down version of what he and Claire had been through. Their violent altercation with a strange beast, which resulted in Claire sustaining a severe injury that put her in a coma. The attack on their base and its subsequent destruction. He finished with Claire's account of her two meetings with Custos. From the horrified disbelief etched across their faces, Dave got a sense that his new allies were having a hard time processing what he had just told them. He couldn't blame them, really. If he hadn't witnessed most of it himself, then it was possible he would have doubted it as well.

The blood seemed to drain out of Emma's face as she stared at Claire, her eyes containing a mixture of sorrow and sympathy. Isaac folded his thick arms across his chest, leaned back in his chair, and stared at Dave with his mouth hanging open.

'By the gods,' Isaac whispered after a long silence. 'I can't imagine the terror and pain you must've felt, my friend.'

'It's not something I would recommend,' Dave replied without humour. He tried to suppress a shudder as the memory of his skin searing came flooding back to him. 'Feeling oneself burning alive is not something I'd likely forget any time soon.'

'I can imagine,' Isaac murmured, giving a slow sympathetic nod.

'I'm so sorry. It's all my fault.'

On hearing quiet sobs coming from somewhere in the room, Dave snapped his head up and glanced over to Claire, but she was still as impassive as ever. He creased his forehead in confusion. Who was sobbing? But as he pulled his gaze away from Claire, he turned slowly to the source and saw the stricken face of Hilaria. He shared a concerned glance with Emma, who seemed to be just as surprised as he was at seeing the silver trail of tears flowing steadily down Hilaria's left cheek.

At first, Dave thought Hilaria's tears were some sort of shared empathy because of his account of being nearly burned alive. But as he gazed at the distraught women, it hit him, and he let out a shocked gasp. They weren't tears of empathy. No, if he didn't know any better, he was almost sure her eyes contained a mixture of shame and guilt. He wrinkled his brow in confusion. What would Hilaria have to be guilty about? She wasn't the one who destroyed the base. It was Oracle.

Hilaria raised her hands and pressed them together in an

imploring, supplicating gesture. 'I'm so terribly sorry,' she continued in a beseeching tone, her voice cracking. 'Colonel Barnes sent the synthroid to attack you in some spiteful attempt to get back at me ... sorry ... General Cooper. I-she knew about it, but didn't want to step in because she wanted to give him enough rope to hang himself.' She buried her head in her hands, muffling her sobs. 'It was some sick game of one-upmanship. They were always trying to outdo each other. Don't you see? It's all my fault. If I had stopped him, you and Claire wouldn't have been injured.'

Dave stared at Hilaria with his mouth hanging open, at a loss for words. Unsure what to do, he glanced over to Emma and Isaac for guidance, but was surprised to see they were staring at Hilaria oddly. At first, he thought he could see a touch of anger in their eyes, but he quickly cast that thought to one side as he realised it wasn't anger he was seeing, it was compassion. As much as he wanted to lash out at Hilaria, Dave realised he couldn't. That would have been like shouting at the puppet instead of the puppet master. From what he'd learned about Hilaria while listening to her story, he understood she'd been just as much a victim of Oracle's machinations as he was, probably even more.

A wave of sympathy overwhelmed him as he stared at the sobbing woman, picturing that small child whom Oracle had abused and manipulated. His sympathy morphed into anger; as far as he was concerned, Custos had just as much blood on his hands as Oracle had. Dave balled his hands into tight balls and struggled to contain his emotions. If those two inhuman monsters kept acting the way they did, both worlds would soon be covered in the blood of the innocent.

Now was not the time for blame though, Dave thought as he drew in a deep breath to rein in his bubbling anger; he rose from his seat. More in control of his emotions, he took several purposeful steps toward Hilaria, coming to a stop in front of her. As he did so, he noticed the concern etched across the faces of Emma and Isaac. Isaac shot up out of his chair, forcing Dave to take a step back in alarm as he realised the burly man seemed to be trying to stop him from approaching Hilaria. It dawned on Dave that it may have been because he still had a murderous scowl on his face.

Afraid he was going to end up a bloody Dave-shaped stain on the

wall, he softened his face and placed a reassuring hand on Isaac's tree-like arm, mouthing a wordless *'it's okay'*. Then, much to Dave's relief, Isaac grunted and bobbed an acknowledgement, then stepped to one side to allow him to pass.

Being careful not to alarm Hilaria, Dave gently touched her shoulder and felt her stiffen in surprise. As she lifted her head out of her hands, he thought he saw a hint of fear and uncertainty on her face. Smiling kindly, he swung Hilaria's chair around and knelt in front of her, clasping her hands in his.

'Hilaria, pet,' he said in a soft but reassuring tone. 'Please believe me when I say I don't hold you responsible for the attack on Claire and I. Colonel Barnes and—'

'B-b-but,' Hilaria interjected, shaking her head. 'It's my fault—'

Dave raised a hand, silencing Hilaria's protestations, and scowled at her. 'I know you feel responsible for the colonel's actions, but you and I are both aware what a conniving bastard he was. Even if you had managed to stop him, he would have still schemed his way around you.'

Peering into Hilaria's stricken face and sensing her vulnerability, Dave was reminded of Wendy – his Wendy – and thought back to one of his last exchanges he had with her. Wendy had also suffered a crisis of conscience after returning from a mission that had gone wrong, which resulted in the deaths of many civilians who had been captured by Oracle's forces. She'd beaten herself up over it, and if it hadn't been for the support of those around her, she would have spiralled into a heavy depression.

Dave leaned forward and squeezed Hilaria's hands, chuckling. 'You may not realise it, but you are very much like Wendy.'

Hilaria's eyes widened in outrage, and she reared back, her head straight in indignation. Dave cringed inwardly as it struck him that he'd once again put his foot in it and, without meaning to, he'd just insulted her. Raising his hands apologetically, he tried to placate the red-faced Hilaria, but a loud shout of exclamation silenced his words.

'I beg your pardon!' Hilaria snapped. 'I'll have you know I'm nothing like General Cooper.'

Dave waved his hands furiously and tried to laugh off the misunderstanding. 'No. No. You've got me all wrong. It wasn't my

intention to offend you. I was simply trying to say that you reminded me of Wendy ... my Wendy. Constable Wendy Cooper. Your doppelgänger.'

Hilaria started and shook her head, spluttering, 'Eh ... what did ...' She held up a finger, frowned and scratched her head, gave Dave a doubtful look, opened her mouth, but paused as if she was struggling to find the words. 'Huh? What?' From the perplexed expression on her face, Dave was struck by the notion that being compared to her doppelgänger was not something she'd experienced before.

'Yes,' Dave answered, smiling. 'From what I was told by Barnes and comparing that information to the person I see before me, I can see you're nothing like that cold, hard-nosed shrew I've heard so much about.' Believing he may have said the wrong thing, Dave gave an embarrassed cough. 'Ahem, no offence.'

The corner of Hilaria's mouth quirked. 'None taken.'

Dave shuffled uncomfortably and felt his cheeks flush as he became aware of the eyes that were locked on him. He swallowed and decided to press on with his explanation – he was already too deep in the hole he'd just dug. 'As I was saying, Hilaria. You may not realise it, but you and my Wendy are very much alike. I'm not talking about your outward appearance; I am talking about what's in here.' He pointed to where his heart was. 'Like your counterpart, you wear your heart on your sleeve. If you're truly anything like my Wendy, then you must share her fierceness and devotion to those who serve with you. In my mind, that sets you apart from your former self. If that is the case, then you can have my back any time.'

From the way Hilaria's face was softening, and her good eye was glistening with emotion, Dave could tell his words had touched her. Her mouth widened into a beaming smile, which covered the whole of her face. 'You don't know what it means to hear you say that,' she said, her voice thick with emotion. 'Up until now, I've been constantly doubting myself. That *she* is still within me, influencing me.'

'Hilaria,' Emma chided, butting in. 'Haven't I already been telling you that you are nothing like General Cooper?'

Hilaria pulled a face and ran her hand through her flame-coloured hair and snorted. 'I know. Even though I was grateful for the reassurance,

a part of me believed you were only saying that to get me on your side.' Emma rolled her eyes and threw up her hands in an I-give-up gesture. Hilaria bobbed her head at Dave and pressed her hands against her chest. 'But hearing Detective Barnes say all those wonderful things, comparing me to my counterpart, it made me realise that's what I needed to hear.' Wiping her hand over her tear-stained face, Hilaria gave Dave a hopeful look. 'Detective Barnes, would it be inappropriate if I asked you if I could give you a hug?'

'No, I would definitely say it isn't inappropriate,' Dave said, grinning. 'In fact, I almost encourage it.' He purposefully lost his grin, lowered his head and pretended to give the impression of sternness. 'However, before you do, I demand you call me Dave. As I once said to a certain red-haired police constable, all this formality leaves me with a headache.'

'Certainly, Dave,' Hilaria replied, beaming with joy.

As he felt Hilaria's arms wrap around him in a tender embrace, a pang of sadness overwhelmed Dave. Hilaria's closeness and smell ignited a memory within him of the last thing he'd said to Wendy before the Castle exploded. A wave of despair enveloped him. He would never get to see Wendy, John, Andy and Sophia again. It had only just occurred to him that he was stuck on this world, with no chance of ever returning home. This was his life now, cut off and trapped on an alien world. He stiffened as he felt Hilaria's arm tighten around him, and it dawned on him that she must have been aware of what he was feeling.

As he welcomed the comfort of Hilaria's warm embrace, Dave became acutely aware of just how different she felt from Wendy. His Wendy was naturally toned and athletic, but this version of Wendy was totally different. It was as if she had been moulded out of steel, giving him the impression of someone who had extensively worked out all their life. For some reason, that only heightened Dave's sense of alienation.

'Hilaria,' Dave whispered, leaning in closer to Hilaria's ear. 'I know you've been second-guessing yourself over how much of you is actually you and not the general. Let me share some words I recently told someone. I believe you are a strong and confident woman with a will of her own. So long as you remember that, I've no doubt you'll be a truly exceptional ally

to those around you. Promise me you'll never forget that?'

'I promise, Dave,' Hilaria whispered back, her voice cracking with emotion. 'Thank you, that means a lot to me.' He felt her body shudder, followed by a melancholic sigh. 'I wish Colonel Barnes had been more like you. If he had, then our relationship may have been a lot different.'

Deeply touched by Hilaria's words, Dave struggled to think of a suitable reply. However, just as he was on the verge of coming up with an adequate response, Hilaria released her grip and pulled away from him and ran a hand down the front of her overall. Her cheeks seemed to be glowing. He guessed she wasn't used to displays of emotion and was trying to hide her embarrassment. But before he could make light of it, he was interrupted by a loud cough. Turning around, he saw Emma staring at him with an arched eyebrow.

'I hope you don't mind me asking a question that has been on my mind since you first arrived?' Emma asked, in a tone that gave Dave the impression she was choosing her words carefully. He gave a silent nod of confirmation, and she smiled as she continued. 'Forgive me for eavesdropping, but you mentioned your encounter with my former husband. I wonder if you could elaborate on that?'

Dave felt his stomach muscles tighten in anxiety. This was what he had feared the most since learning about Emma's relationship with his indomitable counterpart – she would want to know what happened to him. Realising he couldn't put it off any longer, he told Emma of his discussion with Barnes, leaving nothing out, including his theory on the colonel's fate following a cryptic exchange with Oracle. When he was finished, the room was silent while the occupants mulled over what he had told them.

'So, you think he's dead then?' Emma asked flatly.

Dave blew out a slow breath through his pursed lips and nodded. 'Yeah, I would bet my life on it,' he replied glumly. 'Commander Payne and I were in the middle of investigating a lead as to the whereabouts of his body, but we were interrupted by an attack from the creatures you call synthroids.'

Emma leaned back in her chair and stared up at the ceiling for a few seconds before answering. 'I don't mean to speak ill of the dead, but forgive me if I don't shed any tears over my David's death. As far as I'm

concerned, he finally got what he deserved.' She shook her head and let out a bitter laugh. 'I'm only sorry I wasn't there to witness it.'

As much as he wanted to be appalled by Emma's coldness regarding her former husband's death, to his surprise, Dave found himself nodding in silent understanding. After learning what his counterpart had put Emma through, the very thought that he was the colonel's doppelgänger had sickened him. He was sure that for as long as he lived, he would never understand how he could have descended to that sort of level. He shuddered as he realised everybody had a dark half they had kept hidden and secretly wished he'd seen the last of his.

As they sat in silent contemplation, Dave slowly became aware of a strange sensation. It was as if there was nervous energy in the conference room, thickening with tension he could almost cut with a knife. As he scanned the faces of the room, he stiffened as he realised the source of the uneasiness. He cast an eye to his right; Claire was still standing in the same spot as when she first arrived in the room, her face an unreadable, impassive mask. She was literally the proverbial elephant in the room – they could see her, but were unwilling to draw attention to her out of fear of what might happen. But before he could decide what would be the best way to bring it up, Dave flinched in surprise on hearing a loud cough from Isaac, who seemed to be rising from his seat.

'Dave, my friend,' Isaac boomed cheerfully, 'you must be hungry. How about I take you on a tour of this facility? Along the way, we can stop by the hydroponics bay, and you can sample the scrumptious delights of our home-grown food. I promise you it's an experience you don't want to miss.'

Wondering why Isaac would bring up food at a time like this, Dave frowned and was just about to question him, but something in his expression made him pause. Isaac and Hilaria were making discreet jerking motions with their heads. He tightened his eyes in confusion as he tried to work out what they were telling him. They seemed to be gesturing at Claire and Emma. *Eh?* he thought. *Why would ... Oh.*

Then it hit him. They wanted to take him out of the room so that Emma and Claire could spend some private time together. Even though he had doubts whether it was such a good idea to leave Claire because of

his concern about her mental state, Dave reluctantly accepted that if anyone could get Claire to open up, then it might be her own twin sister. Giving his best pretend smile, he nodded and made to follow Hilaria and Isaac.

'Yes, that would be lovely,' he replied in mock sincerity, following Isaac and Hilaria out through the hatch, while trying deliberately to avoid making eye contact with Claire.

Once he was on the other side of the closed hatch, Dave smiled courteously at Hilaria as she placed a hand on his shoulder.

'I'm sorry to dash off, but I've a matter with young Zoe to deal with,' she said, gesturing to Isaac. 'So, I must leave you in Isaac's capable hands. Don't worry, I'll catch up with you both later to see how you're doing.'

Without waiting for a reply, Hilaria swiftly turned on her heel and marched down the corridor. As she disappeared around a corner, he blew out a long breath, glanced at the closed hatch they had just come through, and stared at Isaac with heavy concern.

'Are you sure it's such a good idea to leave those two by themselves?' Dave asked warily.

Isaac glanced at the hatch and gave a thoughtful nod. 'Yes, I think it'll do them some good. Em's been holding on to a lot of pent-up feelings over what happened the night she was abducted.' Isaac smiled and spoke in a tone that had an unmistakable touch of confidence. 'Trust me, this is the right thing to do.'

Unconvinced, Dave screwed up his face and scratched the back of his head. 'Hmm, I don't know,' he murmured with heavy reluctance. 'Claire's been through a lot, and in her current state of mind, I'm not sure a confrontation with her sister might be the best answer.'

Isaac pulled back his head and let out a loud, cheery laugh. 'Hah! Dave, my friend, I like you, but when it comes to the Tulley women, you still have a lot to learn. If Claire is anything like her sister, then I imagine she's also got some steel in her veins.' Dave winced in pain as Isaac's massive hand slapped him on the back and Isaac laughed even louder. 'You worry too much, my friend. What's the worst that could happen, eh? They fight. Lots of blood and so on, yes? Well, that just means we'll have to come back and clean up the mess.'

Trying hard not to imagine the carnage Isaac was describing, Dave turned and gave the beaming giant a sceptical look. But before he could voice any of his reservations, Isaac grabbed his arm and Dave found himself being led down the corridor. While he listened to Isaac's banter, he cast a worried eye over his shoulder to the receding hatch and secretly prayed to himself that Claire would be okay.

-24-

As she watched the conference room's hatch close, Em shook her head in amusement and chuckled to herself. Even though her friends were trying to be discreet, it had been plainly obvious what they were up to. Subtlety had never been one of Isaac's strong points. However, she was grateful for them not making a difficult situation even more stressful than it needed to be.

She had been silently studying Dave throughout their meeting, and she'd found him to be an enigma. Not in a bad way. In fact, it had been the other way around; he came across to her as a genuinely warm and compassionate person – nothing like her Barnes. Whereas her David's eyes had been cold and filled with deceit, his counterpart's eyes were completely the opposite. Yes, Dave seemed to share his counterpart's insightful nature, but there had been no hint of any malice in his eyes. The other thing she found comforting was that Dave had kept casting a concerned eye over to Claire, which told her he was heavily concerned about her. That alone gave her all the insight she needed about him – he might be someone she could have confidence in.

The amused smile on Em's face slowly morphed into a concerned frown as she turned her focus towards Claire's impassive face. She shared Dave's concern about the way her sister was acting. As soon as she had set eyes on her, Em had been equally shocked and troubled. Yes, it had been a long time since she'd last seen her, but Em could still recognise the signs – there was something terribly wrong with Claire. If she didn't know any

better, it seemed as if she was purposely closing herself off from those around her.

Sucking on her bottom lip, Em steepled her fingers and stared at Claire in thoughtful contemplation. If she failed to take action, it was possible Claire would withdraw even further and she would lose her again, probably forever. Em tightened her lips into a thin line and shook her head. No, she wouldn't allow that to happen. She had just been reunited with her sister, and she was determined not to allow her to be taken from her without a struggle.

From her experience of dealing with people who'd acted in a very similar way to Claire, Em was knowledgeable in a variety of techniques she could employ to get through to her. But it needed to be something so irritating, it would force Claire to break out of her stupor in a violent reaction. Em tapped her bottom lip with her finger while she ran through the various options in her head, each one more unsettling than the next. The corner of Em's mouth curled up into a secretive smile as she settled on a solution. Oh yes, if there was one thing she was good at, pissing people off was one of them. She had Cornelius to thank for that. Not only had her devious mentor taught Em everything he knew about intelligence gathering, arm-to-arm combat, he'd also passed on to her his extensive experience in psychological manipulation.

Keeping her eyes fixed on Claire's impassive face, Em loudly drummed the fingers of her right hand on the table's surface, increasing in speed after every minute. After five minutes, she made a loud popping noise with her lips in sync with the drumming of her fingers. Seven minutes later, she upped the ante by trailing the fingernails of her left hand over the surface of the desk.

Drumming.

Popping.

Scratching.

She carried on for several more minutes before she began to notice a reaction. It had been small, but Em was certain she had seen a tremor in Claire's right eyelid, followed by what appeared to be a slight strain in the tendons in her neck. A sense of satisfaction stirred within Em; what she was doing was working.

She stopped the popping of her lips and smiled. Even though she had been successful in getting a reaction out of Claire, that wasn't enough. She needed to make her angry, and the only way she could do that was to provoke her.

Ignoring the pain from her sore knee, Em drew in a long breath, rose from her chair, and hobbled towards Claire, coming to a stop in front of her. Then, quietly singing 'I know a song that will get on your nerves' over and over, she walked in a slow, tight circle around her, every so often flicking the back of her ear.

'Not annoying you, am I?' she said, chuckling as she continued to walk around Claire. 'All you have to do is tell me to stop, and I will.' On receiving no response, Em pulled her head back and scoffed, 'Oh, this is just like you, Cee. You always thought that I was better than you, that Mam and Dad loved me more than you. Jealous because I was more popular than you. Tell me, did Mam and Dad ever tell you how disappointed they were that you weren't the one who was taken? Hmm? I'm sure it looked like they loved you, but deep down, they must have despised you.'

Despite being aware of the emotional toll it was taking on Claire, Em understood she had to be even more ruthless in order to penetrate Claire's barrier of silence. Determined she would not stop until she got a reaction from her, Em came to a stop behind Claire and leaned in closer to whisper into her ear.

'That night, when you saw me lying on the kitchen floor in front of that creature, you must have thought all your Christmases had come at once,' Em sneered, continuing to whisper in the best cruel tone she could manage. 'This was what you had been waiting for, to be finally rid of Little-Miss-Know-it-All. With me out of the picture, you would be the centre of attention. What would all your friends think if they saw you now?' Em leaned in closer and hissed into Claire's face, showering her face with spittle. 'Hah! Friends! I bet you don't even have any.' She cocked her head and pretended to stare at Claire with disdain. 'Tell me, is Dave aware what a monster you are? That at the first opportunity, you'll probably hand him over to Oracle, and turn your back on him the same way you did to me.' Taking a step back, Em let out a loud, scornful laugh. 'You and my David would've made the perfect couple. You're both back-stabbing bas—'

Em's vision went white with pain as something hard connected with the right side of her jaw, taking her by surprise and forcing her to take a step back. Stunned, her vision filled with stars, Em blinked and shook her head while she massaged the side of her jaw. Once the stars had cleared, she saw Claire was standing before her, hands clenched, face tight with fury.

'How dare you!' Claire snarled, her body shaking with rage.

Okay, the tiger has been woken. Now let's see what happens if I rattle the cage some more, Em thought while she continued to massage the side of her face, nodding in approval. 'Impressive, the kitty has claws after all,' she taunted. 'Here I thought you preferred to turn your back while you let others do your dirty work for you.'

'Th-that-that's n-n-n—' Claire spluttered, shaking her head.

'N-n-not t-t-true,' Em interrupted, mocking Claire's voice. She shook her head and laughed, bringing her hands together in a slow, sarcastic clap. 'Oh wow, I'm really loving the act, sis. Never realised you had it in you.'

Even though she had got the reaction she had wanted, Em knew she had to keep the pressure on Claire if she was to make her even more emotional. She needed to turn the screw even tighter, no matter how much it hurt them both. She gave a loud huff of disdain and a dismissive wave of her hand. 'Oh, give me a break, sis. You can cut the act. Back when we were children, you resented having me around. I could see it every time you looked at me. You forget, I saw you standing in the kitchen doorway the night I was taken. I recognised that look in your eyes. You finally had the chance to get rid of me and you took it.'

Tears flowed down Claire's face as she shook her head furiously. 'N-n-no,' she pleaded, her voice cracking with emotion. 'Th-th-that's not true. I-I—'

Not wanting to let up with her emotional attack, Em took a step forward and viciously jabbed her right index finger into Claire's shoulder. 'Stop lying, Claire,' she hissed. 'I saw you. You could have called out for help, but instead you simply turned your back and closed the kitchen door, leaving me alone with the synthroid.' She leaned in closer and stared into Claire's eyes. Claire tried to turn away, but Em seized hold of her face with

her right hand and forced her to keep staring at her. 'How easy was it to turn your back on me, sis? I always wondered whether the guilt over what you did kept you awake at night. Did you ever—'

Suddenly, Claire snapped her head back, breaking Em's grip on her face, and let out a heart-wrenching, anguished howl. 'You lied to me!' she screamed, her bottom lip trembling. Then she collapsed onto her knees, her hands pressed against her chest, face crumbling as she stared up at Em and gave another heart-wrenching cry. 'Why? Why did you do it? You lied to me.'

Not the reaction she was expecting, Em stood frozen on the spot, opening and closing her mouth in stunned shock. Throughout the years, she had envisaged this exact moment in her head – but in her mind she was standing over Claire, who would be on her knees pleading for mercy, not accusing Em of lying as she was now. Em had replayed this moment time and time again in her head and had felt confident about what she would say and do when the time came. She had imagined exchanging some barbed words with Claire, who would then apologise, and all would be forgiven.

However, as Em had learned painfully over the years, events never go the way one expects.

She swallowed, drew out a long breath and slowly lowered herself in front of Claire, taking hold of her hands. 'What do you mean, Claire? How have I lied to you?' she asked gently.

Claire stared into Em's eyes and squeezed her hands so tight, it caused her to grimace in pain. 'All these years I thought you were dead,' she said through long, racking sobs. 'But all this time you were alive and well.' A bubble of snot burst out of Claire's nose and another sob escaped her while she gave Em a gut-wrenching look of betrayal. 'Why did you lie to me, Emma? Was it to punish me for turning my back on you?'

'Cee, I didn't lie to you,' Em insisted. 'I thought you—'

Before Em could finish what she was saying, Claire let out another distressed scream, so loud it tore through Em's soul. She could only watch as Claire snatched her hands back and shot up straight so fast it caught Em unprepared, and she fell back onto her bottom. Speechless, she remained rooted to the floor while Claire paced around the room, waving her hands

and mumbling erratically to herself.

'If you didn't lie to me, that must mean God was punishing me for being selfish,' Claire mumbled, nodding to herself furiously. 'Yes, that's right. God has been punishing me.' She came to a sudden stop and stared beseechingly up at the ceiling. 'I'm aware I made a mistake, but haven't I worked tirelessly to put right what I did wrong by fighting to unravel the conspiracy of silence?' Her face streaked with tears, she threw her hands up and raged at the ceiling. 'How many times must I die before you finally absolve me of my actions?'

Recognising the torment in her sister's voice, Em let out a sharp gasp. All these years, she had assumed that Claire had led a carefree life, shielded from the terrors that Em had been forced to endure. Nevertheless, it was becoming apparent that the events of that night had had an impact on Claire equivalent to those events on her. Em shook her head despondently while she tried to imagine how hard it must have been for Claire to walk around all these years with the guilt and shame churning away inside her like a pressure cooker but without an outlet for release.

But as she studied Claire's stricken face, Em furrowed her brow as she detected something else in her sister's eyes and got a sense that there was something else troubling her. She nodded and tightened her eyes while a seed of suspicion grew inside her. Yes, she was certain there was something more going on here, other than guilt or shame.

She winced in pain as she lifted herself off the floor and made her way over to the sobbing Claire. Without saying another word, she wrapped her arms around Claire and pulled her closer. At first, Claire appeared to resist, but then it seemed as if the fight was draining out of her, and Em felt her body shudder as she buried her head in Em's neck and wept.

'It's okay, sis,' Em whispered in a soothing tone, gently stroking the back of Claire's head. 'Just let it out.'

'For years, I punished myself for leaving you behind,' Claire whimpered. 'After I closed the door and made my way to the bottom of the stairs, I realised what I was doing was wrong, so I turned back to help you. But just as I did so, I knocked over the vase and it crashed onto the floor. I guess the creature must have heard it because next thing I know, it burst through the kitchen door.' She shook her head pleadingly. 'Emma, I

tried to save you. I did. But the creature was too fast for me. It slashed me across my back and then I must have blacked out from the pain. As soon as I regained consciousness, I crawled back upstairs to alert Mam and Dad, but by the time Dad got down into the kitchen, I knew from his screams that I was too late.' Claire's body trembled and she let out a long, shuddering breath. 'I've forgotten how many times I've replayed that night in my head, wishing I could've done something different. Emma, if I could have traded places with you, I would've done so without hesitation.'

'If you'd stayed to help,' Em replied sombrely, 'then we might have both been taken, or worse – we might have both been killed.' She pulled back, wiped the tears from Claire's wet cheeks and gave her a tight, humourless smile. 'But that's not what this is about, is it? A lot of years have passed between us, but I feel I still know you well enough to recognise you're hiding something from me.' The corner of her mouth curled up into a secretive smile and she gave Claire a knowing look. 'It may surprise you to learn I've become quite perceptive in my middle age. During my time on this world, I've had a fairly colourful … career and developed a variety of skills that have come in handy during times like this.'

Claire let out a sarcastic laugh and shook her head. 'Yeah, sure. You're this universe's version of Liam Neeson.' Having no idea who Claire was referring to, Em remained silent but kept her eyes locked on Claire. She guessed there must have been something in her expression because the colour drained out of Claire's face, and she let out a surprised gasp. 'Frack me, you're serious, aren't you?'

'Uh-huh,' Em replied, nodding, and then gestured for her to take a seat. Once they were sitting beside one another, Em reached over and placed a hand on Claire's knee. 'So, are you going to tell what's really bothering you? I can see Dave cares deeply for you and that he's worried about you, too.'

Claire's shoulders sagged as she leaned back in her chair and ran a hand down her face. 'I'm exhausted.' Claire sighed wearily, prodding a finger into her right temple. 'Not physically, mentally. Since the night of your dea— erm … disappearance, I feel like my life has been one constant battle. First, I had to fight to get people to believe me about what I saw. Then, when the government pressured our family to keep quiet, I vowed I

wouldn't stop until I uncovered the truth about what's really going on.' Her eyes shimmered in the warm glow of the room's lighting, and she exhaled a long, frustrated groan. 'But I just feel like I'm treading water and getting nowhere. I've had four near-death experiences and survived a couple of assassination attempts on my life that were meant to stop me from talking.' Claire's voice cracked, and she buried her face in her hands. 'If I am being honest, following the attack by the thing you call the synthroid, it seemed like I was living on borrowed time. Eventually, I just thought, what was the point? I even pushed Dave away. The final straw for me was being caught in a nuclear explosion. As I felt my skin blister, I honestly thought this was my time, and I was finally going to be reunited with you.' She lifted her head out of her hands and stared at them while speaking in a despondent tone. 'But then Custos stepped in to save me and I woke up in this world. This may sound strange, and I know I should've been delighted to be alive, but I felt like I'd been cheated out of the death I deserved ...' Her voice trailed off, but she continued to gaze in silence at her hands.

Her heart breaking from the doleful tone of her sister's voice, Em wanted so badly to ease Claire's pain. Inhaling a deep breath, she lifted her hand from Claire's knee and took hold of her trembling hand; Claire responded by raising her head and smiling gratefully. However, as Em peered into her sister's sombre face, it hit her that she'd seen that same expression many years ago, whenever she used to look at her own reflection. It was of someone who had given up on life. She gave a small nod of acknowledgement. Yes, that explained why Claire was acting the way she was. She must have thought … what was the point of feeling anything, if the universe was just constantly going to punish her?

Releasing Claire's hand, Em leaned in closer and placed her hand under Claire's chin. Claire turned her head and smiled sadly at Em, who spoke soothingly to her. 'If it helps, I understand what you're going through,' she said. 'I went through the same thing as you when I first arrived. For years, I felt numb, not believing I was alive. I would get myself into trouble on purpose, just so that the overseers could punish me. I had this idea in my head that so long as I continued to feel pain, it meant I was still alive.'

Claire nodded in understanding and let out a bitter laugh. 'Would

you believe one of the first things I wanted to do, not long after I regained consciousness, was to snog Dave?' She wrinkled her nose in disgust and stared up at the ceiling. 'What the hell was I thinking?'

'Well, at least you didn't want to get off by encouraging people to use pain sticks on you like I did,' Em answered, smirking and giving Claire a playful nudge. She winked. 'I'm sure you put a smile on Dave's face.'

'Oh god, Dave,' Claire groaned, planting her face in her hands. 'What must he be thinking? I was so nasty to him.'

They lapsed into an uncomfortable silence, and Em leaned back in her chair while she regarded her sister. After a few minutes of pensive silence, she straightened, shuffled closer to Claire, and placed her hand over hers.

'I'm going to share some words of wisdom that were given to me by someone who was very dear to me,' Em said as Claire turned and gave her a quizzical look. 'Life isn't straightforward. It isn't meant to be easy. Every so often, we'll be hit by an obstacle that'll knock us off our feet. It's how we handle these knocks that define us. Do we just lie down and accept it, or do we stand up, brush ourselves down and try again? For years I considered myself a victim, but Cornelius taught me otherwise – I'm a survivor.' The muscles in Em's face tightened as she placed both hands on Claire's shoulders and stared deep into her eyes. 'You've endured and suffered a lot. Yes, they've knocked you down, but they didn't kill you. In my eyes, they only strengthened you.' She jabbed a finger into Claire's chest and spoke with conviction. 'You are a Tulley, just like me. Do you understand what that means?'

Claire was silent for several seconds as if she was considering what Em was saying, then the middle of her forehead wrinkled, and she lifted her shoulder in a half shrug. 'I don't know, does it mean I'm a survivor?' she asked in a hesitant, uncertain tone.

Em shot up out of her chair, folded her arms across her chest and fixed Claire with a steady gaze. 'Is that a question or a statement?'

'It's a statement,' Claire answered meekly, nodding.

Em blinked and pretended she hadn't heard by placing her right hand against her right ear. 'I'm sorry, I didn't catch that. I thought you said it was a statement, but I couldn't hear it over the self-pitying whimpering.'

'I'm a survivor,' Claire replied through gritted teeth. From the scowl etched across her face, Em could tell she was unhappy. *Tough*, Em thought, *I'm not going to make it easy for her.*

'Nope, still didn't hear you,' Em said, waving her hand dismissively. 'I don't think you mean it. I've got better things to do than stand here while you waste my time. Come on, Claire, say it like you mean it. Prove to me you're my sister.'

Her face blazing red with humiliation, Claire bolted up from her chair, balled her fists and glared at Em. 'I'm a survivor,' she snarled.

'Is that the best you can do?' Em laughed, making a sweeping gesture with her hands. 'The universe is laughing at you, Claire. What are you going to do? Shrink in a corner and cry?' She curled her lip and sneered at the seething woman standing in front of her. 'You make me sick. Get away from me. You're not my sister.' Em knew she had probably gone too far, but she needed to make sure Claire meant what she said.

Her eyes incandescent with rage, Claire lunged at Em, stopping just centimetres from her face, then grabbed the lapels of her overall. 'I *am* a survivor!' she screamed, white spittle spraying out of her mouth.

Em broadened her smile, and she wiped her face. 'Louder,' she hissed.

Tears of fury streaming from her eyes, Claire released her grip on Em, took a step back, craned her head back, flung her arms wide and screamed up at the heavens, 'I. Am. A. Survivor!'

'Who are you?' Em screamed back.

'I am Claire Tulley,' Claire roared, her voice nearly hoarse. She sucked in a deep breath and let out a howl of defiance. 'I am the sister of Emma Tulley, and we are survivors.'

Her heart swelling with pride, Em secretly wished their parents were here to see this and fought back the tears as she wondered what it would have been like if Henrietta had been standing alongside them too. Without uttering another word, Em embraced her sister and clung to her tightly, afraid that if she let her go, something might take her from her. She squeezed her eyes shut, but that didn't stop the tears from flowing down her cheeks while she continued to hold her in a tight embrace.

It became clear to Em that she had needed this as much as Claire

had. Although she hadn't intended it, she felt as if they'd both exorcised their demons today. A warm glow filled Em's heart, which spread out to the rest of her body. Blinking away tears of joy, Em kissed Claire's forehead and fixed a harsh stare up at the ceiling.

Let Oracle be aware. No. Let it be known throughout the multiverse. The Tulley sisters are back together again, and heaven help anybody who gets in our way.

-25-

The two women sat in silent contemplation for several long minutes. Claire was aware of the hum of energy passing through the power conduits hidden somewhere behind the walls, alongside the hiss of recycled air being pushed into the room through the ventilation ducts. The noise was calming for Claire, who found it aided her concentration while she reclined in her chair and contemplated what Emma had told her.

The past couple of months had been a struggle for Claire, and she was forced to admit that it had felt like she had been heading down a dark path that seemed to lead to a bleak future. If it hadn't been for Emma's stubborn bloody-mindedness, Claire was afraid to imagine how things might have turned out for her.

She drew in a deep breath and massaged her brow. Even though it seemed as if she was making progress in her recovery, she was certain she still had a long road ahead. However, with the support of those around her, she now felt confident she had enough faith in her heart that she would arrive at her destination victorious, stronger than ever.

As she thought about Emma's timely assistance, Claire tilted her head slightly and cast a surreptitious eye at her sister, and she couldn't help but be impressed by her physique. From the toned appearance of her upper arms and her broad shoulders, she could tell Emma had spent a lot of time looking after herself. A pang of jealousy stirred inside her as she let her eyes wander over the rest of Emma's body and imagined the steel-like abs

hidden under the T-shirt.

What must Emma think of me? she groaned to herself as she pulled her gaze away, focusing on her own stomach. *Compared to her, I must look like a right slob.*

'Hey, what's with the frown?'

Startled out of her self-pitying thoughts, Claire snapped her head back. She realised Emma was looking at her with her right eyebrow raised in concern. It dawned on Claire that she must have groaned out loud, loud enough for Emma to hear, which made her feel worse, and she felt her cheeks warm with embarrassment. That was just great! She cringed inwardly, wishing for the ground to open and swallow her.

'Sorry,' Claire said sheepishly, allowing the right corner of her mouth to lift in a weak smile. 'I was just thinking I must look a right state.'

'Whatever makes you think that?' Emma laughed, her eyebrows climbing up her forehead in surprise.

'Oh, come on, Emma,' she scoffed, turning in her chair and making a wide sweeping gesture over Emma's body. 'Look at you. You look amazing. I would give my eye teeth to have a body like yours.' She bobbed her head at the closed hatch. 'Not only that. You're the leader of this awesome facility, surrounded by people who think the world of you. It looks like you've done pretty well for yourself, if you don't mind me saying.'

Claire realised she must have said the wrong thing. Emma's face darkened, and she shot her frosty look.

'I'll have you know,' Emma said in a curt tone with an edge to it. 'My life here hasn't exactly been a bed of roses. You think things haven't been easy for you? Try to imagine all the horrors and abuse I've suffered over the past forty-odd years.'

Sensing she'd put her foot in her mouth, Claire squirmed in her seat at the build-up of acid in her stomach and struggled to say something that would de-escalate the rising tension. But no matter how hard she tried, her mind was blank and she kicked the right leg of her chair in frustration. *Great, what a time for my brain to take a leave of absence.*

But as Claire stared into Emma's eyes, she saw something that made her pause. It was something she was seeing for the first time. Emma's eyes had a haunted vibe to them. Not only that, but they also seemed to be full of pain, giving Claire the impression that this was someone who'd had been forced to endure a tremendous amount of suffering throughout their life, physically and mentally. Claire felt her heart tighten in sympathy on recalling what Emma had told Dave earlier about losing her daughter.

'Emma, please forgive my poor choice of words,' Claire said, pleading, holding her hands out in front of her in a penitent gesture. 'I didn't mean to upset you. I sometimes have this habit of speaking with my foot in my mouth.'

To Claire's relief, Emma's face softened, and she waved her hand. 'It's fine, Cee. Water under the bridge,' she said, grinning, and then her mouth widened into a mysterious smile and she let out a small laugh.

Puzzled at what Emma was finding so amusing, Claire pulled a face and shook her head. 'What?'

'Oh, I was just thinking that you haven't changed.' Emma laughed. 'It's just like that night all over again. Remember? Your mouth got you into trouble then, too.'

Even though Claire could remember the incident Emma was talking about, she decided to act all innocent and held up her head and sniffed. 'I don't know what you're talking about.'

'Oh, aye,' Emma scoffed, waggling her finger, 'that little miss innocent act doesn't work on me. You know full well what I'm talking about. If you remember, it was your potty mouth that got us both into trouble in the first place.'

'If I remember correctly, you were the one who grassed me up to Mam,' Claire retorted, trying to keep the enjoyment of their playful banter from showing on her face.

'Yeah, well,' Emma said, grinning and nudging Claire on the shoulder. 'At least I didn't answer back to Mam. I can still remember the look on her face.'

Claire shook her head as she pictured the thunderous expression on her mum's face. 'Bloody hell, if looks could kill, I'd probably have died in that bed.'

The two women laughed out loud and slapped each other on the shoulder. Eventually, after several seconds, Claire lapsed into silence as she thought back to that night, as she had so many times over the years. She

stared up at the ceiling, wondering how her life would have turned out if she and Emma had never got into that argument, which had resulted in Emma going down to the kitchen. Claire wrinkled her brow as, for the first time, she thought about how Emma's abductors had chosen that particular moment, when Emma was alone in the kitchen. It had always puzzled her why the creature had killed Emma but had spared her.

Ever since she learned the truth and discovered Emma was alive, an unsettling theory had been gnawing at the back of Claire's mind. Had Emma been targeted on purpose? If that was true, what would have happened if Emma hadn't been in the kitchen? Would the creature have left, or would it have tried again another time? She nibbled on her bottom lip as an even more troubling thought occurred to her. Now that she knew the dead body in the kitchen wasn't Emma's, whose had it been? Over the years, she had discovered people were being replaced by doppelgängers, so she was starting to wonder if that dead person had been Emma's doppelgänger. Claire shook her head in bewilderment. If that was true, then whoever had been in charge of the portal must have ordered the doppelgänger to be killed. Why? That made little sense.

The more Claire thought about it, the more she realised it just led to more questions.

Before she could give it any more thought, she stiffened as Emma's hand touched her arm, breaking her out of her musing. She cast an eye over to Emma, who had shuffled closer to her, and detected a mischievous grin on her face. What was she up to now?

'Cow,' Emma whispered.

'Moo,' Claire replied, repeating her response from their last night together.

'Matter transference displacement with quantum entanglement,' Emma retorted, smirking.

Claire laughed, 'Oooh, who's showing off now?'

Folding her arms across her chest, Emma lowered her head and smiled. 'After forty-odd years, I think I deserve a little payback.' Her smile vanished and she gave Claire a deadpan look, her voice developing a serious tone. 'Claire, how are Mam and Dad? Are they …' Her voice trailed off; it was as if she was unwilling to finish the sentence.

The atmosphere in the room seemed to change. To Claire, it no longer felt jovial, becoming heavier, as if anticipating her answer. She inhaled and let out a long, shuddering breath. From the very moment she had learned Emma was alive, Claire had dreaded being asked this question. Not because she was afraid to answer it, but because she feared how Emma would react to the news.

'Dad ... passed away two years ago,' Claire said, unable to hide the sorrow in her voice. 'Following a short battle with cancer. Mam, she passed away six months later. They say it was complications from a stroke, but in my heart, I knew it was because she missed Dad so much.'

Emma's eyes shimmered, and she nodded slowly, her voice breaking slightly. 'D-did they ever talk about me?'

Her vision blurring, Claire wiped the tears from her eyes and gave a sorrowful nod of acknowledgement. 'They never forgot about you. Mam lit a candle twice a year in your memory – on your birthday and on Christmas Day.' A surge of anger burned within Claire, and she wasn't able to hide the bitterness she was feeling from showing in her voice. 'The night I thought you had died, neighbours took me away while Mam and Dad spoke with the police. When I was allowed to return, I tried to explain to them what I had seen, but they wouldn't listen to me, saying I was only making it up out of grief, looking for attention, et cetera. They didn't tell me until a few years later that they had been pressured into ignoring what I was telling them.'

'Oh, Cee. I'm so sorry you had to go through that,' Emma whispered, squeezing Claire's hand.

'It's okay.' Claire sniffed, shrugging. 'It just made me more determined to uncover the truth.' Straightening her head proudly, she gave Emma a sad smile. 'Just before he died, Dad told me how proud he was of what I was doing, and he made me promise I wouldn't let anything stop me from uncovering the evidence I needed to bring those behind the conspiracy of silence to justice.'

Emma tilted her head and gave Claire a look that contained a touch of amusement. 'So, what are you? A secret agent or something?' Her face turned serious, and she pumped her right hand into the air. 'Agent Claire Tulley, defender of the truth.'

'Hah! I wish,' Claire said, laughing and shaking her head. Composing herself, she held Emma's gaze and spoke in a serious tone. 'I'm actually a history professor. I studied first at Durham University, then at Cambridge. It was there I earned my doctorate. Before I took up my place at Durham, I travelled the world searching for information, developing contacts that would help me uncover those responsible.'

'Wow! Cee,' Emma whistled, nodding, visibly impressed. 'You really are a clever clogs.'

'Pfft,' Claire snorted, giving a dismissive wave. 'It pays the bills. Over the years, though, I've managed to use my network of contacts to uncover information on those behind the global conspiracy.'

'Is that how you met Dave?' Emma asked, her voice thick with curiosity.

'Sort of,' Claire said, smiling as she thought back to their first meeting when he had literally knocked her off her feet. 'Let's just say our paths crossed in a case he was investigating.'

Claire noticed a mischievous twinkle in Emma's eyes, and she did a double take on seeing the self-satisfied smirk on her face. It was the same self-satisfied smirk she had seen on her face when they were children, whenever Emma had something that Claire had wanted. Claire pressed her lips together, remembering that expression had irritated her back then, too.

'Okay,' Claire grumbled, giving Emma the hairy eyeball. 'What's with the look?'

'What look?' Emma answered, eyes widening, and then she pressed her hands against her chest in obvious mock innocence, something which also used to piss off Claire. 'I don't have the faintest idea what you're talking about.'

Claire stood up, placed her hands on her hips, and shot Emma an accusatory stare. 'Cut the crap! You understand perfectly what I mean. You've got that same self-satisfied look you had whenever you got something I wanted. It's that Christmas Barbie all over again.' Screwing up her face, Claire bobbed her head from side to side, speaking in a childish voice. 'Naa-na-naaa-na. I've got something you want. Na-naaa-na-na.'

'Did I really?' Emma said, shaking her head in amazement. 'Well, Claire, you certainly have a better memory than I do, because I've no

recollection of that.'

Bristling at Emma's persistent theatrics, Claire felt her face burn with anger and she raised her right index finger. 'Listen here, you—'

The words died in Claire's throat when she saw the sly smile on Emma's face. The penny dropped, and it dawned on Claire what Emma had been hinting at. She felt her eyes grow wide, and did a double take. No! She couldn't be serious. Surely this hadn't been about Dave?

'Hang on a second,' Claire said, holding her hands up, incredulous at the idea. 'You're having a go at me because I'm with Dave, aren't you?' She thought her jaw was going to drop to the floor as Emma's grin broadened into a beaming smile and she let out an unbelieving laugh. 'Oh my god! It is, isn't it?'

Emma held up her hands with her palms facing upwards and shrugged. 'You always wanted what I used to have,' she said in a matter-of-fact tone, staring at Claire with an arched eyebrow. 'It seems like you have now moved on from wanting my toys to wanting my men.'

Not believing what she was listening to, Claire pinched the bridge of her nose and let out a disbelieving laugh. 'For Pete's sake, Em. You seriously can't believe that? My Dave is completely different to yours.'

Emma held up a finger and spoke in a serious tone. 'Technically, they're both the same person. Can't be a coincidence you slept with the man I married and had a child with.' She tapped her finger on her chin and stared up at the ceiling with a contemplative look on her face, murmuring, 'I wonder whether, because we never officially divorced, that means my husband cheated on me with my sister?'

'What?' Claire exclaimed in disbelief. Could Emma hear what was coming out of her mouth? Surely, she couldn't believe what she was saying? Struggling to get behind her sister's logic, she opened and closed her mouth but was at a loss for how to respond. Emma had to see that they were entirely different men, separated by dimensions. How could someone classify that as cheating? The only reason Claire could think of was that this world had twisted Emma's mind so much it had made her paranoid. Claire nodded. Yeah, that had to be the only explanation, because no sane person would even think of something like that!

'N-n-now j-j-just,' Claire sputtered, pointing to Emma and then to

herself. 'Y-y-you ... m-m-me ...'

She stiffened on noticing a mischievous twinkle in Emma's eyes, followed by the softening of her deadpan expression. Then she realised Emma had been teasing her and embarrassment warmed her cheeks. She planted her face in her hands and groaned. Like she did when they were children, Emma always knew how to push Claire's buttons.

'Oh, I'm sorry, Cee.' Emma laughed, tears streaming down her cheeks as she waved her hand. 'I couldn't resist. You should see the look on your face.' Collapsing back into her chair, she howled with laughter.

-26-

For what seemed like several long minutes, Claire could only stand and stare at Emma, seething because once again, she'd fallen for one of her sister's tricks. It annoyed her that she had walked right into it. But as she stared at the laughing Emma, the corners of Claire's mouth quivered slightly. In that moment, she felt like a child again and she burst out laughing. Back when they had been younger, they could never stay mad at each other for long. Her vision blurred, and her stomach ached with joyous laughter as she plonked herself back into the chair and gave Emma's arm a playful punch. Claire could not remember the last time she'd laughed this much.

'You had me for a second there, sis,' Claire said, wiping her eyes, her laughter easing. She leaned forward and placed a tender hand on Emma's forearm and spoke in a sorrowful tone. 'I'm sorry about what happened to your daughter. It may not have seemed like it, but I was aware of everything you and Hilaria were saying to Dave.'

Emma sniffed, wiped her face, and gave a small nod of acknowledgement. 'Thank you, Cee. That means a lot.' She let out a long melancholic sigh and shook her head. 'In truth, I lost her a long time ago, when my Barnes took her away and gave the order to have her memory wiped.'

'Still, it can't have been easy watching your daughter dying, as well as working alongside the woman responsible,' Claire said, shaking her head in awe. 'All I can say is you must be made of stronger stuff than me.'

Leaning in closer, Claire pressed her hands together and gave a tight smile. 'You understand my Dave is nothing like yours, don't you?'

'Yeah, I know that,' Emma replied, nodding. She ran her right hand down her face and exhaled a weary breath. 'Even though deep down a part of me still can't help feel a stir of revulsion whenever I look at him.' A humourless laugh escaped her and she gave Claire a playful nudge. 'We live in interesting times, sis. We live in interesting times.'

'Humph! You're preaching to the choir here, sis,' Claire said, holding up her hand to allow Emma to fist-bump it.

'I can see he loves you, you know,' Emma whispered, giving Claire a knowing smile. 'Your Dave, I mean. I recognised it as soon as I saw him look at you. He genuinely loves you.'

Claire pulled a sour face and blew out a slow breath. 'Yeah, I'm perfectly aware of his feelings toward me. I would love to say I feel the same, but …' A growl of frustration stirred in her throat, and she slammed her hand down on the table.

'You can't forget what Custos told you,' Emma said, nodding, her voice full of sympathy. 'You're worried what you're feeling isn't real, and you're second-guessing yourself. If you get too close, you're afraid Custos might be manipulating you again.'

Claire snapped her head back and folded her arms across her chest. 'How'd you know about that?' she asked with heavy suspicion. But before she could say any more, a flash of memory stirred inside her and Emma's conversation with Dave came flooding back to her. Nodding in understanding, she arched her eyebrow curiously. 'Oh yeah, you were there too, weren't you? How much of it did you hear?'

'Enough,' Emma answered, giving a tight, sympathetic smile and reaching over to take Claire's hand. 'So I mean it when I say I understand perfectly what you must be going through. But that shouldn't stop you returning Dave's affections.' Before Claire could respond, Emma held up her right hand to silence her protestations. 'Please let me finish. I was there when Custos also told you that your feelings for Dave had always been there. He just helped bring them to the surface. It may even be possible that you and Dave would have eventually got together without Custos's *help*.'

Even though a part of her had a hard time accepting what Emma was saying, Claire screwed up her face and scratched the back of her head. 'So, what? You're saying we're destined to be together?'

Emma leaned back in her chair, steepled her fingers and stared up at the ceiling with a thoughtful expression etched across her face. 'No, I'm not saying that. It may go even deeper than that,' she murmured. Then, much to Claire's surprise, Emma snapped her fingers and looked directly into her eyes 'Bear with me here, but I've been dwelling on this ever since I woke from my coma, so this will be the first time I've voiced it.' Emma cleared her throat, rose from her chair, and paced around the room. 'Cornelius once told me about his theory on fixed moments in time. Things that are meant to happen, no matter if they are good or bad. Now, what if that applies to the multiverse? Surely it can't be a coincidence that my David and I got together, and you and your Dave got together?' Before Claire could respond, Emma continued. 'No, it's because it's a multiversal fixed point – in every universe a Tulley and a Barnes must get together.'

'Holy crap, Em, I know we've experienced some weird shit, but isn't that stretching things?' Claire scoffed, trying to hide the scepticism in her voice. She leaned forward and held up a finger. 'Okay, let's just say what you're saying is true. Doesn't that confirm what I've been saying – we're not in control of our own destiny?'

'No, I'm not saying that,' Emma replied, shaking her head adamantly. 'Just because we're being guided doesn't mean we're not in control.'

Emma lapsed into silence and sucked on her bottom lip. It seemed to Claire she was mulling something over, so she thought it was best to remain quiet. Less than a minute later, Emma's face brightened, and she turned sharply toward Claire.

'Okay, try this,' she said with a touch of excitement in her voice. 'In this reality, my Barnes worked alongside Cooper. From what Hilaria has told me, didn't your Dave also work alongside the Cooper from your reality?'

'Yes,' Claire answered slowly, grimacing at the pressure building in her temples, which had all the hallmarks of a headache coming on from trying to wrap her head around what Emma was trying to explain to her.

'In my reality, Wendy was a police constable while my Dave is, um, was a detective inspector. But wha—' Claire stiffened, and she blinked as a light bulb went off in her head. *Of course,* she thought, *now I understand what Emma's trying to say.* There had to be a balance in every universe. Certain relationships needed to exist, whether they were good or bad, so that they could ... what? Claire frowned and then stared at Emma with an enquiring raised eyebrow. She wondered if Emma was trying to imply that the reason they existed was to combat threats such as Oracle?

Feeling as if her headache was turning into a full-blown migraine, Claire massaged her forehead and groaned. 'So, what you're saying is we're like the white blood cells in a human body. We are the multiverse's defence against other-worldly forces?'

'Possibly,' Emma answered, shrugging. 'How else to explain everything that has happened to us?' She smiled and held up her hands. 'Of course, I could be just spouting horse shit, and it is all just a cosmic coincidence.' Shuffling closer, Emma took hold of Claire's hands, a serious expression on her face. 'Forget about that and listen to what I'm trying to tell you – forget about what Custos told you. Just follow your heart. Understand?'

Before Claire could respond, she found herself being pulled out of her chair by Emma. Not sure what Emma wanted her to do, she blinked and shook her head in bewilderment. Was she wanting to show Claire something? If so, what? As much as she was enjoying Emma's eagerness to show off, she wasn't sure how many more surprises her brain could handle. Ever since she had woken up from her coma, it felt as if she hadn't had a minute to herself to process what had happened to her. How could she tell Emma she needed time to herself to rest and think things over without offending her?

'It's okay,' Emma said, beaming as if she were answering Claire's unspoken question. 'I thought you might like to go for a walk and get some fresh air. Then before I show you to the quarters that have been assigned to you, I thought it might be nice to sit and have a bite to eat.'

'Yes, that would be nice,' Claire said, smiling. She absent-mindedly touched her face to adjust her glasses and then remembered she wasn't wearing any. She inwardly chastised herself for being too self-absorbed to

notice there was something slightly off with her vision. She'd completely forgotten that her glasses had been lost during the explosion that had left her trapped. It was highly likely they'd been vaporised in the nuclear blast.

'Cee, you okay?' Emma asked, head cocked curiously. 'You look a bit annoyed. Something wrong?'

Not wanting to make a fuss, Claire laughed sheepishly and gave a dismissive wave. 'Oh, sorry, Em. I'm feeling a bit foolish for just noticing I'm not wearing my glasses.'

Emma laughed and gave Claire's arm a reassuring squeeze. 'Oh, you silly cow! I didn't realise you wear glasses. We can fix that easily for you. It's just a simple matter of taking you to the infirmary to have your eyes scanned and having a pair of eyeglasses replicated for you.'

'Gosh! You can do that,' Claire replied, unable to keep the amazement from her voice. 'I don't want to put you out by going to all that bother.'

Emma lifted her shoulder in a half shrug, 'It's no bother at all. We can do that right now if you like. We'll be going past the medical level on our way up to the surface anyway. That'll also give me the chance to introduce you to somebody who I believe may be of some help to you.'

Grateful for Emma's assistance, Claire smiled and took hold of her sister's hand. As she followed her through the hatchway, Claire mulled over what they had discussed, and she could see that what Emma had said made sense. Now that she could look at everything that had happened to her from a different perspective, it felt as if a weight had been lifted off her. No longer burdened by the depressive thoughts that had haunted her these past couple of months, she was now even more determined that she was the one in control of her life.

As she followed Emma through the command centre, Claire realised she had wasted too much time worrying whether she and Dave should be together. It was time she showed him how she felt.

A short time later, Claire gently closed the hatch behind her and gazed around the small bedroom. It was very compact, but with a large double

bed. A set of metal drawers stood across from the bed, with a tall narrow wardrobe next to it. Just in front of her was an open door, which she assumed led into an en suite bathroom.

A gentle snoring drew Claire's attention back to the bed, and she smiled at the resting figure of Dave snuggled beneath the grey blanket. His presence did not surprise her since she had just seen Isaac, who mentioned that Dave seemed tired, and he'd advised him to get some rest.

Gently removing her new glasses and placing them on the dresser, Claire crept over to the bed. She stared at the sleeping Dave for a second, then wordlessly slipped out of her overall. Being careful not to disturb him, she slipped under the blanket and placed her arm on the snoozing Dave's shoulder.

'Hmm, hey you,' he murmured, patting Claire's hand.

'Sorry, I didn't mean to wake you up,' Claire whispered in response. 'Emma took me to get some fresh air and then for some lunch. Hilaria turned up with Zoe, who apologised for how she spoke to me earlier. Deep down, when you get to know her, she's actually a sweet girl and thinks the world of Emma. The four of us spent ages talking, eventually losing track of the time.'

'Glad to hear you're getting on,' Dave muttered sleepily. 'So, I guess you've discovered where we are too, huh?'

'Yeah, talk about strange coincidences. An underground base on the exact spot where the Castle was,' Claire said. She had been astounded when Emma opened the door to the outside and revealed their location.

'Humph, yeah, blows your mind, doesn't it,' Dave muttered. He turned so that they were directly looking at one another. The concern in his eyes was clear to see as Claire felt him touch her arm. 'How're you doing?'

'I'm fine. Emma introduced me to someone in the medical bay, Fausta is her name. I think she's what would be classed as a counsellor here. She helped me understand I was suffering from a form of PTSD, so we had a really long chat and helped me get some stuff off my chest. I've still a long way to go, but I'm getting there,' she whispered, edging closer to Dave and brushing her hand over his cheek. 'Sorry about how I treated you earlier.'

'It's okay. You were going through a tough time. We both were,' Dave replied, kissing the back of her hand.

Claire smiled as she felt Dave's arms wrap around her, and she snuggled closer into his body. Not wanting to spoil things, she decided against telling Dave that she'd asked Fausta if she could also talk to him, concerned he may also be suffering from PTSD. She sighed with contentment as his hands slid down her back with deliberate slowness, eventually stopping at her buttocks. Not wanting to spoil the moment, she closed her eyes and nuzzled his chest.

Screw destiny, Claire thought happily as for the first time in years the embrace of Morpheus took hold of her and guided her into his kingdom of dreams.

-27-

The following day, Dave was standing in the centre of a large round auditorium in front of several rows of seats that encircled the entire room. As he stood and stared at the slowly assembling audience, he had a sudden sense of déjà vu. Memories of his university days came flooding back to him from when he had sat inside lecture theatres, chatting with his fellow students and listening to the lecturer.

Unfamiliar faces acknowledged Dave with polite smiles and nods while he cast an eye over the people taking their seats. Although it pleased him that everybody seemed to welcome Claire and him warmly, he still couldn't shake that sense of unbelonging. Ever since he'd woken up and learned where he was, something had niggled away at him from the inside – a sense of unease. It wasn't because he was on a parallel world; it was the idea that he was stuck on this world with no way back home that bothered him. Knowing he would probably never see his friends or his own world again depressed him. Ever since his divorce, Dave had had difficulty sharing his feelings with anyone. He was reluctant to admit his loneliness to Claire because she had her own problems, and he believed it would be selfish of him to tell her what he was feeling.

The sense of depression became even greater when he glanced over to Claire and saw her chatting with her sister. *No*, he thought glumly, *I need to carry this burden myself. It wouldn't be fair to spoil Claire's moment of happiness.* Drawing in a shallow breath, he let out a despondent sigh as he wondered if there was anyone back home still alive. Kendra had most

certainly died in the explosion that had trapped him and Claire. But what about Sophia, John, Wendy or Andy? Were they fighting the good fight or had they also met their end?

'You look like you've lost a denarius and found a bronze aes, Mr Barnes,' a female voice said, breaking Dave out of his unhappy thoughts.

Embarrassed to have been caught daydreaming, Dave felt his cheeks warm as he spun round to see an attractive raven-haired woman smiling at him. Trying to remember if he'd already met the woman, he gave a polite smile and bobbed his head in greeting. 'Sorry,' he said apologetically after failing to recall her name, 'I was miles away.'

'Yes, I could see that.' The woman laughed, placing her hand on Dave's arm in what felt like a compassionate gesture. 'I didn't mean to startle you, but you looked like somebody who has the weight of the world on their shoulders.' Before Dave could respond, the woman took her hand away, pressed both hands against her chest and beamed. 'Forgive me, Mr Barnes. I haven't formally introduced myself. My name is Fausta.'

Out of the corner of his eye, Dave noticed that Claire and Emma had ceased their chatting and seemed to be watching him with curious interest. As he took Fausta's hand, Dave couldn't hide his surprise at the firmness of her shake. It seemed well-practised, like she was used to approaching people this way. For some reason, as he stared into Fausta's eyes, he got a vague sense that she was studying him. No, that was wrong, not studying him. It felt like she was analysing him. It was the same look he'd seen many times when he'd stood next to criminal psychologists. Was she a psychiatrist of some sort?

Dave's detective instincts kicked in and his gut told him something felt a bit off. Had she purposely singled him out? He cast a surreptitious eye at Claire and wondered if she had somehow read his mood and had asked Emma if she could find someone to speak to him.

'Pleased to meet you, Fausta,' he said in a cool tone, deciding to keep his suspicions to himself so that he could see where this woman was leading him. 'But please, call me Dave. Whenever people address me by my surname, my jaw aches.'

The corner of Fausta's mouth twitched slightly; she cocked her head and regarded Dave in silent appraisal for several seconds. 'Is that

because you had a difficult childhood?' she said finally, raising an eyebrow curiously.

Taken aback by the question, a surge of anger swelled inside Dave. Just who the hell was this woman? The muscles in his jaw tightened and he scowled at her. 'Not that it is any of your business,' he said, struggling to keep control of his temper. 'But if you must know, my father and I had an excellent relationship. The reason I prefer people to call me by my first name is that I've never been too comfortable with the formalities that go with leadership.'

If Dave's angry outburst had unsettled Fausta, she didn't show it; instead she bobbed her head slowly and spoke in a tone that told Dave she was choosing her words carefully. 'Is that because you prefer those who serve under you to see you as one of them? That deep down, you believe you're not good enough to lead?'

The last question took the wind out of Dave's sails, and he drew in a sharp intake of air. His mouth opened and closed as he struggled to say something in response. Was she right? *No, it couldn't be that*, he thought. However, before he had time to compose himself, Fausta gave him a sweet smile and gently tapped his arm. Was she flirting with him now?

'Dave, I apologise if I've offended you,' Fausta said. 'I'm quite astute at reading people, which is probably why I'm this facility's unofficial counsellor. When I see someone like you, who looks as if they're struggling mentally, I can't help but step in and see if there's anything I can do to help ease that burden.'

Dave realised he'd badly misjudged Fausta's intentions. A wave a shame engulfed him. All she was trying to do was offer an ear so he could share what he was bottling up. Instead, he'd treated her with suspicion. He wasn't used to a stranger being so direct with him, and even though he had every right to be suspicious, Dave realised Claire must have asked Fausta to approach him because she was concerned for him. He should be angry at Claire for going behind his back, but that would have made him a hypocrite because he'd spoken to Isaac about Claire behind her back too. It wasn't exactly the same, but it was close enough.

'Fausta,' Dave said hesitantly, giving a weak smile. 'I ... uh ... I mean, if it's not too much bother, there is something I would like to discuss

with you.'

But before he could hear Fausta's answer, a loud cough came from the centre of the room. Dave turned and saw Emma was now standing on a raised part of the floor in front of what seemed to be something that resembled an interface. The quiet chatter of the audience settled while everybody focused their attention on Emma.

'If everybody could take your seats,' Emma announced, smiling and making a wide sweeping motion with her hands. 'We're about to start this briefing.'

Taking that as a cue to follow Claire to their seats, Dave gave a silent nod to Fausta and strolled away from her. But just as he did so, Fausta brushed past him and gently tapped his arm. Without missing a beat, she smiled and spoke in a reassuring whisper.

'Call by and see me in the infirmary after the meeting is over.'

Before Dave could respond, Fausta swiftly stepped away and disappeared into the audience. Still unsure as to whether he should take her up on her offer, Dave silently mulled it over while he took his seat next to Claire, who raised an enquiring eyebrow at him. Not wanting to get into a conversation that would eventually lead to twenty questions, Dave wordlessly waved his hand, mouthing, *I'll explain later.* Just when Dave thought he'd got away with explaining himself, Isaac took the other seat next to him and leaned in closer to him.

'Can I give you a piece of advice, my friend?' Isaac whispered, grinning. 'When Fausta wishes to speak to you, I've learned it is best to just do it because once she has your scent, she'll never let up until she has you.'

Dave cringed inwardly and rolled his eyes, wondering who else knew he had a problem. Did he have a sign over his head that said *Hi, I'm Dave and I'm feeling depressed. Please talk to me!* He guessed Isaac must have seen something in his eyes because he let out a loud chuckle and slapped his hand on Dave's back.

'Relax, Davey. It's nothing to be ashamed about. I've even found myself talking to her from time to time.' He waggled his eyebrows and lowered his voice into a conspiratorial whisper. 'It helps that she has a bottle of Hanzi stored in her room. Of course, I can neither confirm nor deny that is the reason I go to see her.' He followed it up with a sly wink.

Not the answer he was expecting, Dave let out a loud barking laugh, earning him a nudge in the ribs from Claire and a death scowl from Emma.

'Would you like to share what is so amusing?' Emma asked curtly.

Dave stifled his laugh but was able to keep his face neutral as he gave a small, dismissive wave. 'No, just thinking back to a joke Isaac told me yesterday, which I finally got the punchline to,' he said, ignoring Isaac's muffled laughter next to him. He held out his right hand and made a gesture for Emma to continue. 'But please carry on, wouldn't want to hold you back.'

From the look of death he was receiving from her, it was clear to Dave she wasn't amused, and he imagined if looks could kill, then it was a good thing he had his life insurance in order. Not only that, out of the corner of his eye, he was aware of the penetrating gaze coming from Claire. It took all his concentration not to groan in pain as she took hold of his left hand and crushed his fingers in a vice-like grip.

'Smooth,' Isaac muttered just loud enough for Dave to hear. 'Very smooth, my man.'

For what felt like an eternity, Dave shuffled uncomfortably under the intensity of Emma's stare before she eventually switched her attention to the rest of the audience. 'Now, is there anybody else who would like to make any jokes?' she asked in a tone dripping with icy sarcasm. On receiving an uncomfortable silence, she gave a small bob of her head and a tight smile. 'Very good. Now, as I was going to say before I was so rudely interrupted, it has been an interesting few months and I wanted to hold this briefing to address the rumours that have been circulating. Not only that, I also thought it would be a good time to properly introduce you to the latest additions to our community.' Emma's top lip quirked slightly in amusement, and her eyes darted toward Dave. 'Detective Inspector Dave Barnes, who has already tried to entertain us with his dry wit. And please could you also give a warm welcome to my twin sister, Claire Tulley.'

Dave felt his cheeks flush with embarrassment as a loud cheer,

followed by a round of applause, rippled around the auditorium. He glanced at Claire as she sank back into her seat and gave a small, embarrassed wave. It felt strangely satisfying to see that she seemed just as unhappy to be the centre of attention. The loud cheer settled after less than a minute and everyone focused their attention back on Emma.

'First the good news,' Emma announced, her tone serious. 'I've received word from the resistance command council that they've assembled all the surviving cells together and are in the middle of preparing to make their way to us. Tomorrow morning, we should expect to receive over two thousand of our comrades as reinforcements.' Loud murmurs of discontent echoed around the auditorium, and Emma gave a small nod of understanding. 'Yes, I know that's not many, but the council have reassured me that those who'll be arriving will not only be the finest fighters in the resistance, but they'll also be under the command of the Warrior of Horath herself.'

'I thought you said this was the good news,' Isaac interrupted in a loud voice, resulting in a chorus of laughter from around him.

'Yes, many of you are aware that, when she was younger, the field marshal was stationed here,' Emma continued patiently once the laughter had settled down. 'I always knew Kaliopi would turn out to be a very capable commander. But I'm sure we all remember she's also someone who has no time for fools or people who waste her time.' She leaned forward and gazed purposely over her captive audience, eventually settling on Isaac. 'So, we're all to be on our best behaviour when she arrives. No jokes or immature behaviour. Is that understood, Sergeant N'Goy?'

On hearing unsettled murmurs and a hushed '*Oh, shit, Isaac's in trouble now,*' coming from behind him, Dave got the impression Emma didn't normally address Isaac that way. But it wasn't until he saw Emma lower her head and shoot Isaac a look that would have curdled milk that he realised. Yes, he'd seen that same look from Claire a couple of times before. If she'd had a pair of glasses, then her scathing look would have been identical to Claire's. Dave tried to stifle a laugh as he glanced at Claire and saw she was staring back at him in puzzlement. Yeah, she would call him Inspector Barnes rather than Dave if she was annoyed at him, too.

Dave watched in silent sympathy as Isaac shuffled awkwardly in

his seat, grumbling, 'I don't know why you're singling me out. It's not my fault she hasn't got a sense of humour.'

Thinking about the audience's reverential reaction to the field marshal's nickname, Dave thought that to get that sort of reaction she must be a truly exceptional soldier, and he stared at Isaac thoughtfully. Curious to know more about his history with the field marshal, he leaned in closer and whispered to him, 'So, I take it you and the field marshal go way back?'

'You could say that,' Isaac murmured in an evasive tone. 'We used to serve together. One day, I wasn't happy about how she seemed to take everything so seriously. So, as a joke, I changed her battle armour's transponder so that whenever anyone looked at her through their heads-up display, it would show her call sign as "The Jolly Maiden".'

'You didn't!' Dave exclaimed, feeling his eyebrows climb up his forehead, and then he cocked his head and gave him a speculative look. 'I'm guessing that's why you don't get on?'

Isaac pulled a face and waved his hand. 'Ah, erm, well …' he said slowly, 'it's a bit more complicated than that.' A mischievous twinkle appeared in his eye and his mouth broadened into a devious smile. 'But then again, it probably didn't help that word of her nickname mysteriously became the stuff of legend and followed her wherever she went.'

Dave was about to ask Isaac to clarify what he meant, but he held his tongue on noticing the strange cloud that had appeared over the big man's face, followed by the exhalation of a long sigh. Dave raised an eyebrow as he thought he caught a glint of regret in Isaac's eyes. Before he could ask Isaac anything else, a loud cough interrupted him, followed by a sharp dig in his ribs from Claire.

Startled, Dave realised he had been so distracted listening to Isaac's story that he'd momentarily forgotten he was supposed to be listening to Emma's briefing. He snatched his gaze forward and found himself on the receiving end of Emma's searing stare. It didn't take a genius to guess from her thunderous expression that she wasn't happy with the two men.

'Are you both finished?' Emma hissed, making a wide sweeping gesture with her hand. 'I'm sure everybody in this auditorium would be only too happy to wait until you two stop jabbering like two drunken men

in a bar. No? Then perhaps we can—'

Dave raised his right hand and coughed politely, cutting Emma off in mid-flow. It wasn't his intention to antagonise his host any more than she was, but there was a question he was desperate to ask and felt that if he didn't ask it now, then he may not get another opportunity. Out of the corner of his eye, he caught Claire planting her face in her hands and letting out a disgruntled groan. From the way Emma was staring at him with her mouth opening and closing, it was clear Dave's interruption had thrown her.

He heard Isaac inhale a sharp breath and whisper to him just loud enough for him to hear, 'By the white hairy beard of Giglamon. Are you trying to piss her off even more, man?'

Any other time, Dave would probably have accepted the advice being offered to him, and he would have stopped himself. But he realised he'd already committed himself by rising to his feet and felt his cheeks flush as he became aware that everyone's eyes were now locked on him. He straightened himself and swallowed. There was no going back now, he thought.

'I apologise for interrupting you, Commander Tulley,' Dave said slowly, choosing his words carefully. He smiled and respectfully bobbed his head. 'But I was wondering why your command council are sending that many additional troops here? Are you planning on attacking the city or do you have something else planned?'

From the wide-eyed shock on Emma's face and the uneasy murmurs coming from behind him, it was clear to Dave that his question had taken everybody by surprise. He felt his throat go dry as he watched Emma narrow her eyes as she silently regarded him for several seconds. But just as he wondered whether she was about to give the order for him to be thrown out of the auditorium, relief flowed through him as her face softened and she gave him a thin smile.

'In some ways you remind me of my Barnes.' Em laughed, shaking her head. 'I keep having to remind myself you're not him. He, like you, also had an uncontrollable desire to question everything. It was really quite infuriating.'

A quiet snort came from Hilaria, who was standing just behind

Emma, and she gave a small nod in agreement. If she'd heard Hilaria's reaction, Emma did not react. Instead, she sucked in a long breath and held up both of her hands.

'Anyhow, that's my problem to deal with, not yours,' Emma continued in a humourless tone. 'But in answer to your question, once we learned from Hilaria that Oracle had assimilated most of the URE's populace and was going to use them to attack your Earth, I sent a proposal to the command council. Because of the threat posed by Oracle, I proposed that the council assemble as many skilled fighters as they could spare to help us seize control of the portal chamber and then travel to your Earth to help in your fight against Oracle.' Emma paused and ran her right hand wearily down her face before focusing her attention back on Dave. 'That is the reason the council are sending everyone they have. It may not be many, but we hoped it would help tip the balance in your favour.'

On hearing that there was a chance he could be going back to his world, a surge of excitement passed through Dave. He leaned forward eagerly and gripped Claire's right hand with his left. But his excitement lessened as something in Emma's voice gave him pause, and he ran over the last bit of her speech in his head. Cocking his head, he frowned in puzzlement. Emma said *hoped*. If they were going back to his Earth, then shouldn't she have said *we hope it will help tip the balance*?

Dave guessed Emma must have recognised the hopefulness in his eyes as she sorrowfully shook her head.

'I apologise if I've got your hopes up, Dave,' Emma said unhappily. 'But recent events have altered things somewhat. There's now the possibility we won't be able to travel back to your Earth after all.' Before Dave could ask Emma to clarify, she turned swiftly to her right and gestured to Hilaria, who had wordlessly taken a step closer. 'To explain further, I'm handing the rest of this briefing over to Hilaria.'

Despite feeling deflated at knowing he wasn't going back home after all, Dave was curious as he watched Hilaria replace Emma on the dais. For the time since seeing her, Dave thought he detected something in Hilaria's expression. It seemed strained, as if she was carrying a huge burden on her shoulders.

Hilaria drew in a long breath and stared at the faces staring back

at her. 'As you all remember,' she said glumly, 'our initial expedition into Pon Aelius did not go exactly as planned.'

Dave cocked his head enquiringly as Hilaria touched something on the dais, and, less than a second later, the auditorium was filled with a warm glow as a holographic image of a vast city appeared a few feet above the stage. His eyes growing wide, Dave was awestruck by the sight before him. Casting a glance over his shoulder to Claire, he saw she was also staring at the hologram in wide-eyed wonder. It was an image of an enormous city, surrounded by what seemed to be an impenetrable defensive wall. For the first time since arriving here, Dave suddenly got a sense of just how technologically advanced these people were. The sheer scale and work involved in building such a huge megatropolis – it simply blew his mind. *What must it be like to live inside such a city?* he thought. *It must be a marvel to behold.*

The image seemed to quiver slightly, and Dave watched in silent wonder as a section of the image blurred. He realised Hilaria must have been focusing on a part of the city as the image changed to one of something that resembled a super-skyscraper.

'When Em detonated her EMP,' Hilaria continued, 'it caused significant damage to the city's power grid. From my experience working inside the portal chamber, I am of the opinion that the EMP likely destroyed the highly sensitive components used to control the dimensional gate device, making it unusable.' Murmurs of concern filled the auditorium, and Hilaria raised her hand to silence them. 'However, we won't know for certain until I can assess the damage for myself.'

'Aren't you worried that some of Oracle's cyber drones are still active?' Dave heard someone in the audience ask, striking a chord with his own worries. He was relieved not to be the one who'd asked. 'Don't mean to sound like a pessimist, but from what Em and Isaac described, I got the impression it was a small number of drones that attacked them.' On hearing the uneasy murmurs coming from behind him, Dave turned around and saw that someone a couple of rows back from him was standing with his hand raised apologetically. 'Forgive my ignorance, but if Oracle assimilated all the children in Pons Aelius, that must mean she held a lot back in reserve. What I'm trying to say is that there could be some in another part

of the city that wasn't affected by the pulse.'

'Yes, I agree,' Hilaria replied, nodding unhappily. 'Which is where the reinforcements come in. If there's still a contingent of drones active, then it's my hope we can keep them distracted long enough for me to get into the chamber, find out if there's anything worth salvaging, then get back out.'

'What losses do you expect to suffer if our forces meet resistance?' another voice called out from somewhere toward the back of the auditorium.

Dave thought he noticed a flicker of uncertainty pass over Hilaria's face as she and Emma shared a look. It was followed by a moment of hesitation and Emma gave a small shrug, which Dave read as *there's no point hiding it*.

Hilaria exhaled a long, dispirited sigh and answered in a low voice. 'If we meet heavy resistance, both from any remaining drones and any synthroids still under Oracle's control, I estimate we could lose at least ninety per cent of our forces.'

From the shocked gasps coming from around him, Dave could tell that number had rattled a few people. If he was honest with himself, he felt a touch of sympathy. Ninety per cent meant that out of the two hundred and fifty present here today, it would be lucky if twenty-five survived. Those were not favourable odds. Which meant that for whoever was going, there was no doubt it would be a suicide mission. He cast an eye at Isaac and from the lack of reaction to the news, he got the impression that Hilaria's news hadn't fazed him, which seemed to indicate that he'd been briefed beforehand.

Struggling to wrap his head around the scale of the losses Hilaria was talking about, Dave wanted Claire's opinion. But he blinked in surprise when he noticed something in her eyes and did a double take. He realised he'd seen that same look in her eyes before – it was a look that said she knew something nobody else did. A sense of dread stirred within Dave as Claire turned toward him and gave him one of her patented secretive smiles.

Dave groaned to himself. Whenever Claire had that look, it usually meant she was about to drag him into something, and whenever Claire dragged him into something, it meant bad news for him. He felt uneasy, followed by the uncomfortable sensation of acid churning inside his stomach. Trying to swallow back the rising bile, he realised one thing for certain was about to happen.

The brown smelly stuff was about to hit the fan.

Suddenly feeling like he was on-board an out-of-control train without a means to get off, he let out an exasperated moan and buried his face in his hands.

I'm getting too old for this shit.

-28-

'Claire, what are you up to?'

Judging from the thick groove between Dave's eyebrows, Claire could tell he was worried. The nervous tic in his eye also meant that he was getting himself worked up. She pursed her lips thoughtfully and wondered what could have got him so agitated. Honestly, the man was such a worrywart. She hadn't even told him her idea yet! The corners of her mouth curled up as she silently appraised him. Yes, he could be overprotective, but his deep, caring nature was one of the things she loved about him.

'What makes you think I'm planning something?' she asked innocently. For extra gravitas, she fluttered her eyelids and gave him her best sickly-sweet smile. 'Why, Detective Barnes, I get the impression you don't trust me.'

Dave leaned back, raised his hands, and laughed softly. 'Oh no, that innocent act doesn't fool me. I know that look too well. You know something, something the rest of us mere mortals haven't caught on to yet.' He leaned in closer and spoke in a soft tone, which had a touch of concern. 'Whenever you get those thoughts, my arse gets twitchy. So, come on, out with it.'

Claire lowered her head and pouted. 'I'm sure they can give you some haemorrhoid cream for that.'

Her glib comment only earned her a frosty glare. *Sheesh! Tough crowd,* she thought and puffed out her cheeks, then blew out a slow breath

in a dramatic show of pretend reluctance.

'Fine,' she moaned, pausing for effect and gesturing for Dave to lean in closer. She lowered her voice to a conspiratorial whisper. 'You remember the experiment the British government ran back in 1932, the one we think was responsible for opening the portal to this world?' Dave gave a small wordless nod and Claire continued. 'Can you remember where it was located?'

'Uh, yeah,' he answered, frowning, 'it was at the isolation hospital in Langley Park. But what does the hospital have to do with anything? Where are you—'

Raising her hand to silence him, Claire cut Dave off. 'The hospital isn't important,' she said patiently. 'It's the location beneath the hospital I'm talking about – the cavern beneath the village. Remember what John told you about what he, Wendy and Sharon found when they investigated the site?'

'Huh-huh,' he answered slowly, nodding, 'he told me they discovered this strange cave filled with weird crystals along with what sounded like a portal.' He shook his head and gave Claire a blank look. 'But what does that have to do with anything?'

Holy crap, for a detective, this man is incredibly dense! Rolling her eyes, Claire pinched the bridge of her nose and exhaled in exasperation, muttering, 'Give me strength.' Her patience just about worn thin, she held Dave's gaze and spoke in a slow, careful tone. 'You told me when you arrived back at the base with your counterpart, John explained to you Sharon's theory about what that cavern could be.'

Dave's brow wrinkled in obvious confusion as he once again nodded slowly. 'Yes, he said something about it being a nexus or something. It was a bit over my head, but—oh.' His eyes grew wide, and he let out a loud gasp of exclamation. 'Holy shit!'

Relieved to see the penny had finally dropped, Claire gave him a knowing smile and nodded in affirmation. *Yes, holy shit, exactly.* However, before she could say any more, Claire paused as she became aware of something. There was a slight disturbance coming from those seated around her. A murmuring, a general intake of air and a shifting of positions in seats.

Detecting movement out of the corner of her eye, Claire glanced toward it and saw Zoe leaning in her seat, looking curiously at her. Turning her head slowly, she stiffened as she realised Hilaria and Emma were now both staring at her; their faces displayed a mixture of annoyance and curiosity.

'Is there something you'd like to share with the rest of us?' Emma asked coolly with an arched, enquiring eyebrow.

Suddenly aware that everyone's eyes were now fixed on her, Claire felt her cheeks warm and she swallowed. 'Um, sorry.'

Awkwardly rising out of her seat, Claire glanced down at Dave, hoping to get some support. Much to her irritation, he gave her a weak smile and raised both of his hands in a wordless gesture, which she read as *Hey, don't bring me into your mess*. It was clear she wasn't going to get any help from him. Imagining the heavy thump of tyres running over her body from the bus she had just been thrown under, Claire shot him a murderous look.

Squeezing her eyes shut, she sucked in a deep breath and prayed she was doing the right thing. 'You don't need to go into the city,' she blurted out, earning her loud surprised gasps from around the auditorium.

Opening one eye, she saw Emma and Hilaria exchanging startled looks before turning back to her. Emma made a gesture for her to continue. Her confidence steadily increasing, Claire took a step forward and acknowledged the two women with a tight smile in gratitude for giving her the chance to be heard.

'Hilaria, tell me,' Claire asked slowly, being careful to choose her words, 'during your … um … the general's time in charge of the portal project, did she ever wonder how it was created?'

Hilaria's head jerked back, as if in surprise at the question. Then she appeared to regain control and gave a slight nod of confirmation. 'Yes. One of the first things the general did was to scour Doctor Drusilla Severan's journals. Because she was the person who came up with the idea of the portal, the general thought reading her journals would help get inside her head, understand the project more.' Hilaria cocked her head and gave Claire an inquisitive side eye. It was clear she was wondering where Claire was going with her line of questioning, but she must have decided to continue with her answer. 'But no matter how much she read Severan's

journals, she couldn't understand how she was able to create a stable wormhole.' Hands raised in defeat, Hilaria shook her head and blew out a dispirited sigh. 'She went over the chamber from top to bottom, even going so far as to inspect every power conduit in the tower. She just couldn't understand where the energy was being channelled from. In the end, she gave up searching for answers and devoted her time to the project itself.'

'Interesting,' Claire murmured, nodding and tapping her bottom lip thoughtfully.

Even though Claire found the whole idea of multiple personalities intriguing, she still found it unsettling that Hilaria was referring to herself in the third person. If she was honest with herself, she would have loved to sit down with Hilaria and put her under hypnosis in the hope of bringing forth the personality locked within Hilaria's mind. What she wouldn't give to speak to the general just so that she could see for herself if the stories about her were true.

Realising she was getting sidetracked, Claire blinked and focused her attention back on the matter at hand. Casting an eye back to Dave, she saw he was now sitting forward as if eager to hear more. He gave a nod of encouragement and shot her a reassuring smile.

The knowledge that she had Dave's support was all she needed. With her hands placed firmly behind her back, Claire cocked her head and gave Hilaria a wry smile. 'During her readings of Severan's journals, did she ever come across the term *nexus gateway*?'

'Yes,' Hilaria said, nodding enthusiastically. 'In one section of her journals, Severan wrote her theories of the multiverse. She theorised each reality intersects with the others by something called a nexus – a cross-dimensional network, providing a pathway to all possible realities.' Hilaria's brow furrowed in puzzlement, and she rubbed the back of her neck. 'Erm, so are you saying that is what our portal is – a nexus doorway?'

'Oh-ho-ho, you were so close,' Claire said, grinning and waggling her finger. 'I had such high hopes for you as well.'

Claire heard Dave give a loud, exaggerated cough, followed by what sounded like a muffled 'be nice'. She felt her cheeks burn as it dawned on her what he was trying to say. But it was only when she cast her eyes back to the raised dais that she realised she may have pushed things a bit

too far. Hilaria's face was now a deep shade of red and Claire noticed there was a twitch of irritation in her good eye. Emma was standing behind Hilaria, hands covering her mouth as if she was trying to stifle a laugh.

'Ahem, pardon me.' Claire coughed sheepishly, hoping to get quickly back on to the subject at hand. She self-consciously pushed her glasses up her nose and laughed nervously. Then she explained the documents she'd uncovered detailing the experiment run by Doctor Selyab and its subterranean location. She went on to explain what John, Sharon and Wendy described seeing during their exploration of the cavern. Pausing to collect her thoughts, Claire held Hilaria's gaze and held up her right index finger. 'I always assumed hydroelectricity was what Doctor Selyab used to power his portal device. However, since my encounter with Custos, I've had time to dwell on it and have concluded that Selyab must've realised the crystals are what's needed to create a stable wormhole. The whole hydroelectric generator set-up must've been for show. The cavern must've been our reality's nexus point, which means—'

'Oh, I see where you're going with this,' Hilaria blurted out, clapping her hands excitedly. 'If what you're saying is true, then Severan must have discovered something similar and figured out a way to bleed energy from the nexus to power the device we used to open portals.' Hilaria let out a loud growl of frustration and slapped her forehead. 'Of course, it was staring at me the whole time.'

Before Claire could say anything else, Hilaria swiftly turned back to the interface and began tapping and swiping, muttering angrily under her breath. Concerned murmurs rippled around the auditorium as Claire approached Emma, who smiled in acknowledgement. Frowning, Claire thought she saw a flicker of admiration in her sister's eyes.

'So,' Emma said, eyeing Claire thoughtfully, 'I thought you told me you were a history professor who got accidentally involved with a secret government agency. But reading between the lines, I can see there's more to you than meets the eye.'

Uncomfortable with being on the receiving end of praise, Claire lowered her head and laughed nervously. 'I didn't do anything, really. I just wanted to pass on information I thought might be of use.'

Em gave Claire's shoulder a compassionate squeeze and nodded

in wordless understanding as she turned to face the audience, hands raised in apology. 'Please bear with us while Hilaria searches for the information she needs. So please chat amongst yourselves until we get this briefing back on track.'

'Hah!' Dave barked loudly, suddenly appearing by Claire's side while everybody in audience started chatting amongst themselves. 'Don't believe anything she tells you, Emma. If it wasn't for Claire, John and Sharon wouldn't have discovered the cavern containing the nexus.'

'Oh, shush, you,' Claire grumbled, feeling her face burn with embarrassment and giving a dismissive wave. 'I'm sure they would have found it eventually without my help.'

Emma regarded her silently and held her gaze for several seconds. As she stared into her sister's face, Claire thought she saw a flicker of emotion pass over her face. At first, she wasn't sure if it was a hint of jealousy, but she stiffened in shock on realising it wasn't jealousy. It was awe, alongside what she thought looked like approval.

She scrunched up her face as she wondered why Emma would be in awe of her. In her eyes, Emma had achieved far more than she ever would. She had survived all the odds, growing up in a hostile world, and had become a skilled warrior and a respected leader of a small community. If anything, Emma was the inspirational one, not her.

Before Claire had time to dwell on it and question Emma, a loud cry of exultation broke her out of her self-pondering and she turned quickly. Hilaria's triumphant smile told her all she needed to know – that she had found what she had been looking for. The holographic image had changed. It was now showing what Claire thought looked like a schematic of a square mechanism that looked strangely familiar. Taking a step closer to get a better look, Claire scrunched up her face and squinted at the image in front of her. Where had she seen it before?

Then it hit her.

Claire touched her mouth in shock and blinked in realisation. She had seen a sketch of a similar device while carrying out research into the conspiracy behind Emma's death. It had been in a journal belonging to a soldier who was present at the site of Doctor Selyab's experiment on the day it had been activated. The soldier had escaped just before the accident

that had presumably killed Selyab and his team. Against orders to destroy all records of the experiment, the soldier had left a detailed account in his journal, along with a sketch of the portal device designed by Selyab.

Dave gave Claire a questioning look, but she raised a finger to forestall any questions. From the way he was tightening his lips, Claire could tell he wasn't pleased. *Oh, he'll get over it,* she thought as she focused her attention on what Hilaria was saying.

'As soon as Claire started talking about nexus energy, I realised it had been staring at me all along and I never knew it,' Hilaria said excitedly, furiously swiping her fingers over the interface. Above her head, the holographic image highlighted the four corners of the device while Hilaria continued speaking. 'I could never understand why Severan had installed four subspace receivers into her design. But now I understand the reason I couldn't locate the power source.' Throwing up her hands, Hilaria shook her head and stared at the faces peering back at her. 'Absolute genius. Insane, but absolute genius.'

Claire wrinkled her brow while she tried to work out what Hilaria was trying to tell them. But had to admit defeat and shared a glance with Dave. On seeing the glazed look in his eyes she realised he was just as confused as she was, and she wondered whether it was because they were from a world that wasn't as advanced as this one. However, her confusion swiftly changed to relief as she cast an eye over the faces of the audience and noticed the puzzled frowns, alongside the scratching of foreheads, glazed eyes and discontented murmurings. It was clear that whatever Hilaria was saying, it seemed to be beyond their understanding too.

'Hilaria,' Emma said finally after a moment of awkward silence, 'for those of us who don't have an advanced IQ, and before we die of old age, would you be so kind as to get to the point?'

'Sorry,' Hilaria answered, shrugging. Taking in a deep breath, she steepled her fingers together and spoke patiently. 'Okay, thanks to Claire, I finally understand where our portal received its energy from. Those four subspace receivers must channel energy from the nexus into the device. My guess is there must be a subspace transmitter somewhere syphoning dimensional energy from the nexus gateway point.' Hilaria turned to Emma and gave her a speculative look. 'My theory is that when you set off your

pulse, it destroyed the subspace receivers, breaking the connection. That may also explain why our scans no longer detect any recognisable energy signatures coming from inside the portal chamber.'

A light bulb went off in Claire's head and she was hit by a sudden epiphany. 'Holy crap!' she gasped. 'That must mean the scientist behind your portal device must've located the site of this reality's nexus gateway.'

A thick groove formed in the centre of Hilaria's forehead, and she acknowledged Claire with a thoughtful nod. 'Yes, that would be my assumption too. Severan must have discovered the site while she was carrying out her research.'

'But why didn't this Severan build her experiment on the site of this reality's nexus whatchamacallit?' Dave asked in a deeply exasperated tone, waving his hand at the image above their heads. 'Forgive my ignorance, but to me, it sounds like she made a lot of work for herself.'

Hilaria, Isaac and Emma exchanged knowing looks, and they all laughed. Claire had the impression that they knew something she and Dave didn't, and wondered if they were amused by their ignorance. Bristling at being on the receiving end of a joke at her expense, Claire folded her arms across her chest and shot them a sharp look. 'What?' she said peevishly. 'What are we missing here?'

'Sorry, Cee,' Emma answered in a sincere tone, 'we're not laughing at you and Dave. We're just laughing because we've got so used to this. We keep forgetting what it must look like to an outsider.' Her smile vanished and her expression became serious. 'For centuries, the URE has been a paranoid and distrustful culture. In this reality, knowledge is power. I believe Severan wanted to keep the nexus's location to herself. Whether it was out of fear at what the URE would do once the location was revealed, or she just wanted to use it as a bargaining chip at a later date, I'm not sure.'

'The question is,' Claire murmured, getting back to the matter at hand, 'where is the location of this reality's nexus gateway?' Her eyebrows climbed up her forehead as an idea popped into her head and she spun around, clicking her fingers excitedly at Hilaria. 'Can you bring up a topographical map on this thing?'

'Sure,' Hilaria answered, smiling confidently. 'Any particular area we're talking about?'

'How about we start with a ten-square-mile area centred on our current position and we go from there?' Claire asked hopefully, exchanging a glance with Dave.

'It's worth a shot,' Dave answered, nodding in approval.

While she waited for Hilaria to perform her magic, Claire cocked her head as she became aware of curious murmurs coming from those still seated in the auditorium. Emma took a step closer and stared at her with a raised, inquisitive eyebrow.

'Care to share what you hope to find?' Emma asked.

'You remember that old creepy isolation hospital back home? How would we dare each other to enter when we were kids?' Claire murmured and smiled when Emma answered with a wordless nod. 'Well, it turns out it was above the cavern I was telling you about. The one containing that reality's nexus gateway.'

Emma blanched, did a double take and let out a loud, mirthless laugh. 'You're kidding?' Claire guessed she must have seen the serious glint in her eyes, because Emma's amusement immediately changed into a look of awe. 'You're not kidding, are you? That must mean you think this reality's nexus gateway is in the same spot?'

'Huh-huh,' Claire responded, beaming.

Emma blinked and shook her head in astonishment. 'Unbelievable,' she muttered in a tone that sounded like she wasn't completely convinced.

Before Claire could respond, she was interrupted by a polite cough coming from the audience, and she turned to see Isaac waving his hand to get her attention. 'I don't mean to sound disrespectful, Sister-Boss-Lady,' he said in a tone that sounded sincere. 'But just because you know where the location of the nexus is in your reality, doesn't mean it'll be in the same place in this reality. From what Em's told me about your reality, the continents on your world aren't the same as they are here, and for all we know, the nexus could be on the other side of the planet. Wouldn't you agree?'

Claire stuck out her bottom lip, silently considering what Isaac was trying to say. His comment didn't annoy her, in fact she found it intriguing, and if she was honest with herself, she could understand his scepticism.

They only had her word that this reality's nexus gateway may be in the same spot as it was in her reality. A troubling thought occurred to her as she wondered about the scientist who had discovered it. If Severan was as paranoid as people said, then she might have set booby traps inside the cavern to stop anyone looking for it. But as she was about to open her mouth to voice her concerns, a small flicker of light distracted her. Turning toward the source, she noticed the holographic image had changed to show a topographical satellite map of an area which she assumed she'd requested. Claire adjusted her glasses and squinted so that she could study it, but a flash of disappointment surged through her as she realised she couldn't see any recognisable features. Even the course of the river looked different. She inhaled deeply and gave her head a dispirited shake. So much for setting her hopes on *X marks the spot*.

'I'm sorry,' she said, deflated. 'There's nothing on that map I recognise.'

'Don't give up just yet,' Dave murmured, placing a reassuring hand on her shoulder. 'There's still one more trick we can try.' He gave her a sly wink and turned toward Hilaria. 'I take it you use something like GPS coordinates here? We use them to express longitude and latitude.'

Hilaria cocked her head and gave Dave an odd look. 'We call it something different, but the principle is the same.'

'Try these coordinates,' Dave said. He ran off a series of numbers to Hilaria.

Without saying a word, Hilaria nodded, turned back to the interface and quickly entered the coordinates that Dave had given her. Claire held her breath in anticipation while she waited for the results to appear. The atmosphere inside the auditorium was almost palpable, and she imagined everyone else was also anxiously waiting with bated breath. However, after several long minutes her excitement grew into impatience, and she wondered what was taking Hilaria so long to verify a set of coordinates. Had these people never heard of using a smart device to ask for something? Then it dawned on her just how ridiculous that sounded in her head. It was because of an AI that they were in this mess in the first place.

Claire anxiously wrung her hands as she continued to wait. But

then Hilaria stiffened slightly, and Claire wasn't sure, but she thought she looked shocked. Her suspicions were confirmed as Hilaria pulled her gaze away from the interface and stared at everyone with her mouth open in amazement.

'You won't believe this,' Hilaria said in a tone echoing her stunned expression, 'but according to these readings, I'm detecting a faint energy signature very close to the coordinates Dave gave me.'

-29-

A stunned silence filled the auditorium. The atmosphere was so thick with tension Claire was sure she could cut it with a knife and wondered what was going through everybody's minds. She cast a speculative eye toward Emma, and from the strained expression on her face, she could tell this wasn't what she'd been expecting; she was probably trying to wrap her head around it before she opened her mouth. However, any concerns Claire had about her sister vanished on seeing the uncertainty in her eyes fade, replaced by the confidence she'd come to see in her since her arrival. Emma gave off a self-assured vibe as she straightened and regarded Hilaria curiously.

'What type of energy signature?' Emma asked

'If I'm reading this right,' Hilaria answered hesitantly, almost as if she was reluctant to pass on the information. 'It's the exact same type of signature a cloaking field gives off, say if you wanted to hide something.'

'Like an inter-dimensional gateway,' Claire said, struggling to contain her excitement as she pressed her hands together in eager anticipation. 'What you're saying is, you think we've discovered the location of this reality's nexus gateway?'

'That's exactly what I'm saying,' Hilaria replied, beaming.

Unable to contain her delight, Claire spun around and slapped Dave on the shoulder, laughing. 'You're a genius.'

Dave gave a nonchalant shrug. 'You're a history professor who's good at digging up stuff. My superpower is remembering useless bits of

information.' He grinned and gave Claire a smug wink. 'I'm not just a pretty face, don't ya know?'

A loud, exuberant cheer erupted from the audience. Although she seemed visibly delighted, Claire thought Emma didn't seem to be as enthusiastic. It was almost as if she was reluctant to accept the good news; her sister raised her hand to silence the crowd. Once everybody had settled down, Emma took her place back on the dais and spoke in a tone that seemed joyful but was also tinged with a touch of apprehension.

'Far be it from me to put a damper on your delight,' Emma said solemnly. 'I don't think I need to warn us about getting our hopes up. We need to tread carefully. First, we must reconnoitre the area and make certain it is what we think it is.'

'I agree,' Hilaria replied flatly, which seemed to indicate she shared Emma's reservations. The centre of her forehead wrinkled, and she gazed unhappily at the image above her head. 'Unfortunately, if it turns out to be what we think it is, we may have another problem. Dimensional travel puts a tremendous strain on the body. The URE were able to counter that by having travellers attach dimensional stabilisers to their wrist communicators.'

Quickly bringing up a schematic of the devices she was talking about, Hilaria turned to Emma, who returned her gaze with a blank stare and a shake of her head. 'I don't understand. Do you think you won't be able to make these stabilisers?'

'Making them isn't the problem.' Hilaria sighed. 'It's the number we need that's the problem. It would take me weeks to make enough stabilisers for over two thousand people. That's time we don't have.' She threw her hands up and shook her head in frustration. 'There's an ordinance room just below the portal chamber in Pons Aelius with boxes full of stabilisers. But I don't know if we can search for them and hold off any hostiles while I'm inside the portal chamber examining the portal and console for signs of damage.'

Isaac gave a polite cough, stood up and raised his right hand. 'Ahem, sorry to interrupt, but I think we have what you need.'

Emma and Hilaria exchanged surprised looks; they turned back to Isaac and stared at him with equal astonished expressions. 'I'm sorry?' they

exclaimed in unison.

Isaac smiled sheepishly and pointed to the schematic. 'During our mission to Pons Aelius, Em, you ordered a group of us to head to the armoury to gather anything that may be useful. Well, I came across dozens of boxes containing hundreds of those things. I still don't know why I did it. I just dumped them onto the sled I was using.'

'Please tell me you brought them back to base?' Hilaria asked, her tone almost pleading.

Isaac straightened and nodded proudly. 'They are currently inside a container in the cargo bay.'

Hilaria let out a jubilant cry of delight and pointed at Isaac. 'Isaac, I could kiss you.'

The corners of Isaac's mouth curled up into a devilish smile as he placed his hands on his hips and puffed out his chest, which reminded Claire of an over-theatrical heroic pose. 'Just think of it as another amazing deed by your finest warrior.' He said, which drew an eye roll from Emma.

'Okay,' Emma said, shooting a disapproving look at Isaac before turning back to Hilaria, 'back to the matter at hand. Before we slap ourselves on the back, we still have to confirm the site is what we think it is.' A serious expression flashed across her face as she straightened and gestured to Hilaria and Isaac. 'I want you both to assemble teams. One will be led by you, Hilaria. Once you've figured out a way to deactivate the cloak and you're certain it is the entrance to the cavern, you and your team are to make your way inside. Isaac, you and your team will remain on the surface to keep an eye out for any hostiles. You'll also act as backup should they encounter any problems. Everybody clear?' Loud murmurs echoed around the chamber as everybody's head bobbed in unison. 'Good,' Emma said, smiling. 'I want teams assembled and airborne in two hours. Get to it.'

It seemed like no one needed to be told twice – excited chatter filled the auditorium, followed by the sound of people rising from their seats and filing out of the room. Claire couldn't help admiring how well Emma had her people trained. There didn't seem to be any hint of nervousness on the faces of those marching past her. Turning to Zoe, who was still in her seat, Claire noticed a flicker of fear in her eyes, something

she could sympathise with. For all her bravado, Zoe was still just a teenager in a strange world. *Hell,* Claire thought, *she's probably just as scared as I am.*

Then a thought crossed Claire's mind, something that had just occurred to her. Hurrying over to Emma, she lightly tapped her shoulder; she turned and cocked her head in surprise.

'Emma, I need you to put me on Hilaria's team,' Claire said adamantly.

Emma reeled back in shock and shook her head. 'Certainly not. It's too dangerous. We've no idea what the team will be walking into.'

'Exactly! All the more reason I should be on the team,' Claire insisted. 'You show me anybody who has spent more time than me researching stuff like this.'

Emma gave Claire a dubious side eye. 'I don't know, Cee.'

Not wanting to take no for an answer, Claire grabbed hold of Emma's hands and stared pleadingly into her eyes. 'Em, trust me, I know what I'm talking about. I've already been inside the cavern back in our reality, so I've a fair idea of what to expect.'

Of course, that was a lie. It had been Sharon and Wendy who'd been in the cavern. But they had described what they had seen. Claire secretly prayed Dave hadn't overheard, or she was going to have a lot of explaining to do.

'Fine.' Emma sighed reluctantly before giving Claire a wry smile. 'You're still just as stubborn as me, I see.'

'Probably even more.' Claire grinned, turning away from Emma.

However, her confident smile vanished as soon as she spotted the unhappy expression on Dave's face. It didn't take a genius to guess the cause of his foul mood. She wondered how much of the conversation he'd heard. Her heart thundered inside her chest as he slid up next to her when she joined the throng of people waiting to leave the auditorium.

'I heard what you told Emma back there,' he muttered just loud enough for her to hear.

'Mm-mm,' she answered, nodding innocently.

'You were lying your arse off,' Dave growled angrily, casting an eye over his shoulder, probably to double check nobody could hear them. 'It was John, Wendy and Sharon who discovered what was inside that cavern, not you.'

Afraid he was going to reveal her to Emma for the fraud she was, Claire licked her lips while glancing nervously over her shoulder, whispering, 'Are you threatening to tell Emma, is that it? Stop me from going?'

She tightened her jaw and braced herself for Dave's response. But it took all her willpower to stop her surprise showing on her face on hearing Dave's response.

'You're kidding, right? I'm going with you. If you think I'm going to let you out of my sight, well, you've got another thing coming.'

-30-

Three hours later, Claire leaned forward in her seat and peered through the aircraft's porthole; they were hovering over a large clearing. From the way they were circling, it was clear the pilot was getting ready to land. A glint of light caught her attention on the edge of her peripheral vision; another aircraft was shadowing them.

Claire's mind drifted, and she thought about how hectic the last few hours had been following the briefing.

As instructed, Hilaria and Isaac selected the personnel they wanted on their teams. After Claire and Dave were fitted with combat suits, which Claire found strangely snug, they were taken to the vehicle hangar where they boarded a transport shuttle.

Claire was impressed by the sleekness of the aircraft's design. Its unique bird-like shape, she guessed, was the reason people nicknamed them eagle transports. Once Hilaria had gone through the emergency procedure, she and Dave were fastened into their seats. Flying always made Claire anxious, and she found herself having doubts about whether it had been a good idea to join the mission. However, any misgivings she had vanished as soon as the transport lifted off and passed through the hangar door into the open air. Even though the journey had only lasted a few minutes, she couldn't get over how comfortable their short flight had been. If she hadn't seen the forest canopy below her streaking by, she would have never guessed they were moving at all.

Claire cast her eye at Dave, who was gripping his armrest tightly. Reaching over to him, she placed a reassuring hand on his arm and gave it a gentle squeeze.

'You okay?' she asked. 'You're not feeling airsick or anything, are you?'

Dave gave a firm shake of his head and acknowledged her with a grim smile. 'No, I'm fine. Normally I get air sick as soon as a plane takes off.' He sucked in a deep breath and let it out slowly. 'As long as I don't look out of the window, I should be okay.'

Hilaria, who was sitting in the seat across from Dave, leaned over and tapped his hand. 'This shuttle is equipped with inertia dampers. They are designed to negate certain side effects of supersonic flight, such as airsickness,' she explained. A wicked grin formed across her face, and she gave Claire a sly wink. 'So long as Gemma doesn't do any sharp turns or combat rolls, I think you should be okay.'

'Great,' Dave huffed sarcastically, 'that makes me feel a hell of a lot better.'

'Hilaria,' Gemma announced from the cockpit, 'I'm about to bring her down in this clearing. You might want to get your team ready – just in case we meet any resistance and we need to bug out in a hurry.'

On hearing the concerned tone in Gemma's voice, Claire felt her heart rate increase and the inside of her mouth went dry; the thought that there was still a chance that at any moment they might come under attack was enough to dial her anxiety up to maximum. The memory of the attack on the Castle still played on her mind; it wasn't something she wanted to go through again. She cast a worried glance at Dave and noticed his strained expression. It was obvious he was thinking the same thing as her. Even though it wasn't an amusing situation, she couldn't help chuckling as she remembered the saying – misery loves company.

If Hilaria had any concern about Gemma's statement, she didn't show it. Her face was a mask of professionalism as she acknowledged the pilot with a brusque reply before rising out of her seat to address the rest of the team.

'Okay, people,' she announced in an authoritative tone, 'you know the drill. As soon as this bird touches down and the doors are open, we move out and sweep the area. We do it by numbers. No heroics, understood?' Swiftly turning back to Claire and Dave, she addressed them in a tone that told Claire it wasn't open to question. 'You two are to remain on-board until I send word to Gemma. If anything happens and the excrement hits the extractor, you're to follow Gemma's instructions to the letter. Is that understood?'

Not used to being spoken to in such a way, Claire swallowed and gave a meek nod. If Dave was unhappy at being ordered around, he didn't show it. He tapped his brow in confirmation and smiled. Claire guessed he was used to receiving orders from superior officers, whether he agreed with them or not.

There was a sudden jarring bump as the transport's undercarriage made contact with the ground. Within moments, Claire felt a chill of cool air filling the cabin as the rear hatch opened. Hilaria and her team rose out of their seats and moved efficiently out of the rear hatch and down the ramp. Despite her anxiety, Claire admired the swiftness with which Hilaria and her team exited the aircraft. She pursed her lips thoughtfully and wondered if their efficient actions were partly down to Hilaria's training. She'd overheard a rumour that Hilaria had been using her vast military experience to teach the base's personnel some discipline and tactics. Judging from the way the team was responding to her commands, whatever she had been doing with them seemed to be working.

For what seemed like several long, excruciating minutes, Claire fidgeted in her seat, eyeing the cockpit nervously while she waited for Gemma to give the signal that it was okay for them to disembark. Glancing to her left, she noticed Dave had his eyes closed, his chest rising and falling as he breathed. Was he asleep? Claire wondered, annoyed at how easily he could drop off. How could he sleep at a time like this? Despite her irritation at him, she noticed how much more at ease he seemed. Shortly after the briefing he'd disappeared with Fausta. She was secretly glad she'd asked Fausta if she could also talk to him, concerned he may also be suffering PTSD, so whatever Fausta had said to him had clearly helped, because he seemed much happier.

'How can you be so relaxed?' Claire moaned, not hiding her irritation. 'All this sitting and waiting is doing my head in.'

His right eye opening slightly, Dave turned his head and smiled. 'It's called experience, love. I've been on so many stake-outs where I've spent endless boring hours just waiting for stuff to happen.' He lifted his shoulders in a slight shrug and closed his eye again. 'This is no different. No point willing things to happen. We just have to be patient. So the best thing you can do is close your mouth and rest that pretty head of yours while you can.'

Irked by Dave's patronising comment, Claire felt the muscles in her face tighten, and her nostrils flared as she shot daggers at him. She

raised a finger and was just about to tell him where he could stick his advice. But then Gemma suddenly appeared by their side, quickly silencing Claire's retort before it could leave her mouth.

'Hilaria's given the all-clear,' she said in a matter-of-fact tone while gesturing to the rear hatch. 'You can disembark now.'

Acknowledging Gemma with a polite nod, Dave yawned, stretched his arms and rose out of his seat. As he did so, he smiled a toothy grin at Claire and gave her a patronising wink.

'See what I mean.'

Holding her tongue, Claire responded with a tight smile, but pretended to adjust her glasses using the middle finger of her right hand. Dave let out a loud bark of laughter and headed toward the rear hatch while Claire continued to shoot daggers at the back of his head as she followed him. The corner of her lip curled up as she silently wished for him to slip and fall on his backside.

Claire squinted and waited for her eyes to adjust to the bright early afternoon sunlight. A gentle fresh breeze brushed over the exposed skin of her face, and she shivered slightly. When she left her Earth, the weather had been typical for a British winter – cold and wet. Even though Claire was aware they were on an island very similar to the British Isles, she wondered if this pleasantly mild day was representative of a British winter on this Earth.

Once her vision had adjusted, Claire stepped off the aircraft's loading hatch and saw that she was standing in the centre of what looked like a large meadow. Turning to take in the view, she could see that they were in a valley like the one her home village had been in. As she took in the scenery, Claire noticed the clearing seemed quite large – she estimated roughly one square mile. But then she frowned; the treeline ran the entire length of the outer edge of the clearing. Was it her imagination, but did it look as if the clearing was a perfect square?

The hairs on the back of her neck tingled, and she shivered. Something didn't feel right. There was something slightly off about this place. A sense of panic stirred inside Claire, and she felt her heart pound against her ribcage. It was as if something was whispering at her

subconscious, heightening her paranoia. Every instinct in her body was trying to go into fight or flight mode, and it took everything she had to ignore it.

'I see you've noticed it too,' Dave murmured, waving a hand over the open space.

'Mm-mm,' Claire replied, nodding. 'You can see the way the treeline runs around the outer edge; it's too precise.' She twisted her face and rubbed the back of her neck. 'It's not just that. This whole place feels wrong. I can't place my finger on it, but something in the back of my mind is screaming at me, telling me to run away.'

'I agree,' Hilaria responded glumly, suddenly appearing in front of them. She gestured for Claire and Dave to follow her. 'I think I can explain why we feel so on edge.'

As soon as she started following Hilaria, Claire immediately realised what she was talking about. Several metres in front of her, in the centre of the clearing, was a strange shimmering effect. It reminded her of a mirage in the desert. But that was only an optical illusion generated by the refraction of light brought on by the extreme heat of desert air. That was ridiculous, she thought, because we are not in the desert. Only as she got closer to it did she notice that the mirage remained in the same position. A normal mirage always looked like it was in the distance. Craning her head to take it in, she saw it was focused over a small area, which gave an artificial quality to it. Pursing her lips, Claire wondered if someone had placed it there as a marker to remind them where something was. Such as an access hatch to a certain cavern, for instance.

The dozen soldiers who made up Hilaria's team all stood just slightly away from the unusual haze. The way they were fidgeting with their weapons echoed the same extreme agitation Claire was feeling. Every so often she would see a soldier lock eyes on the mirage, then instantly look away. Claire had an idea what they must be feeling because every time she looked at the same spot, she had to fight the impulse to look away from it. She couldn't explain it, but the sight of it made her skin crawl.

'That will be the perception filter,' Hilaria explained as if sensing Claire's apprehension.

'Whatever you call it,' Dave answered grimly, 'it's definitely not natural.' He pulled a face and gave a theatrical shudder. 'The closer I am to that weird mirage, the more I get the heebie-jeebies.'

Hilaria cocked her head and gave Dave an odd look. 'I'm not sure

if my translator chip recognised that, but if you're saying you feel a heightened state of fear or anxiety, then I would have to agree.'

With her left arm raised, Hilaria took several steps toward the strange phenomenon, coming to a stop half a metre from it. Her face was a mask of concentration as she activated something on that strange wristband attached to her left arm. Less than a minute later, she took a step back and stared at the holographic readout, nodding thoughtfully.

'It's as I surmised,' she explained, not taking her eye off the display. 'There's a perception filter covering that small area. A cloak, if you will, which is designed to mess with people's senses.' Hilaria thinned her lips and gave a small nod of approval. 'I must give Severan her due. It was genius of her to create something on this scale. She obviously didn't want to make it easy for people to find whatever it was she discovered.'

'Can you disable it?' Claire asked, eyeing the spot warily. It was taking everything she had not to run back into the shuttle and cower. The longer she looked at it, the more it felt as if her heart was racing. She inhaled and exhaled slowly to calm her pounding heart, trying to fight back the impulse to scream.

'I-I-I'm not sure,' Hilaria stammered, turning away from Claire.

Just before she turned away from her, Claire thought she caught a flicker of emotion in Hilaria's good eye. If she didn't know any better, Claire thought she saw a glint of fear. It couldn't have been from the perception filter, because the emotion she'd seen on Hilaria's face looked too natural. Not only that, but she was sure she recognised the look on her face. Claire bunched her eyebrows together and shook her head in confusion. Where had she seen that look before? Why did—

Then she remembered.

Claire felt her eyes grow wide and she let out a soft moan. *Of course, that's why Hilaria's expression looked familiar*, she thought. She'd seen that same expression on Wendy – the Wendy from her reality – many times before. It was the look she had whenever she'd been unhappy at having to do something she really didn't want to do.

'Hilaria, are you okay?' Claire asked, taking a step forward and placing a comforting hand on Hilaria's arm.

Hilaria smiled tightly and gave an appreciative nod. 'Yes, and no. I think I've an idea on how to deactivate this field, but to do so, I need to access something in my mind I've worked so hard to keep locked away.' Pain flickered across her face, and she turned toward the Asian man standing beside her. 'Yuto, if this doesn't work, and she takes over. On your honour, do you swear to me you'll do what is necessary?'

Yuto stiffened and gave a respectful bow. 'Hilaria-San, I give you my word. I will do as requested.' He took a step forward, grabbed hold of Hilaria's hands, and looked her in the eye. 'I also have faith that won't be necessary, noble warrior. Trust in yourself and remain strong. Repeat after me. My will is stronger than hers.'

Hilaria shook her head and held up a finger as if to stop Yuto, 'Yuto, that's not nec—'

'Repeat it,' Yuto cut in sharply and repeated the mantra, but this time in a much more forceful tone.

Hilaria rolled her eye and sighed half-heartedly. 'My will is stronger than hers.'

Much to Claire's shock, Yuto took a step forward and struck Hilaria across the right side of her face. As Hilaria jerked back in shock, Claire was certain she hadn't been expecting it. A large red welt formed across Hilaria's right cheek, and she stared at Yuto with her mouth open. A dark cloud descended over Yuto's face and Claire thought he was going to lash out at his comrade again.

Wondering whether she should step in, Claire was just about to move forward, only to be stopped by a firm hand on her arm. She snapped her head round to whoever was holding her, and was unable to hide her surprise on realising it was Dave. From the serious expression on his face, she knew he was trying to tell her they shouldn't interfere. With great reluctance, Claire turned back to Hilaria and noticed the hesitancy on her face had vanished. She now stood with her head straight, shoulders squared, giving the appearance of someone who was more self-assured.

'My will is stronger than hers,' Hilaria repeated, this time in a louder, confident tone. She bobbed her head and gave Yuto a humourless smile. 'Thank you, my friend.'

Yuto took a step back, pressed his hands together and bowed. 'Do what you need to do, Hilaria-San. You can now enter the battlefield in confidence, with the knowledge that those around you are certain of your ability to emerge victorious.' Then, as if to emphasise his statement, Yuto cast an eye to the rest of his colleagues, who all stood straight, weapons raised, and let out a howl of defiance. 'Ha-ooh! Ha-ooh! Ha-ooh!'

Confused by the almost tribal display being played out in front of her, Claire scratched her head and tried to make sense of what was going

on. She wondered if Hilaria was going to have to go somewhere dangerous to get the information she needed. From the gist of what she'd heard, she got the impression whoever had the information they needed wasn't going to give it willingly. Was it someone she hadn't seen? A prisoner back at the base?

But as she waited for her to move back to the aircraft, Claire frowned as Hilaria lowered herself to the ground and assumed a cross-legged position. Then, with both of her hands resting on her knees, Hilaria closed her eyes and inhaled several deep, slow breaths. Claire sucked on her bottom lip and nodded curiously, finally understanding what Hilaria was doing. It appeared she was going to put herself in a trance and dig into her memory to get the information she needed, which was probably buried in the deepest part of her mind.

To confirm her theory, Claire took a step closer to Hilaria to get a closer look. To gauge her reaction, Claire waved her hand in front of Hilaria's face. The lack of reaction from Hilaria confirmed her suspicions that she was in a trance. Curious to see how deep a trance she was in, Claire couldn't resist the temptation of leaning in so that she could gently prod the unmoving woman's face. But as she was about to do so, she let out a cry of alarm. Yuto had seized hold of her arm, stopping her.

'Many apologies, Claire-San,' Yuto said in a tone that sounded sincere. 'We cannot interfere. This is Hilaria's battle, and it is something she must do alone. Any interference from us will cause her to lose focus and possibly result in her death.'

'I don't understand. What's so dangerous about going into her mind to retrieve some information?' Claire asked, casting a worried eye at the transfixed woman. Apart from the twitch of her facial muscles, Hilaria remained impassive.

Yuto inhaled deeply, and Claire felt herself being guided away from the meditating Hilaria. Dave appeared next to her, and they both listened intently to Yuto explaining what was going on.

'May I assume you know about Hilaria-San's history?' Yuto asked cryptically.

'Yes,' Dave answered carefully, nodding. 'She was previously General Wendy Cooper, but then, after an altercation with Oracle, she took on the identity of Hilaria.'

Yuto wrinkled his nose and waved his hand. 'That's …' he said hesitantly, 'not entirely accurate. Hilaria has always been open about her

past, so she wouldn't mind me sharing this with you.' Yuto paused and gestured for Claire and Dave to walk with him, only stopping once they were far enough away from Hilaria before continuing and recounting what he'd been told about the difficulties the young Cooper experienced in her early days at the academy, including how she'd been altered by Oracle, creating a colder personality and increasing her intelligence. A flicker of sadness flashed across Yuto's face, and he glanced over his shoulder to the spot they had just come from. 'I'm not even sure Hilaria herself truly understands her own capabilities. Hilaria told me she only found this out recently after Oracle reset her back to what she was before.' Yuto shook his head in sympathy while he continued. 'Hilaria hasn't shared with anybody why Oracle did that. But what I know for certain is the constant internal battle Hilaria must wage every day to stop her other half regaining control.'

A wave of sympathy surged within Claire as it dawned on her what Hilaria must be going through. She peered over to where Hilaria was sitting and tried to put herself in her shoes. To constantly have to be on your guard. The toll it would take on you. What sort of life was that?

'So that's why she's put herself into a trance,' Claire murmured, 'to retrieve information her former self has buried.'

'Yes,' Yuto answered, nodding gravely. 'Hilaria warned me she may have to do this just after we landed. It is my understanding that to access the cavern we need to switch off the cloaking field that surrounds it. To do that, we need to input the correct code. Entering the wrong code could likely activate any countermeasures Doctor Severan installed.'

A glimmer of understanding flashed in Dave's eyes, and he gave Yuto a wide-eyed look of disbelief. 'Holy crap!' he gasped. 'I think I've just worked out why she's doing this.'

Still not understanding why Hilaria would put herself through all this, Claire frowned and shook her head in exasperation. 'Well, I don't. So I would be grateful if you would share it with me.'

Dave tapped his bottom lip thoughtfully as he spoke uncertainly, as if he was choosing his words carefully. 'We know General Cooper was the last person in charge of the URE's portal project. So it's safe to say she probably carried out a lot of research into its past.' He glanced at Yuto, who acknowledged him with a polite nod. 'What if Cooper discovered more than she let on to her superiors? She already said she read through Severan's journals, but what if they also contained an account of what she

did here, including the codes needed to access it?'

'I still don't understand why Hilaria has to do all of this,' Claire replied, frowning. 'Surely Hilaria would still be able to remember everything Cooper read?' Sensing a migraine coming on, she winced and massaged her temples as she tried to wrap her head around Hilaria's split personalities. Psychology had been one of her weakest subjects. She'd only taken the course because she needed a subject to make up her grades so she could attend university. The nightmares she'd had the night before her psychology exam had left an impression on her.

'Not necessarily, Claire-San,' Yuto answered in a respectful tone. 'Even my people knew about General Cooper's excessive paranoia. It was well documented that Cooper was highly distrustful. I have heard stories where people have hypnotised themselves to stop them from remembering certain information.'

'Oh, I see,' Claire exclaimed, finally understanding the full picture. 'The general must have learned about the location of the nexus gateway from Severan's journals and hypnotised herself to forget all about it. She didn't want her own superiors to know of it.' Claire massaged her forehead and let out a humourless laugh. 'What a bitch. Fancy not trusting your own people.'

Yuto grunted and nodded. 'That is the reason Hilaria is doing this. She must access the deepest part of her subconscious to retrieve the information we need. Deep in the recesses where her former personality is locked away.'

An icy shiver ran down Claire's spine as she understood the danger Hilaria was placing herself in. By travelling into the deeper depths of her subconscious, Hilaria would be forced to confront the person she most feared. Even though she'd had her share of mental health issues over the years, those paled in comparison to what Hilaria must be going through. Peering back over her shoulder to where Hilaria was sitting, Claire wondered what sort of battle was raging inside her mind. Never had she felt more powerless to help than she did now.

'Do you think she'll be successful?' Claire whispered, afraid that raising her voice might affect the outcome of the battle.

Yuto inhaled deeply and lifted his hands. 'We can only hope, Claire-San. It all depends on whether the general is willing to share what she has learned.'

'And if she isn't?' Dave asked grimly.

Yuto answered with a small, silent shrug. Claire could see her own concerns mirrored in his bleak expression. If the general wasn't going to give information up easily, that meant Hilaria was in for a fight. If she lost, then it was possible that not only would she lose access to the information, but there was a risk she would also lose control of her body. Closing her eyes, Claire sent a silent prayer to whoever was listening in the hope they would give Hilaria the strength to win against an improbable foe.

-31-

For several hours, Claire sat next to Hilaria in the hope her presence might somehow give her strength. But if Hilaria was aware of what was going on around her, she gave no sign. Every so often, Claire would reach over in concern whenever she noticed the odd facial twitch or heard the occasional soft groan emanating from the immobile woman. Now that she understood how the perception filter worked, Claire realised that keeping herself focused on Hilaria offset the effects of the field somewhat. The fear and anxiety still lingered, though it was less intense, like a faint tickle on the edges of her mind.

Yuto helpfully updated Isaac, who was on-board the other aircraft. Once his vehicle had touched down, the big man disembarked and hurried over to see for himself what Hilaria had done, only to let loose with a carpet bomb of expletives. Claire's cheeks burned and a wave of discomfort washed over her on hearing some of the colourful phrases used while wondering if any were anatomically possible. Once Isaac had calmed down, he stomped back to his aircraft so that he could inform Emma what was happening, only to return a few minutes later in an even fouler mood. Claire guessed Emma hadn't taken the news well and had probably chewed Isaac out for not stopping Hilaria.

To keep themselves busy while they waited for Hilaria to wake up, the two teams used the time to set up a defensive perimeter along the entire outer edge of the clearing. Shuttles flew back and forth carrying more personnel, equipment and other military hardware. As they set up several

portable cabins, Claire was impressed by the entire team's efficiency.

For his part, Dave tried to be helpful by assisting those who were setting up the camp. But whether it was because he was in their way or because he just wanted to check up on Claire, he occasionally appeared next to her and offered her a bottle of refreshment. During one of Dave's visits they both heard what sounded like a loud gasp from Hilaria. Turning sharply toward her, Claire couldn't hide her relief at seeing she was no longer in a trance but was now fully alert. Dave ran to summon Isaac and Yuto, while Claire handed Hilaria a bottle containing an energy supplement.

'Thank you,' Hilaria groaned, smiling gratefully and taking a gulp from the bottle.

Several people appeared at once, and Claire was appalled to see that their weapons were pointed at Hilaria. Isaac ignored Claire's questioning look as he knelt in front of Hilaria, regarding her with concern.

'Hilaria?' Isaac asked worriedly.

'Yes, my friend,' Hilaria breathed between large gulps of liquid, 'it is me, Hilaria.'

Isaac shot her a dangerous look and Hilaria thought she detected a trace of scepticism in his voice. 'Forgive me for being slightly sceptical, Miss Cooper, but how do I know it's you and not the general?'

Hilaria waggled her finger and laughed in a tone devoid of humour. 'Well, if I was the general, you would be dead for having the temerity to speak to her. She would have reached over and snapped your neck so fast, you probably wouldn't even realise you were dead until you were in the afterlife speaking to your ancestors.' Hilaria's cheeks flushed, and she gave Isaac an embarrassed smile. 'Not to be disrespectful, Sergeant N'Goy, but she wasn't what you would call tolerant of races she … um … considered inferior.'

Claire felt her chest tighten with anxiety on hearing the racist slur and glanced worriedly at Isaac as his right eye twitched and his fingers tightened their grip on his rifle, and she held her breath while she waited for him to lash out in anger at the insult. But much to her surprise, his face softened. Then he pulled his head back and let out a loud, barking laugh.

'Hah-hah, my friend,' Isaac boomed, 'it's a relief to have you back.'

His cheery mood quickly vanished, and he gestured to those holding their weapons to lower them while he stared at Hilaria with a serious expression. 'Did you get what you needed?'

A frown pinched the bridge of Hilaria's nose, and she gave a small nod of confirmation. 'Yes. It wasn't easy, but I was able to get the codes to deactivate the cloaking field.' The corner of her lips quirked slightly in amusement. 'I have it on good authority that the codes will also grant us access to the cavern.'

Curious to know more, Claire coughed politely and raised her hand. 'Ahem. Mind if I ask, what was it like? I mean, did you ... have to fight your other self or something?'

Claire realised that she may have put her foot in it on hearing what sounded like a strangulated cough from Dave. Turning toward him, she saw his eyes were almost popping out of his head in disbelief. She swallowed at the murderous scowl aimed toward her from Isaac. *Oh crap! Me and my big mouth.* Wishing for the ground to swallow her up, Claire sheepishly lowered her head and stared at her feet. Her heart thundered inside her chest as she waited for someone to grab her arm and march back to the shuttle. However, any concerns were quickly dissipated as soon as she heard Hilaria's weak laugh.

'It's okay,' Hilaria said, laughing and holding up her hand. 'I don't mind you asking. To be honest, it wasn't what I expected. There wasn't any violence involved. The general and I simply talked ... sort of.'

'You just talked?' Claire exclaimed, struggling to hide her disappointment after imagining Hilaria being involved in a brutal psychic battle. 'Why were you making all those strange growling noises?'

Hilaria's cheeks flushed and she rubbed the back of her neck while she laughed weakly, sounding almost embarrassed. 'Yeah, about that. The general is quite competitive, so she set me some challenges in order for me to win the information I needed. Those groans you heard were my frustration at being put through a series of tests.'

Before Claire could ask anything else, Hilaria sighed loudly in resignation and climbed back to her feet. Her face now a mask of determination, she clapped her hands and turned to face the strangely shimmering patch of air.

'Right then,' she said in a tone of heavy conviction, 'enough chatting. It's time we get around to what we came here to do.'

Isaac pursed his lips and gave Hilaria a disapproving look. 'My friend, are you sure you don't want to take a few more minutes to rest?'

Hilaria scoffed and flicked her wrist in dismissal. 'Pfft! I've done enough sitting around. Time is getting on, and I would like this done before any other problems crop up to stop us.'

Then, before anyone had a chance to stop her, she marched with resolute purpose toward the mirage-that-wasn't-a-mirage, stopping barely a metre in front of it. Claire wondered whether she was going to raise both of her hands and call out *Open sesame!* in a loud, defiant voice.

However, much to Claire's disappointment, that did not happen. Hilaria simply raised her left arm, typed something into the strange wrist device on her arm, then made a wide sweeping motion. Claire struggled to contain her nausea as the air seemed to shimmer before her eyes. Then, to Claire, it felt as if a veil was being removed from her eyes; she found herself standing in front of a mountain-shaped edifice. On first appearance, she guessed it must be approximately three hundred metres in height, with an equal circumference, which instantly told her it was too precise to be a natural formation. Not only that, but even her untrained eye could tell that whatever material the edifice was made out of was obviously artificial – what, though, she had no idea. Claire drew her eyes to the bottom of the artificial edifice and noticed a shallow cave, inside of which stood a ten-metre-wide smooth, solid-looking door.

Claire anxiously chewed on her bottom lip as Hilaria took another step forward and pressed her wrist device against an interface panel just to the right of the door. Despite her anxiety, Claire felt slightly cheated at the time wasted just for this. Where were all the futuristic security robots issuing warnings of death and dismemberment? At the realisation that she'd spent too much time watching low-budget science fiction B movies, she let out a heavy sigh and shook her head.

Sometimes reality sucked!

There was a loud rumbling noise and Claire had to grab Dave to steady herself as the ground beneath her trembled. A nerve-jangling grinding noise filled the air as the large door groaned open, sliding upwards

to reveal an ominous-looking opening. Her curiosity getting the better of her, Claire took several hesitant steps forward to get a better look and saw what looked like a steep corridor, which appeared to go on forever, with what looked like a chain of lights dotted along the corridor's ceiling.

Hilaria gestured for the members of her team to take point. The dozen men and women raised their weapons and carefully entered through the open doorway in a two-by-two formation. Turning toward Isaac, Hilaria gave him a polite nod while she removed her wristband and handed it to him. 'If you don't hear back from us in two hours, you're to use this to close the doorway and head back to base as quickly as you can,' Hilaria said bluntly to Isaac, who acknowledged her with a grim wordless nod. She turned and appraised Dave and Claire. 'This will be your last chance to back out.'

Claire shared a look with Dave, who responded with a brief shake of his head. Relieved that he was still willing to continue, Claire straightened and fixed Hilaria with the best confident smile she could manage. 'What? You think I'm going to let you have all the fun?'

As she followed the team down into the steep tunnel, Claire shivered at the sudden unease running down her spine. She wondered if she would live to regret her decision to join the mission. Her unease increased further on hearing the bone-shaking groan coming from behind her. She spun around to see the huge door closing, sealing them in.

They were truly on their own now.

With Yuto and the other soldiers walking ahead of her, Claire followed with Dave and Hilaria on either side of her. Their steady footfalls echoed off the tunnel walls as they continued at a slow but steady pace. Concentrating on her breathing to calm her thundering heart, Claire tried not to imagine how far underground they were going. Although she rarely suffered from claustrophobia, she couldn't help being acutely aware of the confined space around her. The soft lighting only heightened her anxiety, playing tricks on her eyes, causing her to jump at the strange shadows on the edges of her peripheral vision.

'You okay, Claire?' Dave asked. 'You seem jumpy.'

Claire shook her head and spoke through clenched teeth. 'Not really. Normally, enclosed spaces don't bother me, but right now I've this overriding fear that the walls are going to collapse on top of me and bury me alive.'

'Yeah, I know what you mean,' Dave responded glumly, waving a hand around him. 'I'm not sure if it's the lights or something else, but I can't shake the feeling that we shouldn't be down here.'

'It's the after-effects of the perception filter you're feeling. I think the tunnel walls have absorbed it somehow, which may explain the reason for our edginess,' Hilaria explained in a flat tone, pointing in the direction they were heading. 'The effects should weaken the further we travel away from the surface.'

'Mm-mm,' Dave grunted in reply.

Dave's sour face was a clear giveaway that he wasn't convinced, and Claire had to concede that she agreed with him. As much as they would like to trust Hilaria, this world was still unfamiliar to them, and she was sure it would take some time for them to fully adjust. But after about twenty minutes, Claire noticed that the strange foreboding wasn't as bad as it had been, and she felt calmer in herself. She cast an eye to Hilaria, who acknowledged her with a knowing smile.

Now more in control of her emotions, Claire realised she could focus more on her surroundings. Growing more confident and feeling more like her curious self, she moved closer to the wall and frowned. Was it her imagination, or did the walls look too smooth to be a natural formation?

'Hilaria, did somebody build this tunnel?' Claire asked curiously, gesturing to the tunnel wall and ceiling. 'They're too smooth, as if they were created through artificial means.'

Hilaria scrunched up her face, peered at the tunnel and nodded. 'Yes, I agree it does look like it was manufactured.' She stuck out her bottom lip and knelt, then gestured at the strange grooves on the floor's surface. 'These markings could only have been made by drilling equipment, such as the caterpillar tracks from a mobile laser drill. Severan must have used a team of engineers to get to the cavern.'

Claire tapped her bottom lip while she contemplated Hilaria's words. Something in Hilaria's statement troubled her. Yes, Severan could have located the nexus's energy like Hilaria had, investigated, and, finding no natural entry, was driven to using drastic artificial methods to gain access. But that wasn't what she found troubling. How many engineers would she have used?

Claire drew in a sharp intake of air as it occurred to her what she'd found so troubling and spun round to look down at Hilaria. 'Hilaria,' she said carefully, secretly hoping she was wrong. 'According to the reports you read, you said Severan was considered to be a very paranoid person.'

Hilaria rose from her crouching position and gave Claire a puzzled look. 'Yes, according to her psychoanalysis profile, she was classed as a sociopath. That's probably why she never told her superiors her theory about this reality's gateway.'

Dave rubbed his chin, and a distant expression appeared over his face. Claire could tell he was pondering over what she'd said. Then a change seemed to come over him; Claire saw his eyes widen in shock, and he exchanged a startled glance with her. 'By Jove!' he exclaimed. 'I see where you're going with this.'

'What?' Hilaria growled in a peevish tone, frowning. 'What am I missing?'

Claire swallowed and spoke in a heavy tone. 'If Severan was forced to use a team of engineers, then wouldn't they have been required to log their time spent working on this project?'

'Yes,' Hilaria replied, nodding slowly. 'Under URE law, all engineering teams must account for their actions. It's so that ... oh!' The blood seemed to drain from her face, and then she spoke in a low, horrified voice. 'She must have killed them as soon as they completed the work for her.'

A chorus of startled exclamations came from the soldiers, who had come to a stop, possibly out of curiosity so that they could follow the conversation. From their troubled expressions, Claire could tell they were also deeply unnerved at what lengths Severan must have gone to keep the existence of this place a secret. She tried to suppress a shudder as an icy feeling of dread wrapped itself around her heart. A sense of foreboding

stirred within her as she gazed down the tunnel.

What gruesome discovery would they encounter when they finally arrived at their destination?

-32-

The Group continued the rest of the way in an uncomfortable silence. Claire cast a surreptitious eye at Hilaria and noticed her strained expression. It was obvious Claire's theory about what may have happened to the engineering team had disturbed her, something that surprised her. When she was first introduced to Hilaria, Claire had found her cold, and she seemed to keep everybody at arm's length. But the more she got to know her, the more Claire realised Hilaria was trying to keep a tight rein on her emotions, and she wondered if the former imperial officer was afraid to let people get close to her in case she hurt them. Despite her similarity to Wendy – the Wendy of Claire's reality – she could see that was where the differences ended. The Wendy Cooper she knew was much more open with her emotions.

Thinking about the differences between the two flame-haired women, a wave of sadness overwhelmed Claire as she realised just how differently Emma's life had turned out, compared to her own. She thought back to that ill-fated night and wondered how she would have turned out if she'd gone down into the kitchen instead of Emma. Growing up, Claire always considered Emma to be stronger than her. There was no doubt in her mind that if their situations had been reversed, she wouldn't have survived like Emma did.

'Everybody stand back while I look for an access port,' Hilaria's loud authoritative voice announced, breaking Claire out of her unhappy musings.

Claire blinked in surprise; she had been so distracted by her thoughts, she hadn't noticed they had arrived at their destination. Dave's head was cocked, and he was giving her a quizzical look, which Claire acknowledged with an embarrassed smile while she focused her attention back on the present. They were now standing in front of what looked like an enormous round door. It reminded Claire of the heavy reinforced doors used by banks to protect their vaults. Based on its solid-looking construction, she thought there must be several internal bolts that extended into the thick outer frame, locking it in place. It was safe to assume that these bolts could only be released by entering a code into a sophisticated lock.

Claire watched in silent curiosity as Hilaria slowly approached a panel situated to the right of the door. The tendons on both sides of Hilaria's neck visibly tightened when she opened the panel to reveal a flat touch screen, and as she leaned in closer to study the device, her expression seemed to change; Hilaria now looked more thoughtful.

'Do you think you can open it?' Dave asked curiously.

Her forehead creased in concentration, Hilaria gave a small nod and gestured to the touch screen. 'It should accept the same code I used on the surface.' Turning toward Yuto, she pointed to the strange wristband strapped to his left arm. 'May I borrow your wrist scanner? I left mine with Isaac.'

Showing no sign of hesitation, Yuto obediently removed his wrist scanner and handed it to Hilaria, who made strange clicking noises with her tongue while she studied the flat screen for a few more seconds. Claire guessed she was trying to recall whatever command she used on the surface.

For a moment, Claire wondered if Hilaria had forgotten, and she started to get anxious about what would happen if they couldn't get the door open. Her fingers twitched nervously as other worrying thoughts entered her head. What if they were forced to make their way back to the surface, but discovered the outer door was still closed and it wouldn't accept the command from the borrowed scanner? Panic began to set in as she thought back to what Hilaria had said to Isaac about the dampening field blocking signals. Claire's breathing increased as she flicked her eyes

up to the ceiling and imagined the tons of dirt above their heads. If Hilaria couldn't open the door and they couldn't get back out, would that mean they would be trapped and likely die of starvation? Her heart rate quickened as it occurred to her that they might suffocate before they starved.

But just as Claire thought her panic levels were about to explode, relief flowed through her as Hilaria tapped her finger on the touch screen and brought up what looked like the wrist device's holographic interface. Once she'd finished typing in a series of letters and numbers, Hilaria held the gadget against the flat touch screen.

The tension was almost palpable as everybody waited to see if it worked. Claire jumped in fright at the sound of a series of loud clunks coming from within the vault-like door, followed by a loud grinding noise of metal rubbing against metal. Claire winced at the sound of the door squealing, imagining it was protesting at being disturbed from its restful slumber. There was a loud pop like the sound of a vacuum seal being broken, followed by a whoosh of air as the immense door slowly swung open to reveal a strange multicoloured aura emanating from whatever was inside.

As she followed behind the soldiers, Claire wrinkled her nose when she caught the whiff of stale air. But as she made her way through the open hatchway, another smell tickled her nose. Cocking her head, Claire tried to remember why it smelt so familiar to her. Was it her imagination, or did it smell like rotting meat? Had someone left food down here? But before Claire could make any sense of it, her jaw dropped open in awe at the sight greeting her eyes; she was standing inside an immense dome-shaped cavern. It was nothing like she'd ever seen before.

Turning in a tight circle, Claire craned her head back to admire the crystalline surface above her head. Crystals completely covered the cavern's ceiling, wall and floor, filling the chamber with a steady warm multicoloured luminance. The crystals seemed to pulsate toward a spectacular crystal arch in the centre of the cavern. Dave blew out a whistle and ran a hand through his hair as he stood and stared. From the awestruck gleam in his eyes, Claire could tell he was feeling the same as she was. Placing her hand in his, she smiled and nodded in understanding.

'Absolutely breathtaking, isn't it?' Claire breathed, enraptured by

the display.

'I wonder if this is how Sharon, Wendy and John felt when they saw this in our reality?' Dave murmured, waving his hand around the chamber. 'They said the cavern they found was covered in strange crystals too.'

'Might be,' Claire answered, thinking back to Sharon's description. 'I remember her telling me it was full of strange crystals. But the one she described still had Doctor Selyab's equipment in it.'

Claire narrowed her eyes; Hilaria had moved toward the centre of the cavern. She seemed to be studying the archway with keen interest. Moving toward her, Claire lifted her left eyebrow when she saw the troubled expression on Hilaria's face.

'I think we may have a problem,' Hilaria said grimly as soon as Claire and Dave got closer to her.

At first, Claire wondered what Hilaria was talking about and absently-mindedly ran her tongue along the back of her teeth while she studied the archway. Not understanding what she was supposed to be seeing, she was about to open her mouth, but paused as her eyes were drawn to the centre of the archway. There was a strange crackling noise, which was followed by an erratic flickering of light. It reminded her of a TV signal being disrupted during a thunderstorm.

'I guess it's not supposed to do that,' she asked worriedly.

Hilaria replied with a firm shake of her head and pointed to the four corners of the archway. 'See those? I think they might be the cause of the disruption.'

Claire adjusted her glasses and squinted at the strange box-like devices attached to each of the corners of the archway facing toward her. It was obvious that whatever they were, they weren't natural. They had clearly been manufactured, but for what purpose, Claire had no clue but leaned in closer to get a better look and stroked her chin thoughtfully. If she didn't know any better, it looked like they had been purposely placed on each corner of the archway. Not only that, but she could also clearly see that the devices, as well as the crystals they were attached to, looked damaged and burned out.

'These are subspace quantum transmitters,' Hilaria explained

unhappily. 'Severan must have placed them there to transmit the gateway's energy to the receivers she'd set up in the portal chamber in Pons Aelius. The feedback from Em's EMP must have travelled through subspace, blowing the transmitters and damaging some of the crystals at the same time.' She waved an irritable hand at the flickering archway. 'Which explains why it looks as if the portal is acting erratically. If I don't fix it, we won't be going anywhere.'

No, not when we're this close. Claire's vision became blurry, and she wanted to scream out in frustration. Why did it feel like the universe was against them every step of the way? A wave of anguish grabbed hold of her as she struggled to find the words to express her disappointment.

As if sensing her inner turmoil, Dave placed a comforting hand on her shoulder and gave Hilaria a hopeful look. 'Can you repair it?'

A flicker of uncertainty flashed across Hilaria's face. However, before Claire could hear her answer, they were interrupted by a loud cry coming from across the chamber. On turning toward the source, Claire saw Yuto waving his arms frantically, urging them to come over. 'Hilaria-San, I think you need to see this.'

Showing no hesitation, Hilaria hurried across the cavern, Claire and Dave following close by. As she got closer, Claire could tell from the grave expressions on the soldiers' faces that they must have discovered something unsettling. A cold chill ran down her spine, and she felt the blood drain from her face on seeing the ghastly pile of skeletal remains. Judging from the number of human skulls she could see, Claire estimated there must have been a couple of dozen bodies, and from their state of decay, she guessed they'd been dead for at least half a century or longer. A sick feeling churned inside her stomach as it hit her what that smell must have been. It had been the stench of bodies decomposing, and, with nowhere to go, the odour had lingered inside the cavern until the door's seal had been broken. Claire screwed up her face and shuddered as she tried to wipe the memory of the smell out of her mind.

'It appears we've discovered what happened to the engineering team Severan used,' Hilaria said, picking up what looked like the tattered remains of a uniform.

Yuto's brow creased as he knelt and gestured to the skull nearest

to him. 'That looks like damage sustained from a high-calibre weapon being fired at close range.'

'This isn't a cavern,' Claire said bitterly, struggling to contain her anger. 'This is a bloody tomb.'

Hilaria ran a hand down her face and sighed. 'Unfortunately, there's not a lot we can do for them now. Once we return to the surface, I'll arrange for a team to come down and retrieve them, and they can be given the burial they deserve. Right now, we've other pressing issues. The damage to the gateway, for instance.'

Claire shook her head and held up her hands in confusion. 'With your skill and expertise in portal technology, I would've thought it shouldn't be a problem for you to fix it?'

Hilaria smiled and bobbed her head. 'I appreciate your confidence in me,' she said in a humourless tone and exhaled sadly. 'But unfortunately, it's not as simple as repairing a broken quantum resonator or circuit board. I'm positive we've the equipment back at the base to stabilise the gateway. But to ensure we arrive at a safe destination, I need to configure the coordinates of the destination point into the gateway. To do that, I need an anchor, someone we can lock on to. Unless we have that, I'm afraid we won't be going anywhere.'

The corners of Claire's mouth twitched as a devious thought popped into her head. She grinned and held up a finger. 'Actually, I think I can help you with that.'

Hilaria did a double take and gave Claire a disbelieving look. She shared a startled glance with Dave, who had his arms folded his arms and was staring at Claire warily.

'Okay, I know that look,' Dave said, the tone of his voice echoing the wariness on his face. 'You're about to suggest something incredibly risky, genius or both. I'm not sure whether I should be worried or excited.'

'Oh, come on, Dave. When have I ever let you down?' Claire scoffed, winking. She quickly lifted her right index finger, forestalling any sarcastic reply Dave may have planned. 'How about you keep any smart-arse remarks to yourself until after we've finished?'

Without waiting for a response, Claire turned on her heel and marched toward the arch, only stopping when she realised that no one was following her. Placing her hands on her hips, she raised an enquiring eyebrow.

'Well, are you coming or not?'

-32-

Once she was sure everybody was following, Claire hurriedly made her way back to the archway. Stopping in front of the flickering portal, she tried to hide her nervousness as she sensed everybody's eyes were now on her, and she wondered whether she was doing the right thing. Deciding she would look like a fool if she didn't go ahead with what she was doing, she squared her shoulders and drew in a deep breath. *Okay, here goes nothing.*

'Custos, are you there?' she called out, her voice a nervous whisper.

Apart from the crackle of energy coming from the crystals around the archway, there was no other sound. She couldn't hide her disappointment and blew out a dispirited sigh. Was there any point in trying again? After everything she'd been through, perhaps she was hoping for too much in believing Custos would be listening. Maybe it was best she just forget all about it and be grateful she was still alive.

Claire detected movement out of the corner of her eye, and she sensed Dave had moved closer to her. She glanced over her shoulder and regarded him curiously when he wordlessly placed a hand on her arm and gave it a gentle squeeze. Claire smiled gratefully and bobbed her head. No words needed to be said. His encouraging presence was all that she needed to lift her spirits. Feeling more confident, she straightened, held her head high and called out again, this time in a louder, self-assured tone.

'Custos, are you there?'

'Of course, child. Where else would I be?' Custos responded

almost immediately.

Claire exhaled a relieved sigh and pumped her fist jubilantly. Never had she been more delighted to hear that recognisable, condescending tone than she did now. From the startled gasps and unsettled murmurs coming from the others, she guessed that the last thing they probably expected today was to hear a mysterious, ethereal voice speaking to one of their team. Even Dave's normally composed demeanour seemed to be affected and he shuffled anxiously.

'Why didn't you respond the first time?' Claire asked, focusing her attention back on the flickering portal.

'Because I wanted to see how long it would be before you lost your patience with me.' Custos chuckled, followed by what sounded like a heavy sigh, which seemed to contain a tone of regret. 'But then I remembered you have such a foul temper. I thought it best to just give in. Wouldn't you agree, Detective Barnes?'

On hearing the snorts of laughter coming from several people behind her, Claire felt her cheeks burn as she turned to look at Dave. From the wide-eyed expression of shock on his face, it was obvious he hadn't been expecting to be addressed. His mouth opened and closed like a dying fish, and Claire wondered if he was trying to think of something to say that wouldn't get him into trouble.

Several seconds passed and Dave still hadn't responded. At first, Claire thought it might have been the idea of having to address a mysterious entity that Dave was having trouble with. She was certain he'd encountered a variety of difficult people during his years of service in the police force, so she couldn't understand what had got him so worked up. Custos was probably no different to the countless hobnobs, councillors and other difficult people that he'd told her he'd encountered over the years. However, it dawned on her that his reluctance to answer might have been because she had her arms folded and was shooting daggers at him while she waited to hear his response.

'Well, Custos ...' Dave said, laughing weakly. 'You may think that, but for the sake of harmony, I'm sure you understand why I can't comment.'

A thunderous laugh filled the chamber, and Claire was certain the

crystals seemed to glow brighter. 'Oh, very good, my boy. I heartily agree with you.' Custos's tone turned more serious. 'Now, Claire, what is it you need of me?'

'Custos, I'm in no doubt you're aware of what has happened here,' Claire explained quickly. 'The archway looks like it's sustained damage. Hilaria's confident she has the equipment she needs to stabilise the portal, but we need an anchor to lock onto to ensure we arrive at a safe destination.' Claire pressed her hands together and stared pleadingly into the flickering portal. 'I've an idea, which will not only provide us with the anchor we need, but it'll also guarantee us a safe harbour to arrive in. Custos, I know it's a lot to ask of you, but can you connect me with one of my friends back in my reality? Wendy, Sophia, or even John?'

There was an uneasy silence for several seconds, and Claire wondered if Custos had thought her request unacceptable. Had he severed their connection after considering such a task was beneath him? But just as she was about to give up hope, a flash of light caught Claire's eye. It seemed to be coming from the right side of the archway. As she moved toward the flash of light, she blinked in surprise as she realised it was coming from a small part of the archway that appeared to be as smooth as glass. Because it was the size of a small window, Claire had paid little attention to it when she first inspected the archway, having been more interested in the awesome spectacle of the fulgurating portal inside it.

'Hilaria Cooper,' Custos ordered in a blunt tone. 'Please take a step forward.'

Of all the things Claire had expected Custos to do, speaking directly to Hilaria hadn't been one of them. She turned sharply toward Hilaria, whose body appeared to stiffen in shock. It was obvious she hadn't been expecting it either. Hilaria glanced at Claire, who raised her hands in encouragement, mouthing, *'It's okay.'*

The stress lines in Hilaria's forehead deepened as she took a hesitant step forward and waved nervously. 'H-h-hello?'

'Hello to you too, my dear. What a pleasure it is to finally meet you,' Custos answered gleefully. 'Now, do you see that area on the right side of the archway? The one that looks like a small window?'

'Yes,' Hilaria replied, nodding proudly. 'It was one of the first things I noticed when I first set eyes on the arch.'

'Really! Wow, that is incredibly perceptive of you,' Custos said in a tone dripping with sarcasm. 'Although, shouldn't that be *set my eye* on the arch? You do have only one good eye, after all.'

Claire groaned inwardly and planted her face in her hands. She could just imagine Custos using air quotes with his fingers while addressing Hilaria in that condescending tone she found so annoying. She shook her head in rueful sympathy as Hilaria bristled at the slight, shooting the flickering portal a murderous glare so powerful, Claire was sure she could feel the heat emanating from her.

'Thank you,' Hilaria replied dryly. 'It warms my heart hearing that.'

'My pleasure, child, always happy to be of help,' Custos replied. 'Now, be a good girl and hurry. We haven't got all day.'

The throbbing vein in Hilaria's left temple, coupled with her clenched jaw, suggested to Claire that Hilaria was straining to hold back a retort. As the quietly fuming woman moved towards the side of the arch, Claire couldn't help admiring her restraint. The window on the side of the arch lit up, casting a warm glow over Hilaria's face. Claire noticed a strange whispering filling the cavern, almost sounding like a multitude of voices speaking as one. Dave exchanged a startled look with her as the surrounding crystals changed colour.

'No need to worry,' Custos said, as if sensing their concerns. 'This is perfectly normal. You see, the crystals are sentient and are connected by a highly sophisticated neural network to other nexus points in every reality across the multiverse, in a manner similar to the human brain. They are scanning for Hilaria's counterpart, Wendy Cooper. Or to be more specific, the Wendy Cooper from your reality, Claire. Once she's been located, Hilaria doesn't need to worry about her counterpart not being able to understand what she says to her because the nexus will automatically translate what is being said. To Wendy, it will sound as if Hilaria is speaking in her language.'

Just as Custos finished his sentence, a joyous noise filled the cavern. It reminded Claire of a choir. As she listened to the heartening chorus, the image in the window changed to show a red-haired woman. Claire reeled back in shock and felt her eyes grow wide in recognition.

It was the Wendy Cooper from her reality.

Wendy was alive, she was actually alive.

Claire, overjoyed to see her friend had survived the devastating blast that had most surely destroyed the base, couldn't hold back her excitement, and she grabbed Dave's arm. Dave, who seemed just as emotional, let out a soft sob and wrapped his arms around Claire in a tight embrace. But once she'd got over the shock of seeing Wendy alive, she noticed how she was dressed. Although she could only see her torso, Claire could tell Wendy had a towel wrapped tightly around her like she was just about to jump in the shower or had just taken one. Whatever it was, they'd obviously caught her at a bad time.

'Och! What the frig!' Wendy gasped. Claire guessed from the way she was grabbing the top of her towel and pulling it tighter that Hilaria's sudden appearance had startled her. 'Oy, bawbag, who are you and what are you doing in my bathroom mirror?'

Hilaria coughed nervously and held up her hand. 'Um, h-h-hi. I can see this has come as a bit of a shock to you.'

'Naw, this is what my face always looks like,' Wendy said in a tone thick with sarcasm. Her face turning a deep shade of red, she pointed angrily at Hilaria. 'You bampot, of course I'm in shock. Wait until you've got an eyepatch-wearing weirdo pop up in your bathroom mirror, then see how you react.'

'Yeah, sorry about this,' Hilaria answered sheepishly. She straightened and held out her hands as if to show Wendy she wasn't a threat. 'I'm your counterpart from a parallel reality and I need your help.'

Wendy cocked her head and gave her a deeply suspicious look. 'Let me guess,' she said, sneering derisively, 'in your reality you're a pirate queen or something and you want me to join your crew?'

'Of course not!' Hilaria snapped, clearly irritated. 'What makes you think I'm a pirate?'

'Because of the eyepatch, obviously.' Wendy laughed, pointing to her own good right eye. She nodded in approval and gave a thumbs up. 'I

must say, that's a good look. You carry it off well.'

Hilaria touched her eyepatch in a display of self-consciousness and Claire noticed that she was blushing. She had to stifle back a laugh because this was the first time she'd seen her react in such a way. It was obvious she wasn't used to receiving compliments.

'Well, let's just say it wasn't by choice.' Hilaria laughed weakly, shaking her head. She cocked her head, and the corners of her mouth curled up into a mischievous smile. 'If you ever decide to go for a more intimidating look, I highly recommend it.'

Wendy tilted her head and gave Hilaria a sly look. 'Maybe I will. If you are ever in my neck of the woods, as they say, maybe we can discuss it further.'

'Excuse me, ladies,' Custos interrupted in what sounded almost like an exacerbated tone. 'I would appreciate it if you would stop flirting with one another. Although time is infinite, my patience is not.'

Claire had to really concentrate to stop herself from laughing as the two women's faces turned beetroot. Dave let out a soft snicker, and Claire had to nudge him in the ribs to stop him from laughing any harder. Then she noticed the bemused expressions of the other members of the team, and she shot them a murderous glare as a warning to compose themselves. Claire was sure the last thing Hilaria needed was to see her comrades revelling in her discomfort.

Fortunately, it appeared Hilaria was too mortified to notice everyone's reaction because her face had turned a deep shade of red; it also seemed as if she was trying not to look directly at Wendy. Wendy's expression mirrored her counterpart's, although she was sure Wendy's cheeks weren't as red.

'I-I-I,' Hilaria stammered, shaking her head. 'I wasn't flirting, honestly.'

'W-w-who,' Wendy gasped, twisting her head from side to side as if searching for the source of the mysterious voice, 'who's that speaking?'

'Ignore him. He's just a mischievous imp who likes to cause bother,' Hilaria said in a tone devoid of any humour, but she was now looking more composed. She inhaled and spoke in a serious tone. 'Wendy, I'm from the same reality as Colonel Barnes. I'm not sure if he told you

anything about me, but if he did, then you'll probably know I was his superior officer.'

Wendy's eyes narrowed, and a flicker of suspicion flashed across her face. 'Yes, he spoke about you. From what I heard about you, you're a nasty piece of work. So why should I listen to anything you have to say?'

Hilaria pressed her hands together in a placating gesture and spoke in a pleading tone. 'Wendy, I know I cannot give you a reason to trust me, but,' she paused and urgently waved a hand at Dave for him to come forward, 'there's somebody here who you can trust, and they would very much like to speak to you.'

Dave smiled gratefully at Hilaria while she took a step back to allow him to take her place in front of the small window. Raising his right hand in acknowledgement, Dave gave Wendy a tight smile.

'Hi, Wendy,' he said grimly. 'I'm sure I'm the last person you expected to see.'

'Guv!' Wendy gasped in wide-eyed shock. Her shock only seemed to last a second as a shadow of distrust appeared across her face. 'The Dave Barnes I know died in an explosion. If you really are him, how did you end up there?'

Dave raised a hand and let out a humourless laugh. 'That's a long and complicated story, but trust me when I say it is me.' He leaned in closer and spoke in a serious tone. 'Do you remember the last thing I said to you?'

'Yes,' Wendy replied, her voice mirroring the uncertainty on her face. 'You asked me to make you a promise. That I would—'

'Make Oracle pay,' Dave cut in, nodding.

'Oh my god,' Wendy said, her eyes growing wide in shock. 'It is you. What about Claire? Did she survive too?'

'Hello, Wendy,' Claire called out, struggling to hide the delight from showing in her voice. 'It's me, Claire. How are you doing, flower?'

'Cl-Cl-Claire, h-h-how?' Wendy stammered.

'No time for explanations, pet,' Dave cut in. 'We're in a bit of a pickle and we need your help. We plan on sending some reinforcements to you, but to do that we need to make sure the area we are arriving at is secure. That's the reason Hilaria here contacted you. Basically, you're a multidimensional anchor, which will allow us to travel through, safe in the

knowledge that we would be coming through to a safe location. But we need you to prepare to hold a large group of people in …' He stopped, turned and stared at Hilaria enquiringly. 'How long do you think you'll need to get the gateway working?'

'We should be good to go by mid-afternoon tomorrow,' Hilaria responded without hesitation.

'Did you hear that?' Dave asked, to which Wendy nodded. 'Do you think you'll be able to organise a space large enough to hold a couple of thousand people, as well as some vehicles?'

'No problem, Guv,' Wendy answered, nodding furiously. 'I'll discuss it with the others. We should be able to deactivate the frequency jammers in the hangar bay. I'll get them to rig up some sort of large mirror as well.'

'Good girl,' Dave said, grinning. 'All being well, we should see you tomorrow.'

Wendy's face changed into a downcast expression, and she exhaled a long, melancholic sigh. 'Guv, a lot has happened since you've been gone … I—'

'Sorry, flower,' Dave said quickly, holding up his hand in an apologetic gesture. 'We're pressed for time. Whatever you have to tell me, it'll have to wait until we arrive. Speak to you soon and stay safe.'

With that, Wendy's face disappeared, and the strange window went dark. Claire pursed her lips and wondered what Wendy was trying to tell them. From the tone in Wendy's voice, it sounded like she was about to deliver bad news. A knot formed inside her stomach as a feeling of dread gripped her. She just hoped Oracle hadn't made things even harder for everybody back home. She lifted her shoulder in a slight shrug and shook her head ruefully. *Oh well,* she thought. *Whatever it is, we'll learn about it when we get back home tomorrow.*

Just then, the portal shimmered, and Custos's voice echoed around the chamber.

'I don't mean to put a dampener on your celebrations,' Custos said in what sounded like a sorrowful tone. 'But I need to make you aware of something that will most likely affect your decision to repair the archway.'

Oh God, what now? A heaviness settled in Claire's heart, and she

glanced sharply at Dave and Hilaria. There was no missing the alarm on their faces, and she knew they were probably thinking the same thing as her.

'What is it you need to tell us, Custos?' she asked, trying to keep the fear she was feeling from showing in her voice.

'As Hilaria will most likely confirm, when you activate a wormhole, it gives off a tremendous burst of energy,' Custos said, to which Hilaria responded with a wordless nod of confirmation. 'The energy signature is so big it will ring out across dimensions. To put it into terms you can understand, it will be like ringing thousands of church bells all at once. Within moments of activating the gateway, Oracle will detect it, and she will launch everything she has at her disposal to seize control of that reality's nexus.'

The dread Claire was feeling heightened, and she felt the contents of her stomach churn; she suspected that wasn't the worst of it. 'There's more, isn't there?' she asked, unable to keep her voice from trembling. 'Something far worse than us being killed.'

Custos sighed. 'Yes. So far, Oracle hasn't been able to learn the location of this reality's nexus. We've been lucky because General Cooper wiped all records of the location after she read about it in Doctor Severan's journals. I have shielded the location as best as I can, but even I cannot hide the energy signature of a wormhole once it has been activated. But once she learns of its location, she will stop at nothing to gain control of it.'

'I don't understand,' Hilaria said, the expression of confusion on her face echoing what Claire was feeling. 'What's so special about this reality's nexus? I've seen for myself that Oracle can cross dimensions without it.'

'That nexus is so much more,' Custos explained in a despondent tone. 'It is unique because it is the prime gateway. Currently, Oracle can only travel between two realities – the one you're in now and your home reality. But if she had control of that nexus, Oracle could conceivably invade every reality in the multiverse.'

An icy shiver ran down Claire's spine as she realised what Custos was getting at. She felt her throat tighten and she shared a horrified look

with the group of people standing around her. 'I think what Custos is trying to say is we've a decision to make,' she said in a neutral tone. 'Remain here in this world, safe and sound, while Oracle does god knows what to my world. Or we risk opening the gateway and hope we can hold off Oracle's forces long enough for us to get through. Not only that, but we would also need to discover a way to stop Oracle from gaining control of it once we've gone through.'

'Yes, that is it, in a nutshell,' Custos said in a grave, humourless tone.

'What would you suggest we do, Custos?' Claire asked, secretly hoping the entity would have some words of wisdom.

'That, my child, I'm sorry to say, is something that only you and your people can decide,' Custos replied in what sounded like a sincere but regretful tone. 'But whatever decision you all come to, I have faith you will make the right one.'

'Thank you, Custos,' Hilaria said bluntly. 'Now, if you would be so kind as to leave us, we have much to discuss.'

'Certainly, Hilaria,' Custos replied, a touch of sadness still showing in his voice. 'I bid you all farewell, and just to let you know, I'll be watching with curious interest what course of action you agree to take.'

With that, he was gone.

Ever since her first encounter with Custos, Claire had had a strange tingling sensation tickling the edge of her consciousness. She'd been comfortable in the knowledge he was watching over her. But that tickling sensation was no longer there, and a wave of sadness overtook her as she realised that they truly were alone and if they got into any bother, Custos wouldn't be able to pull her backside out of the fire like he'd done before.

Claire swallowed and gazed at the faces around her, wondering what was going through their minds. It was a huge decision to make. Was it even fair to put the responsibility on their shoulders? Did they even have the right to decide on the fate of not just two worlds, but many others too?

'I think we should hold off making any decision,' Hilaria announced as if in answer to Claire's unspoken question. Turning slowly around, she looked every person in the eye and spoke in an authoritative

voice. 'This is a decision that everyone should make. I suggest we head back to base so that everybody can hear what we've been told, and then we can put it to a vote.'

From the murmurs of acknowledgement and the expressions on everyone's faces, Claire could see they all agreed with what Hilaria was suggesting. As she followed them all out of the cavern and into the tunnel, she was surprised to discover she didn't harbour any resentment toward those who would vote against fixing the archway. If she was honest with herself, she could see it from their point of view. Why should they risk themselves for another world's population, who probably weren't even aware of their existence?

One thing was certain, Claire realised, whatever way they voted, it would not only decide the fate of two worlds – it might also decide the fate of the multiverse.

-34-

The vote was unanimous.

The gateway would be repaired.

The following day, Dave was fastened into the rear seat of an open-top cargo transporter, which was gliding down the tunnel toward the crystal cavern. As Emma expertly guided the vehicle, Dave reflected on the events of the previous day.

Upon returning to the base, Emma assembled all personnel in the auditorium so that they could hear Hilaria give the grim news and what was expected of them, highlighting the pros and cons of such a monumental decision. Because it was a decision that would affect the whole of Terra, all the other surviving resistance cells attended the meeting via video link.

The discussion lasted for several hours, and at times became very heated while everyone expressed their opinion. However, when it came time to vote, Emma pulled Dave, Claire, Karen and Zoe to one side to request they remain outside while everyone else voted, her reason being that the four were relatively new to that world and she felt it would not be fair for them to have the stress of being involved in such a decision.

Although disappointed not to be included, the three adults could see where Emma was coming from and reluctantly agreed. Unfortunately, young Zoe did not see it that way and tearfully stormed off in a huff. Claire chased after her, only to return a short time later with the unhappy teen, who reluctantly agreed to Emma's request.

After one long, anxious hour, the door to the auditorium was

reopened, allowing the quartet back inside. Upon hearing that there was a unanimous vote to repair the arch so that the portal to the other reality could be opened, Dave let out a huge whoop of delight. A short time later, he learned that many people had expressed the belief that not to do so would send a message that they were afraid of Oracle. Remembering the grim, resolute expressions on everybody's faces, Dave could clearly see they were anything but afraid.

His thoughts drifted back to the present and Dave focused his attention on the two women in front of him. Claire was sitting in the passenger seat next to Emma and was listening intently to her sister happily chat away while she guided the vehicle down the tunnel.

Dave leaned forward and lightly tapped his finger on Emma's shoulder. 'Have you had any word from Hilaria?' he shouted, trying to be heard over the roar of the vehicle's engine, which echoed off the tunnel's walls.

Her gaze still focused on the tunnel ahead, Emma shook her head, gestured to her ear, and spoke into her wrist communicator. Immediately, Dave flinched as he heard Emma's voice in his earpiece.

'She's kept me up to date as best as she can,' Emma replied. 'But from what I can gather, they've been working tirelessly through the night.'

Dave nodded, recalling what Hilaria had said just before departing with a small engineering team immediately after the result of the vote was announced. He couldn't fault Hilaria for her determination to get everything ready as quickly as possible. However, Dave wondered if she was pushing herself too hard to prove to those around her that they could trust her. It made him chuckle as he realised just how alike his Wendy she was. The Wendy of his Earth also liked to push herself to the brink just to prove something, sometimes coming at a cost.

Dave cast an eye at Zoe, who was sitting next to him with a silent, contemplative expression etched across her face. While they'd been waiting for the result of the vote, he'd made an effort to get to know her. His first impression was that she was a pleasant young lady, if slightly on the moody side. But he put her angst down to the typical imbalance of teenage hormones. But then again, being stuck on a frightening, hostile world would make the most evenly balanced person moody. So he was willing to

cut her some slack.

'How are you doing, Zoe?' he asked, this time remembering to speak through his wrist communicator. 'I'm sure you're looking forward to getting back home?'

Zoe stiffened, whether because of the shock of hearing his voice in her ear or that she hadn't expected to be spoken to, Dave couldn't tell. She turned and gave him a strange look. He wasn't sure how to interpret it and wondered whether she was trying to work out how to answer him. She peered at him for several seconds before responding.

'I-I-I'm,' Zoe said hesitantly into her communicator, 'not sure how I feel, Mr Barnes. I'd got so used to the idea of not going home, I'd begun to think of this world as my home.'

'Well, at least you can look forward to being reunited with your family,' Dave said helpfully, which drew an eye roll from Zoe.

'Yeah, right,' she said unhappily. 'My mam and I never had the best of relationships. I bet you a quid she probably doesn't even realise I'm missing.'

'Hmm-mmm,' Dave replied, nodding slowly as he tried to work out how best to answer her. Then he remembered Wendy's encounter with Zoe's doppelgänger a few months ago. 'I probably shouldn't be telling you this, but two of my colleagues interviewed your doppelgänger at the hospital not long after you were attacked. From what they told me, your mum never even caught on you had been switched.'

Zoe pulled her head back and let out a mirthless laugh. 'See. I told you she probably wouldn't realise I was missing. Well, I hope she treats my counterpart better than she did me, because—' Suddenly, Zoe paused, a vacant look appeared on her face and she seemed to stare at something in the distance. The vacant expression only lasted for a moment, then she blinked, twisted in her seat and looked at Dave directly with her right index finger raised. 'You know what I would love to do? I would love it if I could look my doppelgänger in the eye and give her what for.'

Dave cocked his head and curled one side of his mouth in a wolfish grin. 'Then why don't you?'

'Do what?' Zoe replied, frowning,

'Give your doppelgänger what for,' Dave said thoughtfully,

tapping his finger on his chin as an idea formed in his head. 'Our base in Durham was destroyed, but I'm sure the maglev station based under Durham's county hall building is still active. I'm not sure where Wendy and the team are now, but I'm confident it wouldn't be a problem to catch a maglev up to Durham. From there we can commandeer a vehicle to take us to your home village, and we could do an unofficial stake-out of your home.'

'You'll do that for me?' Zoe beamed, nodding excitedly.

'Sure,' he said, smiling. 'I don't think it'll be a problem. Leave it with me and I'll see what I can do.'

Then, to Dave's astonishment, Zoe leaned forward and wrapped her arms around him in a tight embrace. After she finally released him, Dave could see the joy in her eyes as she shuffled back into her seat. Grinning and delighted he was responsible for that, he focused his attention back to the front of the vehicle.

He felt his self-satisfied smirk vanish as he locked on to a pair of eyes staring back at him from within a rear-view mirror. They belonged to Emma, and from the stern, narrow glare radiating toward him, he was under no illusion he was in trouble. He now realised by making a promise to Zoe he'd overstepped, and he wondered how long it would be before he was on the receiving end of a tongue lashing.

To ward off the tension headache that would be shortly arriving, he groaned inwardly, leaned back in his seat and massaged his temples.

It wasn't long before Dave received the tongue lashing he was expecting. After the vehicle had come to a complete stop in front of the entrance to the cavern, he climbed out and was following Claire and Zoe but was stopped by a firm hand on his arm.

Steeling himself of the worst, he slowly turned around, only to be greeted by Emma's evil eye. Even though he'd been expecting it, the thunderous expression on her face still made him take a step back. Although Emma and Claire had spent their lives dimensions apart from one another, Dave couldn't get over how alike they were, now he saw the

anger in Emma's eyes. Having witnessed that same rage in Claire's first hand, Dave knew he was in trouble.

Giving his best disarming smile, he turned and tried to act all innocent. 'Can I help you, Commander Tulley?' he asked with every bit of civility he could muster.

'Oh, no,' Emma retorted, waggling her finger. 'Don't try that innocent act on me. It may work on Claire, but it won't with me.' Then, as if to emphasise the fact, she angrily jabbed her right index finger into his chest. 'You had no right saying those things to Zoe. She's been through a lot and doesn't need someone coming along and filling her head with useless promises.'

Although Dave respected Emma's position of authority, there was something in her tone that irked him. How dare she speak to him like he was a child? He inhaled and exhaled through his nose and counted to ten. If Emma hadn't been Claire's sister, he wouldn't have stood there and taken it, but for the sake of family harmony, he decided it was best he kept his anger in check.

'With respect … Commander,' he said through gritted teeth, struggling to keep his tone civil, 'first, I think you need to get that finger out of my chest before you lose it. Second, you need to stop treating Zoe with kid gloves. She's stronger than you think.'

Emma snatched her finger back and shook her head in adamant refusal. 'I won't apologise for wanting to protect those under my command.'

'I understand that, Emma,' Dave countered, nodding. 'But there's protecting and there's overprotecting.' He held up a finger to ward off Emma's protest. 'Before you say I was giving Zoe false hope, let me just say that wasn't my intention. I meant every word I said to her.' He gave Emma a warm smile and reached out to place a reassuring hand on her shoulder. 'I've been on the job long enough to recognise when someone is worrying about what might happen. I could see that same worry in Zoe's eyes, so I thought by giving her something to look forward to, it would help distract her, keep her mind active.' He pressed his hands against his chest and gave Emma a sincere look. 'Emma, I wasn't lying to Zoe about taking her home. I believe it might help give her some closure.'

The fire seemed to disappear in Emma's eyes, and her face softened. Dave felt himself stiffen in shock as she reached over and squeezed his arm. 'I'm sorry, Dave,' she said in a tone that sounded sincere. 'I can see you're only trying to be helpful, but there's more going on here than you realise.' Emma glanced over her shoulder; for a moment Dave thought she was checking to see who was behind her. She turned back to him and spoke in a conspiratorial whisper. 'You may think I'm being overprotective, but trust me when I say you need to be careful around Zoe.'

Feeling like he'd missed something obvious, Dave shook his head in confusion. 'What do you mean, I need to be careful around Zoe? Is there something wrong with her?'

Emma held up a hand and shook her head. 'I can't go into it now; all I can insist is that you trust me. Will you do that for me?'

Dave nodded hesitantly and gave Emma a serious look. 'I do trust you, Emma. You have my word. I won't overstep your authority again.'

'Thank you,' she said, her tone echoing the relief on her face. She massaged her brow and exhaled a weary sigh. 'Please forgive me for snapping. The stress of the past few days is making me a bit punchy and causing me to bite people's heads off.'

Dave let out a loud huff and flicked his wrist. 'Pfft! Think of it as already forgotten.' He playfully punched Emma's arm and gave her a wry smile. 'I know only too well the burdens of command and that sometimes we have to let off a bit of steam.'

Emma cocked her head and spoke in a tone that Dave was sure held a touch of admiration. 'I can see now what Claire sees in you. You truly have a heart of gold.'

Dave let out a loud theatrical gasp, drew back and pressed his hands against his face in mock shock. 'Commander Tulley! Are you flirting with me? I'm shocked. What would your sister think?'

The expression on Emma's face registering her disgust, she planted her face in her hands and groaned. Dave kept his face neutral and had to stifle a laugh as Emma turned away from him, muttering something under her breath. But Dave's amusement switched to concern as he caught a glimpse of a pained expression and noticed she seemed to be leaning heavily on her cane. It was obvious she was struggling from the injuries

she'd sustained from the synthroid, and he wondered whether she wasn't pushing herself too hard.

As he followed Emma towards the open hatchway, Claire slid up next to him and gave him a quizzical look. 'Everything okay?' she asked, her forehead crinkling with worry. 'It sounded like you were having an argument.'

'Nothing to worry about,' Dave muttered, waving his hand in a dismissive gesture. 'Just a difference of opinion, but it's all been sorted now.'

A flicker of confusion flashed across Claire's face, and Dave could tell she wanted to know more. Not wanting to get into a long, drawn-out conversation, he raised his hand to forestall her questions. However, as he stepped through the large hatchway into the crystalline cavern, a surprising sight greeted him.

Even though it had only been twenty-four hours since he was last inside, Dave couldn't get over how much had changed. Crates, tools and other pieces of equipment lay scattered around the floor and on temporary workstations, with a couple of dozen engineers beavering away. In the centre of the cave, the crystalline arch was now surrounded by what looked like makeshift scaffolding, holding unrecognisable pieces of equipment that seemed to be connected to the archway. Standing like an island in the centre of a hurricane was Hilaria, with dirt and grease smearing her uniform and face. She was waving a wrench in her right hand at a tall, sandy-haired man, who seemed to be cowering in fear as she berated him.

'How many times have I told you – the right tool for the right job! Are you trying to blow us all up?' Hilaria growled and made a sweeping motion with her left hand. 'If you don't think you can handle it, I'll find someone else who can. Now get out of my sight.'

The sorry-looking man nodded wordlessly and scurried away, towards one of the workbenches. Hilaria ran a hand through her hair and muttered something under her breath. As he got closer to her, Dave could tell from the dark circle around her eye that she mustn't have slept much. He shook his head sadly as he realised once again just how alike she was to her counterpart.

'Hilaria,' Emma called out as soon as they were close enough. 'I've

come to see how things are getting on.'

'What?' Hilaria snapped, clearly irritated by the interruption. But then she stiffened as if realising who was speaking to her. 'Oh, Em, it's you.'

'Hilaria? Is everything okay?' Emma asked, her tone heavy with concern. 'I couldn't help but notice that exchange you had with Malachy.'

'Oh, that,' Hilaria said wearily, waving a dismissive hand. 'Just a minor disagreement. We've a lot of frayed nerves here. Some friction is expected.'

'How long has it been since you've last slept, or eaten, even?' Emma asked, her expression echoing the tone of disapproval in her voice.

'Oh, I'll sleep when I'm dead,' Hilaria replied, laughing half-heartedly.

Dave couldn't help but notice her expression altered slightly as the blood drained from her face. He followed Hilaria's gaze, and he understood the cause for her sudden change on seeing the disapproving scowl on Emma's face.

Raising her hands in a supplicating gesture, Hilaria nodded reluctantly and sighed. 'Fine, I promise to take a break after I've finished talking with you.'

'Good,' Emma replied. She looked at the work going on around them. 'How are things progressing?'

'Very good,' Hilaria answered happily, gesturing to the people working around the archway. 'We've just about finished manufacturing the dimensional stabilisers and my team are preparing the arch so we can connect them. Once we've installed the stabilisers and run a few tests, I estimate we'll be able to transport people through the gateway in three hours.'

'Wow,' Emma exclaimed, clearly impressed. 'That soon.'

Hilaria's lips thinned, and she gave a small shrug. 'It helps when you have a good team of people working through the night.' A touch of hesitancy flashed across her face, and she glanced quickly over her shoulder. 'Em, there's something else I need to talk to you about.'

Dave felt his heart flutter – there was an edge in Hilaria's tone. He wasn't sure if it was the tone of her voice or the fearful glint in her eye, but

it filled him with concern. He glanced at Emma and noted the bleak expression on her face, which only heightened his worry.

'What is it?' Emma asked in a heavily guarded voice.

Hilaria sucked in a deep breath and pointed to something on the far wall. 'While I've been working, I was mulling over Custos's warning about activating the gateway.' A wicked grin formed across her face, and she snapped her fingers. 'Then it hit me. We only need to stall whatever Oracle sends against us long enough for us all to make it through, right? What if we rig the gateway so that as soon as the last person is through the portal, it'll cause a cascade failure in the crystals, sending a power surge into the archway? I have a theory that if the nexus is as sentient as Custos says it is, then it should recognise our intentions and it'll shut the portal off, sealing it and trapping whatever remains in this reality forever.'

'You can do that?' Emma gasped in wide-eyed amazement.

'Well,' Hilaria answered slowly, shuffling her feet sheepishly. 'I've a confession to make. I sort of had a bit of help. As soon as the idea came to me, I contacted Custos to get his opinion, and he helpfully pointed me in the right direction.'

For several seconds, Emma could only gape at Hilaria, looking awestruck. Dave sympathised with her. Even though most of what he'd heard had gone over his head, and he had a vague understanding of what Hilaria was trying to do, he was forced to admit he was also in awe at the way Hilaria's mind worked. She was probably the smartest person on the planet.

Emma blinked, and Dave guessed she must have regained control of her emotions; she gave Hilaria a suspicious look. 'Hang on,' she said, holding up her right index finger. 'Custos told me he wasn't allowed to interfere.' She exchanged a glance with Claire, who gave a small nod of acknowledgement, and turned back to Hilaria. 'So how come he's helping you now?'

Hilaria pulled a face and waved her hand in a vague gesture as she spoke in a slow, hesitant tone. 'Hrrm … I'm not sure whether he was being completely honest with you. Yes, he didn't answer my questions outright, but he was still able to give me very cryptic answers to the questions I asked him. So it was up to me to work it all out for myself.' She turned and

pointed to the cables leading from the arch, which appeared to be connected to several strange-looking boxes attached to a number of crystals in the cavern walls. 'Everything is set up. As soon as we activate the portal, a countdown will start, and we'll have twenty-five minutes to get through. Once the countdown reaches zero, the antimatter compensators will release a massive burst of energy into the crystals, causing them to overload. In theory, that should create an effect like that of a mini black hole. It will only last for about twenty seconds, but that's long enough to destroy this whole cavern and crush anything unfortunate enough to be caught inside the event horizon.'

While he'd been listening to Hilaria, an uneasy feeling stirred within Dave's stomach. Yes, he and at least a thousand reinforcements would be travelling to his reality, but what about those few resistance cells still left behind? If he understood what Hilaria was saying, it sounded like they were going to abandon a lot of people in this reality to Oracle, and that didn't sit well with him. Clearing his throat, Dave felt it was his duty to say something. 'Excuse my ignorance, but wouldn't that trap Oracle in this reality? Not only that, haven't you forgotten about the people who won't be able to come through with us? To me, it sounds like we're talking about abandoning them.'

Hilaria blinked and gave Dave a surprised look. 'I understand your concerns, Dave, because I had them too,' she said, giving him a tight smile. 'But you needn't worry. Oracle is no longer in this reality. While I was talking with Custos, he informed me he believes it travelled back to your reality just seconds before Em activated her EMP. So whatever way Oracle is controlling its minions, it must be doing it in a way Custos cannot detect, which suggests it must have left behind a sub-mind with instructions to carry out whatever Oracle had planned. But as to the other thing ...' She turned her head slightly and gave Em an enquiring look. 'Maybe you should contact the command council to see how they feel about that?'

Em nodded slowly. 'I agree,' she said, the tone of her voice matching the serious expression on her face. 'Give me a few minutes while I confer with what remains of the command council.'

Before Dave could ask how she was going to manage that, Em pulled the visor of her helmet over her face, spun on her heel and walked

hurriedly across to a quiet corner of the cavern. He guessed she must be using her suit's communication system to speak to the council and didn't want to be interrupted. Although he was disappointed Oracle wasn't going to be trapped in this reality, he was also relieved that it would no longer pose a danger here. However, he wondered how Em's superiors would react to the news that they would be trapped in this reality.

To help pass the time, Dave and Claire quietly chatted while Hilaria and her team continued with what they were doing with the archway. As he chatted with Claire, Dave noticed that Zoe was acting oddly, giving Hilaria odd looks, and he wondered whether he should've invited her to sit with them. But before he could do so, a small movement caught his eye and he turned to see Em walking back over to them. Hilaria stopped what she was doing and joined him and Claire; Zoe moved silently toward them. As Em drew closer, Dave felt a touch of relief when he saw she was smiling.

'Sorry it took so long, but I had to wait for some of the council members to join,' Em said, as she came to a stop in front of them. 'However, once I explained what we had planned, they were surprisingly quite happy to go along with whatever we feel necessary. Once we leave, there will only be a couple of thousand left on Terra. If things do go to plan and Oracle's forces are crushed in the event horizon, those who remain plan to join those who've been living on the *Atlantician* island colony, safe in the knowledge they can spend the rest of their lives in safety.' One side of her mouth curled up in a wry smile, and she gave Hilaria a playful nudge. 'They've advised me to tell you that when we get to the other side I'm to award you with a commendation.'

'That's if we survive.' Hilaria sighed. She placed her hands on her hips, stretched backwards and let out a tired groan. 'Ugh! Personally, I would be quite happy to settle for a nice bed and forty-eight hours of uninterrupted sleep.'

'Blessed be the truth, sister.' Emma chuckled, holding her right hand up in a fist bump, which Hilaria returned. Then her face hardened, and her tone became serious. 'I'd better let you get on with it. Field Marshal N'Goy and her team will be arriving shortly, so I'd best hurry back up to the surface to greet her.'

But just as they were about to turn to leave, Zoe coughed politely and stepped forward with her back to Hilaria. Dave shared a surprised look with Emma, who gave the teen an odd look. On seeing the businesslike expression on Zoe's face, he had to keep a straight face, and it took all his willpower to stop himself from laughing.

'Commander,' Zoe said in a curt, almost professional tone while standing rigid with her head held straight, reminding Dave of a soldier on parade for inspection. 'I request to stay behind to assist the general with whatever she needs doing.'

'Oh, you do, do you?' Emma answered with a deadpan expression.

Still mindful of his earlier conversation with Emma, Dave caught Emma sharing the briefest of glances with Hilaria, who responded with a barely detectable nod. It was clear that whatever was going on between the two women involved Zoe. Dave's finely tuned detective senses kicked in and he glanced surreptitiously at Zoe. For the first time he could see there was something going on with her. Every instinct inside him told him she was up to something, and from the way Emma and Hilaria were acting, they recognised it too. The calmness in Zoe's voice felt forced, like she was trying to mask her true emotions. It was clear she desperately wanted to be with Hilaria, but for what reason, he couldn't fathom.

Afraid he'd been staring at Zoe for too long, Dave focused his attention back on Emma, who had her hands clasped behind her back while she gave Zoe an appraising look. '*Cadet* Murray, what makes you think the general needs you? After all, she's got enough people to assist her.' On hearing the playful tone in Emma's voice, Dave thought she was probably trying to lighten Zoe's mood by having a bit of banter with her. Emma turned and stared enquiringly at the straight-faced Hilaria. 'What do you say … General?'

Hilaria scrunched up her nose and tapped her bottom lip thoughtfully. 'Hmm, I'm not sure, Commander. The cadet might get in the way.'

Hands pressed against her chest, Zoe spun round and stared beseechingly at Hilaria. 'Hilaria, please let me stay and help. I'll do anything you ask of me – I promise.'

Hilaria held up her hands and let out a long, exaggerated sigh.

'Fine, you can stay and help. The first thing you can do is run over and check if anybody needs any refreshments.' Before Zoe could respond, Hilaria held up a finger and shot her a warning look. 'But any moaning and you'll be out of here like a shot. Do you understand?'

'I promise you won't regret it,' Zoe replied excitedly, twirling around and hurrying towards where a group of engineers were standing. She came to a sudden stop, turned and gave Emma an awkward salute before dashing back off.

As Dave followed Claire and Emma back to the entrance, he glanced at Emma, who responded with a tight smile and a wordless nod. Then he realised what Emma and Hilaria were up to. Allowing Zoe to remain down here would not only keep her out of harm's way, but keeping her busy would allow Hilaria to keep a close watch on her. One thing Dave was sure of, whatever scheme Zoe was up to, Hilaria would be the one to uncover it.

Dave cast an eye over his shoulder and raised his eyebrows in surprise as Hilaria sank to the floor with her head in her hands. Just as she did so, Malachy, the engineer she'd berated earlier, approached her and sat beside her. He handed the bottle he was holding to Hilaria, who smiled and took it gratefully. The last thing Dave saw as he exited the chamber was the rest of the engineers stopping what they were doing. They strolled over to where Hilaria was sitting and sat around her while Zoe handed them all refreshments.

The sounds of laughter echoed from out of the cavern as Dave climbed back on-board the vehicle.

-35-

Moments later, Dave found himself back on the surface, staring in awe up at the sky. Dozens of eagle-shaped aircraft flew in formation above his head, the sound from their throaty turbine engines filling the air as they descended toward the clearing. Now a temporary campsite, the once grassy fields were now an ugly brown area of churned-up mud with blocks of makeshift shelters filling one area, giving it the vibe of a military camp. Huge armoured vehicles were parked in strategic positions around the camp. Along the edge of the clearing, just in front of the treeline, Dave could make out what looked like heavy-duty cannons being unloaded from transport vehicles.

He squinted and craned his head back as he watched an eagle transporter begin its descent. No matter how many times he saw them, Dave couldn't help but admire the aircraft's sleek lines. What must it be like for those who piloted them? he wondered idly. Even though he suffered badly from air sickness, he would have given anything to sit behind the controls and feel the aircraft respond to his touch. He shook his head and blew out a dejected sigh. Pity he would never get that chance.

'Didn't you say you and the field marshal already know each other?' Dave shouted, trying to be heard over the cacophonous noise.

Emma nodded. 'Yes,' she said, also raising her voice. 'I last saw her a few years ago. I don't know if you're aware, but she's the daughter of—'

Just then, the roar of twin turbine engines drowned out Emma's

words. Dave turned to the south, where the aircraft was beginning its transition from level flight to hover mode. The aircraft's turbines growled like an angry beast as its undercarriage made contact with the ground. Dave screwed up his face and raised his hand to shield his eyes from the dirt and dust being blown around by the air being forced from the aircraft's exhaust.

Once the dust had settled, Dave blinked to clear his vision and saw the transport's rear loading hatch slowly lowering. The aircraft's engines had barely had time to come to a complete rest when an armoured figure marched purposefully down the open hatch. The figure briefly paused, then made its way directly to him.

As the figure got closer, Dave could see it was wearing armour similar to that worn by Oracle's assimilated storm troopers. The armour was quite sleek in appearance and seemed to be moulded to fit the wearer. And like the armour worn by those in Oracle's army, the helmet was opaque, which made it impossible to see the face of the person wearing it.

One thing Dave was certain of, whoever the soldier was, it was clear they were significantly taller than him as well as being broad in the shoulders. But as the figure marched toward him, Dave frowned and cocked his head curiously. There was something almost recognisable in the way the newcomer walked. It was proud and determined. He scratched his head and wondered where he had seen that walk before.

Before he could ponder it further, something on the edge of his vision caught his attention, and he turned his head to investigate. Isaac was standing beside Emma, but there was something in his demeanour that made him do a double take. Isaac didn't look his usual bouncy self. He seemed very serious. No, Dave realised. Not serious, more like downcast. Apprehensive even. He wondered whether he should take him to one side to check if he was okay. But before he could do so, Emma took a step forward and gave a respectful bob of her head to the newcomer, who responded with a rigid salute.

'Commander Tulley,' the stranger announced, their voice distorted by their helmet's speaker. 'I stand ready to relieve you.'

'Field Marshal N'Goy,' Emma said, smiling. 'I stand relieved.'

'Thank Hera we've got that out of the way.' The field marshal sighed, carefully removing their helmet. 'I always find these formalities very

tedious.'

As soon as the field marshal's helmet was removed to reveal the face beneath, Dave inhaled a sharp breath in recognition. The field marshal was the double of Kendra Goynes. Though her face was thinner, and she had a tight box-braid hairstyle, there was no doubt in Dave's mind who she was. He glanced at Claire, and it was clear from her stunned expression what was running through her mind.

She gasped. 'The resemblance is so uncanny.'

If the two women were aware of Dave and Claire's reaction, they gave no sign. A wide smile covered Emma's face and she extended her hand toward the taller woman. The field marshal grinned and she took hold of Emma's hand in a tight, comradely embrace.

Emma grinned. 'Kaliopi, it's been such a long time. Congratulations on your promotion – your mother would have been proud of you.'

'Thank you,' Kaliopi said, nodding as she gave Emma a tight smile. 'Although from the sound of things, you've been ruffling a few feathers too.'

Her warm smile vanished as she appeared to set her gaze on Isaac. Dave thought he noticed a touch of hostility in her eyes. It was so intense, it was almost murderous. But no sooner than it was there, than it was gone. Kaliopi turned toward Dave and her eyebrows lifted in mild surprise.

'By Neptune's trident,' she gasped. 'Even though I was warned about Colonel Barnes's doppelgänger being here, it's still quite unnerving seeing you for myself.'

'You'd be amazed at how often I hear that,' Dave answered with his tongue firmly in his cheek. He cocked his head and gave her a mischievous wink. 'Although I'm probably the more handsome one.'

'Many apologies, Kaliopi,' Emma said irritably while shooting Dave a harsh glare. 'Please let me introduce you to Detective Dave Barnes and,' her irritation was replaced by a wide, beaming smile that covered the whole of her face as she indicated Claire, 'my sister, Professor Claire Tulley.'

'A pleasure,' Kaliopi replied, nodding. The centre of her eyebrows bunched together, and she held up her right index finger and regarded

Dave curiously. 'I noticed your reaction when I removed my helmet. May I hazard a guess and say you've met my counterpart on your world?'

'Yes,' Dave said hesitantly, sharing a worried glance with Claire and wondering whether they should tell her that Kendra sacrificed her own life so that her colleagues could escape. 'On my Earth, she went by the name of Kendra Goynes. She was the head of security at the military facility where she was stationed.'

'Fascinating,' Kaliopi murmured, nodding thoughtfully. 'My family's name was once Goynes, but many generations ago the senate began a vicious rumour campaign by targeting certain families like mine by saying we were a threat to the security of the empire or some other rubbish. My ancestors went into hiding and changed our surname to N'Goy to avoid being persecuted.' She cocked her head and gave Dave a guarded look. 'I noticed you referred to Kendra in the past tense. From both of your sorrowful expressions, may I assume she's no longer alive?'

A wave of despondency overtook Dave as he thought back to the last time he saw Kendra. The base had just been invaded by hostile creatures, and Kendra had led a team to intercept them. Everyone knew it was a suicide mission, and even though Dave hadn't witnessed it, he was in no doubt that Kendra had died in the explosion that had left Claire and him trapped. The grief was clear to see on Claire's face, and he placed a hand on her shoulder as he acknowledged Kaliopi with a sad smile.

'Yes,' he said in a muted tone. 'Oracle launched an attack on our base. Kendra bravely sacrificed herself so that her colleagues could escape.'

Kaliopi's face hardened and she stared at Dave with narrow eyes that had a touch of fire in them. 'I see. Well, I hope one day I'll get the chance to avenge my counterpart.'

'I think you'll have to get behind a very long queue if you want to do that.' Dave laughed.

As if to change the subject, Emma coughed and politely stepped to one side, pointing to Isaac. As before, Dave felt the atmosphere had become slightly frosty as Kaliopi locked her eyes on Isaac, who had been standing in silence.

'I'm sure it has been a while since you set eyes on this ruffian.' Emma said, laughing. 'We can give you some space to allow you to catch

up with your—'

'I'm sorry, Em,' Kaliopi growled, cutting Emma off. 'I've got a lot to do. If you don't mind, I need to check to see if everything is in place.'

Before anyone could say anything, Kaliopi spun on her heel and marched swiftly away, shooting a murderous glare at Isaac as she turned. It didn't take a genius to see there was a lot of animosity between the pair, and Dave wondered if it had anything to do with the stunt Isaac had pulled when they'd served together. But before he had time to process what had just happened, Isaac let out a loud, angry snort and charged after Kaliopi. Emma reached out as if she was trying to stop him, but was too slow.

Confused at what was happening, Dave glanced at Claire, but the puzzled expression on her face only echoed what he was feeling. They both turned to Emma, who held up her hands and exhaled a despondent sigh.

'Kaliopi is Isaac's daughter,' Emma explained, staring sadly at Isaac, who was still chasing after Kaliopi. 'Things have been strained between them since the death of Allison, Isaac's wife and Kaliopi's mother.'

Despite being surprised by this news, Dave felt a touch of sadness at the almost venomous hatred behind Kaliopi's eyes whenever she looked at Isaac. He shook his head and wondered what could have happened for a daughter to hate her father so much.

By the fire of the eternal flame, why did I have to act like that?

Kaliopi seethed in frustration and angrily stabbed her toe into the ground. A knot of anxiety twisted inside her stomach as she thought about the pain and disappointment she'd seen in her father's eyes. That hadn't been her intention. In fact, during the whole time she'd been travelling here, it had been her wish to reconcile with him. Unfortunately, as soon as she set eyes on him, all that pain and resentment she'd built up over the years took control.

A firm hand grabbed Kaliopi's arm, snapping her out of her silent self-chastising. She twisted round, only to find herself staring into her father's beseeching face.

'Kal,' Isaac said, 'please will you talk to me?'

Kaliopi rolled her eyes and groaned. Not like this. Not now. Why did he have to follow her? Couldn't he have waited until she had time to calm down?

'Not now, Dad,' she snapped, snatching her arm back. 'I've got things to do. We can do this later.'

'Damn it, Kal,' Isaac growled, waving his hands in the air. 'I'm your father. Talk to me. You owe me that. Your mother would be turning in her grave if she knew how you were acting toward me.'

Bristling with anger, Kaliopi felt her blood boil. *Oh no, how dare he use Mum like that?* Enraged, Kaliopi felt a red mist descend over her. The strong taste of angry bile hit the back of her throat as she took an angry step forward and jabbed an accusatory finger into her father's chest.

'Don't. You. Dare. Speak. Her. Name,' she hissed with venomous fury. Tears filled her vision as she cut loose and let go of all the years of pent-up bitterness she'd been holding on to. 'You gave up any right to speak her name the day she died. I hate you. I wish you'd died instead of her.'

The words were out of her mouth before she even realised it, and her father staggered back, his mouth dropping open. However, Isaac didn't say anything. He didn't need to; Kaliopi could see the pain and hurt in his eyes. In that moment, the look he gave her said everything he couldn't put into words.

His hands outstretched, his voice cracked as he spoke in a pleading, grief-stricken tone. 'Kal, how much longer are you going to hold me responsible for your mother's death? I didn't ask her to break me out of prison. She knew we had a plan in place, but she still tried to do it on her own.'

'That's the thing, Dad. You didn't have to ask,' Kaliopi retorted, struggling to fight back the tears. 'Have you any idea what it was like for her believing she was second best? Do you? That's why she kept taking all those dangerous assignments.' No longer able to hold back the tears, Kaliopi felt them flow down her cheeks as she held up her right hand and spat the words out. 'No matter what she did, she still believed she wasn't good enough for you. That was why she tried to break you out, because

she thought if she did that, then you might finally take notice of her.'

Isaac's mouth opened and closed in stunned disbelief. 'I-I-I,' he stammered, 'I don't know what you mean. Surely you must know I loved your mum. I loved both of you.'

'That's bullshit, Dad, and you know it,' Kaliopi scoffed, not believing a word her father was saying. 'How long are you going to go on lying to yourself. The only one you were truly in love with was Emma Tulley. Mum saw it every time you looked at her.' Her top lip quivering in disgust, she placed her hands on her hips and regarded her father with disdain. 'Everybody knew how you felt about Em. The way you followed her around like a lovesick puppy. The night before she died, Mum even told me that when she gave birth to me, she prayed that would be the day you would finally realise and be grateful for what you had.' She shook her head and let out a bitter laugh. 'Well, I guess you can imagine how much it broke her heart when you wouldn't even give her that.'

Her father's shoulders slumped, and he spoke in a heavy-hearted tone. 'I never realised everyone could see how much I cared for Em.'

Kaliopi pinched the bridge of her nose and let out a weary sigh. 'Well, it's true. What's ironic is that you and Em spent so much time together. I'm surprised she still doesn't know. I would have thought somebody would have accidentally let it slip by now.'

No sooner had the words left her mouth than she spotted something in her father's body language that gave her pause. It had been barely detectable. If she hadn't been staring at him, she would have missed it. She frowned and cocked her head as she studied his face. Why did he look sheepish? Why would he … Oh!

'By the gods,' Kaliopi gasped, making no attempt to hide the contempt she was feeling. 'She finally found out, didn't she?' Bristling with rage, Kaliopi squeezed her hands into tight balls while she struggled to speak in a calm tone and hissed at him through clenched teeth. 'You must be so delighted to have the woman of your dreams finally know how you feel about her.'

'I-I-I,' he stammered. He closed his eyes and sucked in a deep breath, shook his head and wordlessly raised his hands.

You've got to be kidding me, Kaliopi thought indignantly. The look on

her father's face told her all she needed to know. The bitter resentment she'd been struggling to fight against now swelled up inside her, threatening to consume her. Her jaw tightened, and it took every ounce of willpower she had to stop herself from punching this sad excuse for a father.

'You're pathetic,' Kaliopi snarled. 'You're still a coward. Now you can see why I didn't want to be around you. It wasn't because of that sick sense of humour of yours. It was because I was so ashamed to be your daughter.'

There are moments in every life when feeling overcomes thought, when the walls erected to safeguard the heart crumble beneath the weight of what must be said, and for Kaliopi, this was one of those moments. It was like a valve had been opened and the words came unbidden out of her mouth. All the bitterness and anger flew out of her mouth like an arrow heading towards its target. Kaliopi suddenly felt detached. She could hear the words, but it felt as if they were coming from somebody else's mouth.

'It wasn't the URE soldiers who were responsible for Mum's death,' Kaliopi continued in a flat, emotionless tone. 'In the end, it was your cowardice that killed her. Emma needs to be careful around you, otherwise she'll end up dead too. Just another fatality, with a gravestone bearing the words "Another woman whose life was destroyed by Isaac the Coward". Hell, maybe I should put a gun to our heads right now? You'd like that. Two for the price of—'

Kaliopi's vision went white with pain as something hard struck the left side of her face. Stunned, she shook her head to clear her vision and pressed her right hand against her stinging cheek. It didn't take long for the star field to clear and she blinked, only to see her father staring back at her with his right clenched fist raised. The stunned horror at what he'd done was written all over his face, mirroring her own.

Then Kaliopi realised how much pain her words had caused, and she instantly regretted them. Within moments, any hopes she'd had for reconciliation had been utterly destroyed. Her scalp prickled with shame on noticing the hurt in her father's eyes. What she had said was unforgivable. She may have as well have taken a knife and stabbed him through his heart. But despite everything he had put her through, something inside Kaliopi told her he was still her father. Desperate to make

amends, she reached out and opened her mouth to apologise. But the words would not come; she realised there wasn't anything she could do that could take back what she'd said.

As they stood staring at one another, right before her eyes, in the space of several seconds, it looked like her father had aged. His imposing build stooped slightly as though all the strength had been taken from him, leaving him a broken shell of a man. Tears stung Kaliopi's eyes as she watched the once proud figure of her father, shoulders slouched, turn and walk away. Guilt gnawed at the recesses of her brain as she realised that by destroying her father, she'd become just like him.

-36-

Having watched the heated exchange from a distance, Em swallowed as Isaac walked away from Kaliopi. The pain on both their faces was clear to see. Although she was too far away to hear what was being said, Em could tell from Kaliopi's wild gesticulations that it had involved harsh words. But it was only when she saw Isaac slap Kaliopi across the face that Em realised she should have stepped in to stop it from escalating that far.

A seed of suspicion grew inside Em as she thought about what they must have been arguing about to make Isaac strike his daughter. For a long time, the circumstances of Allison's death had been shrouded in mystery. She never understood why Allison had been so reckless as to believe she could get Isaac out of the detention centre alone, against impossible odds. However, it was only recently, after learning of Isaac's long-buried feelings for her, that it had started to make sense to Em. But that had only been part of the puzzle, and she had a hunch there had to be much more to Allison's death than that.

She tapped her finger on her bottom lip while she replayed the animated exchange back in her head. The only explanation Em could think of for Kaliopi's hostile attitude toward her father was that Allison must have shared her suspicions about Isaac's infatuation with Em. Shaking her head in exasperation, Em blew out a slow breath through her tight lips. Was that the reason Allison had risked her life? She was jealous of Isaac's feelings toward her? Surely, she had to have seen Em wasn't a threat?

The more Em thought about it, though, the more she could see that was the only reason Allison had acted recklessly. A sense of guilt scratched at the back of her mind as it dawned on her that she was the cause of Kaliopi's estrangement from her father. She set her jaw in determination, and she wondered if there was anything she could say or do to repair the damage she had unintentionally created.

Casting an eye on Isaac's receding back, Em knew from his defeatist body language that he might not be in the best frame of mind to listen to her. However, that didn't mean she couldn't talk to him later. All she needed to do was give him time to get his thoughts together, then she would approach him. But Kaliopi was her primary focus. After witnessing their violent altercation, she was more of a concern to Em.

Now she had a plan for the best way to proceed, Em signalled to Claire and Dave to stay where they were. Certain she'd last seen Kaliopi heading toward the shelters, Em took off. It was a long shot, but she was certain that if Kaliopi listened to what she had to say, she was confident she could repair their relationship.

As she moved over the uneven ground, Em puffed through tight lips, trying to ignore the pain coming from her still tender chest and knee. *This would have been so much easier if it had happened a month ago,* Em thought as she stumbled on a loose piece of earth.

After questioning a couple of soldiers to see if they'd seen where Kaliopi had headed, Em soon found herself standing outside the entrance of one of the temporary portable cabins that had been assigned to those who'd just arrived. But just as she was about to give a light tap on the cabin's door, Em paused at the sound coming from within.

Did that sound like someone was crying?

Out of concern for Kaliopi's well-being, Em dispensed with the etiquette of waiting for permission to enter. As Em swung open the door and stepped inside the cabin, Kaliopi jumped up from her cot in surprise at the intrusion. She spun away, looking as if she was wiping something off her face. But as she did so, Em felt her heart tug on catching a glimpse of Kaliopi's tear-stained cheeks and puffy eyes.

'Kaliopi?' Em asked worriedly, taking a step closer, no longer caring that the woman was technically superior to her in rank. 'Are you okay?'

'Of course.' Kaliopi sniffed, her tone defensive. 'Why would you ask that?'

Em folded her arms across her chest and gave Kaliopi a sceptical look. 'Really?'

Sinking back down onto her cot, Kaliopi's shoulders sagged in defeat, and she let out a loud, resigned sigh. 'So, guess you saw it all?'

'Kiddo,' Em answered without humour, 'I think the entire camp saw you and your father going at it.'

Groaning, Kaliopi screwed up her face and gave Em a suspicious side eye. 'I guess my father sent you because of the hateful things I said to him.' She rolled her eyes, placed a hand on the side of her forehead and let out a half-hearted laugh. 'You don't need to say anything to make me feel worse than I already do.'

'Actually, Kal,' Em said softly, lowering herself onto the cot next to the mournful-looking woman. 'He doesn't even know I'm here.'

'Uh-huh,' Kaliopi murmured, her eyes creasing together into suspicious thin slits. 'So why are you here?'

Pressing her lips together into a thin line, Em shuffled around so that she could look Kaliopi directly in the eye. She drew in a deep breath and spoke slowly, choosing her words carefully. 'I'm here because I feel I'm to blame for what happened to your mother. If you should be angry at anyone, it should be me.'

A cloud of anger passed over Kaliopi's face and she shot Em a rage-filled stare. 'Oh, I would love very much to beat the living shit out of you.'

On seeing the incandescent fury in Kaliopi's eyes, Em tensed herself and waited for the inevitable tirade of abuse and violence on her body. But that did not happen. No sooner than the anger appeared than it was gone. The blazing intensity within Kaliopi's eyes seemed to vanish, replaced by a more compassionate warmth as her face softened and she laughed contemptuously. 'Hurting you would only make things worse. If anything, you're just as much a victim here as my mum and I are.'

'How come?' Em answered, frowning in confusion.

Kaliopi threw up her hands and let out an exasperated cry. 'Hell's

teeth, Em. You, more than anybody, know what my father has always been like. He's always been too scared to face the truth and tries to cover it up with juvenile jokes.' She cocked her head and regarded Em curiously. 'I gather you found out how he's felt about you all these years. Tell me, how did he react when he found out you knew?'

Em rubbed her chin as she thought back to how Isaac had acted after she discovered his feelings toward her. 'He avoided me for days, like he was ashamed or scared,' she finally murmured after a moment of silence, nodding.

With her hands held out, the palms facing upwards, Kaliopi let out a loud, bitter laugh. 'I rest my case. The man's a coward.' She rolled her eyes and stared up at the ceiling, shaking her head. 'Mind you, I'm just as bad. Rather than discuss things with him, at the first opportunity I chose to get as far away from him as I could by accepting an assignment on the other side of the world. How ironic is that?'

Even though she hated hearing Kaliopi talk this way about someone she held dear, Em couldn't completely disagree with some of the things she'd said about Isaac. Yes, it was true he could be annoying, but he was in no way a coward. Em strongly suspected Kaliopi's bitterness over her mother's death had tainted her vision of her father and she wished she could make Kaliopi see that.

Nodding sadly, Em leaned forward and placed her right hand on Kaliopi's knee. 'Kaliopi, I'm not saying your dad's perfect. He's far from it. In fact, there are times I would like to strangle him, but he's the only parent you have left.' She pressed her left hand against her chest and stared pleadingly into the younger woman's eyes. 'For years, I let my bitterness toward my sister poison my mind. I was lucky I realised how much it was affecting me before it was too late.' Raising a finger to forestall any protests that may have come from Kaliopi, Em smiled and continued. 'I'm not saying your anger isn't justified, but what I'm saying is, don't let your bitterness poison you. Otherwise, one day you'll wake up alone, filled with regrets.'

A flicker of uncertainty flashed across Kaliopi's face, and then she nodded. But just as it looked like she was about to open her mouth to say something, a loud commotion came from outside, distracting them both.

Wondering what was going on, Em shared a worried frown with Kaliopi and they both shot to their feet.

The cabin door swung open, and Yuto barged inside. On seeing the alarmed expression spread across her friend's face, a sense of dread tingled down Em's spine. Yuto was normally restrained in his emotions, so for him to react this way must have meant something dire was happening.

'Emma-San, Kaliopi-San,' Yuto breathed, his tone urgent. 'We've received word from Gemma that a large number of hostile forces are heading towards us.'

Kaliopi let out a torrent of expletives and shot Em a serious look. 'Oracle's forces must have detected our transports and tracked our flight path.' She raised an enquiring eyebrow at Yuto. 'Was Gemma able to give you a count and an estimate of how long it would be before they reach us?'

Yuto nodded gravely. 'At least four thousand synthroids are advancing toward our location. They are still some distance away, but at the speed they're travelling, she estimates they'll reach us in just over one hour.'

The icy hand of fear gripped Em's heart and she felt her blood run cold; once again, she felt that strange prickling sensation on the back of her neck. It was not the number that frightened her – it was what made up the numbers that scared her the most. Normally, with that large a hostile force made up of human soldiers, there was a chance of holding them off with only a small number of fatalities. But a hostile force made up entirely of synthroids – that was a whole new level of threat. Four thousand synthroids against a highly trained force of two and a half thousand humans – that was the equivalent of being outnumbered by five to one. Not great odds for the humans. On top of that, something else troubled Em. Her mind had locked on to something Yuto had said. A daunted feeling gnawing in her stomach, she swallowed and focused her attention back on Yuto.

'Yuto,' she said in a voice flattened into calm from shock. It sounded to her like her own voice was coming from far away. 'That number you quoted, was Gemma able to tell you if that included anything like those cybernetic children we encountered in Pons Aelius?'

'No, Emma-San,' Yuto replied, frowning. 'From what I can understand from the information given to me, the hostile force is

completely comprised of synthroids, nothing else.'

The neurons inside her brain firing in every direction, Em shook her head in frustration as she tried to wrap her head around what Yuto was telling her. Every instinct inside her screamed at her, telling her something didn't feel right. There had to be something else going on, but she couldn't see it. If the AI had included those cybernetic abominations in the attack group heading toward them, that meant their defences would be overwhelmed in a matter of minutes. Why would Oracle hold them back? What was it she wasn't seeing?

'You know what's strange?' Kaliopi murmured, scratching her head, a perplexed expression covering her face. 'After we received your report about what you had encountered in Pons Aelius, we sent teams into the other cities to see if there was anything similar to what you described.'

'What did you find?' Em asked curiously, even though something inside her told her she already knew the answer.

Kaliopi puffed out her cheeks, blew out a long breath and held up her hands in apparent frustration. 'Not a thing. That's what's strange. The cities were completely devoid of life. All the search teams went through every major city meticulously, but they didn't encounter any assimilated children like you described.' Kaliopi's forehead wrinkled and she held up her right index finger, almost as if it was an afterthought. 'But here's what's peculiar. While accompanying one of the search teams, I came across the skeletal remains of a child. No other bodies, just one child. It looked as if it had been there for a while. At the time, I wondered whether it was the discarded remains of one of Oracle's failed test subjects.'

Of course, that's it. Em inhaled a sharp breath as something in her mind clicked into place, clearing the picture. Her chest tightened, and she felt the blood drain from her face as she finally understood what Oracle had done with the children. It was too horrible to believe, but Em realised, like many times in history, sometimes if it sounded awful, then it had to be true.

'They're all dead,' Em croaked, forcing the words out of her mouth and feeling the blood drain out of her face. 'They killed them.'

Yuto and Kaliopi exchanged startled looks. Kaliopi's startled expression quickly changed to concern. Her eyes grew wide in a horror-

struck expression of fear and Em guessed it was because either she had seen the terror in Em's eyes or had recognised the tone of her voice. Whatever it was, Em was certain Kaliopi had just realised the same thing as she did.

Kaliopi's right hand pressed against her mouth, and she let out a horrified gasp. 'By the ghosts of my ancestors, no,'

'Yes,' Em answered, nodding grimly at the ashen-faced Yuto. 'As soon as Yuto told me who was attacking, something in the back of my mind screamed at me, trying to convince me something didn't seem right. I've never heard of the URE breeding that many synthroids before because it would be too difficult to control their blood lust.' She swallowed and fixed her eyes on Kaliopi. 'It wasn't until I heard you say what you found in the other cities – or what you didn't find – that it finally made sense to me.'

'I don't understand,' Yuto said, frowning, clearly not understanding. 'What does that number of synthroids have to do with missing children?'

'Because, my friend,' Em explained sadly. 'The children aren't missing. They're dead. For Oracle to breed that many synthroids, my guess is it either used the children as genetic material to clone the beasts, or fed them to the beasts as soon as they awoke.'

'By the spirit of Tianzhu,' Yuto exclaimed in wide-eyed revulsion. 'What a monstrous thing to do.'

Em let out a snort of disgust and nodded. 'I couldn't agree more, my honourable friend. My guess is the group of cybernetic children and animals we encountered were only a test. Once Oracle saw how easily they could be disabled, it must have concluded the test was a failure and decided the URE's remaining children were superfluous.'

'But that many synthroids,' Kaliopi said, the bewilderment in her voice mirroring the expression on her face. 'How is Oracle able to withhold their blood lust long enough to prevent them from attacking one another?'

Em tapped her bottom lip thoughtfully, silently considering Kaliopi's question, and her blood ran cold at the horrifying theory taking shape in her mind. 'I might have a theory about that,' she said gravely. 'I would say Oracle has attached some sort of feeding unit to each synthroid,

which slowly injects genetic material into their bodies. That might explain how it can control their blood lust.' She tried to suppress a shudder at the ghastly mental image of children being turned into liquified sludge.

'How long did Cooper say before the portal would be operational?' Kaliopi asked bluntly.

Oh bollocks! Em felt her cheeks flush as she realised that she'd forgotten all about Hilaria. She gave a sheepish laugh, held up her right index finger, and raised her wrist communicator. 'Hilaria, how long will it be before you're able to activate the gateway?'

A holographic image of Hilaria's grease-stained face appeared almost immediately. 'If I go through all the tests,' she answered, giving a tight smile, 'then we should be good to go in three hours.'

Three hours! Em groaned inwardly as she felt the back of her throat go dry at the thought that nothing would be left in hours after the synthroids were finished with them. Reining in her emotions, she tried to keep her tone neutral and stared intently at Hilaria.

'Hilaria,' she said, trying to keep the fear she was feeling from showing in her voice, 'we're about to receive some visitors. I've been advised that a force of at least four thousand synthroids are making their way towards us. We estimate they will reach us in approximately one hour.'

There was a long pause and Hilaria seemed to just stare back at Em. For a moment, Em thought the image had frozen. Eventually Hilaria gave a small nod and replied in a surprisingly calm tone. 'I see. If I don't run all the tests, the best I can give you is two hours. Even then, I cannot promise it will be a smooth ride. If the portal isn't completely stable, we could end up experiencing some time dilation.' Hilaria exhaled sorrowfully. 'I'm sorry I cannot give you better news, Em. That's the best I can manage. Do you think we can hold them off for that long?'

'We'll just have to pray we can. Tulley out,' Em answered bluntly. After disconnecting the link, she turned and gave Kaliopi an enquiring stare. 'Field Marshal, you heard what Hilaria said. Do you think we can hold them for an hour or so, long enough for everybody to make it through the portal?'

'We're about to find out if we can. Some of us may have to stay behind to ensure you make it through, though,' Kaliopi replied glumly. She

straightened to attention, giving Em the formal imperial salute – clicking her heels together and slapping her right hand against her left breast. 'Commander Tulley, there's no point standing around when there's work to be done. So if you excuse me while I brief everybody about what is coming and what I expect from them.' A cruel smile formed across her face, and she slapped Em across the shoulder. 'We'll give our visitors a welcome they won't forget. This will be a day to remember. When this is over, the gods themselves shall sing songs of our bravery.'

Wishing she could share in Kaliopi's enthusiasm, Em bit back a retort but watched in mild amusement as the chuckling woman spun on her heel and charged through the open doorway. Em shook her head sadly and took in a deep breath. Kaliopi was so much like Isaac; it was a shame she couldn't see that. Em turned to Yuto, who pulled a sour face and pointed at the empty doorway.

'That is an unusual woman,' he murmured.

'You don't know the half of it, my friend.' Em chuckled before giving him a serious look. 'We need to help the field marshal with the preparations. You didn't happen to notice where Isaac was, did you?'

'No, Emma-San,' Yuto replied unhappily. 'Before coming to you, he was one of the first people I tried to speak to, but I couldn't find him anywhere.'

Damn it, what a time for him to disappear. Em groaned inwardly. Drawing in a deep breath, she gave Yuto a tight smile. 'Nothing we can do about that, I suppose. We just have to hope he resurfaces.'

Realising there was nothing more to be said, Em gestured for Yuto to follow her out through the doorway. As she stepped out into the bright afternoon sunshine, she closed her eyes to take a moment to enjoy the mild winter air on her exposed face. She opened her eyes and turned to the north, but frowned on seeing the storm clouds forming on the horizon. It was not the storm itself that bothered her, but what was ahead of the storm and the danger it was bringing. There was no doubt in her mind that the upcoming battle wasn't going to be easy. There was a chance many of her friends, or even she, might not survive. But one thing she was certain of, she was determined they would show Oracle what it was to be human. If the AI wanted a war, then war was what it would have. Because they

weren't fighting just for themselves, they were fighting for the survival of humanity. Em was certain that if those creatures got through the gateway, there would be nothing to stop them from wiping out all organic life, not only in her home reality, but in every other dimension, too.

Filled with resolute purpose, Em ignored the odd looks from people as she continued marching, only coming to a stop in the very centre of the makeshift camp. Then, to her surprise, Kaliopi joined her. Em guessed she must have noticed where she was heading and had worked out what she had in mind. They acknowledged each other with a curt nod. Then, no words needing to be said, with their rifles held tight in their hands, they held them up high, pulled back their heads, and let out a cry of defiance to the horizon. Soon they were joined by others, and they all stood united, weapons raised as they joined in the battle cry.

Em's chest heaved; she was out of breath and her throat hoarse. She gazed at the defiant faces of those standing around her.

They had sent their message to Oracle. This wasn't a battle just for the survival of Terra anymore – it was a fight for the life of every single organic being across the multiverse.

The line had been drawn in the sand, and now they had to wait for Oracle to step over it.

To be concluded in Mirror Wars Book 4
The Custos Gambit

ABOUT THE AUTHOR

Born in Hartlepool in 1970. Alan lived in Langley Park, Durham, England for many years before moving to Northern Ireland in 2006. Has been married to his wife, Monica, since 2007. Loves reading fantasy, science fiction, action & adventure and thrillers. Favourite authors are Stephen King, James Herbert, Clive Cussler, Dean Koontz, Audrey Niffenegger and Neil Gaiman. Is a big Marvel Comics fan and enjoys watching movies. Favourite tv shows are Blake's 7, Babylon 5 and Star Trek. He also supports Sunderland AFC.

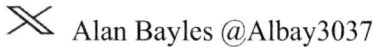 Alan Bayles @Albay3037

Alan Bayles @Albay3037

Facebook.com/AlanBaylesWrite

Printed in Dunstable, United Kingdom

76668000R00231